GATES OF HOPE

RICK PARTLOW

aethonbooks.com

GATES OF HOPE
©2022 RICK PARTLOW

This book is protected under the copyright laws of the United States of America. No part of this publication may be reproduced, stored in a retrieval system, or transmitted, in any form or by any means, without the prior permission in writing of the publisher, nor be otherwise circulated in any form of binding or cover other than that in which it is published and without a similar condition including this condition being imposed on the subsequent purchaser. Any reproduction or unauthorized use of the material or artwork contained herein is prohibited without the express written permission of the authors.

Aethon Books supports the right to free expression and the value of copyright. The purpose of copyright is to encourage writers and artists to produce the creative works that enrich our culture.

The scanning, uploading, and distribution of this book without permission is a theft of the author's intellectual property. If you would like to use material from the book (other than for review purposes), please contact editor@aethonbooks.com. Thank you for your support of the author's rights.

Aethon Books
www.aethonbooks.com

Typography, interior design, print and eBook formatting by Steve Beaulieu.
Artwork provided by Vivid Covers.

Published by Aethon Books LLC.

Aethon Books is not responsible for websites (or their content) that are not owned by the publisher.

This book is a work of fiction. Names, characters, places, and incidents are the product of the author's imagination or are used fictitiously. Any resemblance to actual events, locales, or persons, living or dead is coincidental.

All rights reserved.

ALSO IN THE SERIES

GATES OF HELL
GATES OF HOPE
GATES OF VICTORY

PROLOGUE

Thacia was coming back together before Valon's eyes, a video of a house fire run backward. Leaning against the railing that lined the roof of the Venator fortress, she stared in wonder. She'd been a Venator for ten years, her entire adult life, and had never witnessed the demons penetrating the capitol city, tearing at it like a predator worrying its prey.

Civilians had streamed out of the city in a panic, some even heading through the gates to the colony worlds, something that hadn't happened in decades, during her grandparents' time. She hadn't witnessed it herself, of course. She'd been out in the wildlands, fighting the demons as they streamed through the gate, making a desperate, last-ditch attempt to put a shield over the portal.

Valon had been at peace with the probability of her own death, sure she'd perish along with her civilization in a forlorn hope. Improbably, the endless horde of monsters had... ended. A break in the line, whether it had been permanent or only temporary, had given her and a team of engineers enough time to install a blocking shield, to seal the Hive Mind's minions on the other side.

The end. So her father would have said if this had been one of the stories he'd read to her when she was a child. But this was no story, and a horrible certainty lingered in her gut that this wasn't the end either.

"Primus, it's time."

She nearly didn't turn, still unused to the new rank, but she recognized the voice. Prefect Marcos was a tall, handsome man with patrician features and a close-cropped, black beard, his uniform pressed and spotless in a way she could never match no matter how much time and effort she put into her preparations.

Valon made a face.

"Do I *have* to do this, sir?" It was much closer to a whine than she would have liked. Marcos tsked, shaking his head.

"You're a Venator, and a primus." He cocked an eyebrow. "The youngest primus in the history of the service, so don't make me look bad for promoting you. This is your duty, no matter how unpleasant you may find it."

"Yes, sir," Valon sighed, then fell into step with the man.

The rooftop landing pad was large enough for a dozen of the aircars, but the prefect's was the only one present, painted a deep red in recognition of his rank and importance. Another officer might have been pleased with the thought, thinking that somehow the power and authority would rub off on them just by being seen near the man. Valon knew better. Power and authority meant responsibility, and she already had enough of that.

I'm responsible for the deaths... so many deaths. For the maiming and the wounding and the scars.

When she closed her eyes at night, she could see them, see the faces of the gunship pilots and foot soldiers she'd led to their deaths in the battle against the demons. They'd have died anyway... that was what Marcos had said over and over, him and everyone else. The men and women would have died protecting

Thacia because it was their choice, their destiny, and it didn't matter who'd given the order.

But it was me.

The pilot didn't turn back to look at them, didn't wait for orders from Marcos, just spun up the ducted fans of the aircar and launched them off the roof. Valon loved the thrill of a steep dive in a gunship when she was at the controls, didn't much care for it as a passenger. It probably, she admitted to herself, had something to do with the fact that she didn't trust anyone else's skill at the stick of a flyer as much as she did her own.

"It's coming together quickly," Marcos said, nodding at the reconstruction crews hundreds of feet below them. "The Senate brought the best engineers in for this."

"Yes, sir," she agreed, not trusting herself to comment further. Marcos, as usual, saw through her reticence, his smile thin and knowing.

"And you think they should have put that much effort into our defenses."

"If they had, perhaps they wouldn't have to spend so much on rebuilding. Sir," she added belatedly.

"Oh, I think you're going to do fine today, Primus." Marcos laughed softly. "Just be yourself." Valon raised an eyebrow and the man laughed again, louder this time. "Yourself but… respectful."

Valon sniffed.

"Make up your mind, sir."

"I present to you, the Senate and people of Thacia," Presiding Magistrate Selena intoned gravely, "the Hero of Thacia, Primus Pilus Valon."

They stood as one, clapping and cheering, and Valon's ears

reddened. She kept her face neutral, but it wasn't embarrassment that made her flush... it was guilt.

"Steady," Marcos whispered in her ear, squeezing her arm before he retreated, leaving her very alone on the dais at the center of the auditorium.

This building hadn't been touched by the demons, of course. That would have been too much to ask. Valon cleared her throat, then looked up, meeting Selena's eyes.

"Presiding Magistrate," she said, trying to keep in mind what Marcos had told her about being respectful, "I am honored to be allowed to speak to this august body, and beyond honored to have been awarded the title of Hero of Thacia." She shook her head. "I don't deserve it. I didn't achieve this victory on my own, but through the sacrifice of hundreds, thousands of true heroes. They gave their lives to preserve this body, this government, this civilization. And I feel as if the only way to honor their sacrifice is to make sure this never happens again."

She swept her gaze across the dozens of the most powerful men and women on the planet... on a dozen planets. She recognized far too many of them as the ones who'd dismissed her ideas out of hand before things had very nearly fallen apart. There was a new one off to the side of the presiding magistrate though, a priest by the white and orange of his robes, his head shaven close and clean, beardless, eyes piercing. He was the high priest of Zeus, Hiereus, one of the most powerful men in Thacia, yet also one least likely to take political positions. It was strange seeing him here in the Senate.

"This could have been the end. It came too damned close to it. It could have meant the end of Thacia and, just as devastatingly, it could have set the Hive Mind loose on the galaxy with nothing to keep it in check. We owe it to these fine men and women, all of them heroes of Thacia, to see that their deaths were not in vain."

Dozens of pairs of eyes stared at her expectantly, and Valon sucked in a deep breath, launching into the speech she'd rehearsed in her head over and over.

"There are three courses of action that are imperative if Thacia is to survive and prevail. First, we have to put Venator outposts on other colonies and reinforce them, so they can be ready if they need to support Thacia and help evacuate. This time, when we needed an evacuation route, it was shambolic, chaos, and civilians died. That can't happen again."

Nods all around. This was something cheap and easy, something they could all get behind. A good place to start. That had been Marcos' idea.

"Second, we need to recruit new Venators from the young students to replace our losses. We've experienced twenty-five percent casualties in the last few weeks and our current numbers are not sustainable. If we encounter another threat, even a small fraction of this last one at our current strength, we're not going to be able to handle it. We need more trainers for the new recruits, so we're going to have to recall all reserve and retired Venators to report to the Academy as instructors."

More nods. Again, cheap and relatively painless. But she could sense just a bit of tension, particularly from Selena. She knew what they were thinking, that the first two had been too easy. The corner of her mouth turned up.

"And last, and this will be difficult for you to hear, but it's something that we must consider, no matter how drastic it might sound."

Selena leaned forward and so did that old, crusty relic Photius, as if they wanted to be ready to jump out of their seats and try to throttle her. They were expecting the third to involve the Archaios because she'd brought it up before the invasion. This wouldn't be that bad, but they still wouldn't like it.

"We have to contact the Earthers," she said, dropping the other shoe. It was almost amusing watching the play of emotions on the faces of the senators, the initial relief that she hadn't mentioned the Archaios hardening to doubt and resentment at the mention of Earth.

"This is against our traditions back to the beginning of our people!" Photius blurted, the thought echoed by several others in his faction.

"As does interrupting a Hero of Thacia addressing the Senate," Selena reminded him, and the portly man reddened with embarrassment. She locked eyes with him and held the stare until Photius looked away in surrender. When Selena turned back to Valon though, there was doubt in her eyes. "You know the difficulty of what you ask, Hero?"

"Magistrate Selena," Valon replied, back straight, chin held high, "do you know why I was able to put the shield over the gate and stop the invasion?" Just the slightest of pauses, long enough to force the woman to think about it, not long enough to actually give her a chance to attempt an answer. "Because *something* stopped the influx of demons long enough to give me the chance. I know what it was, Magistrate, I know it as well as I know my own name. The Earthers attacked the Hive Mind from the other side. The man I met on Hades, this Wash Williams, went back to his home and told his people of the threat. He was a brave man, a capable man, a man of honor. He would not allow the existence of such a dire menace to his world to go unanswered."

Another pause to let that sink in, and again there was doubt in Selena's expression, but Valon thought this time it was a doubt of her own, long-held beliefs.

"I know the Earthers are feckless and self-absorbed," Valon went on. "But we've *allowed* them to become so. The Venators have protected them for centuries, given them the luxury of believing that the only threat to their existence was each other. They've built a population in the *billions*, squandered their resources on squabbling amongst themselves, but the time has come for them to pull their weight. We've shielded them from reality long enough. Now, they must join the fight or die."

That seemed to go over better. Even Photius seemed to be considering the idea, and none of them would object to the proposition of the Thacians receiving help, even from the Earthers.

"Thank you for the honor of being able to address this august body," Valon concluded, bowing deeply. "It has been my pleasure to serve Thacia."

"And we have been fortunate to have your loyal service, Hero Valon," Selena acknowledged with a bow slightly less deep. "As well as your sage advice." The presiding magistrate smiled thinly. "Though I would counsel that you keep in mind that asking the Earthers for help is one thing… them agreeing to provide it is quite another."

Valon withdrew to enthusiastic applause, though she barely registered the sound or the faces of those clapping. She was in a haze, as if she'd just survived a battle, her hands shaking as she and Marcos left the chamber, the change in the light seeming to transport them to another world.

"Congratulations, Primus," Marcos told her, offering a confident smile. "You had them eating out of your hand."

Valon nodded gratefully, but all she could think of was Selena's final warning. She believed in Wash, but she'd left out in her pitch to the Senate the fact that he was a young enlisted man in their military reserves, not a general and not a politician. He would tell everyone of the threat… but would they believe him?

And where was Wash Williams right now?

1

"Where the hell are we?" Kyle Washakie Williams murmured.

His eyes darted side to side, the shadows of the towering forest teasing at him with twisted, gnarled shapes that might have been demons from the Hive Mind or older, more atavistic fears like wolves, bear, or lions. He resisted an urge to pull down the night-vision goggles mounted on his helmet, knowing they'd be useless in the patchy light filtering down through the trees from the spring morning.

"I'm thinking Narnia," Warrant Officer Victor Shaw replied from somewhere behind him.

Everyone was somewhere behind him. Wash Williams wondered how the hell he'd wound up on an alien world, walking point for a team of Delta Force operators.

No, it's ACE now. Sgt. Reeves told me it was ACE. Army Compartmented Elements.

It had once been CAG, Combat Applications Group, and among the Joint Special Operations Command it was referred to as *Task Force Green.* But whatever they called themselves, Special Operations Detachment-Delta was the best of the best, men with years of experience in SF or Rangers *before* they were sent to Selection. Most of them were ten years older than Wash, some already twenty-year veterans. And Wash... well, he'd been in the Wyoming National Guard for six years and hadn't had time to get to NCO school before the aliens invaded, or he would have been an E5.

Real special operations material there.

They'd made him an E5 after the Hades mission, of course. That had been the least of what they'd done.

Something moved twenty yards ahead of him up the trail and Wash went to a knee, his M-5 coming to his shoulder, finger taking up the slack on the trigger. Then he let off, letting go of the breath he'd been holding. It was an animal, a large ungulate with striped, brown fur and the stubs of new spring antlers covered in velvet. Its head came up from grazing the forest floor and liquid brown eyes fell on him for a long second before it bolted, crashing away through the undergrowth.

Wash looked back over his shoulder. The team had been traveling in a Ranger file, but they'd broken off into a wedge when he'd halted them, and third on his left was a familiar figure. Master Sergeant Brian Reeves wore the same unmarked combat utilities as the rest of them, his hard-edged, square-jawed face nearly hidden in the shade of his helmet and night-vision goggles, but after the last few months Wash knew his movements like a signature.

Reeves sprinted forward in a low crouch, arriving at Wash's shoulder just in time to catch a glimpse of the ass-end of the animal as it disappeared into the trees.

"I know it's crazy," Wash told the team leader, "but I would swear on a stack of Bibles that was a young bull elk."

"Not that crazy."

Dr. Emil Brooks was surprisingly stealthy for a scientist, and Wash hadn't noticed him creeping up behind them. Brooks couldn't have passed for an operator though, even from a distance. He was short, and not just shorter-than-the-average-operator short, but Hobbit short, just a hair's breadth over five feet and skinny as a rail. He looked like a twelve-year-old playing Army, swimming in the smallest combat utilities anyone had been able to find for him, the SIG 9mm holstered at his waist as big as a 50-cal Desert Eagle would have been compared to Wash.

"Think about it," Brooks went on, motioning like he was lecturing in front of a classroom. "We're talking about gates between worlds, and if what you said about these Thacians is accurate, Sgt. Williams, they had to have come over from Earth through a portal in the last two to three thousand years. That means we've had gates opening between Earth and other worlds for at least that long."

"How do you figure?" Wash asked him, frowning, partially from confusion but mostly because he knew this was not the place to be having the conversation.

"The few words you remembered from their language resemble ancient Greek," he explained, sounding very excited about the whole business. "I mean, I'm a particle physicist, not a linguist or a historian, but…"

"Doc," Brian Reeves interrupted, strained patience plain in his tone, "this is all fucking fascinating, but can we bring this all back on mission? Are you picking up the connecting secondary gate yet?"

"Certainly, certainly," the man said, pulling the detector around on the sling over his shoulder.

To Wash, the thing looked like a cross between a ham radio receiver and an EKG monitor, and he had absolutely no idea how the thing worked except that it detected some sort of radio signal the gates put out. Wash forced his eyes off the thing, concentrating on doing his job, making sure nothing more dangerous than an alien elk snuck up on them.

"It's off to the right a little," Brooks announced, pointing. The little man frowned. "I guess that's... north? Northeast maybe? Anyway, it's close. Maybe a couple kilometers?"

Wash had been required to use the metric system for the last six years, every time he drilled with his Guard unit, but it would never be native to his thoughts. He mentally converted to a mile and a quarter and shrugged. Reeves twisted around, nodding at the back of the line, where Nyland was guiding the motorized cart with the Special Munitions. Wash still shuddered at the sight of the metal cannister, dull gray and featureless, despite the fact that they'd delivered so many of them in the last few weeks.

"The batteries on that thing gonna last another couple miles, Tony?" Reeves asked him.

It was a valid concern. They might have been traveling to star systems light-years away from Earth, but that didn't mean they had magic power sources, and even the best power storage black budgets could buy would only get the cart so far. Sgt. Tony Nyland leaned over the cart, squinting at the readout on the control handle.

"Long as we don't gotta bring it back with us," he assured Reeves.

"Well, shit," Shaw drawled. "There goes our deposit. This goes on much longer, the Office of Management and Budget is gonna run a fucking audit on our expenses. And by the way, why didn't we have this handy-dandy motorized shit when we had to haul that nuke halfway across Hell's creation back on Hades?"

"We were damn lucky we could even find a nuke on short notice for that mission," Reeves reminded him, and Wash still wasn't sure if he was just pretending to be annoyed by Shaw's endless grousing. "And the cart is something the boys and girls at DARPA threw together for us just a few weeks ago, so you should maybe stop complaining and be glad you have it." Reeves clapped Wash on the shoulder. "Move out."

The underbrush was sparse beneath the redwood-size trees,

malnourished from too little sunlight and too little water reaching it from the thick canopy. Hunter's instincts kept Wash's feet on bare ground, avoiding dry branches and roots, though silence wasn't their priority. The demons didn't track by sound but by heat, or at least that was what the biology team had informed them after a few necropsies. They were braver than Wash, because he wouldn't go near one of the things after it was dead, not with the load of corrosive chemicals stored in the tail.

The mile passed quickly, at least quickly for a tactical movement, and the sun was still high in the sky when Wash spotted the clearing... and the odd twisting of the light as they approached it. He held up a fist and took a knee, waiting for Reeves to come up again.

Even the biological data about the demons couldn't override decades of field experience, and Reeves went dead silent, pointing to Shaw and then motioning forward and to the right. Wash might not have been an operator, but he recognized the signal. So did Shaw, and the warrant officer took half the team with him, circling around to the right at the perimeter of the clearing.

Shaw might have been a loudmouth, but he knew his shit and so did the rest of them, and they faded into the woods like ghosts. Reeves tapped his arm and Wash crept forward again, the remaining half of the team following, Brooks at the rear with the Special Munitions. The crunch of the tires on dead leaves seemed thunderously loud in the sudden silence, but nothing came to investigate it, no demons nor elk nor extraterrestrial grizzly bears.

The gate took up most of the clearing, standing nearly straight upright for once. That was no guarantee. Some of them were flat on the ground, some floating in the air, others half-buried in the dirt, but not this one. It was standing straight up, its edge flush with the grass, and the only gates Wash had seen that were that neatly placed had been arranged that way by the Hive Mind. Which meant this one probably had been as well.

Wherever was on the other side of the gate wasn't daylight. The ring was almost solid blackness, nothing visible, but a scent of decay made its way through the portal, dead fish on some salt sea. Wash stayed thirty yards from the thing, wary of the reach of a demon stinger, feeling slightly stupid just standing in the open. But they weren't worried about humans armed with guns. That would have been too simple.

"Nothing over here, boss," Shaw reported, circling around from the other side of the clearing. "We're clear."

"I don't see any tracks," Wash added, motioning at the ground in front of the gate. "None of the demons have been here recently."

"Isn't there something else we can call them?" Shaw asked, shaking his head. "I feel like a fucking medieval peasant talking about demons all the time."

"It's what the Thacians call them," Wash said, shrugging defensively. "I was good with bug-eyed monsters."

"You get the honors, kid," Reeves told him. "Clear the other side and we'll bring the cart through."

"Oh, come on." Greenway. He was one of the replacements for the men who'd died on Hades, though Wash didn't know much more about him than his name yet. "This kid was in the National Guard a few months ago and he hasn't even been through Selection. Can't you let someone else walk point once in a while?"

Reeves frowned at the man.

"Sure, Greenway. I'll let you walk point when you've spent days inside enemy territory with no weapons and been awarded the fucking Medal of Honor. That's a whole new sort of Selection, ain't it? Let me know when all that happens, okay?"

Wash's face warmed. The guy was right, and none of it was

anything he hadn't thought of himself. He gave Reeves a questioning glance.

"Go clear us a gate, Williams."

"Copy that," Wash said. He sucked in a breath. This wasn't as easy for him as it was for the hardened warriors, but he couldn't let them see he was scared.

The M5 was heavy, heavier than the M4s his National Guard unit carried, but there was a comfort to the weight, a knowledge that the 6.8x51mm rounds it fired would do some damage to the enemy. Still, it was a stone bitch to carry around miles through the forest, and not that easy to handle jumping through a gateway in spacetime.

But practice makes perfect.

Going through the gate shouldn't have felt like anything. That's what all the scientists said. But he felt it anyway, just a twisting inside his guts like jumping off the side of a rappelling tower. And then he was through, trading day for night, trading a deciduous forest for... a vision of hell. Another one in this case.

It wasn't Hades, wasn't a high desert like some nightmare version of New Mexico. This time, it was more a nightmare version of the Great Salt Lake, or probably more appropriately, the Dead Sea. It was a salt lake, not an ocean, that much he was sure of, because it was surrounded by jagged mountains on all sides, including behind them. And if it had once been teeming with life, it wasn't anymore. It was too dark to see the decay and death, even the stars concealed behind a thick layer of clouds, but the smell of it was almost overwhelming.

Wash pulled down his night-vision goggles and the darkness evaporated, changed to a low-res version of reality, though at least it had more three-dimensional depth than the older model NVGs he was used to at his National Guard unit. These were the latest and greatest, ENVG-Bs, shit he'd read about but never seen before he'd gone into combat with Reeves and his Delta team. He could actually walk while using them without worrying about tripping over a root or rock because he couldn't make out how far away it was. They took some getting used to, turning the world into a computer animation with artificially drawn black lines at the edges of each shape, each rock and rotted log.

And each of the bug-eyed monsters charging at him through the fog, only fifty or sixty yards away.

"Contact, right!" he yelled, hoping the radio signal or at least the shout would make it through the gate.

He wasn't going to wait around to find out though. The M5 might have been heavy to lug through the boonies, but Wash felt none of the weight now with adrenaline coursing through him. The XM157 mounted on the M5 was a groundbreaking optic, a classic, dumb, etched-glass variable-power scope if the electronics went dead but also a combination laser rangefinder and bullet drop calculator that would allow him or any other shooter to make hits out at a thousand meters.

Wash didn't even look at it. The PEC15 laser mounted to the rail on the side of the forearm was a lot more useful with a half a dozen alien demons galloping over the weathered, slick rock toward him around the lakeshore, less than fifty yards away. With the night-vision goggles on, the laser was a broken line in the fog, settling itself over the chest of the closest of the non-sentient warrior drones, each of them an extension of the Hive Mind. If he'd been shooting at other humans, Wash would have had the weapon set for semiauto, but the demons were a lot tougher than humans and he couldn't count on one round taking them out.

Three rounds of 6.8x51 armor-piercing ammo sliced through the chitinous plating over the demon's chest and the eight-foot-tall monster stumbled three more steps before it crashed into the shallow pools at the lakeshore, spraying plumes of brackish water into the night air. Wash knew he should think about getting back through the gate, but turning his back on the demons this close would be suicide—the demons could run about the top speed of a grizzly bear, thirty-five miles an hour, and they could do it longer. They'd be on him before he could take three steps.

He almost did it anyway. Raw fear surged in his gut like the tide that had once churned the salt sea eons ago, when this had been a living world, fighting against training and knowledge and every bit of logic. It screamed at him to run, to make a dash for perceived safety through the portal. Instead, he trusted the other men in his team and cut down another of the things, this one crashing to the rocks only thirty yards away. They were getting close enough now that Wash readied himself for a mag dump, hoping he'd hit enough of them to slow the pack down, give himself that out to change positions.

It wasn't necessary. The dull thump of suppressed M5 rifles echoed off the rocks behind him and two more demons were hit, but the real fun started when Sgt. Flanders' M250 Squad Automatic Weapon cleared its throat. Three-round bursts of battle-rifle-caliber bullets were all well and good, but full-auto was another language, one that comforted with its unceasing commitment to carnage.

Someone added an HEDP grenade from their pistol-like M320 40mm launcher and the concussion pounded at Wash's sinuses from thirty-five yards away, though it did worse to the bug-eyed monsters, burning a hole the size of a man's fist through the chest of the primary target, while the blast took three more of them off their feet. Wash emptied his magazine into those three, then swapped it out without thinking, the reflexes he'd learned in years of USPSA shooting competitions taking over.

"Cease fire, cease fire!" Reeves called, stepping up beside Wash and waving his hand in front of his face in the age-old signal in case anyone's ears had been too blasted by the fusillade to hear the order. "Nyland, get that bomb through right now. This is an active site."

Active site sounded very sterile and military, but Wash preferred the term Valon had used... *Beast World*. It had a certain poetry to it, besides more accurately describing what the Hive Mind and its minions had done to the planet. The gates, Valon had told him in their brief time together, only appeared on living worlds. She claimed not to know why, but what that meant was this place had once been a paradise, an Eden, but the predations of the Hive Mind's endless army of drones had turned it into somewhere that nothing bigger than a slime mold or an algae matt could thrive, where the food was gone and the air was following.

"There'll be more of the things," he warned. Wash knew Reeves didn't need to be told, but a lot of the team was new, and it bore repeating. "The Hive Mind sees through their eyes, so it knows we're here."

Nothing but a few grunts by way of reply, though he could see out of the corner of his eye the new guys taking up a defensive position. Behind them, the motorized cart lumbered through the gate, a freight train in the dead stillness after the firefight, the scratch and grind of its fat, off-road tires rivaled by the curses from Sgt. Nyland as he tried to maneuver it on the slippery, uneven rocks.

"Get that thing in place behind the portal," Reeves said, "and hurry it up. Three minutes on the timer."

"There's got to be a better way to close these fuckin' gates," Shaw complained, "than blowing up a nuke at every one of them. This is getting pretty labor- and time-intensive, you know? Why can't they just launch a Tomahawk through every gate until they reach an active site and then detonate it?"

"Because they're *nukes*, Vic," Reeves ground out, his patience obviously wearing thin. "People get nervous when you start slinging nukes around, and even more nervous when they're on missiles. We're like their ultimate safety, making sure they're not accidentally zigzagging a missile through multiple gates and winding up somewhere in Siberia or Tibet."

"Oh, and it wouldn't work anyway," Brooks added. Wash looked over his shoulder at the physicist, surprised he hadn't stayed back in the forest. The little man was looking over Nyland's shoulder as the Delta op programmed the warhead. "Tomahawks work on either inertial or GPS guidance, both of which require accurate mapping of your target. We're flying blind here, which I guess is why they keep sending in you guys and the SEALs and people like that."

"There's water here," Sage, one of the newbies commented, waving at the dead salt lake. "Surprised the fucking SEALs didn't try to grab onto *this* op."

"It's set," Nyland announced. His voice was muffled, distorted, the edge of the portal interfering with the sound waves. "T minus three minutes and counting, as they say at NASA."

"Vic," Reeves said, motioning to Shaw, "take Brooks and half the team through and set up a perimeter back in the clearing."

"Yeah, yeah, I've heard this song before," Shaw said. "Come on, boys. I never thought setting off nukes would get boring, but damned if it isn't."

"Goddamn, Shaw, if someone gave you a Ferrari, you'd complain about the gas mileage."

Shaw snorted and shot Reeves a bird as he disappeared through the portal. His middle finger had barely disappeared when Greenway shouted a warning.

"Contact, left!"

The demons had come up the opposite side of the lake this time, emerging from the fog like ghosts in a horror movie. Brenda didn't like horror movies, but Wash had dragged her to a few in retaliation for her making him see the *Star Wars* sequels, eight hours of his life he would never get back. The revenge for *The Last Jedi* had been a movie called *The Fog*, and it hadn't been much, but he'd rather have faced the ghost pirates than the demons. There was something about those red, bulbous, multifaceted eyes that were much more intimidating than any specter.

But at least he could shoot these things.

"Flanders!" Reeves snapped, and the weapons specialist went to the prone, resting the bipod of his M250 light machine gun on the rocks and laying down a field of fire.

"Too many of them, boss," Flanders said, and he was right. There were dozens this time, swarming like the insects they resembled.

Wash pulled the grenade launcher around off his back and aimed it one-handed, squeezing off a shot by instinct, barely needing to bother with elevation at this distance. The launcher kicked like a sawed-off shotgun and the round barely had time to arm before it struck one of the demons at the legs, blowing the thing in half and taking out two next to it. Wash didn't bother to reload, knowing the things were too close for grenades now.

"Get through!" Reeves ordered, firing from the hip as he backed toward the portal. "Everyone get through, now!"

Wash knew Reeves was talking to him just as much as the others, but he hung back anyway, waiting for the rest to go through first. He wasn't sure why. He sure as hell *wanted* to be the first through. Maybe it was the fact that the others didn't think he belonged here, the ones who hadn't been with them on Hades. Maybe he had to show them he was worthy despite not being Special Forces qualified or having gone through Selection. Whatever the reason, he kept firing while the others retreated, using the red dot from those high-tech sights transmitted wirelessly to his NVGs.

The closest was forty feet as the seconds counted down, and when he killed that one, the next was past it almost immediately. Thirty feet. Wash backed up a step, firing until his bolt locked back, knowing there wouldn't be time for another reload. He took one last, big step backward, cutting it to the last second... and slipped, one foot going out from under him. Not much of a delay, but enough, and that jagged, scorpion-sting tail was flicking toward his face, just twenty feet away.

Something grabbed him by the casualty handle on the back of his armored vest and yanked him to another star system. He was back in the forest, Reeves hauling him upright, but there was no time to feel relieved. The demons were following them through, concentrated fire from the rest of the team dropping the first of them almost at Wash's feet.

He scrambled backward, conscious of the gunfire coming from the edges of the clearing, careful to stay out of its way as he dropped the spent mag and swapped it for another. Heavy-caliber rifle rounds and 40mm grenades plunged through the gateway, but it wasn't going to be enough. The things were too tough, too fanatical. A talonhed hand reached through the gate... and dropped, severed cleanly at the elbow as the portal disappeared.

"I don't care what you say, Shaw," Wash panted, hauling himself to his feet as he stared at the slight sizzle in the air where the gate had been only a second before. "That never gets old."

2

Master Sergeant Brian Reeves rubbed at his eyes and tried to focus on the laptop screen, but the words swam in front of his vision.

"Tired?"

Reeves squinted up at Victor Shaw, then grinned at the steaming cup of coffee the man was holding out to him.

"Thanks." He didn't attempt to answer the question until after he'd taken a couple sips of the drink. It tasted like shit, being Army coffee, but it was hot and he badly needed the caffeine. "I swear to God, if I'd known back on Hades that there was *so much* Goddamned paperwork involved in setting off a nuclear weapon, I'd have let the fucking demons kill me."

Shaw nodded, testing his weight against the cheap, folding plastic table that held Reeves' laptop as well as six others devoted to the other officers and higher-ranking NCOs who called the temporary base home.

"Hopping from one time zone to another every time we go through the gates is the worst part," Shaw said, gesturing out the entrance to the canvas tent, where the sun was just setting. "We left Elmendorf at dawn, went through the gate out in Chugach

State Park about mid-morning, hit the forest planet sometime before noon, then got into that salt sea area in the middle of the night, and by the time we got back to Anchorage, it's just getting dark. Not to mention we just got off the plane from Europe like an hour before this mission." He snorted. "When I left the barracks tent, the snoring was loud enough to wake the dead."

"What about you?" Reeves wondered. "Why aren't you sleeping?"

Shaw was about the same age as Reeves, but in that moment, the warrant officer looked a dozen years older.

"Ah, you know. I think I'm getting to the point where sleeping is harder than staying awake."

"Yeah, I copy that." Reeves sighed. "Trying to fill out this bullshit, I think I'm gonna nod off any second, but if I try to hit the rack, I'll just lie there staring at the ceiling."

"It's not as bad as it could have been." Shaw's voice was bleak, his stare going somewhere a thousand yards beyond the walls of the tent. "We could be burying half the team again, like Hades."

Reeves blinked. He'd known Shaw long enough to be aware the man's pain-in-the-ass whiner persona was an act, but even with Reeves, Shaw was rarely that open.

"I told the colonel I'd make the notifications," Reeves said by way of reply. "But he insisted on it. Said it was his duty."

"How's Chappie's wife?" Shaw asked. "The kids? I haven't heard nothin' from them since the funeral." He winced. "I mean, the ceremony." There'd been no internment because there'd been no body to bury. Chappie and the others had been left behind on Hades, cremated in the nuclear blast that had buried the Hive Mind's fortress under a mountain.

"She's living with her parents." Reeves closed the laptop, giving up on the reports for now. "Up in Maine. Augusta, I think. I need to stop by and visit, if we ever get a chance."

"I wanna know why Chappie didn't get The Medal," Shaw grumbled, arms crossed. "Not that I begrudge the kid, you understand... but Wash lived through it and even got the girl, lucky bastard. Our guys left behind their families and kids and died on some shithole planet no one'll ever see again."

Reeves nodded. He understood the anger, even if he didn't agree with it.

"I think they will. Colonel Dos Santos put them up for it, and the rumblings he's getting from the White House is that they're leaning toward approving it over the next few months. The kid..." He shrugged. "You gotta understand, Vic... everyone's scared shitless after what happened in LA. It was important the White House gave the impression that we had a handle on this, that we'd already won this fight, had our heroes and were handing out the fruit salad. Wash was a likely face to put on the whole thing. Young, good-looking, indigenous..."

Shaw rolled his eyes.

"It *matters*," Reeves insisted. "This is politics we're talking about here. I'm just surprised they let him get assigned to the team after that. Getting your newly minted hero killed fighting an enemy you're selling that he already defeated would be bad PR."

"You don't mind having him along?" Shaw asked, frowning doubtfully. "Greenway is a douche sometimes, but he's not wrong. The kid hasn't been to SFAS, he hasn't been to Q school, he hasn't been through Selection... hell, he hasn't even gone to fucking *Ranger* school."

"You know as well as I do that we have non-qualified personnel attached to us all the time," Reeves argued, though he felt the weakness of the words even as he said them. And he knew Shaw wouldn't let him get away with that.

"Walking fucking *point*? Kicking in doors?" Shaw pushed away from the table, leaving it wobbling precariously while he paced the pavement that was their floor. "You don't put non-qualified personnel up front kicking in doors, Brian, you know that as well as I do."

"He hasn't been through the schools," Reeves said mulishly, jaw set, "but I'll be damned if he's not qualified. We're not slotting Tangoes in Syria, Vic, we're killing fucking alien monsters, and he has more experience dealing with them than any of us." He shrugged. "He'll go to all those schools when he gets the chance, when all this shit dies down. Unless he just wants to go back to working on ranches and competition shooting."

"Hell, *I* would," Shaw opined. "He could fuckin' sell his story, ghost-write a book about it like he was a Navy SEAL, and never have to work a day in his life. Maybe be a consultant for the movies that are gonna come out of this." He smiled broadly. "Who d'you think they'll get to play me?"

"Oh, don't go fooling yourself, Vic," Reeves warned him, laughing. "You and me and Colonel Dos Santos will get conflated into a single character and they'll get some Australian dude to play our role. And we'll die at the end, just to add to the tension and make Wash look more heroic."

"That sounds about right."

Reeves' issue phone beeped at him and he sighed, pulling it off the clip on his belt.

"Go for Reeves."

"It's me." Colonel Dos Santos. Reeves wouldn't let anyone else get away with that vague of an answer. "Get everyone up and into the operations center in thirty. High-level briefing, mandatory attendance. We have a problem."

"Roger that, sir." But the colonel had already hung up. Reeves frowned. That was something *else* he wouldn't have let anyone but Dos Santos get away with. He sighed and replaced the phone. "Go wake everyone up, Vic. The movie's gonna have to wait."

Wash rubbed at his hair, still unruly from his too-quick shower and too-short sleep. He needed to get it cut. Sure, the Delta operators let theirs grow out even longer than his was now, but they'd earned the right. Cutting it would make him stand out even more from them, but he felt like they'd look down on him more if he grew it out.

Damn, this is complicated. Maybe I should just see if they'll let me go home.

And the truth was, none of the others seemed to be paying any attention to him at all. They'd all been rousted out of their makeshift barracks and called into what was presumably the main operations center for Elmendorf Air Force Base, though he hadn't been there long enough to receive the grand tour. Wash thought about grabbing another coffee but decided against it. He was still a bit shaky from the adrenaline dump, and more caffeine probably wouldn't help.

The operations center was old-fashioned and lacking the sorts of high-tech projection equipment Wash had seen in Los Angeles, but the flat screen monitor on the wall was sufficient to show a map of the United States. Red dots infected the land mass like an outbreak of smallpox, and even without anyone present to explain them, Wash had a troubling idea of what they represented.

The door scraped open and everyone prairie-dogged, rising in their seats and looking around, but it was Reeves and Shaw, neither of whom would likely know the purpose of the meeting yet.

"No, don't get up," Shaw said dryly, smirking as he and Reeves found a seat near the front. "I insist… it's okay."

"You know, boss," Nyland said, a sour exhaustion in his voice, "I'm as hoo-ah as the next asshole, but we *did* just get back from a firefight with monsters and setting off a nuke on an alien planet. You'd think they could let us get a solid eight before dragging us out of bed for a briefing."

"*Another* briefing," someone muttered, though Wash couldn't tell who.

"Y'all know me," Reeves drawled, leaning back in his chair, hands behind his head. "I'm not one to defend unnecessary bullshit. But the colonel said this was important, and I haven't known the man to blow smoke up my ass."

"Team!" someone barked near the back of the room. "Attention!"

Wash was on his feet before the second word had come out, used to the preparatory command when an officer came into the room. The Delta operators might have been lax about showing the usual deference to officers' ranks, but that didn't extend to Dos Santos. The colonel strode into the operations center, back stiff, chin against his chest like he was expecting to get into a fistfight, waving at them as he passed.

"As you were."

The man trailing after him was skinnier, his dark hair frizzy and disheveled, his clothes looking as if they'd been slept in. Wash had met him in LA, before the mission to Hades, but he hadn't seen Dr. Miguel Huerta since then, and everything he knew about the man Reeves had told him. Huerta had been part of the experiment that had caused all this, the ones involving the crashed UFO, and the particle physicist had been rescued from an underground bunker by the Delta team before Wash had met any of them. Wash wondered if the man had always had the haunted look to his eyes, the sallow hollowness to his face, or if those had come thanks to his encounter with the demons.

"I know none of you want to be here," Dos Santos growled, moving behind the podium, leaning against it until the wood creaked. "And I wouldn't pull you out of bed right after an op if it wasn't crucial. I just flew straight here after an in-person briefing at the Pentagon with the Secretaries of Defense and State and the president's National Security Advisor. Everything they and Dr.

Huerta told me is need-to-know, compartmentalized, and the same goes for what we're about to tell you. Clear?"

Dos Santos, Wash decided, wasn't looking directly *at* him when he gave the warning, but close enough.

"Clear, sir!" Reeves said with enthusiasm, and the others echoed him with less of it, and less volume. They were all professionals and probably didn't need to be reminded, while Wash knew the warning had been for him and resented it.

It must have been enough for Dos Santos, because he turned his attention to the laptop open on the podium, tapping the screen. The image on the monitor retained all the red dots but grew some blue ones, and their location was familiar enough that Wash could guess this one too.

"These are the gates you and the other Delta and SEAL teams have closed in the last few weeks. A significant enough amount that it's run our stock of Special Munitions low and the DoD has had to resort to stripping the warheads off retired medium-range and tactical missiles."

"Just doin' our part for world peace and nuclear disarmament," Shaw muttered, earning a dirty look from the colonel.

"Together, the infiltration teams have done an admirable job of closing down active site gates as quickly as they've been discovered," Dos Santos admitted. "But that's just here." He touched a control on the laptop and the United States scrolled off the screen, revealing Europe and Asia, which seemed to have a red dot for every fifty miles.

"Holy shit," Wash blurted, and Dos Santos nodded agreement with the sentiment.

"While we've been shutting down gates here, they've been spreading through Asia and, to a lesser extent, Europe."

"As near as we've been able to tell," Huerta spoke for the first time, hands stuffed into his jacket pockets as if he didn't know what to do with them, "when the initial gate appeared in Nevada, the phenomena first spread out like the blast wave of an explosion, as far east as Riverton, Wyoming." He nodded to Wash as if acknowledging that he should know that. "But once the Riverton gate was closed through the use of the nuclear warhead on Hades, the effect didn't just end... it began spreading slowly on a new vector. Westward."

Huerta's right hand came out of his pocket and gestured to east Asia. His hand was shaking just slightly, barely enough for Wash to notice, but it was there.

"Now, there's mostly ocean for thousands of kilometers after the US west coast, so it took weeks for the wave of new gates to reach the mainland. Now that it has, we're getting reports daily of new incursions. Though we got no official report since it's technically part of the Russian Federation, social media videos have been uploaded indicating the first incursion was on Kunashir Island."

The map zoomed in on an island north of Japan, and Wash frowned.

"The Russians control Japanese islands?"

"World War Two," Dos Santos reminded him, smirking. "The Kuril Islands were claimed by the Soviet Union after Imperial Japan's defeat and Russia still holds on to some of them to this day." He shrugged. "Not that Japan is happy about it."

"Fortunately, there's not much the Hive Mind can do with Kunashir," Huerta continued as if neither man had spoken. "There were images of demons taken near the small settlement, but they never returned. We *think* the next series of gates opened in North Korea."

The map slid to the left, bringing the Korean peninsula into view.

"We can't say for sure, obviously," Dos Santos interjected, "because the North Koreans aren't going to tell us. But satellite imagery has shown EM signatures consistent with three of the gates spread out from just across the DMZ to all the way up at the Chinese border. Not to mention huge troop movements to those areas in the last few days."

"Oh, well," Greenway said. "Guess it's gonna suck to be North Korea. I mean, more than it did already."

"It's also gonna suck to be *South* Korea, Greenway," Reeves told him, an edge of annoyance in his voice. "The DMZ will help, but some of us have seen exactly how Goddamned many there are of those demons. If the Hive Mind makes a concerted push into the south, there's no way we'll be able to get enough troops there to keep it out. And the north ain't exactly gonna let us go tote a nuke into the gates on their side of the border."

"The North Koreans have nukes already, don't they?" Wash asked, then tried not to shrink under the attention of thirteen pairs of eyes. "I mean, shouldn't we be telling them how to close those gates?"

Greenway snorted.

"You think they'd listen to us?"

"You didn't hear this from me," Dos Santos said, eyeing Greenway beneath hooded eyes, "and if anyone repeats it, I can pretty much guarantee a court-martial, but we told them." He shrugged. "Whether they'll believe us is another story."

That shut Greenway up, which Wash appreciated. The rest of the team were the stereotypical quiet professionals he'd expected from Delta, except Shaw and Greenway. Shaw was a joker, but a competent one, as if he was determined to combine that Delta stereotype with the one for Army warrant officers. Greenway was just abrasive, at least to Wash.

"Anyway, there's not much we can do about North Korea, and even if the whole peninsula falls, it won't affect us strategically. But the gates have spread into China and India, and that's bad."

There were an impressive number of the red dots spread over the two countries, along with a few blue ones inside China.

"The Chinese have already started closing gates," Wash noted.

"Very good, Sgt. Williams. They're getting their asses kicked doing it." He shrugged. "And being the Chinese Communist Party, they aren't at all hesitant to use airstrikes against their own people to push back the demons. But they've closed a few of the portals, though they had to break a couple treaties to do it."

Another touch on the computer and a satellite image replaced the map, showing an unmistakable, sun-bright flash.

"Did the fuckers actually nuke their own territory?" Reeves asked, his eyes going wide.

"They did. And I have a feeling it won't be the last time we see that happen." Dos Santos's voice was grim as a preacher at an atheist's funeral. "India has nukes and they've had a much harder time getting them through the gates. Sooner or later, they're going to be tempted to use their bombs against the demons to get to the gates. If this goes on, we won't have to wait for the Hive Mind and its drones to make our planet uninhabitable. We'll do that all by ourselves."

"This is all pretty heavy shit, sir," Reeves said, eyes narrowing, "but it's nothing that couldn't have waited until morning. What's the other shoe?"

Dos Santos nodded.

"You're right, Master Sergeant. We aren't going to be allowed to intervene in any of those incursions. But the gates are still spreading westward, and we've had our first confirmed report of one opening in Europe."

The map shifted again, this time to eastern Europe.

"They've probably appeared in the 'stans,'" Dos Santos reasoned, and Wash recognized the slang term. His father had used it regularly to refer to the near-eastern nations just west of China—Uzbekistan, Kirgizstan, Kazakhstan, etc. ... "But a lot of those countries are filled with impassable mountains and trackless deserts and very little civilization between the cities. The odds are, if the Hive Mind sent scouts through in there, it'd probably just pull them right back out again and blow the whole place off. Lucky for us, the wave of new gates opening skipped over Turkey, because I don't even want to think about the shit-show *that* would have been."

"So, where are they, sir?" Reeves prompted. Wash didn't know the man *that* well yet, but he would have been willing to bet the master sergeant was getting impatient with Dos Santos.

The map stopped over a shape Wash didn't recognize by sight, though the big, red dot in the north-central part of the country was obvious.

"Romania. Specifically Transylvania, not very far from the resort city of Brașov."

"Shit," Nyland said. "The bug-eyed monsters weren't bad enough, now we gotta deal with vampires too."

"Romania's a NATO member," Reeves mused, ignoring the round of chuckles Nyland's joke had engendered.

"And they're *very* eager to have this threat dealt with," Dos Santos confirmed. "Eager enough that they'll allow us to bring nukes onto their soil."

"Not complaining or anything, sir," Shaw said, "but why us? Surely there's gotta be a team closer than fucking Alaska."

"There is. But the president trusts you with this… and so does *their* president. You all in general because of the publicity the Hades mission received, and *you* in particular, Sgt. Williams."

Wash gulped, sensing that Dos Santos wasn't happy about that development, but it didn't stop him from asking the question that had been bugging him. He felt a ridiculous urge to raise his hand like he was back in high school, but restrained himself.

"Dr. Huerta, can I ask you something?" At the physicist's cocked eyebrow, he continued. "This wave, the one that's creating these gates… where's it coming from? Why is it still active? It's been months since the accident."

Reeves' eyes narrowed and he glanced at Huerta, as if annoyed he hadn't thought of the question himself. Huerta squirmed, obviously uncomfortable.

"I've run scans of the accident site with my research team. There are still strong EM and gravitational waves coming from deep underground there, from where the equipment was buried from the bombing. It's my opinion that the phenomenon created in the accelerator experiment is still active and creating the new gates."

"Well, fuck," Shaw said, shifting in his seat as if he wanted to take off running immediately. "Why don't you like, go dig that shit up? Maybe put a nuke down there and try to shut it off?"

Huerta scowled at the man, anger overruling his earlier embarrassment.

"The last time we fed the thing energy," he said, slowly, as if speaking to a child, "it began ripping holes in the fabric of space-time. Do you know what will happen if we detonate a nuclear weapon on top of it? Because I sure as hell don't."

"Okay," Shaw acknowledged, settling back into his chair. "Good point."

"We need to get help from Valon's people," Wash declared.

"Maybe," Dos Santos allowed, "but we've been traveling the gates for weeks now and haven't run across any. For now, this is our problem." He sighed. "You asked why I woke you up. It's so you wouldn't miss any of your leave. We may be doing this for a while without a break, particularly if the gates keep spreading through Europe. You've all got seventy-two hours leave and then we'll all report to Edwards Air Force Base for the flight to Romania. There's a flight leaving here in an hour that'll take you back to Los Angeles, and I've already booked you all seats to your home states from there. Use the time wisely." He shook his head. "I can't say when you'll get the chance again."

3

"Things are getting worse," Valon declared before the door to Marcos' office had closed behind her.

Her helmet was tucked under her arm, and the dent was clearly visible. She knew Marcos would notice—she was counting on it. The prefect's eyes narrowed and he looked her up and down. Valon knew she was a mess and hadn't bothered to clean herself up between the roof landing pad and here. Black ichor stained her armor, the only clean places the harsh, white lines on her shoulder where talons had come just fractions of an inch from ending her life.

"You're a primus," he reminded her, the tone of his voice chiding rather than alarmed. "And a Hero of Thacia. You should be running these battles from your gunship, not on the ground with the engineering units."

"The shields have to be put in place," she said, waving the criticism aside impatiently. That was presumptuous, though she wasn't sure if it was her new station speaking or her exhaustion. "We have a grand total of one engineering unit experienced at erecting the barriers in combat, and I can't keep dragging them out on every mission."

"Yet you'd drag *yourself* out." Marcos stood, pacing around his desk and putting a hand on her shoulder. "Valon, how long has it been since you slept?"

She sighed, sagging at the weight of his hand.

"I can't remember that far back."

"You think you're going to win this war by yourself?" Marcos tsked. "I taught you better than that. Sit down." He nodded to the chair in front of his desk. Unlike most senior officers in the Venators, Marcos didn't have a stiff, high-backed, uncomfortable seat in front of his to keep his subordinates at attention, but Valon eyed it suspiciously just the same.

"I believe if I sit down," she told him, more honestly than she'd intended, "I may not get up again."

Marcos pushed her into the seat and Valon's whole body seemed to melt into the padded leather. It was all she could do not to fall asleep the moment her back touched the cushion.

"Maybe you're taking this Hero of Thacia thing too literally," Marcos advised, sitting on the front edge of his desk. "It's a title, not a job description."

"If I'm such a hero," she said, fighting not to slur her words, "why the hell can't I get the Senate to listen to me? They *still* haven't decided whether to contact the Earthers." A surge of anger gave her focus, banishing the exhaustion momentarily. "Sir, you've read the reports. You know what it's like out there. There are new gates opening every few days... maybe every day, and we just don't know about most of them because they're in inaccessible locations. This isn't sustainable. Even if I trusted every single one of our engineering crews, we won't be able to close them all."

"This is the Senate we're talking about," Marcos pointed out. "Nothing is ever done fast. We're fortunate they implemented the other two parts of your plan so quickly."

"They're going to wait too long," she warned. "If this is

happening to us, it has to be happening to the Earthers as well, and they lack the shield devices. Soon, they'll be in no condition to aid us because they'll be too busy fighting their own battles, and it'll be too late." She rested her chin against her fist, staring at the floor, knowing she must look like a sullen child but past caring. "And then, there'll be no other choice but to use the Archaios."

Marcos barked a laugh, shaking his head.

"The Senate may vote to contact Earth, Valon, but they'll *never* willingly use the Archaios. It would mean the end of everything."

"The end of what we know," she corrected him. "That's the prophecy, isn't it? What they told us so many centuries ago? That it would be the end of all that we know. Everyone assumes that's some horrible thing, but my word to the gods, Prefect, is all that we know that wonderful? All I've known since I was a girl is battle and death."

"Go get some sleep, Primus," Marcos told her. "That's an order. And perhaps after you've rested, you'll leave off such irrational thoughts."

"I'll sleep, sir," Valon told him, rising slowly, laboriously from her chair, straightening her back and facing him, chin upturned. "Since it's an order. Rest, I'm not so sure of. But when the world is crashing down around our ears, perhaps irrational thoughts aren't so irrational after all."

Marcos sighed, eyes downcast as she grabbed the handle of his office door.

"I'll speak to them again," he said. "The Senate. I'll ask them to speed up their decision."

Valon nodded before she slipped through the door. Other officers stared at her as she passed in the corridor, though whether for her status as a Hero or the charred, disheveled state of her armor and uniform, she wasn't sure. She wanted to feel hope from

Marcos' words, but hope was in short supply. Everything seemed to be, except demons.

There were always plenty of those.

"The house looks nice," Wash said, setting his overnight bag on the floor beside the couch. "You've done a lot of work."

"Thanks," Brenda Sands said, peeling off rubber gloves and the baseball cap she'd been wearing, letting her blonde hair fall down around her shoulders before she kissed him.

She looked pretty damned nice herself, even dressed in old, faded work jeans and a t-shirt. Wash savored the taste of her lips for a long moment, the warmth of her pressed against him, still not sure if it was real. So many years it hadn't been, and now...

"You sure you're okay with this?" he asked her, pulling away just slightly, needing to breathe but not willing to let her go. "With staying here in the old house?"

Wash nodded at the interior of the ranch house... well, what had *used* to be a ranch house. The ranch was long gone, sold off to pay his mom's medical bills after the cancer had claimed her, and all that was left was the fenced-in acre around the old building. It had looked like shit for years, his father's disability and Wash's multiple jobs leaving neither the money nor the opportunity to fix it up, but since Brenda had moved in after the Hades mission, it could have been a different house entirely.

The furniture had been replaced, nothing incredibly expensive but much better looking than the ripped upholstery and gouged wood of the old stuff. The walls had been repainted, the wood floors polished till they almost looked new, and Brenda had even managed to fix the old, loose boards in the porch steps. The pictures of Wash with his mom and dad were still on the fireplace mantle, though she'd obviously dusted them.

"Of course," she told him, shaking her head, loose strands of her hair teasing at his cheek. "Where else would I stay?" she chuckled, letting loose of him and walking into the kitchen, pulling open the fridge, which was also new, and grabbing a twelve-ounce can. "Would you like a beer? I know it's barely noon, but I'm dying of thirst... been painting the guest bedroom all morning."

"Yeah, thanks," he told her, sinking into the couch. He'd been sitting in a plane seat for hours and had figured he'd stand for a while, but the new furniture felt *so* good. "But I meant, I know your mom wanted you to move back in after... what happened."

What happened. That seemed like a nice, euphemistic way of putting it. What had happened was that her fiancé, Jimmy Bonner, had fallen into the same gateway through spacetime as Wash and they'd both wound up on the Hive Mind homeworld of Hades. Wash had been lucky enough to run into another human, the woman Valon who was apparently from some weird human colony, however that was possible. Jimmy had been captured by the Hive Mind, but he'd been such a stubborn, bloody-minded son of a bitch that when the alien blob had tried to absorb his consciousness into it, Jimmy had taken the damned thing over. Which had been a *bad* thing for Earth in general and for Wash and Brenda in particular.

Jimmy had sent his pet demons to kidnap Brenda and bring her through to Hades to make life there more comfortable for him, and when Wash had gone through with Reeves and the Delta team to nuke the Hive Mind gate room, he'd gone to rescue Brenda. It hadn't worked out *quite* like that, of course.

Brenda offered him a beer and a raised eyebrow.

"You really think I'm gonna go live with *Mom* again after she pressured me into getting engaged to Jimmy to begin with?" She sucked down about half the can in one gulp while Wash sipped at it carefully. He'd never been much of a beer drinker, and couldn't keep any alcohol at all in the house because of his father. "After what happened... after what I could even *tell* her about what happened, I could tell she blamed me for it somehow. At first she was convinced I was throwing my life away staying with you, until she realized you could make a few million dollars off the book and movie rights once you got out of the military."

"Oh, Christ," Wash moaned, leaning his head back, staring up at the ceiling. "I really don't want to think about that. Some of the guys on the team already think I'm attached to them just because of the publicity I got."

Brenda smacked him on the arm hard enough that he winced and frowned at her.

"Who do those assholes think managed to find Hades in the first place?" she demanded, anger knitting her brows. She looked way too much like her mother when she was angry. "How the hell do they think they would have found their way back to close the gates if it hadn't been for you? I mean, how many of them have a Medal of Honor?"

"*You* deserve the Medal," he told her, shaking his head. "You saved all our asses."

"You came back for me." Brenda grabbed his face between her palms and looked hard into his eyes, her azure gaze piercing right through him. "You knew what the place was like, that you'd probably die if you went back there, but you still did it for me, after the way I'd treated you. I will *never* forget that." She kissed him hard, as if making a point. "And I don't want you to forget it either."

Wash smiled, setting the beer down on the coffee table and slipping his arms around her.

"I promise I won't. Have you heard back from the office?"

"Bobby called yesterday," she said, shrugging. "He said I can come back to work whenever I'm ready."

"You don't *have* to," he said, "if you don't want to yet. I'm making enough to cover the bills after…" A muscle in his cheek twitched as he suppressed the sob still threatening to burst through even after so many months. "… after Dad's insurance paid off."

"I can't just sit around and play house all day long." Brenda waved at the walls. "I mean, it's bringing out the realtor in me, trying to make this place into something I could sell if we had to, but I can't keep this up much longer before I go a little nuts. I need to talk to people, you know?"

"Have you…" Wash shut his mouth, wondering if he should bring the subject up. "Have you talked to the Bonners?"

"No." Brenda sank back into the couch, taking another long drink from her beer. "I've thought about it. They've called, left messages, texted me. But I just can't face them. Not after I killed their son."

"You didn't have any choice. He was insane." Wash grabbed her hand, squeezed. "I don't think anyone could have stayed sane hooked up to the Hive Mind. If you hadn't shot him, he would have killed both of us."

"I know." The words didn't match her expression. "Really, I do. But I still can't face them. Not without telling them, and there's no way they'd understand." Brenda hesitated. "Wash, is there any way… is there any way you'd consider leaving this place? Leaving Riverton? I feel like there's nothing here for either of us anymore."

Wash said nothing for a moment. The whole business about fixing up the house made sense now. Irrational anger tried to work its way up from his gut, but he'd had enough experience hiding his anger to keep it under control until he could examine it.

What *was* there in Riverton for him? Memories. A few friends, though not close ones. There wasn't much time for hanging out with friends when he was working three jobs, and most of the ones he'd had in high school had drifted away, gone off to college, joined the military, or gone to jail. There were a depressing number of that last one.

There were his mom's relatives up on the res, but they'd never liked his dad, and he wasn't sure if they'd be happy to see him if he turned up on their doorstep.

"Where would we go?" he asked, finally.

"Anywhere," she said, enthusiasm lighting up her face. "We can go *anywhere*. I mean, for right now it would have to be somewhere they station you...w hether that's temporary or permanent. But once all this is over, once they close down all the gates, we can live anywhere we want." Brenda hesitated, tugging at one of her curls. "I mean, if I was going to live on whatever base you were stationed at, I guess..."

"We'd have to be married," Wash finished for her. A grin slowly spread across his face. "Is that something you want to do?"

An arched eyebrow and a scowl answered him, and Wash knew he'd screwed up.

"Oh. Uh, sorry." He slipped off the couch, kneeling on the floor. "I don't have a ring... I guess I could run out and buy one real quick."

Brenda still had the scowl, but it broke up like ice on the river in spring and laughter burbled up to replace it.

"Oh my God, Wash, get off the floor!" Brenda put her forehead against his, still laughing. "I'm not trying to make you propose to me. But yes, I love you. And that *is* something I want to do, when the time is right."

"Maybe we should do it now," he said, not getting up. She blinked, staring at him. "I mean it," he insisted. His mouth was suddenly dry and he licked his lips. "I'm not supposed to tell anyone this, and if it gets out I might get court-martialed, medal or no. But things aren't looking so good."

"I thought you guys were closing all the gates!"

"All the gates *here*," he corrected her. "But the effect is

Gates of Hope

spreading, and they don't know how to stop it. It's already happening all over Asia, and most of the countries over there would never admit to it and definitely wouldn't let us haul nukes around to close their gates. Now, it's all the way to Europe. I only have like two days here, and then I have to head back to Edwards to catch a flight to Romania."

Brenda's face went ashen and she stared past him, perhaps seeing the same grim future he'd been imagining.

"I love you too," he added, putting a finger on her cheek and bringing her attention back to him. "And I don't want to waste any more time."

"You only have two days?" she asked. Wash nodded and Brenda stood, pulling him up and leading him toward the bedroom. He frowned at her, confused, and she grinned over her shoulder. "Like you said, let's not waste any time."

4

"Can you tell me," the Vulturi NCO asked in broken, accented English, "what is in the box? I have asked the others but no one will tell me."

Sgt. Teodor Petre was a slim, wiry little man, his nose aquiline, chin narrow, with dark hair cut nearly as long as Wash William's. His eyes were a liquid brown that would have seemed more at home on a psychotherapist or a talk show host than a member of the most elite special operations unit in Romania, the *Batalionul 610 Operații Speciale*. "Vulturi" was Romanian for "eagles," though Wash would have been willing to bet that Petre had never been to Philadelphia or heard "Hotel California."

Wash hadn't known much about Romania in general before arriving in the country two days ago, and knew even less about their armed forces, but the Vulturi were supposed to be the equivalent of the Navy SEALs or something... the whole organizational thing had been complicated and not that relevant to the mission. They were allies and their president was kindly disposed to letting Reeves and his team into the country with a nuclear weapon. As long as they didn't tell *anyone* about it. Including the

Vulturi platoon assigned to escort them through the mountains to the gate site.

Reeves and the others, even the garrulous Shaw, hadn't seemed to have any trouble turning aside questions from the allied troops, but unfortunately Wash was stuck in the cab of a Polaris ATV next to Petre, while two more of the Romanian troops were in the front, though neither had shown any propensity for English. And Petre was a very curious man.

The *box*, as Petre had put it, was in the back of the lead vehicle, driven by Nyland and guarded by Reeves and Sage, while Dr. Brooks rode with them probably with the idea that they couldn't trust the scientist not to blab something top-secret by accident.

But they trust me.

"I'm afraid I can't say anything more than was included in the mission brief, Sergeant," Wash replied, smiling to take the edge off the words.

He *hoped* Petre could see the smile. It was pitch-black outside, a new moon and an overcast sky keeping even the stars from illuminating the narrow dirt road. Well, calling it a *road* was a gross exaggeration. It was more of a hiking trail, which was why they were in the ATVs rather than real trucks or Humvees, or whatever the Romanians used in their place. The headlights from the small vehicles barely seemed to penetrate more than a few yards into the Stygian night, no further than the rear bumper of the vehicle ahead of them.

It would have been easier using night vision, but the Romanians had insisted on running with visible lights on. Something about animals or villagers or hell, maybe vampires for all Wash knew. There were ten of the Polaris four-wheelers in all, and at least Wash was in one near the front, where he could tell what was going on.

"This seems pretty remote," he said, changing the subject pointedly. "How did you ever find out about the gate?"

Gates of Hope

"There's a village up here." Petre waved forward. "It's isolated. There's a road, but it comes in from the other side and takes much longer to get there. We thought about flying to it, but there is much tree cover and we could only get small helicopters up there, not big enough to take these ATVs, and the gate is far into the woods. Would have taken hours to walk to it." He smirked. "And your box looks heavy."

Wash pressed his lips together against the laugh trying to work its way out, wondering how Shaw would have reacted to that. Shaw had already gushed in private about how happy he was to have the ATVs instead of trying to lug the bomb around in a cart, even a motorized one.

Something flashed across the trail, gray and furry, and Wash leaned forward, trying to get a better look, but it was gone.

"What the hell was that?" he asked.

"Wolf." Petre smirked at his reaction. "The Carpathians are home to three thousand of them. Have you never seen one?"

"I'm from Wyoming," he said. "I see wolves all the time... just didn't expect one over here."

"We have bears too. And lynx. It's a beautiful place. In the day. Here, in the night, it's... what's the word? Spooky."

"Glad you said it first," Wash told him, shaking his head. "This feels like a really good place to find demons."

"The people of the village would not agree. The ones still alive."

"Sorry." Had that been mentioned in the briefing? Everything had been fast and furious since the minute they got off the plane from Edwards.

"Four died," Petre told him. "Older men in a hunting lodge. The grandson of one of them was able to get away and reported it back. We were lucky the gate appeared so deep in the woods. If it was near a city, the demons would likely have swarmed across it by now, but they seem to be still scouting the area."

"I read somewhere," Wash told him, "that only about three percent of the Earth's surface is covered by urban areas, so the odds of a gate appearing in one aren't that high. You got lucky, but Los Angeles didn't."

"It is interesting," Petre said, eyeing him sidelong, "that the first of the gates was in the United States. I read the stories about you, Sgt. Williams, when you were awarded your Medal of Honor. There was a gate in your little town in… Wyoming, you said? And there were reports of the monsters in Las Vegas. This whole thing seemed to start in the American west." The corner of his mouth quirked upward. "One might be forgiven for wondering if this whole thing had been caused by your government."

A ball of ice solidified in Wash's gut, fear not just that he'd been asked the question but that it was obvious enough that some Romanian Army sergeant could guess at the truth. He hoped he'd been able to keep the alarm out of his expression, though he'd never been much of a poker player.

"This is alien technology," Wash said, choosing his words very carefully. "It's all controlled by some ancient alien blob brain that uses rips in space so it can suck planets dry all over the galaxy. Do you *really* think that somehow, the United States government can create holes in reality? Do you think we'd be having so much trouble fighting these demons if we had that kind of technology?"

That was something his dad had taught him, that it was much easier to lie to people if you asked questions instead of answering them. It hadn't been a good lesson, and not one Harry Williams had meant to pass down to his teenage son, but Wash had been listening when his dad had talked to the cops, to all the different doctors he'd been trying to get painkillers from. It had worked on them, and it worked on Petre. The NCO nodded slowly.

"Yes, I suppose that is so. Perhaps this Hive Mind attacked you first because you are the most powerful nation on Earth."

Yeah, that sounds plausible.

"Tell me," Petre went on, "you have been over there twice, to this Hades place."

"I don't think it's an active site anymore, but yeah." Wash's tone was conversational, but he was still wary of the man. Petre was a lot smarter than he'd given the man credit for.

"Do you really think we can beat this Hive Mind?"

There it was. A question he couldn't answer, not because he was forbidden to, but because he didn't know. But did Petre really want to hear that? Or was he looking for reassurance? Wash knew *he'd* be looking for reassurance.

"I believe we can," he said, and it wasn't *exactly* a lie. He had to believe they could win, or there was no point to any of this. "I definitely believe we can take care of your problem here."

"With your box, eh?" Petre winked at Wash. "You don't have to tell me. I know what it is."

The driver saved Wash. The ATV had slowed, but he'd barely noticed—they'd been forced to slow almost to a stop at some of the sharp curves and switchbacks in the trail as it traveled up the mountain. Now they *did* stop, and the Romanian soldier twisted around in his seat and said something to Petre in their native language.

"We're close," Petre translated for Wash. "Your Sgt. Reeves wants to stop here and reconnoiter the area."

Wash couldn't open the door fast enough, eager to get out into the darkness and danger and away from any more questions. The headlights were still on, but Wash pulled down his ENVG-B goggles anyway, not trusting the paltry glow from the ATVs to warn him of impending danger. Reeves was already out of the lead vehicle and Wash jogged up to the man, taking a moment to rack a cartridge into the chamber of his M5.

"Where do you want me?" Wash asked.

"Up front," Reeves said as if it was obvious. He was preternaturally calm, and Wash really wished he knew how the man did it. "You, Greenway, and Flanders take Dr. Brooks and scout up ahead another kilometer. Call when you find it and set up a watch, we'll bring the vehicles up if it's clear."

"Yes, Master Sergeant." Wash eyed the two Delta operators and the physicist, wondering if he was supposed to be ordering them around since he was in the lead, but Reeves had, apparently, anticipated the question.

"Greenway, you ride herd on the Doc. If there're any Tangoes up there, you get him back to our main force ASAP. Otherwise, both of you follow Williams and get ready to lay down support if you have to withdraw. Hooah?"

"Hooah, Master Sergeant," Flanders said, and Greenway mumbled something less enthusiastic.

"We should go as well," Petre suggested, motioning to Reeves. The Romanians had their night-vision gear on now, though the goggles seemed old-fashioned compared to what the Delta team was using. "I will take a squad and accompany your scouting group."

Wash exchange a look with Reeves, the doubt he was feeling mirrored in the face of the team leader.

"I'm not sure that's a good idea, Sgt. Petre," Reeves said, speaking slowly as if choosing his words carefully. "Our units haven't trained together."

"This is our country, Sgt. Reeves," Petre said. English wasn't the man's first language, so Wash couldn't be sure, but he thought there was a hint of a threat in the words. "We have invited you here to help, but we have not given up our sovereignty."

Reeves sighed, face twisting into a scowl.

"Right. If you're going, you need to follow thirty meters behind in a squad wedge. You know what that is?"

Petre stiffened as if Reeves had personally insulted him.

"We are the *Vulturi*, Sgt. Reeves. We may not be your Delta

Force, but we are the best in Romania, the best in eastern Europe. I believe we are competent with squad infantry tactics."

"My apologies, Sgt. Petre," Reeves said, raising a hand in surrender. "I meant no offense, I just wasn't sure the term would translate."

"Of course." Petre nodded to Wash. "Lead on, Sgt. Williams."

"That's it," Dr. Emil Brooks announced, looking up from his detector.

Wash shot him a look that was probably wasted behind the barrier of his ENVGs.

"You think, Doc?"

The gate was parallel to the ground, floating about four feet above the clearing. Well, sort of a clearing. It had once been dotted by European beech trees, but now their stumps lined the underside of the fifty-foot portal like support columns. What had once been the remainder of their length carpeted the forest floor beneath the gate, piles of branches, leaves, and shattered bark. The interior of the gate glowed stark white in Wash's night-vision goggles, though when he slipped his ENVG-Bs up, the color faded to a dull gray. Dusk on the other side, or a moonlit night.

"Get down," Wash told Brooks, holding up a fist to send the same message to Greenway and Flanders.

He took a knee, scanning the woods surrounding the gate. They were way too close, but there wasn't much to be done—the woods were too thick to see it from more than forty or fifty yards away. The trail had narrowed to only six feet across before Wash had led them off of it, unwilling to take the path of least resistance while he was trying to scout out possible enemy action. They were thirty degrees around the perimeter from where the trail intersected the clearing, and if there were demons in the area, that was where they'd be heading.

Wash had the patience of a lifelong hunter, and he remained stock-still, waiting... but there was nothing. Not even a wolf. He was still looking when one of the Romanians high-crawled through the brush to squat beside him.

"There is nothing out there." It was Petre, of course. The man seemed to be connected to him at the hip. "Do you think they have left this place?"

"Maybe." He touched the mic key. "Icarus One, this is Icarus Three, do you copy? Over."

"Three, this is One," Reeves replied. "Copy five by five, over."

"We have the portal, but there's no sign of enemy activity. Recommend you bring up the vehicles. Over."

"Roger that. We'll be there in five mikes. Over."

"Icarus Three, out," Wash said, then turned to Petre. "The others are on their way. Could you take your squad and secure the end of the trail?"

"Yes, will do."

Whether or not the Romanian Vulturi were actually the best special operations force in eastern Europe, Petre was damned good at moving through the brush stealthily. Wash barely heard him as he backed out of their position and wouldn't have seen him without the help of his NVGs.

Reeves had said five minutes, but to Wash it felt like an hour sitting in the dark with only Dr. Brook's labored breathing to keep him company. He was about to radio back and make sure there hadn't been a problem, but just as his hand was going to the mic, the sound of thick, rubber tires scraping against roots and leaves reached him. The engines of the ATVs were nearly silent, their position hard to fix until the first of them peeked out through the trees on the other side of the clearing.

Gates of Hope

"Come on," Wash urged, waving forward.

Hair stood on the back of Wash's neck as he skirted the phenomenon, and from what Brooks had said, that was an effect of the static electricity, not just his nerves from being this close to a gate through spacetime. There was a temperature differential on the other side as well. It was chilly in the Carpathian mountains, the gathering winter pushing its way into early autumn, but a warm wind blew through the gate, bringing with it a slight haze of fog, barely visible even with the night vision gear.

Remembering the experience of dropping into a gate parallel to the ground, Wash kept a careful eye on the portal, knowing that if the demons *did* come through, they'd fly out like they'd been launched from a catapult.

"What's wrong, Williams?" Greenway asked quietly, backing into the clearing, watching behind them. "You look like someone just walked on your grave."

"Naw," Wash said, not even thinking about it, just going with the same back-and-forth bullshitting he was used to at his National Guard unit. "I just got a little worried thinking how far Delta Selection standards must have fallen lately."

Greenway surprised Wash by laughing softly.

"You're not so bad, Williams. For a leg."

"Well this sucks," Shaw said, not trying to keep his voice down. The warrant officer was standing beside the lead ATV, staring at the gate. "There's no way we can drive through that."

"Nope," Reeves agreed. The corner of his mouth turned up. "Sgt. Petre, you were so eager to know more about that box... how about you detail a squad to help carry it through?"

"*Cacat*," Petre said, and Wash was fairly certain it was a curse word. "How much does it weigh?"

"A hundred and twenty kilos, give or take."

Petre snapped orders at his men and eight of them hurried to the back of the Polaris, not bothering to ask again what was in the shielded case. Wash didn't envy them. Not that he was worried about the radiation coming through the shielding—he figured he had a much better shot at dying hopping through space fighting demons than getting cancer from being around a nuclear warhead. But the damned thing was heavy and awkward and he wouldn't have wanted to be hauling it around, unable to shoot back. They'd brought along a push cart, though they hadn't been able to get their hands on the motorized version on short notice, but it still took three of the Romanians to unload the case from the back of the ATV.

More jabbering back and forth that Wash couldn't follow at all, but finally, Petre flashed Reeves a thumbs-up.

"Ready."

"Nyland, get the drone ready."

Wash had used the RC-airplane style drones in the Guard, but this was different, a tiny quadcopter that looked like something he could have picked up at Walmart. He had to assume it was more durable than it looked, because he'd seen it work under rough conditions, and he wondered how many tax dollars had been poured into developing it.

Nyland held the drone high until the motors spun up, then tossed it into the portal. The quadcopter wobbled at the influx of warm air, then steadied and disappeared.

"Got it," he said, finger tracing a line on the screen of his tablet.

Wash edged behind him, looking over Nyland's shoulder and watching the video from the multiple cameras. The view was surprisingly stable, and what it showed was even more surprising. The world on the other side could have been Estes Park, Colorado, or even these same Carpathians in the daylight, verdant and forested, with snow-capped mountains in the distance. The local star was low in the sky, a shade of sunrise gold in a halo around the distant peaks. No demons, but...

"Check that shit out," Nyland said, angling the drone downward just on the other side of the portal.

"Those are vehicle tracks," Wash said. The ground was wet, probably from a snow melt, and the ruts dug into it were clear, coming from off to the left and heading through a gap in the woods.

"Yeah, not tires though. Treads maybe."

Reeves pushed Wash aside and tilted up his night-vision goggles, peering at the screen.

"Treads or tires," he said, "the fucking demons didn't make them." Reeves twisted around, looking a question at Petre.

"It wasn't us," the Romanian insisted, letting his rifle hang on its sling as he spread his hands in a helpless shrug. "And how would we even get a vehicle through it like it is?"

"It's not one of the Beast Worlds," Wash pointed out. At Reeves' baleful glare, he corrected himself. "Not an active site. It's got to be connected by at least one other gate. It could be the Russians or the Chinese, or…"

"Yeah, I know who else it could be," Reeves said. "Bring the drone back, Tony," he told Nyland. "Williams, Greenway, Flanders… get your asses through that gate."

Greenway shot Wash a grin.

"Want me to take point, kid?"

"Next time," Wash told him. He looked at the height of the portal, then clambered up the side of Reeves' ATV, standing on the hood, the edge of the portal coming to his shins. He tossed Reeves an offhanded salute. "See you on the other side."

He jumped.

5

"I've never seen this place before," Centurion Diodorus murmured, his eyes darting from one side of the trail to the other.

Valon barely heard him over the rumble of the engineering vehicle's tracks over the muddy, uneven ground. They'd hit this place in the spring, and there were still patches of snow deeper into the shade of the trees, the runoff from the melt turning the path into something almost impassable.

Had she made the comment, it wouldn't have been saying much. Prior to her misadventure on Hades, she'd never been off Thacia, and even since, she could still count the worlds she'd visited on her fingers and toes without running out of digits. But Diodorus was a veteran, twice her age, and by rights he should have outranked her, and would have if not for a spotty disciplinary record. The man had visited at least fifty worlds and thrown dozens of gates up in his day, which was why Marcos had assigned him to her unit. If he hadn't seen a world…

"The gates are opening farther out," Valon declared, the picture sharpening in her thoughts. "This effect is spreading, not stopping."

"I'd like to say it's an opportunity for us to spread more colonies and Venator outposts," Diodorus mused, "but we're not the only ones who see it as an opportunity."

The centurion didn't have to tell her what he meant. She could see the tracks as well as he could—bipedal, holes in the dirt from the talons digging in, the occasional twisting scratch of the tail brushing the ground. And worse, the quadrupeds, larger than elephants, their tracks so wide they didn't even wipe out the others.

"Where are they coming from?" Valon wondered. "And do they know the string of gates leads back to Thacia? Or are they just here to gather resources for the Hive Mind?"

"They come from *that* way," the centurion cracked, pointing ahead of them, his sarcastic insubordination evidence of why he hadn't advanced higher in rank. "And maybe we can ask them when we get there."

Valon's eyes narrowed, but she kept her instinctive, angry retort contained, knowing it was just what he'd expect.

"You think I'm too young for my rank, Centurion?" The question was casual, neutral.

"Not my place to say." He kept his attention on the steering yoke, but the frown he wore as he stared out the windshield spoke volumes.

"Speak freely," she ordered, nothing casual about the command.

"Yes, ma'am." He met her eyes, no surrender behind his hard-edged expression. "I know you've performed heroically in battle, ma'am, and I do not gainsay your awards for it. But there's more to being a primus than bravery. If there weren't, I would have been one three times over by now."

"You believe I lack the experience and maturity for the rank."

"I make no judgement of you as a person, mind," he insisted.

"I don't know you. But I believe it's not possible for an officer your age to be qualified for the rank of primus."

He was honest to a fault, she gave him that. Perhaps it had kept him from being promoted, but it could make him valuable as a subordinate.

"You may be right, Centurion," Valon acknowledged. "If you were, I'd likely not be experienced enough to recognize my failings. But that's why you're here, isn't it? I can count on you to keep me from screwing up too badly, can't I?"

Diodorus smiled, and Valon thought the older man recognized what she was doing and appreciated it.

"Yes, ma'am. Yes, indeed you can."

Valon wondered if that was how Marcos would have handled things and decided the prefect probably never had to worry about it. She leaned out the cab's open window, craning her head back to glimpse at the rest of the convoy. They'd had the rare luxury of flat, even land through the two gates back to Thacia, and she'd decided to take advantage of it by bringing along an entire armored combat team to escort the engineering unit. They were spread out as wide as possible on the muddy game trail, which wasn't very far, a dozen armored assault vehicles stretched out over a hundred and fifty yards, their main guns alternating directions.

Another of the tracked vehicles was out on point, thirty yards ahead of the engineering truck with the shield emplacement unit, running off to the left side of the road by her orders so as not to obliterate the evidence of the demons who'd come through here not long ago. Mud spattered the side of the truck, a few flecks striking her in the face, but she resisted an urge to wipe them off. Image did mean something, particularly for the youngest primus in the history of the Venators.

She frowned, shielding her eyes from the wind and sun, trying to look around the upcoming curve in the road. Withdrawing back inside, she touched the comms button.

"Convoy Lead, this is Convoy One, security halt immediately."

Diodorus glanced aside at her curiously before squeezing the brake lever, taking the initiative and slowing the heavy truck even before the assault vehicle stopped.

"There's something up there," Valon declared.

"You sure?" The centurion leaned forward, squinting through the windshield, then activating the wipers to try to clear some of the mud splatter. "I don't see nothing."

"Convoy One, this is Convoy Lead." The pilus commanding the lead vehicle was a young man, even younger than her, though he had combat experience. "What's the situation, ma'am?"

"Convoy Lead, I picked up... movement ahead, at the curve." That was a half-truth. She hadn't seen movement so much as just a vague sense of the other, leaving her unsure whether there'd been a shadow, a motion, or perhaps just a tree trunk with a darker color than its neighbors. If she was wrong about this, she'd look ridiculous in front of Diodorus and the others, but the rumbling in her gut told her she hadn't been jumping at shadows.

A small herbivore burst out of the tall grass to one side of the game trail and trotted across it, disappearing from view. Valon let go of the breath she'd been holding, her shoulders sagging with relief. But Diodorus showed no such sign of releasing tension, his stare still fixed on the path ahead.

"What?" she asked him.

"This is a game trail. That deer might run off it when he saw our convoy, but why wasn't he *on* it to begin with?"

She nodded, hit the microphone key again.

"Convoy Lead, I want you to fire three rounds into the trees at the corner ahead."

"Say again, Convoy One?" The track commander's name was

Lykon, Valon recalled, and she resolved to have a talk with him later.

"Fire three cannon rounds into the trees." Valon allowed some small portion of the impatience she was feeling with the pilus into her tone. "Now."

"Yes, ma'am."

The turret traversed slowly, the maw of the cannon fixing on a line leading just to the left of the trail, into the midst of a thick stand of trees. Tension wrapped itself around her spine and squeezed, and she was certain this was going to be a waste of time and ammunition.

The cannon thumped, a line of smoke connecting it with the trees for a split-second before the warhead detonated. Wood splinters exploded, a few smacking against the hood of the engineering truck from two hundred yards away. A spider-web crack appeared in the windshield, and Diodorus flinched away from the impact.

"Damn it," he murmured, "that's coming out of my pay."

"I'll write the expense voucher," she assured him, sliding her carbine out of its rack between the seats.

The trees were burning already, but Lykos did as he was told and fired again. This time, instead of just wood exploding, a flood of demons exploded out of the smoke, dozens, moving faster than the armored cars had been able to drive on the muddy road, and Valon *nearly* froze up despite expecting the attack.

There were only two responses, and one of them was unworkable, since there was no room to turn around for at least half a mile back the trail.

"All Convoy units, open fire and assault through!" she yelled into the mic. "Diodorus, keep to the center of the trail! All assault vehicles, go around the engineering truck!"

And that was the extent of the leadership she could provide, leaving her free to lean out the window, the stock of the carbine tucked into her shoulder. The cannons opened up as she pulled the trigger and the tiny, spin-stabilized rockets from her weapon seemed futile and inadequate beside the heavy artillery. The drumbeat of the gods themselves pounded into her head and into the oncoming horde of Hive Mind warrior drones.

A wall of smoke and fire rose between the convoy and the demons, impenetrable, invincible... at least in Valon's imagination. None of the demons made it through, and the rest of the assault vehicles rumbled past the truck, dutifully adding their firepower to the carnage.

Keep going. Pour it on.

She wanted to scream it over the radio, but they knew their jobs and they were already doing them well. Demons were torn to pieces, spreading noxious ichor across the mud, turning it black. A few got through. Not many, but they swarmed over one of the assault vehicles, their stings stabbing into the tracks, acid splashing over the truck, acrid smoke rising from the melted metal. It was off to the left, out of Valon's field of fire, forcing her to clamber out of the cab and climb to the roof of the truck, holding on with one hand, firing the carbine with the other.

"Ma'am!" Diodorus yelled. "Is that a good idea?"

The crew of the assault vehicle leaned out firing ports and added their own carbines to the conversation, demons falling away under a hail of automatic-weapons fire. The last of them went down, but the righthand track was disabled and the crew piled out. Valon waved at them to climb onto the engineering vehicle.

She was staring right at the vehicle when the spike hit. She hadn't even seen the elephant-sized spiker, and only saw it now as a blur of black and purple carapace and a flash of segmented legs. The jagged, six-foot projectile sliced through the wedge-shaped nose of the assault vehicle, the sheer kinetic energy turning the car's own armor into shrapnel, cutting down the fleeing crew. Valon happened to be looking at the horrified face of a tall, lanky

Gates of Hope

woman. The face disappeared in a spray of blood as a fragment of hatchway passed through her head, then banged off the side of the truck.

Valon tried to climb down, tried to get to the radio and order the vehicles to speed up, but it was too late. The next spike passed right through the cab of the engineering vehicle, the impact throwing her off the roof. The fall *should* have broken her neck. It was long enough for her to have time to expect it, but the mud saved her, a foot deep by the side of the road where she hit.

The breath exploded out of her lungs and deep, concussive pain slammed into her with the force of a bomb. Her carbine lay at her side, and she knew she should try to pick it up, but she couldn't move, not yet. All she could do was lie on her back and watch as spikes ripped apart one assault vehicle after another, killed more of her people.

Diodorus was right. I'm not ready for this… and now he's dead because of me. They all are.

She could almost see his homely, craggy face hovering over her, a ghost of her regrets.

"Come on, ma'am!" Diodorus yelled, grabbing her arm and hauling her to her feet. Most definitely *not* a ghost then. He'd survived the hit somehow, though blood was streaming down the side of his face from a nasty cut on his scalp. "Grab your rifle and let's go!"

He wasn't dead, and he wasn't alone. The crews of the wrecked and trapped assault vehicles swarmed around them, looking for leadership. Looking to her.

Forward or backward? If they turned and ran back the way they came, it would take two or three hours in the muddy track, and the demons would dog their trail, still three times as fast as a human.

"Into the trees!" she ordered, putting all the strength she had into the command, yet still only managing a hoarse squawk. "Get off the road!"

"Back to our entrance gate, ma'am?"

"No," she said, jaw clenched in anger... or perhaps just bloody-minded obstinance. "To theirs."

6

This place *wasn't* like the Carpathians, Wash decided after only five minutes on the other side of the gate, and it wasn't like the forests of the Rockies either. It was more like the Cascades. He'd only visited once, on a trip with Mom and Dad when he was a kid. They'd both loved hiking, and Wash would never forget sinking up to his ankles in mud on that trail.

"This," Sgt. Petre said with conviction overriding his accent, "is bullshit."

Wash looked behind him and noted without surprise that the cart had gotten stuck again. It was a lost cause, and the Romanian soldiers looked as if they knew it. Wash had a feeling he was going to learn a few Romanian curse words by osmosis on this trip.

"We'll just have to carry it," Reeves suggested, coming up behind them.

They weren't even attempting a textbook infantry formation on the narrow, muddy pathway, sticking with a tight Ranger file. It made sense, given that they weren't fighting a human enemy with guns and explosives. The ten-meter interval between soldiers had been established to make sure no more than one would be hit by a grenade, and the wedge formation was to allow a unit to spread out and avoid missing a hiding enemy. Neither was likely while fighting eight-foot-tall bug-eyed monsters with acid stings in their tails, but even walking a close line formation strung them out for over a hundred yards.

"What do you mean *we?*" Petre asked, waving his hands like an Italian used-car salesman. "You mean *us*. You mean my people will carry it, carry your nuclear warhead for you."

"I can either confirm nor deny what's in the case," Reeves said, wearing a cat-that-ate-the-canary smile. "But I do appreciate you volunteering to lug that heavy sucker through the mud for us."

Another phrase Wash couldn't have even repeated, much less translated, but it was accompanied by an order to the Vulturi squad. Four of the men maneuvered themselves around the cart and managed to lift the thing up to shoulder height, each taking a handhold. Shared by four, the weight wouldn't be unmanageable, but keeping four men in step on the rough trail was going to be a challenge. Wash was glad it wasn't him.

Once the Romanians had the Special Munitions moving again, Wash picked up the pace.

"How long do you think this will be?" Petre asked, walking up beside him. "We have some food and water, as your Sgt. Reeves suggested, but only enough for a day, perhaps two."

"I've never been gone longer than three," Wash told him, keeping his eyes on the trees, scanning for shadows and movement. "Not with Sgt. Reeves' team, anyway."

"Yes," Petre said, grinning slyly. "I read about your adventures on the Hive Mind world... Hades, is it called? How you met that alien girl?"

"Valon. She's not an alien though. She's human."

"You saved her, and then you went back again for *another* woman! Are you sure you're not French, Sgt. Williams?"

"I don't know if I saved Valon," Wash said, shaking his head. "We kind of saved each other. But yeah, I went back for Brenda."

"Are you still with this Brenda?" Petre shrugged. "She is quite good looking."

"Yes, I am." Wash tried to keep the irritation out of his voice. Different culture, different manners. He kept telling himself that.

"Good for you! I hope you make it. Me, I have been married three times, and I think my current wife and I are not long together. I spend too much time away, you know?"

"You know, Sgt. Petre," Wash said, stopping in his tracks and facing the man, "for a member of the most elite special operations unit in the whole country, you're not big on stealth, are you?"

Petre snorted.

"I can be as stealthy as a ninja, but what is the point here? We're not sneaking up on Taliban in Afghanistan, we're hunting giant bug monsters! You think they're going to hide in a hole and jump out at us?"

Wash was willing to admit that Petre had a point, but it was the principle of the thing.

He turned back to the front... and stopped. Something up ahead was different. He couldn't make it out clearly through the trees, but there was an unnatural shape that didn't fit in with the rest of the background. He raised a fist in the air to call a security halt, then made a face as he realized that meant he was going to have to go to a knee in six inches of mud.

Petre looked at him as he began to crouch, shaking his head and giving no indication he was going to go anywhere near the ground. Wash sighed, turning back and waiting for Sgt. Reeves to make his way up the line.

"I think we've got vehicles up ahead," Wash told him. "No

motion, no sound, but I see squared shapes, and I'm willing to bet we haven't stumbled across a port-a-john on the trail."

"It could be Russians," Petre warned. "Those assholes might start shooting at us."

"Then maybe we should stop yelling about it," Wash told him, rolling his eyes.

"It's not the Russians," Reeves decided, sniffing as if he could smell them from here. "You ever been near Russian military vehicles? You can smell the exhaust a mile away. Whatever those are, they don't run on diesel." He eyed Wash. "And you know what that means."

He did.

"You want me to go scout it out?" Wash asked, more eagerly than he'd intended.

"I think it'd be safer if we all went," Reeves decided, smiling thinly. "Wouldn't want your friends to think we're hiding anything."

They'd barely made it another hundred yards before Wash saw the bodies. Or rather, *pieces* of bodies. The smell hit him first, giving him an idea of what to expect. He'd smelled death before, human death just since this whole nightmare had begun, but other kinds of death before. He'd hunted, he'd helped butcher cattle. All death smelled the same, yet this stench hit him harder, made his stomach twist into knots. Wash pulled his go-rag up from around his chin, over his nose. It didn't shut out all the smell, but it let him move closer without puking, let him separate himself from the carnage and examine the corpses with a detached, analytical eye.

Some had been ripped apart by demons. He knew the signs of it. The others... they looked like they'd been hit by bomb shrapnel, which confused Wash until he saw the remains of one of the spikes. He'd only seen them on Hades, but there was no mistaking the things. They reminded him of an elephant's tusk, but straighter and made up of something dark-gray and shiny, like the legs of an insect. The spikers could launch the things at hundreds of feet per second, using some weird combination of the muscles in their spongy hides and chemicals produced in their organs. He wasn't sure how something like that could breed and didn't really want to think about it.

The bodies weren't identifiable except that they'd once been human, but he'd seen the markings on the wrecked vehicles before.

"Those are the same as on the aircraft where I found Valon," Wash told Reeves, pointing at the side of some kind of tracked cargo truck. They reminded him of the Greek alphabet, and the researchers back on Earth had assured him that was exactly what they were. "These have to be Thacian troops."

Wash had felt embarrassed about having to pull up his neck gaiter to block out the smell, but Reeves had done the same, and so had the Romanians at the front of the line.

"They're not Russians, that's for sure," Petre commented, squatting on his haunches over one of the bodies, yanking at the tatters of the uniform top. More Greek alphabet. "This isn't Cyrillic." He picked up the sidearm that had fallen beside the dead man, making a face at the blood splashed over the weapon. "And I sure as hell have never seen this sort of weapon before."

Wash held his hand out and Petre passed the gun to him. Wash was wearing gloves, but the blood added a wet tackiness to the metal grip. He hit a catch on the side, popping out the magazine, and showed the end of it to Petre, then Reeves.

"Rocket cartridges. Like the old Gyrojet pistols." Except these were about fifty caliber. He'd fired one himself back on Hades.

"Well, now I know what *I* want for Christmas," Shaw said, taking the magazine from him and examining the rounds.

"We got a survivor over here!"

Flanders was beside one of the armored vehicles, what looked like a cross between a Bradley APC and a light tank. The thing was on its side, multiple holes punched through it by the spikes, including one through the gun mount. It had an abbreviated barrel with a maw bigger than any tank main gun Wash had ever seen, and he assumed it used the same sort of rocket-assisted rounds as the handguns. Flanders knelt just around the wedge-shaped nose of the thing, fingers at the neck of the survivor.

The man was young, no older than Wash, dressed in the same sort of deep forest green as Valon had been, though the green was stained red from a deep wound in the side of his head. The soldier's eyes were open but unfocused, his hands shaking.

"Looks like a bad concussion," Flanders reported. "He needs to be medevacked now or he's not going to make it."

"Any other survivors?" Reeves demanded. "Everyone spread out and look around."

Wash circled the perimeter of the zone of destruction, going past the last of the vehicles until he came across dead demons, each of them chewed apart by cannon rounds or multiple streams of automatic fire. Plenty of Thacian corpses among them, but no living. Others on the Delta team and the Romanian Vulturi checked the vehicles but all came out shaking their heads or making chopping motions sideways.

No joy, as his father used to say.

Wash did find one thing though, clear as an after-action report inscribed in the fresh mud.

"There are tracks leading into the woods," he yelled to Reeves, pointing off to the right. "Human tracks, at least thirty or forty people."

Some of them were scraped deep, like the soldiers had been dragging their feet, and droplets of blood were still fresh, blending in with the dark mud. Reeves stared at the markings, then moved up the trail, eyeing the *other* tracks, the ones not made by humans.

"The Thacians are going after the demons," he declared.

Wash nodded.

"That fits. Valon was pretty hardcore, and if the rest of the Venators are like her, they wouldn't give up just because their vehicles got blasted."

"They're gonna get their asses handed to them again," Reeves told him, "if they go up against the demons with small arms." He shook his head, then pulled down his neck gaiter and spit off to the side. "Damn."

Reeves walked back to the wrecked vehicles and the rest of the team, waving a hand to get everyone's attention.

"Okay, listen up!" he yelled. "Sgt. Petre, I'm gonna need a fire team from one of your squads to take the survivor back to the gate and get him to a hospital. He's the only one of these Thacians we've seen, and I don't want to lose the chance to have a talk with him. Jansen." Reeves pointed a knife-hand at the Delta team's medic. "You go with them. Make sure this fucker doesn't die *en route*, you got me?"

"Copy that, Master Sergeant," Jansen said with a nod. He stripped off his backpack, pulling out the folding poles for a portable stretcher. Wash had been told that Delta medics had as much in-depth training as most civilian doctors. If anyone could get the wounded man back alive, it was Jansen.

Petre didn't question the orders, just detailed off a team to accompany Jansen and the wounded Thacian. The team medic slung his M5 and his whole demeanor seemed to change with the weapon out of his hands, turning him from a warrior to a healer in one motion. Wash shook his head in wonder, trying to imagine being able to make that transition. Dos Santos had mentioned sending him through training if and when all this ever calmed down... maybe he could try for medic qualifications.

"What about the rest of us?" Shaw asked. "Where are *we* going?"

Reeves nodded off the road, through the trees where the Thacian footprints led.

"We're going after them. We're supposed to make contact if we can." Reeves grinned broadly. "And I can't think of a better way to open diplomatic relations than to save their asses."

7

"What the hell are we gonna do when we find the things, ma'am?" Diodorus asked.

Valon glanced sharply at the man, then looked at the rest of the unit, clustered close together as they made their way through the trees, wondering if anyone had heard him. No one showed any sign of it if they had. Diodorus was walking less than an arm's length away from her, positioned in case she needed support, which she definitely had when they'd started on their foray into the brush.

"We don't have the shield," he added. "We don't have enough high explosives to bury the gate from the other side. What are we going to do?"

"If nothing else," she told him, her voice tight with the lingering pain in her back from the fall off the truck, "we'll find out where they're going. If they're heading for one of our colonies, we have to know."

Their exchange was interrupted by a tight squeeze between the trees, complicated by tanglefoot vines and fallen branches in the gaps. Valon braced herself against the rough bark, shaking insects off her hand as she scrambled through, making room for the others to follow her. They were moving too slow, but too many were banged up, including her, and she didn't think she could push them any faster.

"Besides," she went on, struggling for breath, the bruised and strained muscles in her back sending spears of pain through her chest with every gasp, "there weren't that many of them. We must have killed dozens during the attack, and we would have wiped them all out if they hadn't brought the spikers. If we stay behind cover in the trees where the spikers can't get to us and the demons won't be able to move as freely, we can make sure, wherever they're headed, they won't have the numbers to do anything when they get there."

"That's what I love about you officers, ma'am," he told her. "You're just so damned optimistic."

Valon tried to smile, though the most she could manage was a grimace.

"We have to do our duty anyway, Centurion. May as well keep a good attitude about it."

She turned, checking on the others. They were moving as fast as her, which wasn't saying much, but all of them seemed determined to press on... or at least were afraid to stop, which would work just as well. She saw a young man with a field bandage wrapped around his leg stumble near the back of the line, and she frowned.

"Keep them moving forward, Centurion," she told Diodorus. "I'll be right back."

It was a tight squeeze back through the line, full of murmured apologies until she finally reached the man. Valon couldn't remember his name, which she considered a failing, but his rank was obvious on his collar. A tiro, a new recruit who hadn't even been in the Venators for six months.

"Are you all right, Tiro?" she asked, grabbing the man by the arm and helping him walk.

He reddened, no helmet to cover his embarrassment. He'd probably lost it in the attack on the convoy.

"Yes, ma'am," he insisted. "I just got a little banged up."

The bandage on his upper leg was stained red, which suggested he was more than a *little* banged up, but he was able to put weight on his leg, so it was likely not broken. He'd kept hold of his carbine, if not his helmet, and he gripped it tightly in his hand as if it were a totem against the evil lurking in these woods. And perhaps it was.

"If you're having trouble walking," she told him softly, "you won't be of much help in the battle to come. There's no shame in being wounded, Tiro. I've been there myself. I don't want your death on my conscience... there are too many there already, and I have no room for more. Be honest with me and with yourself. Can you keep going, or are you going to drop back because your leg won't make it and force me to leave someone with you? Because if that's the case, I'm going to detail one of the other walking wounded to take you back to the gate and report our situation back to Prefect Marcos."

She was giving him an out, but perhaps, she thought, she should just give him an order. The tiro hesitated and Valon was about to just send him back, but he pulled away from her arm and stood straight.

"It hurts, ma'am," he confessed, "but it's just the pain making me limp, not the leg. I can keep up."

Valon nodded, clapping the man on the shoulder.

"All right, Tiro. Make me proud."

Which seemed *so* arrogant that Valon could barely stand herself, but she knew it was what the young man wanted to hear. She'd barely taken a step back to the front of the line when she heard something... an unfamiliar chatter, sounds vaguely similar to small arms fire, but subtly different. Not the *whoosh-crack* of the mini-rockets their carbines and handguns shot, but something sharper, more abrupt. Something she'd never heard before.

Her breath caught in her throat as she realized what that meant. Valon ran for the front of the line, not nearly as polite as her journey to the rear, almost knocking over several Venators on the way. Diodorus waited for her at the edge of a clearing in the woods, one that stretched all the way to the game trail.

"Where?" she asked, lacking the wind to say more.

The man pointed down the road.

"That way," he said, all business now. "A quarter of a mile at most."

Turning back to the others, Valon was greeted with the same fear and determination and, amazingly to her, respect.

"Venators!" she said, pitching her voice to carry. "The battle is here! Our allies fight the demons, and we must aid them!" She held her carbine over her head, ignoring the jets of pain shooting through her back.

"Follow me!"

"Contact, front!" Wash yelled, heels skidding in the mud-coated dirt.

"*La naiba!*" Petre exclaimed in counterpoint, and by this time, Wash knew it was Romanian for *shit*.

He couldn't blame the man. He'd reacted more strongly than that when he'd first seen the demons, and that had just been one of the things... this was a whole company of them, more or less, and the two of them walking point had nearly run straight into the back of the demons' formation as they turned a corner on the trail.

The things turned as one, all controlled by the Hive Mind through the gate ahead of them, standing vertically across the trail, or perhaps one connected to it. No sort of human emotion was readable on their insectoid faces, yet somehow, Wash sensed the malevolence behind those red, faceted eyes, as if the Hive Mind recognized him personally and wanted to kill him.

Yet the demons didn't worry him as much as the spikers. There were three of them in the enemy column, elephants in Hannibal's army, except these mountains weren't the Alps and the Romans hadn't been equipped with automatic weapons. Wash let his M5 fall on its sling, pulling the grenade launcher off his back, letting Petre take the first shots. The Vulturi had come prepared, even if they'd never encountered the demons before, and the M110 designated marksman rifle Petre had carried with him barked its displeasure.

The weapon was generally outfitted with a telescopic sight, but Vulturi had switched those out for Aimpoint red dots for closer-range work, and it was a damned good thing, because the first pair of demons was barely twenty yards away before Petre opened fire. 7.62x51 wasn't quite as hot as the 6.8s the Delta team carried, but the round did the job, chopping through the neck of the first of the creatures, then bursting the eyes of the second.

The two alien corpses slid in the mud after they collapsed, ending up nearly at Wash's feet, but he shut the sight out, shut out the possibility of one of them taking a last, spiteful, disemboweling swing of its talons. He concentrated on the sights of his grenade launcher, trying to find just the right spot on the spiker.

There.

He pulled the trigger and the short-barreled thumper kicked like a sawed-off shotgun in his hands. It kicked the spiker a lot harder. The M433 high-explosive, dual-purpose round was a shaped charge meant to take out light vehicles, but it was enough to blast a hole through the skull of the spiker. The black sludge that streamed out of the ragged, smoking hole was the same consistence and color as the ichor that ran through the bodies of the demons, though he couldn't imagine how the two sorts of creatures could be related. The massive creature stumbled, its column-like legs stumbling and skittering sideways, then it collapsed, the vibration shaking the ground.

It had been a calculated risk, and as the demons charged their position and Wash desperately tried to transition from his grenade launcher to his rifle, it seemed like it would be a fatal one. But he had an effective platoon backing him up, and he'd been counting on them reaching him before the demons did.

"Get down!" Wash heard Reeves' yell through the air and over his earphones and acted on instinct, grabbing Petre by the back of the man's daypack and yanking him to the ground as he fell backward.

The hail of lead and arcing 40mm grenades flying over the top of them reminded Wash of the machine guns being fired over his head while crawling through the obstacle course in basic training. He didn't just sit there watching it though. Wash rolled off Petre and onto his stomach, the M5 coming to his shoulder. But the demons weren't charging anymore, weren't ready to overrun his position.

They were running. He hadn't seen this before, didn't know why they'd bother. Neither Jimmy Bonner nor the Hive Mind had shown any propensity to conserve forces in his previous encounters with them. But instead of trying to swarm over the American and Romanian troops, the demons retreated through the gate. Wash took one of them out with a burst into the back of its head, and then they were gone.

"Cease fire!" Reeves yelled, waving a hand in front of his face, and once he was sure everyone had listened, Wash jumped up, pointing after the enemy forces.

"That's gotta be heading back to one of the hives."

Wash expected an argument. Hell, *he* would have argued if someone else had said it, and he was sure Shaw had something to say about the idea of following the enemy through the gate

Gates of Hope

blindly. There was none, and whether that meant that Wash was thinking more and more like Reeves or that Reeves trusted him that implicitly, either possibility was frightening.

"Get through!" Reeves yelled, waving the unit forward. "Get through before they can get ready for us! And bring the damn nuke!"

Wash didn't wait to be told he was on point, mostly because he was afraid the position would get taken away from him. He got his feet beneath him and sprinted for the gate, reloading his grenade launcher on the run. He'd only had a couple months of practice with the M302 but was still able to reload without looking at the process.

The barrel snapped into place twenty yards from the gate and Wash fired it through blindly. It was probably some sort of safety violation, but so was jumping from one star system to the other, chasing bug-eyed monsters. The concussion of the explosion was distant, echoing, telling him a story about where he was heading... indoors, enclosed. And hopefully full of just enemies.

The bottom of the gate was about three feet off the ground, and Wash jumped at the last second, hurdling the edge of reality and then *falling*...

It wasn't a far enough drop to break anything, but it also didn't give Wash enough warning to do a controlled fall. His lead foot slammed into the stone floor and drove his knee into his chest. It wasn't as bad as if he hadn't been wearing body armor and a tactical vest loaded with rifle magazines and grenades, but his ribs still creaked and the wind went out of him in a whoosh, his vision filling with stars.

The floaters cleared in less than a second, just in time for him to see the eight-foot demon turning on him, its scorpion-like tail whipping through the air as fast as the end of a bullwhip. Chance saved him. His father had warned him never to depend on it, that chance was a fickle friend that would let him down when he needed it the most, but this one time, chance came through. He had his M5 up at high port, across his chest, and when the jagged spike hit it missed his chest, missed his arms, and caught the SIG rifle in the receiver.

The bad news was that it ripped the weapon away from him with enough force to snap the tactical sling and send him rolling across the floor. The good news was, the roll got him out of the way, giving Sgt. Petre the opening to fire a quick three rounds through the demon's chest... and giving Wash his first look at where the gate had taken him.

It was a huge cavern, a hundred yards across and at least as tall, and not one with the convenient bioluminescent algae of the ones on Hades, but he didn't need it. The gates provided plenty of light to see by. There were at least twenty of them, lined up in a semicircle, each with an underlying ring of some different kind of material than the natural floor of the cave. He'd seen that before on Hades, but briefly enough that he hadn't attached any significance to it. Now, he had the thought that it had something to do with the method the Hive Mind used to move gates and erect them.

That thought fled from his mind along with all others at the sight of what was happening in the huge cavern. Demons were swarming from one gate to the next, like they'd been brought here just like the ones they'd followed, sent through for the purpose of going to this one portal. So intent were they on their task, they barely paid attention to the humans streaming through from the mud world... until the shooting started in earnest.

Automatic weapons fire hammered at his ears even through his noise-cancelling earbuds and he couldn't place who was firing or even in which direction, but the effects were clear. Some of the demons fell, but others shrugged off rounds that hit nothing vital and spun out of their queue and attacked, a swarm of the insects they resembled.

Wash's rifle was gone, thrown somewhere on the other side of the cavern, a hole through its receiver, but he still had the grenade launcher… somewhere. It had twisted around, hooked under his day pack, and he scrambled against the closest rock wall to make sure nothing snuck up behind him as he tried to get at the M302.

The nuke was through the gate, light from one of the portals glinting off the gray metal of its case as it tumbled off the shoulders of the Romanians. They'd panicked at the sight of the oncoming horde of warrior drones, dropping the bomb and going for their rifles, and Wash flinched at the crash of the Special Munition on the stone floor. He knew on an intellectual level that it couldn't go off from rough handling, but it was harder to convince his gut of the fact.

"Shaw, get the bomb set!" Reeves yelled, firing a burst off from his M5 without even looking, because how could he miss? "We have to get out of here!"

Wash agreed with the sentiment and finally got his grenade launcher untangled from his pack, breaking it open, the spent casing flying over his shoulder. He slipped another HEDP round home and snapped the thing shut like one of the oldsters at the range shooting skeet. Petre was heading his way across the cave, firing at the demons as he went.

"Come on, Wash!" the man yelled, his accent thicker with the stress. "Get back to the gate!"

The spike snapped across the hundred yards from the other side of the cavern in-between eyeblinks, the massive, insectoid beast not even pausing in its shuffle from one gate to another, just cutting loose with a barrage of the biological cannon rounds. One second Sgt. Petre was rushing toward Wash, trying to help, trying to cover him, and the next the Romanian soldier was gone, pieces of him tumbling in every direction, painting the gray stone of the floor with his blood.

Wash froze, bile rising in his throat, and not just because of

Petre. The spikes were hitting the opposite wall and shattering stone and themselves into deadly shrapnel, ripping apart the Romanian platoon. Men went down screaming, while others died where they fell, and not just Romanians. A figure in American camo pattern combat utilities had collapsed in a pool of his own blood, and with each man lost, the suppressive fire fell away.

We're fucked. It wasn't the first time Wash had the thought since he'd joined the team, but this was the most conviction he'd felt about the statement.

He raised the M302, aiming for one of the spikers, knowing it would be his last shot when the demons noticed him alone, on the other side of the chamber.

Something else hit the spiker, multiple trails of smoke lancing into its head, black fountains erupting where the rounds touched. The spiker lurched, thrashing back and to the right, falling atop a dozen demons and partially blocking one of the gates. Wash couldn't help watching the thing go down before his gaze followed the smoke trails back to their source. He wasn't familiar with the weapon, big and drum-fed, but he knew the uniform of the man holding it, as well as the others pouring through the gate from the mud planet.

They were Thacians. Reeves had wanted to rescue *them*, but it looked like the reverse was happening. His mouth fell open, and he nearly forgot about the grenade launcher in his hand. At the head of the Thacian formation was a tall, stern figure firing a carbine version of the rocket launcher, yelling orders, or perhaps just a feral battle cry.

It was Valon.

8

Another gods-cursed cave. Why in the nine hells did the Hive Mind like *caves* so much?

There was probably some scientific reason for it, having to do with the temperature regulation the creature required, or maybe something to do with how they were good defensive positions back when the Hive Minds were fighting each other thousands of years ago, but Valon just wished, for once, they'd run across a nest of demons on a tropical island.

But the fates and the Archaion willed otherwise, and she refrained from sharing her complaints with the men and women following her, literally, into hell. She didn't say anything, for one because no one would have heard. The weapons of the Earthers were *loud*, ear-damaging, and she wondered why anyone would design such things, though they had an admirable effect on the demons. There weren't enough of them though, and she feared there might not be enough of *her* forces either.

Rather than yell orders no one would hear, she screamed her defiance, more to herself and her own pain than to the creatures before her, who wouldn't have appreciated it. The carbine ran empty in seconds, but they'd driven the enemy back through the simple expedient of piling up bodies between her forces and the demons. Valon paused to switch magazines, and in the moment of that action she found one of the Earthers staring at her, a strong-jawed, thick-chested man perhaps ten or fifteen years her senior.

She ran over to him, keeping her carbine pointed in a safe direction, trying to get close enough to be heard over the chaotic din.

"Do you understand me?" she asked, speaking the English the hypno-teacher had programmed into her memory months ago on Hades. "I am Valon, a Venator of Thacia. We are your allies."

"Well, it sure as hell seems that way," the man yelled his reply, then paused her with a finger held up and drew a short, stubby weapon off his back, loading it through the breech and firing it off-handed, as if he'd done it so many times, he no longer needed to aim.

The weapon didn't *bang* like the others, instead issuing a chest-deep *thump*, the projectile it fired moving so slow she could follow it with her naked eye. It hit the legs of an onrushing demon, and the blast from its detonation was much worse than the *bangs* of their firearms. A grenade launcher then. And the warhead was quite effective, taking down three of the demons with one round.

"Do you have a way to close this gate?" she demanded, pointing behind them.

"That." The man pointed off to the side, to where two others dressed in like uniforms and armor were pushing a heavy-looking metal box behind the gate through which they'd entered. "If we can buy them a couple minutes, they can set that thing and it'll take down this whole cavern."

A cough racked Valon, sending spasms of pain through her back and costing her time she didn't have to waste. The cavern was filling with acrid smoke and the bitter stench of demon ichor, and if the interior of the place had started out at the cool of a cave deep underground, the heat had raised with the discharge of the weapons and the press of bodies... and the ambient heat coming from the gates.

Valon was about to respond to the man when she finally noticed the insistent vibration in her thigh pocket. It was her tablet, and she would have ignored it, except there was only one reason the device would be trying to get her attention. It had detected a signal from home... through one of the gates. She pulled it out, and the indicator was plain to read. The gate straight across the chamber led to Thacia, to somewhere within range of one of the Venator outposts or even the city itself.

A plan gelled in her thoughts, and she didn't question it, going with her gut.

"Take your people and fall back to that gate," she told the Earther, pointing at the portal they'd entered through. "My people will push forward and draw the enemy's attention, then go through that gate directly across from us. Once we're through, use your weapon to bring this place down and go back through the portal."

The man was smart and quick on the uptake. He didn't argue with her, just flashed her a thumbs-up that Valon thought was a positive sign.

"Copy that," he said. "Give us five minutes if you can... if you can't, well... it was nice meeting you." He grinned. "Wash has told me all about you."

"Wash?" she repeated, pausing in mid-motion as she was about to turn away. "He's here?"

"Across the chamber, there," Reeves told her, pointing to the other side of the massive cave, near the farthest of the gates. The illumination from the gate was the only reason she could pick him out through the shifting mass of demons, blocking the way, just seconds from swarming all over them the second they found a clear path across the cavern. "I was about to take a couple of my guys and try to get him back to the gate."

A quick scan around them showed Valon that the Earther's forces had already shrunk to less than twenty, dead bodies scattered across the polished, stone floor, and yet he was as calm as if the whole thing was a training exercise, ready to take a portion of his dwindling unit to rescue Wash across the killing floor. A leader worthy of the Venators.

"No," she told him. "You don't have enough people left for this. Pull back to your bomb and I will collect Wash and send him back to you." The man seemed doubtful, as if he were about to tell her no, that it was his responsibility. "You have my word," she assured him, putting a hand on his shoulder… or on the rifle magazines there, more accurately. "I owe Wash Williams a debt, and I will not let him die here."

There was no time for soul-searching, and the Earther did none. He nodded.

"Don't let me down."

"Venators!" Valon yelled, raising her carbine over her head. They all stared at her, pausing in their suppressive fire for just a moment. Their faces blended into one, and she made herself focus on Diodorus… and the tiro with the wounded leg. "Home is *that* way!" She used the weapon to point toward the gate glowing a faint green just over a hundred yards away. "We must cut through the enemy to reach it! Diodorus will lead you through, and I will watch your backs! Are you with me?"

"Ma'am," Diodorus said, alarm written across his broad features as he jogged up to her. "What are you doing? You lead us! I'll watch the rear! The troops need you."

"On the other side of that gate is home," Valon told him. "Once you're through, set up a defensive perimeter and wait for me. I have a debt to pay. Follow my orders, Centurion."

"Yes, Primus."

Though the man didn't look happy about it, she had faith he would do the right thing. But they'd taken too much time... less than a minute, enough for the demons to find a path through the rows of their dead, around the pair of collapsed spikers.

"Venators, follow me!" Diodorus bellowed, his voice a foghorn on a misty night at sea. And they did, though whether that was because they considered him a natural leader or because they'd been told that safety was through the gate, Valon couldn't be sure.

The Earther had already moved out, joining the rest of his team back at the device, a few of them working on getting it into place, the others either providing covering fire or retrieving the bodies of their dead. Valon thought the custom odd... would the spirit of a hero not rest better if it could see the ground it had fought and died for?

Her focus was on the living... on Wash. She moved laterally, scooting out of the way of the press of demons trying to get to the Venator force and the Earthers. Two of them saw Valon and broke from the pack, coming after her, forcing her to drop to a knee and lay down a long burst of fire from her carbine. Both went down, but the shooting had drawn even more attention, clusters of the things breaking off and heading her way.

"Damn."

Valon ran, giving up on stealth for speed. She'd lost sight of Wash, the far end of the chamber lost in a white haze as explosions and gunshots pounded walls of raw sound off the stone walls as if reality itself was conspiring to confuse her. It was short sprint, barely sixty yards to reach the spot she'd last seen Wash, but with the pain and the smoke making every breath a labor, with the muscles in her legs cramping from the abuse and overstraining of miles walked in the clinging mud, it seemed to stretch out endlessly, like in a nightmare.

The real nightmare was, no matter how fast she ran, the

demons could run faster. Six of them were on her tail, broken off from the pack, ignoring the pounding thump of the Earther weapons and the desperate charge of the Venators, concentrating on the one Thacian who'd gotten away. Just twenty yards to go, but they'd be on her before she reached the far wall.

Wash stepped out of the glowing haze at the edge of the gate, a grenade launcher like the one the other Earther had used tucked into his shoulder, the barrel yawning, aiming right at her face.

"Duck!" he yelled.

She didn't duck... she slid, the stone floor slick with the black blood of demons, a coat of oil that took her nearly to Wash Williams' feet before he fired. Valon covered her ears, but the detonation still banged a drumbeat inside her skull, adding another layer of haze and smoke to what was already nearly impenetrable. There was no time to indulge in the physical or emotional shock of the blast though, because it hadn't killed all of the group chasing her.

The first three were laid flat, unmoving, while another tried to crawl, dragging itself on skittering talons, its legs mangled beyond use. But two of them were still on their feet, staggered yet advancing. Valon's magazine was low, she knew that much, though how many rounds were left she couldn't say without checking the readout on the side. She aimed carefully for the head of one of them and fired off a short burst, blowing apart the thing's eyes and coring through its skull, blowing inky black out the other side. The rifle's bolt had locked empty and the last of the demons was only ten yards away, far too close to allow her the opportunity to reload.

Valon threw herself off to the right just ahead of the whip of an acid stinger, the point of the biological weapon scraping across the stone, leaving a trail of foul-smelling smoke as it ate into the rock. Valon hit on her shoulder, the impact sending spasms through her back, the carbine falling free of her hand against her will, stars crossing her vision.

How many times had she been sure she was about to die in her career as a Venator? How many times in just the last few months? She wasn't sure she'd ever been more certain than she was at that moment... and again, Wash intervened. He didn't have a rifle, hadn't had time to reload his grenade launcher, but he'd pulled out a handgun, an Earther design she'd never encountered before, ugly and plastic but with the look of deadly effectiveness. The thing barked like a small dog warning of an intruder, unrelenting until the slide locked back, and she couldn't imagine that the small caliber would do anything to the demon.

But Wash was a steady and accurate shot, and the bullets pierced through the eyes, not killing the demon but blinding it. The thing's tail swept through the space where Wash had been a moment before, but he hadn't stayed in place after emptying his magazine, dancing backward... and falling through the gate.

Valon *should* have left him, should have followed her people through the gate back to Thacia. It was her duty, they were her responsibility, it was the right thing to do. Valon shot a look back at them, saw they were almost through the Thacia portal, though two or three had fallen to the demons. The Earthers had the bomb set up and were already jumping back to the mud world. Except for the one she'd talked to, who was still standing just this side of the gate, laying down fire with his rifle, waiting, looking at her.

"Go!" she told him, waving demonstratively.

Then she turned and leapt through the gate after Wash.

The heat and haze and choking stench of the cavern was washed away by a cool wind, the harsh, blue glow of the gates replaced by the gentle darkness of a moonlit night, the rays of the moon shining through the thick boughs of a tree canopy overhead.

Valon had a half a second to enjoy the stillness of the night before she realized she was falling, and then another half a second before she hit the water. The air had been cool—the water was unrelentingly *cold*, bone-chilling, taking her breath away just as her head went under and there was no more air to be had. Her uniform and body armor dragged her down, as if the Venators were trying to drown her for abandoning her people and following her heart.

And maybe she deserved it, but that didn't mean she was going to let death pull her into its arms without a fight. She kicked as if striking out at the water in anger, the bitter cold deadening the pain in her back, giving her the energy to stroke with her arms as well. Water spewed from her mouth in an uncontrollable cough as she broke the surface, gasping for air, but she kept swimming, knowing she didn't have long to get to land before the cold sapped the strength from her.

Blinking to clear her eyes, Valon thought she could just make out a swell of dirt twenty yards ahead, and she added a burst of desperate speed to her stroke. The cold had soaked through her clothes, through her chest, and the numbness that had taken away the pain in her muscles now made it harder to take a breath. She had to rest, tried to tread water and couldn't... because her feet touched the bottom.

Cursing in a low mumble that was all she could manage, she splashed out of the... was it a pond? A lake? The lines of the body of water were blurred, merging with the darkness of the surrounding trees even in the brightness of a night lit up by *two* moons. She decided on calling it a lake to make herself feel better for nearly drowning in it. The gate hovered fifty yards out into the water and twenty feet above it, and Valon decided she was grateful for the lake, because a fall from that height onto rocks or uneven ground might have broken her neck.

Wait... Wash. Where was Wash?

"Valon?" The voice startled her, brought her around sharply, her sidearm leaping into her hand, though a moment's thought told her how silly that was, how unlikely it would have been for a demon to be calling her name.

Wash stood from the shore of the lake, his helmet off, face white from the cold of the water, eyes wide with what might have been disbelief.

"I can't believe it's you," he said, shaking his head. "But why the hell did you follow me through?"

She sighed, lowering her gun, though she didn't reholster it.

"Well, *that's* gratitude," she sighed. "I followed you through because your commander had to see to setting the charge to close the gate and I promised him I would keep you safe."

"Master Sergeant Reeves," Wash said. "Is he okay?"

"I told him to go through the gate back to the mud world. Come," she said, waving back at the lake. "We have just a couple minutes to get through before the bomb goes off!"

Unfortunately, something *else* came through before she could finish the thought. A demon, and in the dull, red glare of the chamber, the flat, mushy shape of the head told Valon it was the one Wash had blinded. The creatures didn't make any sound other than the constant chittering of their mandibles, but this one thrashed around as it fell through the gate, swiping with talons and whipping its tail around like a bolo, and Valon could imagine it roaring and screaming if it had the ability.

A fountain of black water sprayed upward as the demon hit, its head still sticking out of the water, tail still flailing about, searching for targets it couldn't see. Wash grabbed her arm, waving the other direction, into the woods.

"Come on!" he urged. "We aren't going to make it in time!"

She frowned, resisting the pull.

"I can shoot it," she insisted, leveling her handgun. Normally it would be hard to take down a demon with the pistol, but this thing couldn't see them to try to dodge.

"No!" Wash yelled, grip tightening on her bicep. "The bomb!

It'll kill anything facing the gate." He pointed to the woods behind it. "We have to get *that* way, and fucking fast!"

Valon wanted to argue, but Wash had been with the ground who'd brought the weapon and knew more about it than her.

"Go!" she said, pushing him ahead of her.

The glow from the gate faded as they ran, the shadow of the trees swallowing them up, the overhanging branches shutting out some of the light from the twin half-moons in the night sky. Wash was moving quickly but cautiously, hunting for solid, flat ground, and she tried to follow in his footsteps, but she couldn't help looking back at the lake. The demon had made it to the shore, still lit up by the glow from the gate, though they'd come around to the backside of it, the out-of-focus blur not visible against the background blackness of the surrounding wood.

It was going to come after them. Even blinded, it wouldn't stop, not until it ran out of energy and starved to death. She needed to kill it now, no matter what Wash thought. She took a step back in the direction of the lake and the world exploded.

A flash of light, blurred out by the intervening gate and yet still so bright that she squeezed her eyes shut and raised a hand to shield them out of instinct. Afterimages exploded inside her eyelids, but before she had the clarity of thought to wonder if her eyes had been damaged, the heat washed over her in a rush of wind as if she'd opened an oven. The sound hit the hardest, crackling, rumbling thunder that went on for seconds... and then, nothing.

Valon stumbled backward, rubbing her eyes and praying to all the gods that they cleared, real fear gnawing at her guts for the first time since this mission had begun. If she was blind out here, light-years from home with no supplies and no support, she was dead.

"Valon!" Wash's arms wrapped around her shoulders, holding her still. "Relax. It's okay."

Gates of Hope

"I can't see," she told him, trying to keep the panic out of her voice. "I can't see, Wash."

"You're okay. The gate shielded us from the flash. Just open your eyes and give it a second."

Valon did as he said and slowly, over the course of thirty seconds, her vision cleared and she could make out the glint of the moonlight on the lake... and the fires crackling in the trees across from where the gate had been. The demon was gone, along with everything that had been on the shore—a stand of young trees, a pile of driftwood washed ashore, all gone, leaving only fiercely burning flames.

"What the hell *is* that thing?" she asked, looking back at Wash.

"Right now," he said, "it's the only weapon we have that works." He waved around them. "I don't suppose you have any idea where we are?" She shook her head, not trusting herself to speak yet. Wash sighed. "It's not that cold, but we're both soaked... and I don't want to hang around those fires to warm up until we know what might be drawn to them." He nodded up at the twin moons. "There's plenty of light. Maybe we should keep moving?"

"Yeah," she agreed, looking not at him but at the fires. "We should get as far away as possible." Valon smiled thinly. "Don't take this the wrong way, Wash... it's good to see you again. But you're really becoming a pain in my ass."

9

Brașov, Romania was a beautiful city, a resort town full of eastern European charm, replete with churches and castles and surrounded by the Carpathian mountains. But for Brian Reeves, the most significant landmark in the ancient capital of Burzenland was Mârzescu Hospital. The building itself was pretty enough, but Reeves had barely spared it a glance on the way in, too concerned with the stretchers the paramedics were pushing ahead of him.

Reeves ignored the stares. He'd expected them. There'd been no time to change into civilian clothes and no safe place to store their weapons, and the sight of American and Romanian special operations troops bristling with guns and gear walking through a civilian hospital in the middle of the day was bound to draw some attention. He hoped the Vulturi troops could keep their mouths shut. They were professionals, but they were also pretty shaken about the loss of so many of their brothers.

They hadn't believed. They'd seen the documentaries, the news reports, the pictures and videos, but they hadn't believed until they'd seen with their own eyes, until the reality of the demons had punched them in the face. Reeves sympathized, remembering the empty feeling in his gut when he'd returned from Hades missing nearly half his team.

This time... they'd lost Greenway. Hadn't even been able to bring his body back with them. It had disintegrated in a nuclear blast on some planet they couldn't even identify, whose sun they hadn't even seen. And yet it hadn't hit him as hard, not because Greenway was kind of an asshole... well, not *just* because he was kind of an asshole. It hadn't hit him as hard as last time because he hadn't gotten to know the newbies yet. He'd actively avoided it, and even now, with another of the newbs, Flanders, being pushed into the emergency room alongside four of the Vulturi, his main concern was still Wash Williams, who wasn't dead. As far as he knew.

The realization disturbed him, but not as much as the look on Dos Santos's face as he stalked down the corridor toward him.

"Is that him?" the colonel demanded, pointing at the gurney being pushed through the doors of the operating theater.

The Thacian looked much like any of the other wounded soldiers, apart from his uniform. He even wore a close-cropped beard, which wasn't much different than the Delta team, though God only knew what the doctors would find when they started poking around, but that was above his pay grade.

"Yes, sir," Reeves said. "He's gonna live. Lost a lot of blood and has a concussion, but they think he's gonna live."

"Well, that's one fucking positive then." Dos Santos sighed, rubbing a hand over his face. Neither of them had slept more than an hour the last three days, and Reeves couldn't have honestly said whether his own trek through the forests and firefight with demons was more stressful than Dos Santos' dealings with politicians and senior Romanian military officers. "I'd sure as hell like to know how to tell General Dobre that I got half a platoon of his best special operators killed."

"Umm... sirs." Reeves turned at the timid yet insistent voice, found it connected to a tubby, bearded man in hospital scrubs. He looked between the two of them, the harsh, white glare of the fluorescent lights glinting off the thick lenses of his glasses. "I am Dr. Tzara, the chief resident here, and I am afraid I have to insist that you take your weapons out of the emergency room. We don't allow them in this hospital." He shrugged apologetically. "It upsets the patients, you see."

Reeves rolled his eyes, gave Dos Santos a pleading look.

"Doctor," Dos Santos said, voice filled with strained patience, "I have authorization from your government to be here, and if you have a problem with it, I suggest you contact the local police. They're very much aware of our presence. Also, I have to ask that you and your staff only work on stabilizing the patients. Our own doctors are on their way by chopper and will be on site in less than half an hour."

"This is highly irregular," Tzara protested, waving his arms like an orchestra conductor during the crescendo. "This is our facility!"

"And we very much appreciate the use of it, Doctor," Dos Santos assured him. "Now, if you'll excuse us…" he made a shooing gesture.

"I will, of course, be checking on this," Tzara huffed, pulling a cell phone out of his pocket.

"I'd expect nothing less."

Tzara shuffled away, already calling someone… either the hospital administrators or the police. Reeves didn't know and didn't care. Dos Santos waited until the man was out of earshot before turning his attention back to Reeves.

"What's the story with Williams?"

"We were cut off by enemy forces." Reeves tried to make the report antiseptic, unemotional, but the guilt made it through the mask and his voice quavered just slightly. "He'd gone through first along with the Vulturi platoon commander, Sgt. Petre, and they'd run into trouble immediately. By the time the rest of us transited the gate, Petre was dead and Williams was all the way across the chamber." He shook his head. "We took casualties immediately and, God's honest truth, sir, I thought we were all dead and I was just hoping we could set off the Special Munitions before the demons got us."

"You said it was like Hades?" Dos Santos asked. "Like the gate room there?"

"*Exactly* like it. And I'll tell you what, sir...." He took a step closer to the officer, his voice pitching lower. "If they'd wanted to overwhelm us, they could have killed us at will and there's nothing we could have done but run back through the gate. It was like they were busy with something more important and they only really started concentrating on us once we really chopped into them. Shitloads of those warrior drones and the big, fucking elephant things with the spikes, moving through a few of the gates and out the other."

"Any sign of where they were going?"

"Not that I could see. I know it wasn't the gate to this Thacia place because that girl Valon told me so."

"You *met* Valon?" Dos Santos asked, eyes lighting up. "I'll be straight with you, Reeves, I wondered a little whether she was even real, like Williams was catfishing all of us."

"She's real, sir," Reeves said, pushing down a surge of irritation. "And she's got balls enough to be a CAG team leader. She and her troops came in there banged up, after getting their asses handed to them in an ambush on their convoy, and they just laid into the enemy to take the heat off us. I was going to go after the kid, but she told me she'd do it, she'd get him back to us while we set the Special Munitions." His lips skinned back from his teeth in a snarl. "I should have gone after him myself, sir. She got to him, but one of the demons was coming after them and he went back through the gate at the far end of the room. Valon went after him

Gates of Hope

and by then, the clock was ticking." Reeves squeezed his eyes shut. "I waited as long as I could, but there were too many of the things between us and that gate, and we only had a minute left. I had to get us out of there and clear of the other side before detonation."

"You did the right thing." Dos Santos clapped him on the arm. "Your duty was to get your team back and get that gate shut down." He sighed and rolled his eyes. "Though now I get to call the fucking president and explain to him how I managed to lose his golden boy."

"Blame it on me," Reeves said bitterly, fighting an urge to spit on the floor, not wanting to piss off Tzara. "It was my fault."

"Yeah, I wish. It doesn't work that way. You're under my command, so if it's your fault, it's *my* fault." He nodded at the operating theater. "I have to go make a call. You stay here and keep an eye on our guest. If he starts talking, let me know immediately."

"Yeah, that reminds me," Reeves said. "Do we have any terps who speak Greek?"

―――――

"Wonder how long it is until sunrise here," Wash said.

It was a casual question, since his ENVG batteries were still holding a good charge and the trail was wide enough that he could have followed it without them. It was also wonderfully free of mud, which made it a vast improvement on the last forest he'd walked through.

"Some worlds have rotational periods hundreds of hours long," Valon said, the first words he'd heard from her since they'd left the lake. Her tone was neutral, almost a drone, as if she were answering a question in a college class. "Others just ten or twelve. No way to tell."

Wash paused, glancing back at her.

"I'm not incredibly happy about being here either, you know," he told her. "I was already lost once on an alien planet with no obvious way home and could have lived without going through that again." He shrugged, looking around at the dark but by no means foreboding woods. "Though I gotta admit this place has it all over Hades. But it seems like something else is bugging you."

"What are you doing here?" she demanded, going from zero to sixty faster than any sports car he'd ever seen. Wash paused, turning back to her, pulling up his NVGs.

"Sorry, Valon," he said, spreading his hands. "I know it was stupid to fall through the gate, but I was off-balance…"

"No, you idiot!" she interrupted, jabbing a finger at his chest. "I mean why are you wandering around Beast Worlds carrying a gun? When you went through that gate back to your world from Hades, I thought you'd be smart enough to stay away from all this!"

"I couldn't." Wash sighed, the weight of everything that had happened since the last time he'd seen Valon crashing in on him. "You know about Jimmy? You saw how he was controlling the Hive Mind?"

"Your romantic rival from the town of the River?" she said, frowning, as if trying to remember the name. "Yes. It was uncanny."

"Well, Jimmy being in charge of the demons made shit a lot worse back home. Unlike the Hive Mind, Jimmy actually knew everything about our society and a lot about how to bring it down. Things were bad when I got back, and there were demons hitting our power generation, water treatment, law enforcement, medical services… everything that glues our society together, you know?" His mouth was dry, and Wash took a moment to grab a sip from his camelback. "And worse, he knew where Brenda lived."

"The girl?" Valon asked. "The one Jimmy was betrothed to?"

"Yeah. Well, he decided he wanted to bring her back to Hades to keep him comfortable. My father happened to be there when the demons came through back in Riverton... and they killed him."

"Oh, gods, Wash," Valon gasped, putting a hand against his chest, though he couldn't feel it through his tactical vest and body armor. "I'm so sorry." He didn't acknowledge the sympathy any more than he let himself acknowledge the lingering pain over his father's death.

"The military needed me as a guide to plan the nuke in Hades, and I *had* to go along and try to get Brenda back."

"You used one of these 'nukes' on Hades!" she said, looking as if he'd told her she'd won the lottery. "I knew it! I knew when the demon swarm ceased to pour through the gate to Thacia that you Earthers had shut down the gate." Her smile disappeared, concern showing through on her face enough that Wash could see it without the night vision. "What happened to Brenda?"

"She's fine," Wash assured her. "She... she wound up killing Jimmy when he tried to kill me."

"A true warrior, then," Valon observed, nodding satisfaction. "And since she saved your life, are you together now?"

Wash frowned, though he wasn't sure why. Maybe because Valon made it sound like such a natural thing.

"Yes, we are. We're probably going to get married. But I'm also in the military full-time now. They put me with a team sealing off the gates."

Valon rubbed her eyes with a thumb and finger, then shook her head.

"I apologize for snapping at you. I've had... too many young men and women die under my orders since we last met, and I didn't want your death to be on my head as well."

"Sorry to hear that." Wash started walking again, pushing

down his goggles, and Valon followed. "What happened after you went back?"

"The demons invaded through the new gates. It was a bloodbath... hundreds of Venators were killed in the battle to keep them out of our cities." Her tone reminded Wash of how his father had used to talk about Iraq. "I lost an entire squadron of gunships and was shot down myself, only surviving through sheer luck. I took command of a shielding unit and closed the gate once the demons ceased coming through." She sniffed derisively. "For that, they promoted me to primus and awarded me the Hero of Thacia, as if I'd accomplished anything other than wasting the lives of the men and women following me."

"People die in wars, Valon," he said, "and there's nothing you can do that'll change that. My father taught me that... and so did Master Sergeant Reeves. He's the one you talked to back in the gate chamber. He's a pretty smart guy. He lost half his team on the mission to Hades, and I was just as wrecked by it as he was, felt guilty because they died on the mission while I lived and got Brenda back. But he told me that they did what they did because they knew the mission was more important than their lives, that I was robbing them of the choice they'd made by trying to take the blame. That made a lot of sense."

"He sounds like my prefect, Marcos. Maddeningly right most of the time."

Wash waited a beat, walking in silence for a few steps before asking the question burning at the back of his mind.

"Valon," he finally said, "I'm really grateful for you helping me out of that jam, and I know you told me last time that you couldn't tell me anything, that you weren't allowed, but I have to ask..." he squeezed his eyes shut, trying to order his thoughts. "Look at this place. It's like every other planet we've stumbled on that wasn't an active site... sorry, a *Beast World*. It looks almost like Earth, and I really want to know how that's possible. I wouldn't have thought of it myself—I'm not into science stuff. But we've had physicists, biologists, astronomers, just about everyone go along with us on missions, and they've all said how impossible this all is. How impossible *you* are. How did you get out here? And why do all these planets look so much alike?"

"I *shouldn't* tell you," she agreed. "I'm not supposed to. I've been trying to convince the Senate to go to you Earthers for help, but they haven't approved it yet." Valon snorted. "They're short-sighted politicians who've lost focus on our reason for being. I'm committing treason by telling you this, but I've come to believe that the only other alternative is extinction. For us *and* for you."

"The linguists I talked to said you speak a language related to Greek," Wash told her. "They thought you crossed over to... wherever Thacia is sometime back around Alexander the Great."

"Perceptive of them." For someone who'd decided to tell him everything, she still seemed close-mouthed. Wash said nothing, waiting for her to expound, letting her wrestle with her conscience. Finally, she went on. "Our histories tell us that we came to Thacia from the Kingdom of Epirus, founded by one of Alexander's generals after his death."

Which was interesting, but Wash didn't know much at all about post-Alexandrian history. All the reading he'd done had been about gunpowder militaries, starting with Napoleon, and the only ancient history he knew anything about was the Roman empire. He stayed quiet, letting her decide how much to tell him.

"The only clue we have of when all this occurred was that Epirus had just fallen to the Romans, and our city was one of the last to defy them. They drove us out of its walls to our death in the screaming wilderness. This was all over two thousand years ago, so all we have are the old histories, written by men who couldn't have imagined the gates or envisioned that they led to worlds around other stars. They thought of the gate as a portal to the realms of the gods, and perhaps they were right. Because worlds like Thacia, worlds like this one... they didn't evolve naturally. Your scientists are correct about that."

"How do you know that?" he asked, unable to contain himself from interjecting. "You told me your people crossed over two thousand years ago. Everything already had to be there, just like it is now, right? The biologists said that everything they studied had been there for tens of thousands of years." Wash cursed under his breath. He sucked at this. He was telling her more than she was telling him.

"Yes," she acknowledged. "The trees, the plants, the animals... it was all what we were used to back home. I imagine that, if things had been allowed to continue as they were, we would have assumed all this was exactly what our ancestors thought it was... a realm of the gods. We would never have developed science or technology beyond what we'd brought with us."

"What changed?"

"The Archaion." Valon hissed the word, as if she expected lightning to strike out of a clear sky and cut her down for saying it. "They visited us while we were still in wattle huts, giving us our purpose and guiding us with the technology you've seen. They told us to use it to protect the world from which we'd come, to take the battle to the Hive Mind, slay its demons and seal off each gate we found to the Beast Worlds."

"The Archaion," Wash repeated. "And what are those?"

"All we have are images, engravings, drawings." He shook her head. "And what they told us of themselves. They claimed to have been fighting the Hive Mind and those like it since before the ancestors of humanity had descended from the trees."

"Aliens?" Why it sounded so ridiculous to Wash, he wasn't sure. He'd traveled through gates to other worlds, fought demons that had never evolved on Earth, yet for some reason, he didn't want to believe the story. Maybe it was because the idea of *benev-*

olent aliens sounded unlikely, given the existence of the Hive Mind.

"You would call them that. They were much like us, but different enough that even our primitive ancestors knew they weren't the same. They thought of them as gods, though the Archaion assured us they were not. Their powers were godlike though. And the gift they left us... or perhaps the curse. Have you heard the story of Pandora's box?" Wash nodded and she went on. "The device they left us is called the Archaios, and it is kept by the priests in the holy temple, tended along with the altars to Zeus and Athena, kept away from the public eye... and from temptation."

"What is it? Do you know?"

"I know what it's for. The scriptures say it was left to us as one last desperate hope, if we were about to be overrun, if there was no way to keep the demons out. Only then were we to activate it. We were told it would destroy all the gates within its range, hundreds of light-years."

"You say that like it's a horrible thing." Wash laughed softly. "Until a few months ago, I didn't know the gates existed, and I wish I still didn't."

"They're our reason for being, Wash. Not just the Venators, but Thacia. We wouldn't exist as a people if not for them. Our colonies will be cut off, the people there left to fend for themselves. It's not something the Senate will approve, not without demons breaking down the doors to their own houses."

Wash snorted.

"I guess it's good to know that politicians are the same everywhere."

10

"He says his name is Lykon, and he's a Venator," Georgi Bellios announced, stroking his oiled mustache.

Bellios dressed, Reeves thought not for the first time since meeting the man, like a Parisian pimp, his clothes too fancy for his salary as a cook at the local Greek restaurant. Which was because he had a second job spying on the local extremist factions for the Romanians and the CIA, and he was too Goddamned stupid to try to hide the extra income.

At least he'd come when he was called, though Reeves wasn't sure who'd called him. Dos Santos had seemed just as nonplused by the man's appearances as Reeves, so his guess was that it had been the CIA. The colonel had probably called the local case officer asking for a Greek interpreter, and this was the best they'd been able to come up with.

Just another thing I have to thank the fucking Company for.

"A Venator," Reeves repeated, looking between Dos Santos, the terp, and the man who'd called himself Lykon.

Lykon looked a damned sight better now than he had when he'd been brought into the hospital yesterday, the wound in the side of his head bandaged and his eyes actually focusing. Though if the Romanian docs had their way, they likely wouldn't have let anyone see him for another couple days. His uniform had been cut off and the man seemed uncomfortable in the hospital gown, pulling the sheet over himself whenever one of them turned his way.

"It means 'hunter' in Latin," Bellios supplied, smiling genially. "I took Latin in college... I wanted to be a teacher, but you know how these things go." He waved a hand dismissively. "There was an incident with a woman, she was married, her husband a city councilman..."

"Venator," Reeves interrupted, glaring the interpreter to silence, "is what Wash said Valon called herself. He said he thought it was like their version of a military."

Bellios said something to the wounded man in Greek, and again, Reeves wished he'd taken the time to learn that language between Spanish, Russian, and French. Lykon frowned, motioning for the man to try again, and Bellios repeated the words slowly. The Thacian nodded and replied.

"He says that's right, that the Venators are the military force of Thacia."

Bellios shrugged expressively. "He does not say where this place 'Thacia' is. Do you want me to ask?"

Dos Santos' forehead wrinkled ,and Reeves had the sense he *didn't* want the man to ask because he was worried the terp wouldn't be able to keep his mouth shut, but those were instincts from before a bunch of bug-eyed alien monsters had rampaged through Los Angeles.

"Yeah, ask him," Reeves encouraged.

Another long exchange, and it was several minutes before the two of them came to some kind of understanding.

"I apologize," Bellios said. "This man speaks some kind of Greek that is, well, not just ancient, but also feels like it has some kind of slang I have never heard before. Thacia is a planet, but also a city, which seems very confusing." His eyes widened. "This man is from another planet! How amazing!"

"Mr. Bellios," Dos Santos ground out. "Just report what the man says."

Reeves glanced around the room. It was just the four of them, and he wondered if he could get away with smacking the terp upside the head, and whether Bellios would object more to being struck or to having his carefully coifed hair messed up. His gaze fell on Dos Santos' phone, propped up on a side table, recording everything, and Reeves decided a court-martial was too likely a result and kept his hands to himself.

"Yes, yes," Bellios acknowledged. "He says Thacia became their home... I think he said two thousand years ago. They were from a place called Epirus, which I have never heard of."

Reeves held up a hand, pulling out his phone and doing a quick web search.

"It was a kingdom in the Balkans," he told Dos Santos, "founded by one of Alexander the Great's generals. It fell to the Romans, and the city rulers sent their families out to escape the Roman soldiers so they wouldn't execute them. And these people... they were going through a mountain pass and they wound up on Thacia through one of the gates." Bellios shook his head. "My God, this means those gate things, they were around two thousand years ago! This is incredible!"

Dos Santos inclined his head toward the man and Bellios sighed.

"Yes, I know." Another exchange with Lykon, and by the end Reeves was checking his watch. It was well past lunchtime. "He says they didn't realize they were on another planet until the Archaion came."

Reeves' ears picked up.

"The what?"

"The Archaion," Bellios repeated. "It's a word I've never

heard before. It may mean something like 'the ancient,' but I can't tell."

"Ask him what the Archaion is," Dos Santos instructed, stepping closer to the hospital bed, arms crossed, staring down at the Thacian. The wounded man looked up at him with what Reeves thought was defiance mixed with intimidation.

Bellios sighed and launched into another complicated back-and-forth with lots of head-shaking and slashing gestures from Lykon. At the end of it, Bellios grabbed the pitcher of water from beside the bed and poured himself a cup, taking a long drink before he proceeded.

"Okay, he will not say." The terp threw up his hands at Dos Santos' glare. "I can't help it. He will not say except that it is something he is forbidden to talk about. I told him we are his friends, that we are trying to help him." He cocked an eyebrow at Dos Santos. "This is true, no? Not that I mind lying, but it would help if I knew."

"Yes, we're his allies," Reeves said, staving off the inevitable explosion from the colonel. "Tell him the demons have invaded our world just like they have his and all we want to do is fight them."

"He says," Bellios related after another few minutes, "that the mission of the Venators has always been to protect Earth from the Hive Mind, to erect shields between them and the Beast Worlds. They are our friends, but he still has his orders and he can't say any more."

As if demonstrating how firmly he believed that, Lykon folded his arms, set his jaw, and rested back against the pillow.

Reeves shared an exasperated look with Dos Santos.

"Now what?"

The colonel retrieved his phone and motioned for Reeves to follow him.

"Mr. Bellios," Dos Santos said, pausing at the door, "you can go grab yourself a coffee or lunch in the hospital cafeteria, but I'd appreciate you sticking around a bit longer in case we have more questions for our guest."

Bellios rose, straightening his purple tie, and made a sour face.

"I may indulge in their coffee," he announced, "but I would not touch their hospital food. I am a man who appreciates the finer things in life, and without good food, we merely *exist*."

Dos Santos waited out in the hallway for Bellios to leave the room before closing the door behind them. Reeves turned to one of the two US Marine NCOs standing outside the door, M4 carbines held at low-ready across their chests. They were on loan from the US embassy and Reeves would have felt more comfortable using his own people to guard the man, but his team needed downtime, especially after losing Greenway. Hell, *he* needed some downtime, not that he was going to get it.

"Don't let anyone in there other unless one of the two of us is with them," he told the senior of the two, a baby-faced young man with bad acne. "Not even police, not even doctors. Not even military, ours or theirs. If they want to check on him, you call me and let me know." Reeves held up his phone. "You both have my number, correct?"

"Yes, sir!" the Marine sergeant barked, coming to attention. Reeves sighed, but didn't bother telling the young E-5 to relax. It wouldn't have done any good.

"Be polite, though," he cautioned them. "Don't act like assholes to the doctors or the locals. Just tell them you have to call your superiors."

The jarhead grunted acknowledgement, but Reeves had already followed Dos Santos down the corridor. The colonel was striding quickly, a purpose to his pace, which was never a good sign.

"Don't tell me," Reeves said, catching up to the man and

falling into step with him, "let me guess. Now we get to play that video for some people who won't like what Lykon had to say?"

Dos Santos grunted, and Reeves thought that might be the only response he would get, but the colonel expounded in a low voice, soft enough that the hospital personnel staring at them as they passed wouldn't hear.

"SecDef, Director of the CIA and National Security Advisor. And I don't like any of those motherfuckers."

"You need me there?" he asked. "I still haven't contacted Greenway's family."

"Sorry," Dos Santos said, and Reeves thought the man genuinely was. He might have been a colonel, but sometimes the man was actually human. "But yeah, I need you there." He snorted a humorless laugh. "If for nothing else, then to keep me from winding up cashiered and court-martialed."

"I wonder if he might be more forthcoming," CIA Director Chris Janus mused, rubbing thoughtfully at his chin in his corner of the four-way video chat screen, "if we used enhanced interrogation."

Reeves chomped down on the visceral reply welling up in his gut, counting to ten before he opened his mouth again. The comms setup in the unmarked white van was fairly basic, a laptop with a plug-in camera, but it would surely pick up any smartass remark he might let slip.

"Director Janus," Dos Santos said, voice carefully neutral, "we're trying to cultivate the Thacians as allies against the Hive Mind. They have *centuries* of experience fighting the demons and they've managed to keep them in check until *we* opened up all those damned gates with the experiment." Reeves watched the eyes of the government officials carefully, looking for signs of alarm or confusion, wondering if any of them didn't yet know about the Nevada experiments, or if any thought the *others* might not know. But if so, they were just as good actors as any other politician he'd ever met. "To that end, I would rather *not* start off our first official encounter with one of their soldiers by *waterboarding* him."

"I'm inclined to agree," the Secretary of Defense, Melissa Endicott, put in. She was younger than Reeves had imagined, something of a *wunderkind* in politics. A former Air Force fighter pilot, though he tried not to hold it against her, with dark, unreadable eyes and the sort of even keel that most zoomies had in the cockpit. "It would be unwise, not even mentioning the ethical considerations. Or the physical ones, giving that he's recovering from a nasty concussion." She was wearing a fashionable, tan pants suit and the cuffs of her jacket shot when she spread her arms, her hands going beyond the video pickup, out of the frame on the laptop. "Perhaps we should be thinking of this as an opportunity for building relationships rather than gathering intelligence."

"I thought you were the Secretary of *Defense*, Melissa," Janus murmured, "not the Secretary of *State*. Shouldn't military advantage be your first thought, not your last?"

"Having allies *is* a military advantage, Chris," Vernon Barclay declared, sitting back in his leather chair, hands resting on his ample stomach. The president's National Security Advisor was the stereotypical politician from all of Reeves' cynical imaginings of the Beltway, old and gray and fat and established as a tick in a dog's armpit, yet for some reason, he couldn't help like the man at first blush. "Right now, we're shuffling nukes around the parts of the world that will *let* us, dropping blind into one deadly situation after another and listening to Russia and China lie to us that they have no problems while they set off their *own* nuclear weapons right on the surface. We need allies who know the enemy, who can direct us so we're doing something useful, not just flailing around blindly."

"Is that what the president thinks?" Janus asked sharply. "Because I haven't heard him express any such notion in my presence or in official correspondence."

"You think he wants *anything* on the record after LA?" Barclay shot back, laughing in what could be disbelief or perhaps mockery. Or both. "We were invaded by fucking *alien monsters*, Chris! Jesus Christ! The mayor of LA, the governor of California, and the entire House and Senate are throwing a shit-fit, not to mention the fucking press! Maybe you didn't see all this from your offices in Foggy Bottom, but the political fallout from this has been a nightmare. The *last* thing the president wants on the record is that we're worried about anything like that happening *again*. This all has to be taken care as far away from American soil as possible and as *quietly* as possible." Barclay had been looking to his left, as if he knew the exact order the video frames would be arranged in on everyone's screen, but now he looked straight ahead, at Dos Santos and Reeves. "That includes you gentlemen as well, by the way. There's already some press sniffing around this because of the uniformed soldiers and the guns in a tourist city hospital. *Nothing* about this leaks, you get me?"

"If it does, sir," Dos Santos said, not showing the slightest hint of intimidation at the man's girth or importance, "it won't be from us. But I can't control the Vulturi, or their commanders, or Romanian politicians." He shot a baleful glance at Janus. "Not to mention the fucking restaurant chef that the local CIA section chief gave us as an interpreter. And you know what that means... some of this *will* get out."

Barclay snorted, the sound of a horse in a stall who didn't care for what the vet was doing to his ass and getting ready to kick in protest. But then he sighed, as if accepting the inevitable.

"Well, as long as the rumor mill has it happening over *there* and not back *here*, I suppose that's the best we can expect."

"If we can get back to the business at hand," Endicott interrupted, a tightening at the corner of her eyes and mouth giving Reeves a clue that she didn't care for Barclay's blustery, good-old-boy ways. "I think we need to get this Lykon somewhere more secure as soon as possible."

"Back to the states?" Dos Santos asked. "I have a plane on call…"

"That would be inadvisable. Mr. Barclay is right about one thing—this needs to be kept insulated from domestic politics. Director Janus, do you have anyplace suitably secure?"

"It'll have to be a US military base," Janus suggested. "I have plenty of safehouses, but the man needs medical attention, and I can't guarantee it in some anonymous apartment in Gdansk."

"Landstuhl." The word had burst free from Reeves' lips of its own accord, and he tried not to shrink at the attention of the three politicians. "It's a first-rate medical facility, and special ops types wouldn't even warrant a second look."

"Good thinking," Endicott acknowledged, nodding to him. "I'll have a couple SEAL platoons brought in for extra security."

"Do you *have* to?" Reeves murmured, and he was sure he'd whispered it softly enough that none of them heard it, but Dos Santos gave him the stink-eye.

"After that… well, the mission was a success, wasn't it?"

Reeves couldn't help it… he didn't realize he was staring at her until he'd been doing it for a couple seconds.

"We set off the Special Munitions in a Hive Mind gate hub," he said, finally, "but we lost most of a platoon of Romanian special forces as well as one of our own men, Sgt. Greenway KIA. Four more were badly wounded and Sgt. Williams disappeared through one of the gates and is currently MIA."

"That's unfortunate. He was a brave young man."

"He still *is*, as far as we know," Reeves said, barely able to keep from snapping at the SecDef. "He was accompanied by an officer of these Thacian Venators, someone named Valon, who he'd encountered last time."

But Endicott was shaking her head.

"I'm sorry, Master Sergeant, I know you're fond of the boy, but they're on their own on an alien world that might be crawling with enemies, equipped with little ammo, little food, little water... and no way to find a gate back. Sgt. Williams may not be dead yet... but it's inevitable."

11

"Wake up."

Wash blinked, sitting up sharply, his Canik jumping into his hand, then stopped himself when he saw Valon hovering above him, backlit by the noonday sun.

Noonday star. The Sun's a long way away.

"How long was I asleep?" he asked, pushing himself up from the loamy dirt, then wincing as his neck tightened up. He'd slept against a tree, using his day pack and helmet as a pillow, which hadn't been the worst sleep he'd ever had, but still wasn't comfortable.

"Four hours," she said, shrugging. "More or less." Her eyes were bloodshot, her red hair tangled, but she was alert and awake, which was more than he could say for himself.

"I said to wake me up after three." They'd waited until daybreak to rest, worried about wildlife, but they'd seen nothing all through the night, even with his ENVGs. Wash picked up his pack and rifled through it, digging through the remains of an MRE. "Want something to eat?"

"I wouldn't turn it down."

"Chili and macaroni," he announced, tossing her the pack. "I got a heater for it, if you want."

"That's okay. I doubt I'd taste anything at this point." She ripped it open, then accepted the plastic utensils he handed her. After three bites, she paused and made a face. "Okay, I take it back, I just *wish* didn't taste anything. You people actually eat this shit?"

"It's a delicacy," he told her, biting into a dessert cake. "Trust me."

The forest was bright and cheerful in the early afternoon, warmer than the night but not by that much. Wash estimated by the color of the leaves that it was sometime in the fall, though that was just a guess. Things could be totally bass-ackwards here... though the sun *had* come up within a few hours of the moonrise, so this place wasn't that different from home. Well, not *home* home, not Wyoming.

"This reminds me of one time when I was really little," he told Valon, "and my dad was stationed in Germany. We took a family trip one weekend to the Black Forest. This is kind of like that, but a little... younger, maybe. Like it hasn't been here as long."

"I don't know much about your world," she admitted, still digging into the main meal despite her complaints. She shrugged. "Before Hades, before we met, I hadn't been offworld except a couple times to the colonies during training. Since then... I feel like I've been to a hundred planets, and honestly, they begin to run together. The Archaion created them all. Or that's what they told us."

"Created them?" he repeated, stuffing the dessert wrapper back into his pack, then grabbing a sip of water. Maybe, he reflected, he should ration the water... but this place seemed to have plenty of ponds and streams, and he always brought a survival straw in his daypack, just in case. "How do you mean? I thought you said they weren't gods."

"Compared to us, they might as well be." She waved around them. "Planets like this one... when the Archaion found them they weren't alive, not like they are now. Some of them were cold rocks with no life at all, while others had seas filled with algae and land covered with fungus. They brought life to them all, to all the worlds you've seen."

Wash stared at her, wondering if she was screwing with him.

"How the hell did they do that?" He shook his head, the day pack halfway to his shoulder. "I mean, all the life looks like home." A horrible thought struck him, ice down his back. "Did they do the same thing to Earth?"

"I don't know." Valon picked the last few bites of the meal out, then handed the package back to Wash. "All we have of them is in the scriptures our people recorded, and at the time, we had no concept of evolution or planetary biology. All we knew of the universe was what they told us." She jerked her head down the trail. "Come on, we should get going."

Wash ran his tongue over his teeth, debating whether to take the time to brush them, but Valon was right. They'd spent too much time in one place. He slipped his daypack onto his shoulders, buckled his helmet in place, and checked the load in his Canik. He hadn't been that attached to the gun before all this. It had been the best he could afford at the time, and if it had won him quite a few matches, he still would have replaced it with a Staccato 2011 in a heartbeat if someone had given him the three thousand dollars to buy one.

Then his father had used the Canik to try to save Brenda from the demons when Jimmy had sent them after her in Riverton. The man had died with it in his hand, and now Wash couldn't bring himself to leave it behind on combat missions. 9mm wasn't much against the demons, but neither was .44 Magnum, so there was no point in carrying a heavier sidearm. And now it was all he had. One 9mm pistol, three full magazines, a combat knife, and his swinging cod, and each of them less effective against the enemy than the last.

"How many spare mags you have for that rocket gun?" he asked Valon.

"Two." She shook her head. "This isn't a Beast World. Maybe I won't need them."

"Your lips to God's ears."

The trail had widened out sometime during the night, and as they traversed another curve through the trees, the river they'd passed by at various times during the night became a permanent fixture, traveling beside them. Wash made a mental note to fill up his water bladder from it when they got the chance. It would be a pain in the ass to rig up a way to use the survival straw with the thing, but better than dehydration. Or giardia.

Did they even *have* giardia on other planets? Maybe they had other micro-organisms that would kill him outright if he drank untreated water. The biologists hadn't found any yet, but that didn't mean they didn't exist. There could be anything out here.

"Wait," Valon said, holding up a hand, eyes fixed on the bend in the river.

Wash went down to a knee by instinct, the Canik jumping into his hand as if he were at the beginning of a US Pistol Shooting Association match. He scanned the banks of the river, searching for whatever Valon had seen... and there it was.

Smoke. A thin trace of it rising up against the deep blue of the afternoon sky.

"That's not the demons," he said. "The only fires I've seen from them are the ones they leave burning after they destroy something." Wash met Valon's eyes. "Could they be your people?"

"It's possible," she allowed. "It's not a permanent settlement

—I know all of those. But we send out scout teams through new gates once we determine they don't lead to a Beast World. They might be camped here... and if they are, they'll know the way back."

Wash stood, letting the gun fall to his side.

"Is there any reason we shouldn't be busting our asses to get there as quick as possible?" he asked Valon, glancing between her and the smoke.

"Just because I can't think of what else it might be," she cautioned, "doesn't mean it might not be something else."

Wash nodded.

"You wanna do a recon? then?" He nodded off to their right, into the thinning woods. "We can't get across the river, but we could skirt the tree line and try to come in quiet."

"How much stealth do they teach in your army?" she asked, eyeing him with he took for skepticism.

"I've been stalking game since I was eight," he told her, bristling at the insult.

She smiled, though he couldn't tell if she was convinced.

"Then you go first."

"Yes, sir," Brenda Sands said with as much cheerfulness as she could force, "we can definitely do a walk-through at ten tomorrow morning. The owners are both at work, so that shouldn't be a problem."

Of course, they'll have to bust their asses to get the place cleaned up and find someone to watch their dogs, and they'll hate my guts for asking, but what else *am I gonna say?*

The California accent on the other end blathered on for another few minutes, an annoying buzz in her Bluetooth earpiece, and Brenda only half-listened, paying just enough attention to pick up any keywords that would mean she had to answer a question. Most of her focus was on the messages Wash had sent. He'd told her back before he'd left to download the Signal app on a prepaid phone and not to use it for anything else. She'd thought that was a bit paranoid but understood he didn't want to get in trouble and be removed from his position.

As if that was the worst thing that could happen.

Arrived in Romania. Transylvania, actually. I'll keep my eyes open for vampires. Heading out to search for the gate tomorrow. Love you.

The message had come through days ago, and it was the last one. Her reply had been succinct, if heartfelt.

Love you too. Be careful.

She scowled, and the realtor at the desk across the room raised his eyebrow at her expression. The office was too damned small since Bobby had hired two people to replace her, and she was shoved into a corner beside Carl and Joanne, neither of whom she especially cared for. If there weren't so many damned Californians like the idiot on the line right now wanting to move somewhere that wasn't California, Bobby wouldn't have had work for her, even though she'd been his best realtor back before... everything.

She hadn't scowled at the Californian, she'd been unhappy with her reply. *Be careful.* How inane. Wash was going to other planets to find monsters and use nuclear weapons against them. Being careful had little to do with it.

She blinked, realizing the Californian had said something to which she had to reply.

"Of course, Mr. Stanhope. I'll see you in the morning."

The line went dead and Brenda sighed in relief. She picked up her work cell and tapped the appointment into the calendar. Not that she would have forgotten. Carl over there was in his fifties and forgot people's names, hometowns, appointments, and just

Gates of Hope

about everything else unless he wrote it down, but Brenda still had the semi-eidetic memory that had gotten her straight As through high school and a 4.0 in college. Would she be like the older man in another twenty-five years? Like her mom?

No. Not like her mom. Not after having gone through three husbands in thirty years, driving everyone away including her daughter. She'd come as close as she ever would to being her mother when she'd been engaged to Jimmy. She wondered what the woman would think if Brenda told her she'd wound up putting a bullet in her fiancé's brain.

Shaking the thought off, Brenda scrolled through her work phone, trying to find the number for the homeowners. She had to break the bad news to them that they had just a few hours to get the house ready for the buyer. Or maybe it was good news, since they desperately wanted out of Riverton. Brenda knew exactly how they felt.

The phone vibrated in her hand and a call notification popped up, the number too long for a domestic call. Europe? Maybe Romania? She slid her thumb across the screen to take the call.

"Wash?" she asked, a smile slowly spreading across her face.

"Brenda, it's Brian Reeves."

The air went out of her, her stomach dropping as if she'd dropped off the top of a skyscraper, realizing what this call meant.

"No," she whispered, wanting to hang up on him but lacking the strength.

"He's not dead," Reeves said quickly. "Not that we know of."

"That you *know* of?" she hissed, anger warring with relief inside her chest.

"I'm going to tell you more than I'm supposed to. We were in a Hive Mind cavern… *somewhere.* I don't even know where. We were planting the device to take it down when we came under attack. Wash got cut off from the rest of us and wound up having to retreat through another gate. We don't know where it went and we have no way of finding him. He's got a transponder, but we're not getting any sort of signal from it on any of the worlds we left repeaters on. He's going to have to find his way to another gate and try to get back to us on his own, unless we stumble on him the next time we go through a gate."

Brenda leaned against her desk as if it was the only thing keeping her from collapsing into a heap on the floor. Carl was staring again, and if she'd had the strength, she would have told him to go screw himself.

"But he's alone? Trapped somewhere you can't find him and he's all alone?"

"No." Reeves hesitated. "This is something *else* I'm probably not supposed to tell you. Wash told you about the woman, Valon, that he met on Hades?"

"Yes."

"She was there, along with about a platoon of her people. They'd come searching for the same thing we were and they helped us out. Valon went after Wash when he gated out. Wherever he is, she's in the same place."

Brenda wasn't sure if that was better or not. True, the woman had helped Wash survive the first time he'd wound up on Hades, but they knew nothing about Valon or her people, where she came from or what she wanted. But at least she could breathe again.

"Thanks for calling me, Brian. If you hear anything..."

"I'll let you know immediately. Brenda, I know this kid. He's a survivor. He's going to be okay. And if there's anything I can do to get him back, you know I'll do it."

He hung up. Brenda stared at the phone until her hand shook so badly that she had to either set it down on the desk or drop it.

"Brenda," Carl said. He'd gotten up from his desk and she hadn't noticed it. He wore his hair too long for a man his age and she was sure he dyed it black, given the gray in his beard, and she despised that Godawful bolo tie he wore, but the look on his lined, tanned face was one of genuine concern. "Is everything okay, sweetheart?"

Is it okay? It was a damned good question. Wash was alive. The situation wasn't good, but he'd surely been in worse before and come through. She had to believe he was coming back.

"No," she told Carl, smiling gratefully. "But I think it will be."

12

"That's not a camp," Wash declared. "It's a village."

Valon nodded, though she didn't look away from the scene laid out two hundred yards away. The trees thinned out from here, dwindling to small seedlings until they gave way entirely to tall grass that persisted until the clearing reached the edge of the settlement and the grass had been trampled down to bare earth. Wash would have liked to get closer, and if he'd been alone he might have tried it, but he knew Valon was more a pilot than an infantry soldier, for all the shit she'd given him doubting his stealth.

They were close enough for him to tell that the cluster of wattle huts gathered around the central fire was a lot more permanent than some scout team bivouac. Nor were they the home of anyone who'd grown up in a technological civilization. Wash had seen recreations of frontier settlements on school field trips, and none of them had looked as primitive as this place. The huts were small, squat, round affairs, none of the roofs over eight feet tall, none of them bigger than twenty feet in diameter.

None of them had a chimney either, though he supposed they could have smoke holes to allow an interior fire in the winter. The main fire for the village was at the center, and it looked as if it was kept going on a permanent basis. Surrounded by large stones that had to have been brought in from the river, the shaved and polished trunks from small trees buried in the dirt provided the support for a latticework covering, pine boughs threaded through them to protect the fire from the rain. A metal pot hung over the fire, steaming, tended by a short, slender figure wrapped and hooded in fur and rawhide skins.

"They're not demons," Valon said. "But the gods know who they are."

Their faces wouldn't have been visible at this distance even if they weren't all hooded and cloaked, but Wash judged the tallest of them wasn't near his own height, while the shortest barely cleared four feet. They went about their tasks unhurriedly, some hauling water up from the river in clay pots, others carrying plants in sacks fashioned out of animal hide. A few seemed to have been off fishing, returning to the village with pots filled with their catch. He counted a few dozen out in the open, but there could a hundred more in the huts, or off in the woods, or down by the river.

If they were talking to each other, Wash couldn't hear them at this distance, and none shouted or sang or made any other sound that carried across the two hundred yards. Wash couldn't put his finger on it, but there was something unnatural about the scene, one of those images that shifted as the viewer shifted positions, except he couldn't get the right point of view to see the real picture.

"What do you want to do?" he asked Valon, motioning toward the distant figures. "We can just sit here until the sun goes down and then sneak out... but we'll be right back where we started."

"You're right," Valon said softly. "We have to go down there. We have to try to talk to them."

He agreed, but he was still surprised to hear it. She seemed reluctant to reveal themselves to the villagers. Wash understood—these people were an unknown, and the unknown always came with dangers. He hadn't noticed any weapons, and given how primitive everything looked, he didn't expect guns. Maybe bows and arrows, spears? But one of those could kill them just as dead as a demon's talons. Maybe *he* was the one who was being unrealistic, but he couldn't think of anything else as dangerous after walking through hell itself.

"I'm wearing heavier armor," Wash told her, "and a helmet. Walk slightly behind me. If they have any sort of ranged weapons, we can lay down suppressive fire and run back for the trees."

Wash thought she might try to argue the point, but she simply nodded. Her expression was troubled, and he had the sense she shared his feeling of something about these people being off. A tingle between Wash's shoulder blades joined the twist in his gut in protest against standing up and walking into the open, and he tried to seem friendly, casual, not as if he was ready to grab his pistol and open fire at the first sign of trouble.

The helmet restricted his peripheral vision, limited his hearing, and he wanted to ditch it, instincts born in the woods long before he'd gone to infantry AIT arguing with military doctrine. But he kept it on because he'd used it as an excuse to walk point, and Valon didn't strike him as a woman who would put up with being protected, particularly by someone she considered a novice compared to her. She followed him a few steps back and slightly to his left, and if her shoulders seemed tense, her gun hand ready to draw, Wash knew he probably looked about the same.

The tree line fell away behind them, tall grass and sage tugging at Wash's fatigue pants on the way through to the clearing, and still none of the villagers seemed to notice them. They went about their business, not looking up, not looking to the woods. Poor situational awareness was his first thought, but then he considered he might be judging them too harshly. There were probably people heading in and out of the clearing all day long. Wash slowed his pace, giving them more time to see him, not wanting their sudden appearance within the confines of the huts to be a surprise.

One of the people attending the fire was the first to notice. Even less than a hundred yards away, Wash couldn't determine whether it was a man or a woman, but the eyes were bright, almost glowing beneath the hood, staring straight at the two of them. The figure stood, arms spreading out to its side, and finally, someone spoke. Sort of.

The language wasn't English, which was no shock to Wash, but nor was it the ancient Greek of the Thacians. It wasn't any language he'd ever heard, not even in National Geographic documentaries about tribes on tropical islands who hadn't had contact with the outside world until modern times and had developed in total isolation. This reminded him more of a video he'd seen of two lynxes having a fight in the woods of Ontario, Canada, a very catlike yowling punctuated with mewls and sharp exclamations. It didn't sound human.

By the time the hooded figure had ceased the yowling, the entire village stood staring at them, all of them stock-still, their eyes glowing under their head coverings, and Wash stopped less than fifty yards away from the closest of the huts, waiting. More of the villagers were streaming in from the river, out of the woods, out of the huts, until there was more than a hundred.

"Still no weapons," Valon observed quietly, not sounding anywhere as close to freaking out as Wash was, which didn't seem fair.

"There're dozens of them," he reminded her. "If they all used sticks and stones, we're still dead."

"After we kill the first few, the rest will likely run."

Wash spared her a wide-eyed glance, wondering if she was actually that cold-blooded, but then decided he didn't want to know. He turned back to the crowd of villagers and raised a hand, fingers spread in what he hoped was a universal signal that they came as friends and weren't holding weapons.

"Hello," he said loud and slow, wincing internally as he realized he sounded like the stereotypical American thinking that foreigners would understand English if he just said the words slowly enough. "My name is Wash. This is Valon. We come in peace." Another wince. At least Valon wouldn't know how cliched that was… and these people probably couldn't understand him at all.

They did react to his words though. The one who'd called the others out to the central square reached up and pulled back their hood, and as they did, Wash got a good look at their hands for the first time. The fingers were impossibly long and seemed to have an extra joint. And there were six of them on each hand.

The hood fell away, and Wash stared in disbelief. Those eyes that had glowed from beneath the hood were much clearer now, green and catlike with vertical irises, and there was a vaguely feline impression from the face, though it wasn't covered with fur and lacked whiskers. The nose was turned up, the mouth small and curved, the ears just slightly pointed. It certainly wasn't human, though he wasn't sure why that shocked him. He already knew there was other intelligent life out here—the Hive Mind. The fact there could be still more species shouldn't have been a surprise, yet it was.

Wash let out the breath he hadn't realized he was holding and tried to think of something to say. Valon beat him to it.

"Blood of the gods," she hissed as the rest of the villagers pulled back their hoods as well, revealing a sea of alien faces. Valon grabbed at his arm, her nails trying to dig through his sleeve and he turned to stare at her. Her eyes were wide, face gone pale. She looked away from the aliens for just a moment, meeting his gaze. "I know what they are. I've seen them before."

"Where?"

"In the drawings from the scriptures." Valon's mouth worked but no words came out for a moment, and she had to try again.

"They're the Archaion."

"Thank you," Wash said, smiling and nodding to the cat lady as he accepted the steaming plate of what he'd decided was stew.

He wasn't sure she understood either the words or his expression, but at least he was fairly certain that the one handing it to him was a woman. It had taken a while, but he'd finally figured it out when the children had come out. Wash forced himself not to think of them as *kittens*, but it was hard. They didn't have tails or fur, but the resemblance was uncanny. When the mothers had come out with their babies, some were suckling, which had been a big clue they were female, and he'd been able to identify the difference in clothing between the males and the females.

The males hung back and didn't engage with Wash and Valon, though it didn't seem to him that they did it out of fear or distaste... it looked more like *deference*. The females were in charge. It was a guess, but he would have been willing to bet a few beers on it. The one who'd given them the food seemed to be the matriarch, streaks of gray in her brown hair, deep lines accentuating the feline features of her face. She'd invited them into the village with gestures and mewling sounds he couldn't understand, but if these people weren't humans, their expressions were similar enough for him to presume she was at least hospitable if not friendly.

"This is better than your MRE," Valon told him, taking a sip of the stew from the clay dish.

"Yeah, but at least my MRE comes with spoons," Wash

retorted, handing her a set of plasticware salvaged from one of the meals. She nodded and took the package.

The... well, *she'd* said they were Archaion, and it was as good a name to give them as any, unless he wanted to call them *cats*. The Archaion females stared at them in what might have been wonder or possibly horror as they used the plastic spoons, like they were all French restauranteurs watching crude Americans drink the finest Chardonnay out of a red Solo cup.

The food was good, he had to admit. He didn't know what the meat was and probably didn't want to, but the vegetables tasted a lot like carrots and squash and the gravy was, at least, salty. The hot food and the glow from the central fire warmed him up against the gentle whisps of the evening wind, but the sun was setting fast and taking the afternoon heat with it.

"I wish we could talk to these people," Valon said. "I have so many questions. How the hell would the Archaion end up here? Living like this? They transformed *worlds*. If they didn't build the original gates, they at least mastered how to use them. There are even hints that they were able to build ships that could travel through space using technology they adapted from the gates."

"That must have been what they had in Nevada," Wash said around a mouthful of stew. Then he nearly choked on it as he realized what he'd said. *I hope she didn't hear it, please, God, I hope she didn't hear it.*

"What?" Valon asked, pinning him with a glare, killing that hope and proving yet again that, if there was a God, He didn't much care about Wash's prayers. "What did you say?"

Wash swallowed the mouthful of food, and with it, the lump in his throat. He was risking more than a court-martial by telling her about the experiment—he was risking her *hating* him, or at least hating his country and maybe his world. And yet. And yet, Wash couldn't bring himself to lie to her. Valon had saved his life and he'd saved hers. She deserved to know.

"I'm going to tell you something," he said, slowly and deliberately, unable to meet her eyes. "that I'm not supposed to, and by all rights, I probably *shouldn't*, but I owe you the truth."

He sucked in a deep breath and put off the inevitable by taking a drink of water. The crackling of the fire and the shuffling of the Archaion villagers drowned out his thoughts.

"The new gates," he said. "You and your people are probably wondering what's causing them, right?"

"The new gates threaten our very existence," she said, eyes still boring into him, full of doubt and suspicion. "We'd assumed the Hive Mind must have found some way to generate new gates in order to destabilize our control of its worlds."

"It was an accident." Wash nearly whispered the words. "My government... I didn't know about any of this, not until after Hades. They found what I guess was a starship buried under the ice at one of our poles, decades ago, and they started experimenting with it in secret. One of those experiments happened in the desert part of our country, in a region called Nevada, way out away from anyone, on a secret military base. They used the technology from the ship to build a particle accelerator." He shrugged. "I'm not a scientist and I don't know what the hell they were trying to figure out, but I got the impression they thought they could use it to develop the same drive the ship was using."

"Blood of the gods," she murmured, staring at him, features slack.

"That's what started it. There was an explosion and the entire complex collapsed in on itself. One of the gates formed in the hole and demons started coming through. At first they thought that was the only problem area, but then new gates started forming, north and south at first, but then spreading east and west." Wash motioned expansively. "When we set off the nuke at Hades, it stopped the formation of any new gates on our continent, but the effect was already spreading… under the oceans at first, they think, but then reaching land again."

Valon's eyes sharpened and she speared him with a perceptive glance.

"If the effect started with the gate in Nevada, maybe if I could get a Thacian shield team there…"

"They bombed the site to bury the gate," Wash interrupted her. "It would take weeks of excavating to get to the bottom of the pit, if the machinery is even down there. They've debated nuking it, but they're afraid it would just make things worse."

Valon spat words out that Wash couldn't understand, and he got the impression she was cursing heartily in her own language, because cursing in a foreign language was never as satisfying.

"We don't know what's going to happen when the effect circles back around the planet to the source," he added. "Or if they *think* they know, they aren't telling me."

The Archaion were eying them, speaking softly to each other in their own strange tongue and cold fingers tapped a pattern down Wash's back, an irrational suspicion that they knew what he was saying.

"You damned fools," Valon finished up in English, pressing her fingers against her eyes as if she had a migraine. "It's partially our fault." The words came out like when Wash had gotten in big trouble with his mother and, after the yelling and raging, she'd calmed down as if to convince herself that he was still her son and she still loved him. "We left you on your own, told you nothing. Why should it be a surprise when you do something so monumentally *stupid?*"

"It's not like we knew there were Hive Minds or demons waiting out there," he said a little defensively. "But yeah, it was pretty reckless." Wash sighed. "We wanted to get to the stars."

"This is worse than I thought," Valon said, her expression more bleak than angry. "If the Hive Mind had done it on purpose, we might have been able to stop it. But if this ship you found *was* made by the Archaion… and if the drive is what's making the gates…"

She closed her eyes, shoulders sagging.

"It might already be too late."

13

"How the fuck did the gates jump from Romania to France so damned fast?" Shaw asked, yelling to be heard over the *thump-thump-thump* of the helicopter's rotors.

Brian Reeves winced, knowing Shaw had been around plenty long enough to understand that the headsets they both wore cancelled out the engine noise and made yelling unnecessary. Shaw liked to be a goofball, and Reeves understood. The man was a warrant officer, after all, and had a reputation to uphold. But sometimes, he felt like Shaw was doing it just to piss him off. He took a breath and counted to ten.

"It's not that far," Reeves reminded his friend, speaking in a regular tone even though he couldn't hear himself talk, hoping to be a good example. "Maybe a thousand miles from Metz to Braşov. And a lot of what's between is the Swiss Alps. Gates could have opened up on mountain passes and the demons wouldn't have been able to get anywhere if they did come through."

"Yeah," Shaw whined, "but why fucking *France*?" He eyed the other occupants of the helicopter, and Reeves had to agree with the sentiment.

The NH90 transport seated twenty, which meant the ten of them—down two thanks to Wash's absence and Greenway's death—and ten special operations troops from the French First Marine Infantry Paratroopers Regiment. Not that Reeves had anything against French soldiers. Contrary to stereotypes, they were very good troops, professional and tough. They certainly looked the part in their body armor and helmets, faces painted with camouflage, HK417 7.62x51 battle rifles tucked between their knees.

But it was *France*. Which meant that, even though there were *demons* rampaging through the ancient streets of Metz, the Pentagon had basically needed to beg to allow Reeves and his Delta team along on the takedown. It also meant that the Special Munitions they'd brought along for this mission was a French weapon, under the control of a French officer, being flown on one of the other two helicopters, guarded by French special operations troops.

Reeves supposed he understood, as a matter of principle. France was a sovereign country with a long history of going their own way politically and militarily, and it would take more than the potential end of the world for the frogs to ever change how they felt about that.

"Master Sergeant Reeves."

The voice came over the headphones, tinted by a French accent, but it took Reeves a few seconds to figure out who was speaking. He'd only met the Marine Infantry Paratroopers platoon a few hours ago and barely remembered any of their names, much less what faces they went with. Then he noticed the team's NCOIC motioning to him.

"Yes, Major Canet?"

The French rank structure was weird, and *major* had no relation to the American O-4 officer rank. It had more in common with the American warrant officer rank, like Shaw, but also sort of overlapped senior NCO ranks in a way Reeves couldn't quite keep straight in his head. Basically, this guy was the chief NCO of the French special operations platoon, which was kind of the equivalent of Reeves' position, but unlike the Delta team, the French Marine Infantry Paratrooper platoon was led in the field by an officer, the *commandant* on the helicopter with the nuke. And just to make things more confusing, "commandant" was the equivalent of the US major rank.

"I watched the documentary about you," Canet said. Then he shrugged, face splitting in a self-conscious grin beneath his camo paint. "It was entertaining, but I have wondered since then... how much was true and how much was government propaganda? I mean, the entire bit about this Wash Williams rescuing his girlfriend... it smacked of action movie bullshit."

Reeves tried to return the man's smile, but his face wouldn't cooperate.

"It was all true. Williams was a fucking hero. The kid had balls that wouldn't quit."

"Really?" The man seemed surprised. "And is he off in Wyoming now, living happily ever after with his blonde princess?"

Reeves wanted to tell him. He wanted to talk about it to *someone*, because he couldn't talk to Dos Santos about Wash without wanting to punch the colonel right in the face. Dos Santos was parroting what the SecDef had said, that Wash would have to find his way home on his own. As if the kid hadn't fucking saved the world.

But Canet didn't want to hear that.

"Something like that," he said. Then he nodded out the window of the chopper at the quaint medieval city below them. Metz might have popped out of a time warp from four or five hundred years ago, except for the cars parked on the narrow streets. The appearance of the town had been preserved over the centuries by a rigid zoning code. "I'm not seeing anything down there. I thought this was an urban incursion."

"Not in the historical district, thank God," the man told him.

"There's something besides the historic district down there?" Reeves laughed. They were flying over the river, with the cathedral rising up above the city like the other buildings were bowing down to it.

"Maybe it will all look historical to *you*, American. But yes, there are modern hotels and apartments. And the incursion is right in the central courtyard of the Plaza Hotel in *Nouvelle Ville*, the commercial section of town. We'll be there in minutes."

Reeves nodded. He could see it now, the line of demarcation between the historic buildings and the newer chain stores and apartments clear from the air. It didn't seem natural to be flying into a combat zone in the middle of the afternoon. These kinds of things should happen at night. It should be some rule of the universe that death only happened at night.

The other stark difference obvious from the air was the lack of automobile traffic in Nouvelle Ville. Police barricades kept the cars out, and the only motion he saw at the borders of the district were those same police along with platoons of conventional infantry stationed at every intersection, gathered around APCs or tanks, playing containment.

Which would work just as long as the demons let it. Right up until the Hive Mind decided that it really wanted Metz and it was ready to send a few thousand of the warrior drones through to take it. Though God alone knew what the Hive Mind wanted or what it would do now that Jimmy Bonner was gone. He'd been guiding the tactics and strategy of the things before Brenda Sands had killed him, but Reeves hadn't noticed much difference in the MO of the things since the kid's death.

A different voice in Reeves' headphones this time, speaking French. The man spoke quickly, running his words together the way all romance languages did, but Reeves was familiar enough with the language to understand him.

"Hatchet team, this is Overwatch One. We have targets in sight in the street outside the Plaza Hotel. Permission to engage? Over."

It was a helicopter pilot, but not the pilot of *their* helicopter. Hatchet team was the codeword for the Marine Infantry Paratroopers, while Overwatch was the squadron of Tiger attack helicopters covering their assault. Reeves squinted out the side window of the NH90, trying to find the targets... or even the hotel.

There.

There was nothing special about the hotel, just another tourist trap like a million others in France, except for the demons streaming out of the main entrance. Even from three hundred feet up the things looked huge, though there was something unreal about them from this altitude, like they were special effects in a movie.

Another voice in French answered the attack helicopter pilot, and this one Reeves recognized as the officer in charge of the special operations platoon, Commandant Amalric. He had a deep, sonorous tone, like an opera singer.

"Overwatch One, this is Hatchet One Actual. Engage targets, guns only. Over."

"Roger that, Actual. Overwatch, out."

The Tigers slipped below the altitude of the transport birds, sleek and deadly, with the angular lines of a boot knife. Puffs of smoke came off the chin turrets and matching showers of dust and debris from the street below. The demons twisted and writhed as the cannon rounds impacted, chopping through the creatures. Not all of them. The demons were totally lacking any sense of self-preservation, but that didn't mean they'd waste themselves sitting still for an air barrage. A handful of the things lay dead or dying on the ground, but the rest had retreated back through the main entrance, leaving trails of black ichor behind them.

"If only the bastards would come out into the open so we could shoot them all down from the air," Canet lamented, shaking his head. "Or drop in artillery."

"The hotel's not that pretty," Reeves offered. "Why not just pour a couple dozen Hellfire missiles into it and then burying the gate under concrete?"

"If it were up to me, I would. I think Commandant Amalric agrees. But that would take a decision by the president, and he's not inclined to destroy one of our own cities." Canet smiled thinly. "That is why *we* are here, no?" Canet's eyes took on a distracted look, as if he was listening to a transmission in his headphones. He responded, but Reeves couldn't hear him until the French NCO adjusted the settings of cord attached to his headphones. "Inform your people, Reeves. We're going in."

"Go!" Reeves said, slapping Shaw on the arm.

The warrant officer charged around the corner, his half of the team hot on his heels. Canet and Amalric had done Reeves and his team the huge honor of allowing them to be first through the door. At least, they'd *acted* like it was a huge honor, though Reeves got the idea that the French were more interested in avoiding casualties from their own platoon. If a few Americans died after their government insisted they come along, then maybe it would teach the pushy Yankees a lesson and save Commandant Amalric a lot of paperwork and a few awkward phone calls.

Anything for our brave French allies.

The Plaza Hotel was probably a nice, well-appointed place when the front entrance wasn't riddled with bullet holes and covered in black alien blood. Chunks of the demons decorated the front walk, and though Reeves was by no means a squeamish man, he did his best not to step on the remains. The black shit stank like a cross between roofing tar and a Camp Doha outhouse, and he didn't need to smell that for the next two days.

At least the doors were already open. The demons had torn them off their hinges and left them lying in a pool of human blood from the remains of three gendarmes and two hotel employees. Or maybe three. Reeves only saw two heads, but that didn't mean there wasn't another that had rolled off under the front desk.

"Clear!" Shaw called from the other side of the check-in desk.

Reeves waved his half of the team forward, filling in the gaps in Shaw's perimeter, two men on each of the exits from the lobby. More blood on the floor, but he didn't look for the source. Dead humans were unfortunate, but they weren't a threat. No threats presented themselves, which was good for the short term but troubling in the long run. The demons were *somewhere*.

"Clear!" he called back to the French paratroopers.

Boot soles tromped on the floor behind them, but Reeves didn't move until Canet slid in beside him and touched him on the shoulder.

"Covering."

Reeves went first this time, four other operators falling in behind him, and he debated pulling down his enhanced optics but decided against it. The lights were still on, the windows still open, barely a shadow to be seen, and despite the incredible technology in the ENVGs, Reeves still found they added a layer of unreality to his perceptions of the world. He didn't even especially care for wearing a helmet in combat, though he usually didn't have a choice in the matter.

The M5 sights *wanted* him to use the ENVGs, but that was something else he didn't care for, very much preferring to shoulder the rifle and get a sight picture with the red dot. He didn't tell the others what to do, and he knew Shaw had his own sights down. Whatever worked.

Reeves ignored the closed doors in the hallway between the lobby and the courtyard. The demons didn't bother opening doors, much less closing them—they just battered them down and left them laid waste. There might be civilians inside, but this unit wasn't equipped to help them, so leaving them in place was the only option. The main area of concern was the gate, and getting the nuke on the other side of it was a time-sensitive operation.

The corridor ended in a set of glass double doors set into floor-to-ceiling windows. It *had* ended in them. Now the doors were gone, the floor a carpet of tiny, crystalline pebbles, what remained of tempered glass when it was shattered, the twisted, metal frames that had once held the glass tossed aside into a corner. Through the ruined entrance were twin rows of hedges, and Reeves cursed them, wishing the demons had ripped those down as they'd destroyed the doors. He couldn't see a damned thing through them.

No point in putting it off. He held a hand up to pause the rest of the team behind him and took a moment to pull his M320 around to his front, dropping the M5 on its sling. The thing was heavy, and before they'd encountered the demons he hadn't really liked the weapon and had avoided carrying it on operations that didn't require long-range capabilities. Now, of course, they needed the damned things to penetrate the carapace of the monsters.

A deep breath to settle himself, then he rushed forward. Tempered glass crunched under his boots, loud enough to alarm even the Hive Mind warrior drones, and before he'd even reached the front end of the hedgerow, motion from the left caught his eye.

"Contact, left!" he yelled, throwing himself into a shoulder roll out of instinct.

It was the right instinct. A scorpion stinger the size of a machete cracked into the pavement where he would have been if he'd stayed on his feet, and Reeves had a half a second to take in the situation before pulling the trigger. There were two dozen of the demons gathered around a gate, this one oriented vertically, just a few inches off the ground, very convenient as far as the demons or they were concerned. They'd been motionless before he'd come out into the courtyard, as if waiting for instructions.

That had so many implications about the leadership of the things, the thought that was going into their strategic guidance, but he didn't have time to think about it, just had time to pick a target. The one that'd tried to kill him was the obvious one, but it was also the wrong one. The goal line was the gate, and they needed it cleared. Four of the things were clustered right in front of it, and that was the place to put his first round.

He didn't use the sights. They were less than fifty meters away, and he'd fired the launcher enough to know where the round was going to go. It bucked against his shooting glove, a streak of smoke connecting the end of the barrel to the center of the four demons. And it would have been the last thing he ever did. Whatever limitations the demons had intellectually, they were fast as hell, and it only took a tick of the clock for the one that'd tried to kill him already to whip its tail in the opposite direction.

The grenade struck just as a muffled stutter came from behind him and the demon jerked from a burst of 6.8x51mm armor-piercing rounds through its chest. Flanders jogged forward, the business end of the suppressor on his M250 Squad Automatic Weapon glowing red. He and the rest of the team barely reacted to the detonation of the grenade, expecting it.

The grenade had taken one of the bug-eyed monsters directly in the chest, blowing a hole through his carapace the size of a fist, the blast taking the two next to it off their feet, though not killing them. The Delta team laid down a mad minute, emptying their mags, pouring hundreds of rounds into the twenty remaining alien monsters, but there still would have been too many if the French hadn't been with them. The things surged against the initial burst, running at them despite wounds that would probably prove fatal, but three more grenades arced in from behind, the bass notes to accompany the staccato beat of the paratrooper's HKs.

Some small part of Reeve's mind that wasn't engaged with tactical considerations took a microsecond to appreciate the irony of the French special forces team arming itself with German weapons, but mostly he appreciated the wonderful job their barrage of 7.62mmm NATO did to the last surviving demons. One of them collapsed just feet from Reeves' position, its talons nearly touching the toe of his boot, and he sucked in a breath, forcing his heart rate down to something normal before he moved again.

"Shaw," he snapped, leaping up to his feet. "The gate."

"Got it."

Shaw was all business when the bullets started flying, which was why he was still in Delta after nearly ten years when so many others had fallen by the wayside. He was pushing forty in a business where men operated at ten-tenths capacity for days at a time with no sleep with all the damage that could do to the human body, but he still moved with the smooth grace of a professional baseball player sliding into first.

"Grenades!" Shaw barked to his group, leading the way with a pair of them, plucking them off his vest and tossing them through the gate before ducking off to the side.

The other four with him did the same, the last one arcing through the gate just as Shaw reached cover. The other side of the gate was gray, twilit, just a hint of cold coming through with a wisp of fog, as if the atmosphere was transitioning from a warm autumn here in France to an early winter wherever the portal went. The fog was blown away in a billowing cloud of white smoke and a kettle-drum, chain-fire roar of detonations. Heat washed back through the gate, though none of the shrapnel made the return trip.

Reeves didn't wait for the echoes to die down, waving his group forward, this time letting Flanders and his light machine gun get ahead of him. There was an indescribable sensation going through the gate, and Reeves didn't know if it was a physical thing. Whatever it was didn't stop signals going through the portal, didn't affect electrical cables laid from one end of the gate to the other, and the scientists they'd brought along insisted there was no biological change going through. But Reeves knew what he felt.

It wasn't debilitating, but it was distracting, like a haze over his mind for a fraction of a second before his feet hit the ground on the other side. Enough to get them killed, but the grenades gave back the time the crossing robbed them of. Reeves' boots hit sandstone, the air full of cordite atop a high-altitude bite, and he found himself in the middle of a cloud-wrapped night, the only light coming from the glow of the gate.

Two of the demons were sprawled across the gentle slope stretching out in front of the gate, down the face of a sandstone cliff, descending into a twisted, shadow-wrapped forest. It was hard to tell where the sinister, looming shapes of the trees ended and the mass of demons began until Reeves swept his ENVGs down over his face and everything cohered into sharp, black-lined clarity.

There weren't as many as he'd feared, but more than he'd hoped. Twenty, he estimated, about as many as had been on the other side of the gate, though these hadn't been at rest. They'd been marching up the slope, heading for the portal, and he had the sense that the ones in the courtyard had been waiting for their arrival to make a rush out the front. The targeting reticle from his XM157 optics floated across the image in his ENVGs, yet Reeves brought the M5 to his shoulder anyway before pulling the trigger, and this time, the reflex betrayed him.

The closest of the demons had gone into motion the instant they came through the gate and was only a few feet from Reeves when he opened fire. Reeves moved forward with each squeeze of the trigger, dropping under a swipe of the thing's talons, trying to stay close enough to it that the tail couldn't reach him. Ichor splattered against his chest armor, and any hope of avoiding the smell shattered along with the thing's carapace. It staggered from side to side and Reeves scuttled along with it, the thing's tail smashing into the ground all around him as it tried in vain to reach his position between its legs. Another burst up through the demon's stomach and it finally gave up the fight, collapsing backward.

Reeves spit out gobbets of ichor, wiping the black blood off the lenses of his ENVGs as he scrambled out from under the dying monster. By the time his vision had cleared, the image might have been of a new world. The rest of the Delta team had emerged from the gate alongside the French platoon, the muted thunder of suppressed battle rifles and light machine guns laying down a thick enough barrage that even the demons couldn't get through it. Most of them.

Motion out of the corner of Reeves' vision turned him away from the cliffside of the trail and toward the ledge hanging out over the slope. Two of the demons had gone off the trail, skittering across the bare, orange rock, digging talons in, using their tails for balance… and coming around behind the gate.

"Contact, rear!" Reeves yelled, bringing his M5 up but unable to get off a shot with the French paratroopers in the way.

They'd brought the nuke through, the cylindrical, lead-lined case resting in a specially designed skeletal cradle fixed to the back of the sort of three-wheeled, motorized cart Reeves was used to seeing on the streets of Asian countries, one of the hardcore French paratroopers looking like a four-year-old on a tricycle driving it. Reeves didn't care about the man's embarrassment but more about the fact that he couldn't open fire on the alien monsters with the cart in the way... and neither could the others.

Cursing, Reeves sprinted back toward the gate, trying to get a clear shot, but the demons were already around the backside of the portal, running so much faster than any human could. The gunfire didn't *quite* drown out the screams coming from the other side of the French formation, and the ENVGs were all too efficient at showing Reeves the body parts flying through the air. *Now* the guns turned the other direction and the shooting started with no regard to how many friendlies were in the way. He wanted to rush in, wanted to scream at them to cease fire, but it was already too late.

It took five seconds to put the two creatures down, an eternity in combat, and all Reeves could do was stand there and wait. The rest of the demons were dead, his own people finishing off the few that still moved, no casualties from the Delta team that he could see, most of them focused on their own battle and not even aware what had happened on the other side of the French positions.

Except Flanders. He'd moved up beside Reeves at some point, his M250 searching for a target, his jaw clenched in frustration that mirrored Reeves' own. When the smoke cleared and the screaming and shooting stopped, when the last, fitful, dying motion of the two enemy warrior drones had ceased, a dozen bodies littered the stony ground. A few moved, writhing in agony, though Reeves couldn't tell whether they'd been shot or mauled by the demons.

There was a near silence, broken only by the moaning of the wounded, before multiple voices shouted in French, half the words curses. Calls for casualty reports, trying to find out who was dead and who was alive. None of the voices belonged to

Canet or Amalric. Reeves turned away from the carnage, checking on his own people.

"Shaw, we have any casualties?"

"Negative, boss," the man said, turning back toward him, rifle propped against his side.

"Get the team on a perimeter defense and send Jansen over to help out with the Frenchies."

"Roger that."

The paratroopers were beginning to unfuck themselves, one of their senior NCOs having taken charge, still barking out orders at the survivors. Those didn't include the driver of the cart. The nuke was still sitting there, undamaged, but the man who'd been behind the handlebars of the trike was sprawled beside it, the blood pouring from the bullet wound in his throat having slowed to a trickle because there was none left.

"Who's in command?" Reeves asked, racking his brain for the correct French phrase. Understanding it was a lot easier than speaking it. No one answered the first time, and he repeated it louder.

"I am," a tall, lantern-jawed man announced, the upper half of his face invisible behind his night-vision gear. He glanced back and forth as if reluctant to look away from his wounded. "Chief Sergeant Perrault. You are Master Sergeant Reeves?"

"Yeah. What's your situation, Perrault?" If Reeves was curt, it wasn't because he didn't sympathize with Perrault, but more that he couldn't remember how to say it.

"We have twelve KIA," Perrault said, the words coming out as if someone had cut his guts open and extracted them with pliers. "Including Major Canet and Commandant Amalric. Six wounded, three of them badly."

"This one needs immediate evac, boss," Jansen called, kneeling over one of the wounded.

Reeves sighed. He knew the answer to the situation, but he wasn't sure what Perrault would think of it.

"You take your people back through," he told the NCO. "Leave the nuke with us, along with the trigger. We'll follow the track of the enemy warrior drones and plant the charge on the other side of their gate."

Perrault's mouth fell open and he tried to talk, sputtered, tried again.

"There is no way I can leave a French nuclear warhead in the hands of foreigners!" he said, outrage making his words harder to understand. "We will set the bomb to go off here and then retreat back through the gate!"

"This isn't a Hive Mind world." Reeves motioned around them. "This is a living planet, maybe even with humans on it. The Thacians have colonies on habitable worlds, and for all we know, this is one of them. We're not setting off a nuclear weapon on what could be friendly territory." Perrault looked as if he meant to argue, but Reeves cut him off. "Particularly not when that friendly nation might take it as an act of *war* against them." That brought the Frenchman up short. "Now, if you just *can't* turn over control of the charge to us… then send one of your people along. Someone with the authority and expertise to set the thing off when we get it to where it's supposed to go."

Perrault pulled up his night-vision goggles and so did Reeves, letting the man see his eyes by the light of the gate, letting him see how serious he was about this.

"Sgt. Daudet!" Perrault yelled finally, pulling his goggles back over his eyes.

One of the platoon's squad leaders rushed over from where he'd been helping treat one of the wounded. The man was skinny and angular, looking lost in his fatigues and body armor, like a kid playing army.

"Daudet, I'm leaving you in charge. I want you to get the wounded out first, quickly and carefully, and bring in one of the helicopters to evacuate them. Once they're on their way, come back for the dead. Then send word back to command that I've accompanied the Americans to try to shut down the gate back to the active site." Daudet's expression was unreadable, but Perrault must have sensed hesitation in the man, because he grabbed him by the arm and shook him slightly. "Just do as I say. Tell the colonel that, if he doesn't hear back from me in three hours, or if any more of the demons come through, they need to bury the gate under a few tons of concrete."

"Yes, Chief Sergeant," Daudet said, started to turn away then hesitated. "Good luck."

Perrault glanced over at the bomb, then back to Reeves.

"I'm *not* driving that Goddamned tricycle."

"Hey, Shaw!" Reeves yelled, the corner of his mouth turning up. "I've got a job for you!"

14

"A gate," Wash repeated, making an expansive gesture, shaping a ring with his hands. "We're looking for a gate."

The Archaion female stared at him as if he were talking in a foreign language. Which, of course, he was. Wash sighed and looked over to Valon, who still sat beside the fire, warming herself against the morning chill. They'd spent the night in a hut apparently used for storage, huddled on either side of a pile of recently-cured hides, though Wash hadn't slept much... there were rats in the hut, and it was all he could do not to shoot them. He could have done it too, with his night-vision goggles, but there was no point in alarming their hosts. Valon didn't look as if she'd slept any better than he had, her eyes bloodshot and baggy.

"Hey," Wash called to her. "You think these people are the Archaion, right?" Valon's response was a blank look. "Well, why don't you try talking to them in *your* language?"

"What good would that do?" she demanded, her tone and her expression sullen.

"Well, think about it!" Wash tried not to yell, though it was difficult. "If the Archaion are the ones who dumped you in Thacia and gave you all your technology and shit to use against the Hive Mind, they must have had a way to talk to you. They're a hell of a lot more likely to know your language than mine."

A nursing mother walked by, her infant squalling from hunger until she affixed it to her breast, speaking softly in what sounded like nothing so much as one of the old barn cats at his parents' ranch when she'd had a litter of kittens. The matriarch smiled at the woman and baby, stroking the little one's hair as they passed by.

"Listen to them," Valon said. "You really think they speak Thacian?"

"And that's a good reason to not even try?"

Wash suspected Valon hadn't attempted to talk to the Archaion because she feared she was right, that this was all that was left of the race that had given her people their purpose. That they'd fallen away to nothing and the Thacians would soon join them in obsolescence. The woman sighed and stood from the tree stump she'd been using as a stool.

She spoke slowly and clearly to the matriarch, and though Wash couldn't understand it, he got the sense it was short and simple. Something along the lines of *hi, how are you?*

The matriarch's expression changed. Wash couldn't read it, but it was different than when he'd tried to talk to the female. Maybe not understanding, but definitely recognition.

"Try some more," he encouraged. "Tell her we're looking for a gate that leads out of here."

Valon frowned at him, looking to Wash as if she resented being told what to do by someone who was barely an NCO while she was already a senior officer, but she did it. The words were different, but the pantomime was the same that he'd used, a circling motion, then miming stepping through the ring. The matriarch's mouth was a straight line, her eyes narrowing, brows closing in on each other.

Gates of Hope

"It's working," Wash said, encouraging.

Another burst of pseudo-Greek, and this time, Momma Cat responded. At first Wash thought she was speaking more of their meow-meow yowling, but a pattern emerged, something recognizable. She was *trying* to speak Thacian. How successfully, he wasn't sure, since he couldn't make heads or tails of the language when a *human* was speaking it, and the feline's voice box was definitely not designed for Greek.

"What's she saying?" he asked once the matriarch had stopped for a breath.

"I'm not sure," Valon admitted, brows knitting, leaning forward as if somehow being closer to the Archaion would make her easier to understand. "It's hard to understand, and I think she's speaking some older version of our language. But I think…"

The matriarch interrupted her, making a motion and taking a few steps down toward the river.

"I think she wants us to follow her."

"Shit," Wash murmured, running back to the storage hut to grab his helmet and armored vest. Last night, he'd stripped the spare rifle magazines and 40mm grenades out of the vest and reluctantly left them behind, lacking any weapon to shoot them through and unwilling to haul the extra weight around any longer. It was a hard decision for the frugal-minded westerner who'd spent the last several years working multiple jobs to keep a roof over his head, but the armor felt a ton lighter without all the 6.8x51 hanging off of him. Unfortunately, he'd also run his camelback bladder nearly dry last night, intending to refill it this morning.

There was no time to do it now. Valon had already turned to follow the Archaion and Wash had to jog to keep up with them, nearly slipping on the smooth rocks beside the river. A trail picked up down there, padded down by generations of feet, and some of the younger Archaion were on it now, carrying baskets of

"Somebody woke up on the wrong side of the hut."

"I don't even know what that means."

"Somehow you learned English in a day and you don't know what that means?" Wash frowned. "You never did tell me how you managed to do that, by the way. Is that some of that alien technology too?"

"It's called an imprinter. We use it to teach complex systems to our technicians. We don't use it much for languages since we all speak Thacian, but I knew it could work."

"Pretty smart, being able to think of that on the fly." He took a sip of water, knowing he'd miss it when he was gone. "You've been doing this a long time, right?"

"Preparatory school for Venators begins at age twelve. I started at eleven." She shrugged. "I convinced my mother to lie about my age. I've never wanted to do anything else."

"Eleven? Jesus. And I thought I had it tough, having to work right out of high school. Not much time for a personal life, huh?"

Valon glanced at him, eyes narrowing.

"If you're asking if I have ever had a relationship, the answer is yes, of course. I'm dedicated, not stupid."

Wash laughed.

"That's good. I was beginning to think your people were kind of fanatics."

Valon glared at him, but before she could form a reply the matriarch stopped abruptly in the middle of the trail, and both of them had to step to the side to avoid running into her. The path curved away from the river and widened out, the trees thinning, the ground rocky and uneven. And floating above the uneven rocks, vertical and just off the ground, as if it had been placed there purposefully, was a gate.

"Thank the gods," Valon sighed.

The Archaion matriarch turned to Valon and took her by the

arm, looking deep into her eyes, then said something in the same garbled Greek as before. Her hand slid away, she gave one brief nod to Wash, and then headed back up the trail.

"What'd she say?" he asked Valon.

"She said, 'you're welcome.'" The woman shuddered. "Perhaps I should have prayed to her that this leads home."

"There's only one way to find out." Wash pulled out his Canik and sighed. "Damn, I wish I had a rifle."

Valon slid the rocket pistol from its holster and nodded.

Wash stepped through the gate, out of the mosquito-infested rain forest and into...

...another mosquito-infested forest.

"Did we *go* anywhere?" he blurted, looking around into a sea of green, thick enough it filtered out the afternoon sun.

"Yeah," Valon said, wiping at her forehead. "It's hot as hell here." She pointed off to the north, a smile spreading slowly across her face. "And unless I'm mistaken, that's a road."

Wash exchanged a hopeful look with the woman and broke into a jog, all the weariness and hunger banished with the adrenaline of expectation. Sounds teased at the edges of his hearing, a distant rumble...

Through one last barrier of brush and then into daylight, and onto the edge of a four-lane highway. Wash didn't need to see anything else to know they were on Earth, and not just Earth but the United States. He'd seen roads in other countries, and there was a qualitative difference to them, the way they were built, the way the lines were painted.

And then there was the cityscape just a couple miles away down the road. He didn't know the place by sight, but he knew it was an American city. He and Valon were at the edge of a stand of trees next to the highway... just before a bridge over a river. It could be anywhere, but he had the sense it was in the south, and not just because of the hot, humid climate in late September. That *could* happen in the Midwest.

But there were palm trees on the other side of that bridge.

"This has to be your world," Valon said, staring at the buildings as if judging the quality of the architecture, "because it surely isn't mine." She sniffed the air and made a face. "What is that *smell*?"

A lifted Ford pickup rumbled by with a diesel roar and a cloud of black smoke, and Wash grinned.

"That's internal combustion," he said, squinting at the license plate but unable to make it out through the cloud of smoke. "I need to make a call."

He fished his cell phone out of his pocket and hit the power button… and then swore loudly as the battery symbol flashed bad news at him.

"Son of a bitch!" he clarified. "The damn thing is dead. I never got the chance to charge it after the flight to Romania."

"Perhaps whoever this is can put us in touch with the authorities," Valon suggested, gesturing behind them, away from the bridge and the city.

Wash turned just in time to catch the flash of red and blue lights as the white SUV rumbled into the gravel at the side of the road. The door opened up and a sheriff's deputy in a white shirt and green pants jumped out, his gun already drawn and pointed their way.

"Do not move!" the chubby, florid-faced man bellowed. "Put your hands behind your head and get on your knees! If you make one move toward your guns, I *will* shoot you!"

"Shit," Wash murmured, raising his hands. "Do what he says," he told Valon, interlacing his fingers behind his head and sinking down to his knees.

As he knelt, he was finally able to read the writing on the driver's door the deputy was using as cover.

Hillsborough County Sheriff's Department.

"Is this how your people treat their soldiers, Wash?" Valon asked, imitating his movements.

Wash sighed, surrendering to the inevitable as the deputy came out from around the door, yelling at them again not to move.

"Welcome to Florida."

15

The lighter grays of false dawn peeked out from above the red blisters of the eastern hills, and Brian Reeves wondered how long it had been since they'd come through the gate. He wanted to look, wanted to check his watch, but realized it wouldn't do any good. He couldn't remember what time it had been when they'd gone through.

It *might* have been forever. The darkness held a surreal quality, even with the light-enhancing filters in the ENVGs—maybe *especially* through the ENVGs, which seemed to turn everything into a video game, complete with the sharp outlines of a Japanese anime. Walking, even at the brisk pace they were making, felt like it took no effort, like this was one of those dreams where he could run forever through the darkness without ever getting tired. It reminded him of training for a marathon, waking up well before dawn to get the long-distance run in before the heat of the day. Until Shaw spoiled it, pulling up beside him on that ridiculous French nuclear tricycle.

"Are you sure we're going the right way?" the warrant officer asked, jerking a thumb over his shoulder. "I mean, those demons *could* have been coming from uphill."

"The tracks went this way," Reeves insisted. It was a weak objection. The trail was mostly stone, and while the little sand there'd been on the ground back by the gate did show the trace of the alien monsters, there hadn't been any sign of them since.

Shaw let the question hang between the for another few seconds, silent, his eyes invisible behind the multiple-lens night-vision goggles, and Reeves sighed.

"If we don't see anything by the time the sun comes up, we'll turn back."

It wasn't a decision he *wanted* to make, and not just because it would make him look stupid to Perrault. Reeves didn't want to admit it, even to himself, but desperation was creeping into his decision-making. They'd set so many of these bombs, closed so many gateways, yet things didn't seem to be getting any better. Somewhere out here was an answer, and every day he didn't find it was a day less the world had to live.

"I hear something," Perrault announced, coming to a halt in the middle of the trail, forcing Shaw to let off the accelerator of the motorized trike and screech to a stop inches behind the Frenchman.

"I hear it too," Flanders agreed, looking upward, as if the sound was somewhere out in the firmament and not farther down the mountain.

It wasn't gunfire, not from the guns used on *Earth* anyway, but Reeves had heard it before and didn't need to be reminded. Of course, Shaw reminded him anyway.

"That's those Thacian rocket guns," he said. "They're fighting the demons."

"I didn't know you'd been promoted to captain, Vic," Reeves growled. "Or that you'd changed your last name to Obvious." He waved at the rest of the team. "Double-time! The fight's down there!"

The slope grew steeper, the stone slicker, and Reeves gritted his teeth, half running, half sliding down, turning his boots to the side like ice skates every few steps to gain traction. The brakes on Shaw's overloaded tricycle squeaked and squealed in protest, and Reeves half-expected to see the awkward vehicle go tumbling down the hill, out of control, and taking their nuclear charge with it.

Then, abruptly, like a good-news, bad-news joke, the slope gentled and widened into a plateau, surrounded by trees. At the center of the plateau was a gateway, this one horizontal to the ground, hovering just inches above the rock, surrounded by the corpses of bug-eyed, alien monsters... and humans. The demons poured through the gate, clambering upward like they were having to climb through, which meant the gate they were entering had to be overhead, which Reeves hadn't seen yet.

The Thacians had taken up positions in the trees, using the constricted surroundings to hold the demons back... or trying to. They'd piled up the enemy dead three deep coming out of the gate, but all that had done was provide cover for the rest to come through. *This* was why the demons back in France had gone back through the portal there rather than stay and fight—the fight was here, and if they lost it, there'd be no chance for an incursion on Earth.

"Form on me!" Reeves yelled. "Echelon left!"

Which was an infantry formation he hadn't ever thought he'd actually use in combat, since it involved everyone swinging around in a line to his left, a particularly stupid move when the enemy was shooting guns at you. Not so stupid when they were demons armed with acid stingers and the only way to keep them from killing you was to lay down more fire than they could wade through.

"Push them back!" he amended, as if the others weren't already smart enough to figure out what he had in mind.

Firing on the run was tricky, but less so with the XM157

optics. The targeting reticle floated in his vision, connected wirelessly between the optics group and his ENVGs, and the key was to pull the trigger between steps, when it had settled onto one of the ravening, nightmarish demons. The buttstock kicked against his shoulder, though he barely noticed the recoil, his concentration split between aiming, keeping an eye on his team, and not losing his footing on the loose dirt and slick rock.

Reeves very nearly let himself be distracted by the sight of Victor Shaw off to his right, driving that stupid motor trike right into the demons, his M5 resting across the handlebars like a shooting rest as he fired full-auto.

"Shaw!" he bellowed at the man, but to no avail. *Fuck it. Go with the flow.* "Advance and cover him!"

If he'd been counting on the orders to penetrate the din of the battle on the sheer force of his voice, Reeves might as well have been shouting into a storm, even with the report of the battle rifles muted by their suppressors. But each of the team wore noise-canceling earbuds linked to their radios, and the command went through. Which meant Reeves had to run even *faster*, because that trike had picked up quite the head of steam running downhill and was going at least twenty miles an hour.

Reeves was fifty yards away from the gate when his rifle went dry and, rather than attempting to reload it, he swung his M302 around off his shoulder and fired a round through the gate. The detonation of the HEDP warhead seemed far off, but the white smoke drifted through the gate, along with the unmistakable fog of warmer air mixing with cold.

The team's suppressive fire sliced through the demons, adding to the firefly swarm of miniature rockets coming from the Thacian positions, dropping the things in their tracks, stacking the dead all the way back into the gate. But those tiny red glows riding skinny smoke trails weren't stopping, and Shaw was heading straight into them...

Shaw must have noticed that right after Reeves, because the shout telling the man to halt was still forming on Reeves' lips when Shaw threw himself off the side of the trike, tumbling to a halt about thirty yards from the gate, just shy of the firing arc of the Thacians. What *should* have happened then, given that the gate was a few inches off the ground, was that the tricycle should have run up against the side of the gate and come to a sudden stop. They'd done experiments with other gates, and running into the edge of the things was like fetching up against a brick wall.

But that didn't account for the speed the trike had built up… or the ramp constructed of dead demons. The trike bounced and tossed left to right as it hit the spiky limbs of the creatures… and then wobbled precariously over the top of the last pile of corpses and disappeared through the gate.

"Fuck!" Reeves yelled, catching up to Shaw and grabbing him by the arm, pulling him clear as a Thacian rocket trail nearly intersected the warrant officer's head. "Vic, what the hell were you thinking?"

"The brakes wouldn't work," Shaw protested, reloading his SIG rifle as he stumbled after Reeves. "At least I got the bomb on the other side of the gate."

"Yeah, but not *us*!"

He wanted to yell at Shaw some more, just to make himself feel better, but the demons hadn't given up despite their losses, and three of them bulled their way through the Thacian gunfire, shrugging off what would undoubtedly be fatal wounds in a fatalistic attempt to get at Reeves and Shaw. Shaw braced his rifle against his hip and fired from there, knitting a line across the chest of one of the things, piercing a carapace already cracked and splintered by Thacian mini-rockets. The demon collapsed, its thrashing blocking the other two just long enough for Reeves to load a fresh magazine into his SIG… but not enough to bring it around before one of the two leapt over his fallen comrade, tail swinging, ready to impale the two humans.

A stream of smoke trails intersected the thing's head and it pitched sideways, slamming into the third before Reeves and Shaw brought it down in a hail of 6.8mm slugs. Reeves turned, looking for the source of the shots that had saved his life, and found himself looking up at the chiseled, patrician face of a Thacian soldier. The man could have been a recruiting poster for whatever they called their army, and Reeves hoped he was the one in charge.

"We have to get to that bomb," he said, pointing at the gate. "We can close that thing, but we have to get to the other side."

The Thacian answered in their weird dialect of Greek, which Reeves had been afraid of. He cursed and pulled his cell phone out of his thigh pocket, bringing up the translation app he'd had the CIA create for all of them just in case. He repeated the phrase into the phone and it spat out something he hoped was closer to the bearded man's language.

The Thacian's eyes lit up and he gabbled a response. Reeves whispered a prayer to the gods of bureaucracy that the Agency hadn't fucked up again, that the app would actually work. Reeve's phone spoke to him in a pleasantly-generic female voice, robbing the words of the urgency the Thacian had given them.

"We've lost half our force, and we're low on ammunition, but we can make one last surge, if you can do what you say."

"Give me thirty seconds," Reeves told him, letting the app translate it. "When you see us heading for the gate, move forward and distract the demons."

The Thacian ran back to his people and the force moved out from their positions behind the trees, revealing there were even less of them than Reeves had thought, platoon strength at most, and half of them looked to be walking wounded. A surge of doubt clenched his gut that the Thacians could even hold the demons off

Gates of Hope

long enough to get to the bomb, but it wasn't as if they had a second option.

"Perrault!" Reeves yelled, sliding in beside the French paratrooper NCO. Perrault fired off the last few rounds from his HK417, sending a demon tumbling back through the gate before his bolt locked open.

"*Oui?*" the man asked matter-of-factly, twisting around to reload his weapon as if this was all a training exercise.

"You're going with me and Shaw through the gate to set the bomb. The Thacians over there are going to cover us. You ready?"

"*Oui.*" A man of few words, which suited Reeves at the moment.

"Nyland." The man was fifty yards away, on the far end of the line, but he waved acknowledgement of the transmission. "Shaw, Perrault and I are going into the gate. Move up and try to force the demons back through, give us an opening."

"Copy. We're down to about two mags apiece though, and Flanders just loaded up his last drum. We better get this shit done."

More of the demons were clambering over the edge of the gate, some hit and dropped immediately, but enough coming through that with each wave, they got closer to the human positions less than a hundred yards away. It would only be a matter of minutes before they were all too low on ammo to hold them off.

Reeves clapped Shaw on the arm and broke into a loping run, crouched low enough to break up his outline against the piles of demon corpses. Theoretically. He had no idea if the things could see into the thermal range or how they saw at all through those bulbous, multifaceted eyes. But it made him feel better and might keep him from getting shot in the back just in case the Thacians didn't have proper fire discipline.

He was about to find out, because the thirty seconds was up

fish back to their village. They acknowledged their leader with a bow, the males bowing more deeply than the females, and the matriarch returned each with a simple nod of her head.

Yet she didn't slow down. Wash was used to keeping up with the Delta team, who were typical military hard-chargers, fast-walking everywhere just to show they had purpose to everything they did, but the matriarch had a pace that put them all to shame. How Valon was keeping up without running, Wash didn't know, because he couldn't do it. He tried not to pant too heavily, not wanting to embarrass himself in front of Valon, but after ten minutes of a steady ten-minute-mile pace, he'd totally lost track of which direction they were going and was just hoping like hell that wherever it was happened to be nearby.

The woods had closed in on the edge of the river, trying to push them in, and finally the cat lady slowed down enough for Wash to catch up.

"Where the hell are we going?" Wash asked no one in particular, although Valon was the only one around who could understand him.

"Hopefully, to a gate," Valon answered unhelpfully.

Wash slapped at a mosquito, cursing. Now that they'd slowed down, the things were swarming all over them.

"If this place is engineered by the Archaion," he said, waving the insects away, "and they actually *live* here now, why the hell would they bring mosquitos with them?"

"They're part of the food chain." She sounded unimpressed that they bothered him. "Don't they have mosquitos where you live, Wash?"

"Yeah, but they're not alien mosquitos. Those bite harder."

"Perhaps we should keep it down so we don't frighten anything off."

Wash eyed her sidelong.

and both groups of human soldiers advanced, the Americans in silence but the Thacians with some incomprehensible war cry. Even the ones with bloody field bandages wrapped around gruesome wounds from the talons of the bug-eyed monsters charged into the fray screeching like the ancient Celts, missing only the blue body paint and handlebar mustaches.

These people had spirit and about as much regard for their own lives as the demons, though Reeves wasn't sure if that was a good thing. Then again, *he* was the one about to throw himself through the gate into the heart of the enemy.

He spared a glance back to make sure Shaw and Perrault were following and hadn't been picked off by one of the demons snaking their way toward the humans, using their own dead as cover. But the pincer attack seemed to be working, driving the Hive Mind's warrior drones back toward their gate, a gap in the middle of them just big enough for the three of them to squeeze through.

Reeves sprinted the last thirty meters, rifle clutched across his chest with his right hand while his left plucked a grenade off his vest. He'd never actually tried pulling the pin of one of the things out with his teeth, had considered it a cliché of old war movies, but lacking a free hand, he did it anyway. He didn't break a tooth, but he could tell it was a near thing, and as he tossed the grenade through the gate, he resolved to check with a dentist if he lived through this.

"Grenade!" he yelled, and his call was echoed by Shaw, the warrant officer's own M68 arcing from behind him into the portal.

The concussion of the twin blasts smacked Reeves in the face, though no fragments came through, and the smoke hadn't cleared before Reeves jumped through the gate. He'd been expecting a drop, but this one lasted a two count, and when his feet impacted he went into a parachute landing fall by instinct—soles of his boots, calf, thigh, butt and side, distributing the impact across his body, and the fall was still hard enough to drive the wind out of him in a loud gush.

It was twilight on this side of the portal, the sun sinking below the horizon, the brightest light coming from the gate itself, which hung eight feet above him. It was definitely an active site, what Wash had told him the Thacians called a Beast World. He could tell by the utter devastation out to the horizon, the lack of any sign of life bigger than thorny scrub. That *could* have been just a natural badland... if it weren't for the horde of warrior drones and spikers lined up like shoppers at the door of a department store on Black Friday until their numbers merged with the blackness opposite the western horizon.

The grenades had bought them twenty or thirty yards of space, but that wouldn't last—the wounded demons were already surging back in, ignoring the cracks in their carapace oozing ichor. Reeves sucked in a pained lungful of the stale, chill air and worked his rifle free of where it was trapped under his body, taking down the closest of the demons before his magazine ran dry.

"I've got it!" Perrault yelled in accented English.

Reeves twisted around, reloading by feel as he searched for the French NCO, found him all the way on the other side of the gate, limping toward the overturned trike, its handlebars twisted into uselessness, smoke pouring off its engine as oil leaked onto the block. The nuclear charge had broken free of its cradle and rolled off against a rock ledge of black basalt, but the case didn't seem to be cracked. Shaw had come down between Reeves and Perrault, though he didn't seem to have landed as badly as the Frenchman and had his shit together enough to fire his grenade launcher into the midst of the demons advancing on them.

Reeves retreated a step, movement out of the corner of his eye turning him to the right just in time for the blur of a sprinting demon to solidify into a target. His finger jammed down the trigger in a burst of adrenaline nearly as explosive as the burst of heavy rifle bullets, stitching the thing from chest up to blood-red eyes. This time he'd waited too long, and talons that could cut through sheet metal swiped the rifle out of his hands, the tips ripping through the spare magazines on his tactical vest and scoring lines through his body armor's ceramic plates. Reeves tumbled backward, the rifle gone, his hand going automatically to his sidearm.

He'd left the Glock 9mm behind for this mission, going with something larger. Shaw had made fun of him for it, saying that if he was in shit deep enough to be using a handgun it wouldn't matter what caliber it was, but the thing wasn't *that* much heavier. The Glock 40 was a long-slide version of their 10mm offering, and Wash, who had a lot of experience in grizzly country, had mentioned that the hunters there carried 10mm pistols loaded with Buffalo Bore 220-grain hard cast lead bullets for bear defense. The demons were a hell of a lot deadlier than a pissed-off grizzly, but the 10mm was better than harsh language.

The gun had jumped into his hands before his back hit the ground, just in time for the Trijicon RMR red dot to fall over the head of the warrior drone hopping over the corpse of the one who'd slashed at him. The heavy, 220-grain lead rounds had kicked like a forty-four Magnum when he'd tested them at the firing range, but in the moment, Reeves barely felt the recoil. The demon felt it though, the slugs ripping through its eyes and penetrating the thinner carapace of its skull from beneath its chin.

Reeves rolled out of the way as it crashed to the ground, its tail flailing wildly in death, the jagged point ripping across the gravelly soil only inches away from his leg before it went limp. Acid sprayed up from the end, a few drops falling onto the armor plate over Reeves' left thigh, white smoke rising as the ceramic bubbled away... and fierce, burning pain erupted from below the armor. Reeves didn't scream, but he did yell incoherently, dropping his handgun and pulling the curved karambit from its sheath across his chest, slicing through the straps holding the leg armor in place, then tossing it away.

The fabric over the ceramic plate had already dissolved, and the ceramic was disappearing in a crater two inches across and growing, but Reeves barely paid attention to it, tearing open his pant leg and checking the bare skin beneath. There was an angry, red welt there, but the acid hadn't burned through. He would have sighed in relief, but there were so many other things closing in, more likely to kill him than acid eating its way through his femoral artery, like the unending swarm of demons racing across the lifeless, blackened soil and bare rock toward the gate. They might have been coming for the portal to the other side rather than him, but he'd still be just as dead when they arrived.

Shaw knelt beside him, firing off short bursts, taking down two of the demons at seventy yards, then letting the SIG fall to his side and pulling out his Glock 34 9mm.

"I'm Winchester on rifle ammo," Shaw told him, yelling over the blast of the 10mm as Reeves chanced a long shot at one of the monsters and wasted a round on its thick shoulder armor. "You got anything?"

"I don't even have the vest anymore!" Reeves shouted back. "You got any grenades?"

"Fresh out."

"Fall back to Perrault!"

Five more rounds of 10mm, along with however many Shaw fired from his nine to the head of another of the demons approaching from the right, and Reeves' slide locked on an empty mag. He didn't try to reload on the run, just sprinted past the wrecked motor trike, putting it between him and the incoming enemy. They weren't that bright, and he was hoping like hell they'd go for their primary target, the gate.

Perrault and the nuke were hidden behind the thing, and he'd been hoping the Frenchman had the thing activated... until he saw the three dead warrior drones clustered all around the nuke and Perrault lolling, covered in blood.

"Jesus!" Reeves switched magazines on the Glock, which left him with one spare, and settled next to Perrault.

The man gasped for breath, eyes flickering open, grabbing at his rifle, but the weapon was locked open, empty, the magazines on his chest rig torn to bits, the spare rounds spilled out around him, stained with his blood.

"I'll get you out of here," he told Perrault, speaking French, not knowing if the man would recall his little English with his chest ripped apart. "I'll get you back."

The Frenchman shook his head and droplets of red scattered from his mouth and nose.

"No. Get out." He cast a glance toward the metal cylinder. "I activated it. You have five minutes."

"Fuck!" Shaw blurted. Reeves hadn't seen the man coming up behind him. He pointed eight feet up at the gate. "How the hell are we gonna get out of here in five minutes?"

Reeves sighed. There were two grenades still nestled in the remains of Perrault's vest. He grabbed them and handed one to Shaw.

"We're not."

16

Wash Williams had visited jails before, to bail his father out of them, but he'd never seen the inside of a cell until now. This one wasn't actually at the county jail, thankfully, just a holding cell in the Hillsborough County Sheriff's Department station on... well, he didn't know the name of the road. He'd never been to Tampa before and hadn't noticed much in the way of landmarks from the back of the SUV, except that it smelled horrible and handcuffs were very hard on his wrists and shoulders.

The holding cell didn't smell much better than the back of the cruiser, though he imagined it was cleaned more often. He'd even managed to grab a quick nap, but he had no idea what time it was and he needed to make some calls. Unfortunately, the deputies hadn't let him make any, though they'd promised to call MacDill Air Force Base and check on his story.

"Didn't you watch the documentary?" he'd asked the deputy, hating himself for the words. "I'm Kyle Washakie Williams...you know, the guy who fought the alien monsters?"

"Maybe you are and maybe you aren't," the man had allowed. "I don't know until I check your story. But I *do* know for a fact that the state of Florida doesn't allow open carry of firearms, and you don't have a valid Florida concealed weapons permit."

And that had been that as far as Deputy Charles was concerned. They'd searched him thoroughly, taken his body armor and holdout knife and even his bootlaces, fingerprinted him, taken his picture ,and stuck him in the cell. At least it was quiet this afternoon and none of the cells around him were occupied. He had no idea where they'd taken Valon, nor how they were going to handle the fact that she wasn't in the system and didn't exist as far as the United States of America was concerned.

What would happen if they shipped her off somewhere, like a psych ward, and she got lost in the system?

Wash paced the tiny cell, a caged lion, feeling as confined and cut off here as he had back on the Archaion planet. He *needed* to let Brenda know he was okay. They would have told her he was missing, maybe even said he was dead, and she'd be going nuts by now. Wash eyed the clear plastic front wall of the cell, considered pounding on it and demanding to talk to someone.

It might backfire. Cops were just as human as anyone else, and if he acted like an asshole, they were just as likely to keep him stuck in here as long as they could get away with. But there was also the chance they were sitting on their hands, waiting for a call back from some idiot public relations officer at MacDill when they *should* have been talking to SOCOM headquarters.

Five more minutes. He'd give them five minutes, then he'd start squawking. Except he didn't have a watch, didn't have a phone, didn't have any way of finding out when it had been five minutes. He could count. It was juvenile and tedious, but what *else* did he have to keep himself busy?

Wash had reached two hundred seconds in his head when he finally just decided to go ahead and start banging. He had his fist cocked back, poised to hammer on the plastic, when the outer door to the holding area opened and a deputy stepped through.

Not Charles from before. This guy was taller and beefier, biceps straining against his short-sleeved white shirt, a circa-1970s pornstache homesteading on his upper lip. The tall deputy pulled out a key and opened the cell door, surprising Wash.

He'd seen other doors opened since he'd arrived, and the protocol was always the same, involving ordering the prisoner to turn away from the doors and put their hands behind their heads. None of that this time.

"Let's go, Sgt. Williams," the man said, nodding down the hallway.

Sgt. Williams this time. Wash stood slowly, not wanting to push his luck.

"Did somebody finally call?" he asked, following the man out into the hallway.

"No, someone showed up from MacDill and confirmed your story. He's waiting for you out in the station."

Wash shouldn't have been surprised to see Colonel Dos Santos standing in the waiting room, arms crossed, impatience writ across his craggy face, but he was.

"Williams, I can't say as I ever expected to see you again, but I suppose I should have known better." He shook his head, smiling ruefully, then extended a hand. Wash shook it a little hesitantly, unsure whether the man was welcoming him back or about to sucker punch him. "Glad you're here, son. The team is off in Europe, but I'm sure we can get you over there with them once you're debriefed…"

"Sir!" Wash interrupted, grabbing the man's shoulder, then letting go when Dos Santos stared at his hand like it was a venomous snake. "Valon is here! She was picked up with me!"

"Valon?" The Delta officer frowned. "The Thacian woman?"

"We escaped the active site together!" Wash nodded, pointing back at the holding cell. "They arrested us together ,but I didn't see her back there in the holding area. You've gotta get them to turn her over to you. She's trying to get the Thacian government to work with us, and there's some other stuff she told me you really need to hear."

"All right, all right," Dos Santos said, raising a hand to stop him. "I'll talk to the sheriff. You wait here."

Wash fidgeted as the man headed off past the reception desk, waving off the desk sergeant's questioning look as he made a beeline for the back, presumably to the office of the actual sheriff. Porn-stache cop gestured for Wash's attention, holding a collection of plastic evidence bags in one hand and his body armor in the other.

"I got your stuff here, Sergeant," he said, holding the things out.

"Thanks." Wash grabbed the bags one at a time, tucking his wallet away and threading his belt into his pants, feeling slightly guilty about keeping the deputy waiting, but not *too* guilty—they'd arrested him, after all.

The Canik was locked open on an empty mag, and several heads turned when he dropped the slide and tucked the gun into its holster.

"The ammo is in here," Porn-stache said apologetically, handing over another plastic bag. "I'd appreciate if you wouldn't reload it until you're out of the building, if that's all right."

"Sure." Resentment gnawed at him, and he had to make a determined effort to banish it. He understood the deputy's caution, but he couldn't help think that they'd trusted him to go to alien planets and plant nukes but couldn't trust him to have a loaded gun in a police station. The train of thought derailed totally when he came to his cell phone. Still dead. "Excuse me, deputy, but do you have an android charger?"

Brenda Sands stared at the microwave dinner and wondered if she shouldn't have tried to cook something. She *knew* how to cook... if her mother had accomplished nothing else as a parent, she'd at least taught Brenda her way around the kitchen. But cooking for one was depressing, and Brenda had found herself eating out too much. Not that they were hurting for money, at least not since she'd started working again, but drive-through food was usually bad for her, and she really didn't want to gain weight and stop taking care of herself and become her mother.

Microwave meals, she decided, were *not* the answer. They all tasted like cardboard.

What if he doesn't come back this time?

The thought intruded, unwelcome. She'd tried to force herself not to consider the possibility, to push the whole thing down until she heard from Brian Reeves again, but it kept creeping back. Brenda blew out a breath and tossed her fork down on the table, hands curling into fists.

All right. Let's just deal.

If he didn't come back, if Wash was really gone for good, she had to get out of this town. They'd been talking about leaving anyway, and there was absolutely no reason for her to stay without him. The scenery was nice here, and she supposed the town had a certain charm, but it also had way too many single-wides and meth-heads and not enough jobs. She didn't see herself selling real estate the rest of her life, and putting her degree to work for her here was nearly impossible.

Denver, maybe. It was expensive there, but she had a friend from college who lived there who'd offered her a spare room if she visited. She could find a job, maybe pay Karley rent for a while. She didn't want to be alone, not right now. Not without Wash.

I am *alone. No Jimmy, no Wash, no Mom.*

She'd never been alone in high school, in college. There'd

always been friends around. Her friends had left town though, left her behind. Brenda grabbed her cell phone and scrolled through the menu. There was Karley's number. She should call her, should talk to her, make sure that room was still available, just in case.

No. She set the phone down. She wasn't ready to give up, not yet.

"Brenda."

The voice was soft, so faint she thought she'd imagined it, and she looked at her phone in alarm, sure she'd accidentally dialed someone, but the home screen was undisturbed. Frowning, she looked around the room.

"Brenda."

Clear this time. Not coming from her phone. Panic surged in her stomach and Brenda snatched up her purse from the kitchen counter, pulled open the Velcro flap in the side and ripped the SIG 9mm out of its holster. The P365 was a tiny thing, barely large enough for her to get a good grip with her last three fingers, and Wash had questioned the choice, wondering if she should pack something larger and easier to control, but she'd shut him up by completing one of his USPSA stages with the little gun without a miss.

She held it in what Wash had told her was called an Isosceles stance, the gun at the point of a triangle with her body as the base, and backed out of the kitchen into the downstairs bedroom. It had a walk-in closet that was a good defensive position, a place she could see anyone and have a shot at them before they could get to her.

"Brenda, it's me!"

A pleading note to the voice, fading into distortion at the end, as if it was coming over a line with a bad cell connection. Brenda cursed under her breath and checked right and left, then behind her. The words had seemed to come from all around her.

Gates of Hope

"Who are you?" she demanded, trying to keep her voice steady.

Nothing for a moment, just a sense of the speaker gathering his strength, his breath, for one more word.

"It's me... Jimmy!"

The blood congealed in Brenda's veins and she stumbled backward a step. Her trigger finger had curled inside the guard of the handgun, and she forced it back out.

"Shit," she hissed.

Wash had talked to her about PTSD, about what his father had gone through, had worried she might experience it herself. Here it was. She was losing it. Brenda walked slowly and carefully back out to the kitchen and set the gun down by her purse, placing her palms flat beside it and leaning heavily against the counter. Breath came short and sharp, right at the edge of hyperventilation despite her best efforts to control it.

"I didn't hear anything," she said aloud, an attempt to get her respiration back to normal. "I didn't hear him. I was just imagining things. I didn't hear anything."

It was a Gregorian chant, a Buddhist mantra, words she seized onto and tried hard to believe. Brenda repeated it again into the silence, afraid if she didn't keep saying it, she'd hear Jimmy's voice again. She kept saying it until her throat went raw and her mouth filled with cotton, and only then did she stop and grab the glass beside her forgotten microwave dinner, gulping the water down, not stopping until it was gone and she was gasping for air.

Silence. Blissful silence. Hands shaking, Brenda went to the refrigerator and pulled a beer from the twelve-pack she'd left there earlier in the week. It was bitter and lacked the bite she needed, but Wash didn't want anything stronger in the house, not after what alcohol had done to his father.

Did it really matter what he wanted anymore?

"I could go to a bar," she said, still talking to herself, afraid what she'd might hear if she didn't. "But I don't think I could drive back. Maybe a taxi or a rideshare?" She snorted. "Not in this town, not without waiting an hour."

She'd just about convinced herself to drive to the liquor store and grab a fifth of Jack Daniels when the phone rang and she jumped back, snatching up her 9mm and pointing it at the device for a half a second before she managed to calm down.

"God*dammit*, girl, get a grip."

Brenda put the gun away in her purse this time, closing it before she took the time to check the phone. The number on the caller ID belonged to Wash. Hyperventilation threatened again as she swiped the screen to answer the call.

"Hello?" She barely hissed the word out, her hand shaking so badly she couldn't hold the phone still.

"Brenda, it's me." The words echoed her earlier hallucination, and she nearly threw the phone down, but this was no spectral voice. "It's Wash! I just got back."

"Oh, my God," she gasped, falling into the chair at the kitchen table, the strength gone out of her legs. "Oh, Jesus... Wash, is it really you? They told me... they told me you were missing on some other planet."

"Yeah, I'm really sorry, hon," he said, actually sounding embarrassed. "I got separated from the others and I had to get out any way I could. But I found a way back. I'm in Florida."

"Florida?" she blurted. It was, she thought, utterly ridiculous, but she found the idea of him being in Florida more outlandish than him being on another planet.

"Yeah, Tampa. We wound up here from the other gate we found."

"We?" Brenda made a face at her own words. She was starting to sound like a parrot.

"We ran into the Thacians out there." Wash hesitated, and she wondered if he was supposed to be telling her this. "Valon escaped through the gate with me... she's here on Earth. They're gonna debrief us and I don't know what's gonna happen after that, but I'm okay. I'm not hurt, though I do smell pretty bad at the moment."

A laugh burbled upward through the stress and fear, uncontrollable.

"You worked on a ranch in high school, Wash... I think I'm used to it."

He shared in her laugh, sounding relieved. Was he that worried about how she'd react?

"Are you okay, Brenda?" he asked. "I'm sorry I put you through this."

"I knew what I was getting into," she insisted. She considered for the space of a heartbeat telling him about her hallucination, but decided against it. He had enough on his plate without thinking she'd lost her mind. "Just come back as soon as you can." She sucked in a breath at the thought of being here alone until whenever that might be. "Or tell me when we can meet and I'll fly out there. To Florida or wherever, it doesn't matter."

"I'd love that," he assured her. "I'll call you again when I know anything. The colonel is coming... I have to go. I love you."

"Love you too."

The line went dead. Brenda set the phone down, feeling like she'd been run over by a semi. Wash was alive. All she'd put herself through and he was fine, not hurt. Relief washed over her, so great that it was almost as overwhelming as the worry and fear.

For some reason, she needed that drink even more now.

"How the hell," she wondered aloud, "am I going to do this?"

17

"I wonder," Victor Shaw yelled over the spiteful crack of his 9mm, "whether the demons will get us first or the nuke. Personally, I'm hoping for the nuke. I always wanted to die in a fucking mushroom cloud."

Reeves didn't reply, concentrating on popping the bulbous red eye of one of the warrior drones with three rounds of 10mm hardcast lead. That was the end of that magazine. He loaded the last and racked the slide. Fifteen rounds. Well, Perrault had a handgun, some kind of HK, if he wanted to wade through what was left of the man's chest to find it. He didn't think he'd have the time. The grenades they'd scavenged from the man had bought them space and a few seconds' respite, but the demons were closing in again, funneled around twin outcroppings of sharp rock into two approaches, one guarded by each of the men. The enemy corpses were stacked in ragged clusters, but the damned things just wouldn't stop coming.

Something smacked Reeves in the shoulder and he spun around, expecting to find a demon that had somehow snuck up on him and was about to slice him to ribbons. Instead, he found the end of a rope. Brian Reeves was a well-trained operator, a man who'd been shot at so many times he'd stopped bothering to count, who'd killed people on every continent and been to a dozen different planets, but he still stared at the rope for a good half-second before he realized what was going on.

It helped when Flanders leaned out over the edge of the gate, one hand gripping the rope, the other shoving his M250 machine gun out against its sling, firing full-auto at the oncoming hordes of demons.

"Get up the rope!" he yelled, which was, perhaps, the most unnecessary advice Reeves had ever heard.

"Go!" Reeves yelled at Shaw, waving him at the rope.

Shaw grimaced like he wanted to debate the issue, but he must have known better than to think Reeves would go before him. He tucked his Glock into its holster and lunged to grab the rope six feet up, pulling himself hand over hand until someone reached through from above and pulled him out. Reeves emptied his last magazine, taking down a demon that was close enough that its tail brushed his shoulder before jamming into the side of the overturned trike, then ran up the side of the ruined cart and wrapped his fist in the rope.

"Pull!" Flanders yelled up at the others, still firing his machine gun into the oncoming demons, the mass of them only twenty yards away.

Reeves dropped his Glock and lunged upward with the now-free hand, locking the rope between his boots and clambering up even as someone above began yanking it through the gate. The shift in light was subtle on the other side, from a dark gray twilight to solid night, but the feel of the air wasn't. Everything on the other side had been stale and dank, but back on the sandstone plateau there was a fresh, chill bite to the night that seemed to make his breath come easier.

Or maybe that was just the hands pulling him out of the gate, his feet back on solid ground.

"Grenade!"

Who had yelled it, Reeves wasn't sure, but everyone on the team except him and Shaw tossed an M68 through the portal, then ducked away. Reeves didn't need any encouragement, falling into a crouch, hands over his ears inside his helmet. A rolling chorus of kettle-drum banging sounded from the other side and a taloned hand reaching through the gate fell backward.

"Get away!" Reeves yelled, waving at his own people and the Thacians who'd crowded around the gate. "Get back! Get to the trees!"

The Thacians might not have known what his words meant, but they followed the example of the Americans, scrambling away from the portal and taking cover deep inside the tree line. Reeves hung back just a few steps, limping on his burned leg, making sure everyone made it... and to his surprise, so did the Thacian commander, the one he'd spoken to through his phone translator. The man nodded to him as they picked their way through the roots and ducked behind twisted, gnarled trees.

Reeves tried to figure how long it had been, but he'd lost track of the time since Perrault's dying warning, and all he could think was that demons were going to come streaming through the unguarded gate in seconds, and there'd be no way to hold them back from this far away with everyone low on ammo... but there was nothing else to do about it.

"Eyes down!" he yelled at the others, then pantomimed covering his eyes to the Thacian until the man shouted his own command.

Reeves didn't wait to see if they obeyed, just buried his helmet in the dirt, hands over his ears, and rooted for a nuclear explosion to beat the demons to the punch. His eyes were closed, helmet blocking his view, dirt cold and slimy against his face, and *still* the light sent flashes through his retinae, the sound momentous and apocalyptic, like a god of old stomping his foot into the earth.

And then nothing. The sound ended abruptly, and no heat, no shockwave accompanied it, just dead silence. Reeves risked a look upward and where the gate had been was... nothing. A ring of smoke hung in the air above the plateau, a hundred yards across and growing as it drifted upward and began to dissipate. The Thacian stared at in awe and murmured something that sounded like a curse.

"Is everyone okay?" Reeves said. "Sound off!"

"Yeah, I'm good," Shaw said, getting slowly to his feet from behind a tree about twenty yards away. "Though God alone knows how."

The others echoed the response up and down the line, coming out from behind cover, relief in the set of their shoulders. Reeves shared in the feeling, not just that he'd made it out —again—but that the whole team had survived. Guilt followed hard on the heels of relief as he thought of Perrault dead on the other side, vaporized. He'd been a brave man and a good soldier.

"What the fuck now, boss?" Shaw asked. He nodded back the way they'd come. "We heading back up?" He checked his watch. "We got like forty-five minutes before the French start bombing the other gate. We might make it if we bust ass."

Reeves looked between Shaw and the Thacian. The tall, noble-featured officer was staring at him, something close to awe in his expression... and maybe gratitude. Gratitude was good, and awe wasn't bad either.

"Vic, take the team back and get through. Tell the colonel I'm going with the Thacians to try to establish contact with their government."

Shaw goggled at him for a moment, mouth dropping open.

"You *sure* about this, Brian?"

"Get going." Reeves jerked a thumb behind him. "You don't have much time."

"You heard the man, guys," Shaw bellowed, waving his finger in the air. "Back to the gate! Double-time!"

Flanders paused before following Shaw, pulling his sidearm from its holster and handing it over, butt-first. It was another 10mm, this one a SIG, and Reeves nodded, replacing the Glock in its holster with Flanders' sidearm, then accepting the man's spare mags.

"Good luck, boss," Flanders told him, patting him on the shoulder then jogging up the trail to join the others.

The Thacian commander was frowning in confusion as he watched the Americans leave, a question in his eyes as he turned back to Reeves.

"Hope this works." Reeves sighed and pulled out his phone, bringing up the translation app. He offered the Thacian a smile. "Take me to your leader."

―――――

This wasn't, Wash decided, that much of an improvement over jail. True, they'd brought him coffee and hadn't taken his shoelaces, but the chair was less comfortable, and at least in jail they'd pretty much left him alone.

"Let's go over this again, Sergeant Williams," Dos Santos said with a sigh, leaning onto the table between them, the cheap plastic creaking under his weight. "Starting with when you and Valon went through the gate. How far did you have to walk to get to these… what was the word you called them?"

"Archaion." Wash was doing his dead-level best to maintain his patience, but it was getting thinner with every minute he spent in this damned, featureless, windowless room going over the same details. "And I don't know exactly. Maybe five or six hours walk, but I can't swear to how fast we were walking. Part of it was at night." He rubbed at his eyes. They felt like sandpaper, and he wondered what time it was and how long it had been since he slept. "If I had to guess, maybe twelve to fifteen miles."

"Right. So, you two walked nearly fifteen miles before you encountered the Archaion." He made a face. "These *cat* people."

"I didn't say they were cat people," Wash insisted. "Sir," he added, belatedly. "I said their features looked kind of feline to me. That's just me. Someone else could look at them and see, I don't know, a fox or a squirrel. The point is, they aren't human and you can tell."

Dos Santos grunted assent, though he didn't seem convinced.

"Did the two of you talk?"

Wash kept from rolling his eyes. Barely. What did the colonel think, that the two of them had walked for six hours and never said a word?

"She wanted to know why I was there," he said. "Why I hadn't just gone home and stayed there, and I explained to her about Brenda and Jimmy."

"You had no clearance to share that information with her," Dos Santos reminded him, though with only mild reproof.

"We made a *documentary* with that information, sir. She's an ally—she saved my life more than once. Who are we keeping it a secret from?"

Wash shut his mouth, realizing he was getting way too close to insubordination, but Dos Santos showed no anger.

"You explained it to her, and how did she react?"

"She understood. She was happy that I'd been able to rescue Brenda. She told me that when we set off the nuke, we saved her world from invasion. That she'd been able to put up what they call a shield over the gate the demons had been using and she was promoted to something called a primus." Wash shook his head. "I'm not sure, I don't think it translates into our rank structure, but it sounds like it's something close to a major or a light colonel."

Dos Santos' eyebrow shot up.

"She seems very young for that rank."

"Youngest primus in the history of the Thacian Venators, she told me," he agreed. "And they named her a Hero of Thacia, which is like some kind of big honor. Like the Medal, maybe."

Dos Santos snorted a sharp laugh.

"Both of you came out of that with the Medal then, except you didn't get to be an officer."

"Thank God, sir." Wash looked back at the room's single door, frowning. "Where is she, anyway? She should be here. I won't be able to remember everything she said, and she's got some really important intel you have to hear."

"She's being questioned in another area," Dos Santos said, shrugging with what Wash thought might be discomfort with the words.

"Questioned," Wash repeated, something about the word striking him as out of place. "You mean debriefed?" When Dos Santos said nothing, Wash rose from his chair, the legs scraping against the floor. "Sir, please tell me that Valon isn't being treated like she's some kind of enemy spy. She's an ally! The Venators only exist to fight the Hive Mind, to keep Earth safe from it!"

"So she's *told* you," Dos Santos corrected him. "We have another source of information." The man seemed reluctant to elaborate, but seeing Wash's stubborn stare, he relented. "Master Sergeant Reeves rescued one of their wounded and we've been talking to him. According to this man, Lykon, the Thacians have their own political issues, factions, some of which don't care much about Earth and are only concerned with maintaining their power." There was a tinge of bitterness to his laugh. "Not too different from here, don't you think?"

"Their politics don't have anything to do with Valon," Wash

insisted. "She's a soldier, like me, like Reeves." He didn't say like Dos Santos, because the man was a bird colonel, by nature a political animal. "She'd do anything to defeat the Hive Mind. They've been keeping it under control for centuries... they *still* would be if it weren't for us! We never would have known the damned thing existed if we hadn't been fucking around with that starship!"

Dos Santos erupted from his chair and stood nose-to-nose with Wash, his face going from that oily politician to a rage-driven Delta operator in a fraction of a second.

"You'd damned well better not have said anything about that to *anyone*, Sergeant! I hope you *remember* the fucking NDA you signed, and exactly how many fucking *years* you'll spend in a federal detention center if you violate it!"

"I know exactly what I signed, sir," Wash shot back, not giving an inch. "And I know what Valon is risking by being here and sharing the information she's giving us. And I damned well know that we shouldn't be treating her like she's the enemy."

"You're in the military, Sgt. Reeves," Dos Santos reminded him, his voice lower but his tone just as coldly ferocious. "You're a member of the Wyoming National Guard, here by a special dispensation of the president, the request of Brian Reeves, and the forbearance of *me*. And by God, if you don't care to keep this arrangement up, I can send you right back to Bumfuck Wyoming where you came from, Medal or no."

Wash glared at the colonel, the stubborn streak running back through his mother and father and into his ancestors on both sides not wanting to give in, willing to call his bluff. And he was sure the man *was* bluffing. Beyond the Medal of Honor, there was also the little matter of bad publicity, which he was sure the president wanted to avoid and which they could only be sure of controlling if they kept Wash on active duty.

But he also knew that if they did kick him off the team and

out of the operation, there'd be no one to look out for Valon. He owed it to her to get her out of this.

"Can I at least *talk* to her? She's gotta be kind of freaked out by all this. Just let me tell her everything is going to be okay. Please, sir..."

Dos Santos took a breath, as if trying to calm himself down, and his eyes narrowed in thought.

"In a while," he said finally, his shoulders relaxing as if he'd accepted Wash's peace offering. "She's over in Building B for right now and they don't allow outside visitors, but once they're through with initial... questioning, I'll see if I can get you in. It'll be under observation, of course."

"Of course. Thank you, sir."

"Now," Dos Santos said, sitting back in his chair and motioning for Wash to do the same, "let's get back to the debriefing. Tell me more about these Archaion..."

18

"Wow," Brian Reeves murmured, staring down from the landing pad on top of the Venator headquarters. "This is some place you got here."

Thacia was like no other city Reeves had ever visited, something otherworldly and anachronistic about it... or no, not anachronistic, but totally outside of time, something that wouldn't have fit at any point in history. He'd seen artistic representations of ancient cities in Greece and Rome, and while this was reminiscent of them, it was more as if someone had taken such a city and followed it through time to the present... but not *his* version of the present. He couldn't put his finger on what was different about it at first until it finally struck him. This wasn't a city built around the automobile. There was no accommodation for them. Instead, there were trollies that went in a checkerboard pattern, laid out before him as if it were a gameboard.

"Are your cities that different from ours?" the man who'd introduced himself as Prefect Marcos wondered.

The man spoke English with no accent... *No, that's wrong.* He spoke English with the faintest trace of the same western accent Wash had. Had he learned English in the same mysterious way that Wash had explained Valon had done? He wanted to ask, but there were more pressing matters to discuss.

"They are. Yours looks more... planned, to me. Like you built it from scratch all at once. Ours are more patchwork, because different parts of the city were built at different times."

Reeves felt odd talking to the man like this was a vacation with his wife to Europe instead of a trip to another planet. Certainly, nothing else about the trip here had been so casual and matter-of-fact. He'd followed the Thacian commander—whose name, he'd discovered, was Demas and rank was pilus, which he thought but couldn't be sure was some kind of NCO—back through the forest and into a riverbed to the gate out of the sandstone plateau, which had taken nearly three hours on foot. It might have been faster, but half the remaining Thacians were injured and they'd had to go at the pace of the slowest of them.

That gate had taken them to a blue-sky world at a seashore, a place that had reminded him of the Pacific Northwest, and another two-hour hike into the hills to the portal back to Thacia. Thacia was the planet as well as the capital city, which had taken Reeves a few go-arounds with Demas to understand, and the gate had dropped them off at an outpost somewhere in the mountains a good five hundred miles from the capital.

They'd wound up sitting around the outpost for nearly a day until someone had sent out an aircraft to pick them up, typical military efficiency no matter what planet they were on. The aircraft itself had been an eye-opener. Reeves had read about the concept of ducted-fan helicopters, but he'd never seen one in person, much less on the scale of the aircraft the Thacians used. Flying in one of the things had been exceedingly strange, like riding a hovercraft over the water.

He glanced back at the transport sitting on the rooftop landing pad, its metal surfaces pinging as they cooled, the reds and whites glistening in the late morning sun. It was a pretty bird, something cool and futuristic about it, though he knew from what he'd read that it wasn't any more advanced, really, just a different path taken to the same effect.

"Well, we *do* have a divine purpose," Marcos told him, and the casual way the man seemed to accept that concept disturbed Reeves. "We were put here for a purpose, which is, I suppose, another way our two cultures differ. But you've had a long journey, Sgt. Reeves." He waved at the door to a stairwell off the roof. "Perhaps you'd like to go to my office, sit down and enjoy some refreshments while we talk."

"Would it be all right if we stayed up here for a while?" Reeves asked, motioning at the mountains in the distance. "This is a really beautiful view, and honestly, I've been sitting in one of your airplanes for hours. I'd like to stand for a few minutes, get the blood circulating."

And keep this guy off-balance, though he didn't say that. This Marcos guy was smooth, almost oily, a politician despite his military rank. Reeves had a nose for politicians, no matter what they called themselves. He was probably at home behind his desk or testifying in front of their version of a House subcommittee, but not so much thinking on his feet.

"Of course," Marcos acceded readily, spreading his hands. "I often come up here when I need to get away from the press of the office and sort out my thoughts. I find it puts everything in perspective."

"Let me ask you something, Prefect," Reeves said, still looking out at the weathered peaks. "How did you guys learn to speak our language?"

"It's a piece of technology that I don't understand well enough to explain," Marcos told him, "and am not at liberty to do so, even if I could." He smiled with all the sincerity of a used-car salesman. "Sorry, hope you can understand."

"Completely." Reeves returned the same sort of smile. "But if our two nations are going to cooperate, we're going to have to learn to trust each other."

"Trust is *earned*, Sergeant." And this time, perhaps, behind that fake smile was a real edge of impatience.

"Then perhaps I can share something to earn yours. We have one of your people. A man called Lykon. He was wounded fighting the demons and we stumbled across him at the site of a battle."

Marcos seemed like a man who was used to keeping his emotions hidden, but he couldn't manage it this time, tension putting new creases next to his eyes and the corners of his mouth.

"He's going to be okay," Reeves went on, hoping to reassure the man. "He's in one of our hospitals recovering. As soon as we can establish some sort of arrangement between our peoples, we'll get him back to you."

"What about his commander?" Marcos asked, not sounding relieved at all. "A woman called Valon. Do you know anything of what might have happened to her?"

"As a matter of fact, I do." The explanation of what had happened on the active site took a while, and Reeves started to wish he'd taken Marcos up on that offer of a chair and a drink. By the end, the Thacian prefect was nodding, his breath seeming to come easier.

"There is hope then. She's alive and she wasn't alone." The corner of his mouth turned up. "Valon spoke to me of this man you call Wash Williams. She was quite impressed with his courage and composure."

"So are we. He was given our highest award for his action in closing off the gates to one of our country's largest cities from the world you call Hades."

Marcos glanced his way sharply.

"I've been told you have some sort of weapon that can do this." Told via a radio report from Demos, most likely.

"We call it a nuclear warhead." Reeves wasn't sure if he should be telling the man. No, scratch that, he was sure he *wasn't* supposed to, that Dos Santos would shit a brick if he found out about it, but Marcos had been right about trust being earned. "It's based on the idea of splitting the atoms in radioactive material. They're big and heavy, and so far we've had to deliver them by hand rather than using aircraft or missile because we don't know where we're planting them until we get there. It's inefficient and dangerous, but yes, it does allow us to close gates."

"Not a worthless thing, the gods take witness." Marcos shook his head. "But more and more gates seem to be opening, and at a rapidly-accelerating pace. We're mystified as to the cause." He speared Reeves with a stare. "I was hoping perhaps your people knew."

"I'm a soldier, not a scientist." It wasn't really an answer, but then, it hadn't really been a question. "We have much better delivery methods for our nuclear weapons. If we could work together, we could do more with them than simply close gates to your Beast Worlds. We could wipe them out, devastate the entire planet."

That seemed to pique his interest. Marcos' eyes clouded in thought, as if he was considering the implications of such a weapon.

"The Hive Mind makes its lairs deep underground. Can these weapons penetrate this far?"

"Probably not," Reeves admitted. "Not unless we can guide them into the lair itself. I was at Hades and I don't know how we could do that without it being a suicide mission." He sighed, trying to piece together strategies on the fly, and brightened as he came up with one. "But Wash told me that the Hive Mind needs food. That it has drones that go all around the planet and through the gates to other worlds looking for biological material. Right?" Marcos nodded. "The nukes can kill tens of thousands of the drones at a time, with just one or two weapons. I know there's a lot of the damned things, but pretty soon, the Hive Mind is gonna be getting pretty hungry. And maybe the lack of troops would make it harder for the Hive Mind to invade you guys."

Marcos folded his arms, regarding Reeves carefully.

"You're proposing that we work together on this matter?"

"You know which gates lead back to the Beast Worlds. We could put our people with yours to guide the missiles in, even through multiple gates." Which would be tricky, but Reeves had at least three different ways it could work spinning through his mind already.

"I'll have to present this to the Senate," Marcos said. "It will not be a quick decision for them, I warn you ahead of time."

"They're politicians," Reeves acknowledged with a shrug. "I wouldn't expect anything else."

Marcos snorted a cynical laugh.

"We have a room prepared for you." He tilted his head in apology. "I'm afraid you'll have to be sequestered away from everyone except authorized Venator personnel until the Senate makes their decision. I hope you understand."

"Of course." Reeves figured they'd be doing the same for Lykon in Germany, or wherever they'd wound up stashing him. "Like I said, I wouldn't expect anything else."

"Ma'am," the uniformed female said with exaggerated patience, "we want to let you leave here, let you go someplace and freshen up, but you need to answer our questions."

Valon glared at the woman, despising her bland, vapid expression, despising the sullen, trollish man sitting next to her, wearing some sort of dark, ill-fitting business suit. He hadn't said a word, sitting there like he was supposed to be threatening.

"I came here as an ally," Valon ground out, then rattled the handcuffs against the bracket set in the stainless-steel table. "You have put me in chains, kept me in this tiny, windowless room under these hot lights, refused me water, and interrogated me like a criminal. Why should I answer anything?"

"You *say* you're an ally," the woman corrected her. She shrugged. "I'd like to believe you. But I have no evidence that the state you claim to represent even exists, much less that its interests are aligned with our own. The only extraterrestrial life we've encountered are the creatures you refer to as 'demons,' and we know that the intelligence behind them has the capability of controlling human minds. You look just like a human from this world, and you speak like someone from the Mountain West. How do I know you're not this Hive Mind intelligence trying to infiltrate us?"

Valon gritted her teeth. It wasn't a bad line of reasoning on its face, but she knew exactly what the woman was trying to do.

"Wash Williams has told you what I've done," she shot back. "I helped him to escape Hades. We fought shoulder to shoulder against the demons. How does your idiotic little fantasy account for this?"

"It's my job to make sure you're not a threat to us," the woman said, not taking the bait. "And the only way I can do that is if you answer my questions."

"And I won't answer a one," Valon ground out, "until you take off these gods-cursed chains."

She rattled the cuffs again and sat back in her chair, closing her eyes against the harsh overhead lights.

"Ma'am, it's in your best interest to cooperate."

The woman kept droning on, but Valon ignored her, picturing a sunlit meadow, a pleasant breeze, and the babble of a brook in the near distance. And the touch of Atreus. He'd been a fellow student at the Venator school, and after five years of study and training together, she'd finally given into her attraction for the man. He'd died in battle three years ago and she hadn't been able to make that sort of commitment again.

"Very well," the woman said finally, standing from her chair. The man in the suit did the same, still silent. "You'll be taken back to your cell until you decide to cooperate."

The door to the room swung open and a pair of armed men stalked through, one keeping the barrel of his rifle trained on her while the other unfastened one of her wrists and slid the cuffs out of their brackets, then put her hands behind her back and shackled them there. They weren't overly tight, but there was an edge of discomfort to them, as if they were taking her right to the borderline of pain, a promise of things to come if she didn't comply.

The cell was down the hall, and perhaps it was an exaggeration to name it such. It certainly hadn't been built for the purpose of imprisonment and certainly not for the long term. It appeared to be an unoccupied office, bare except for a threadbare, cloth couch and a flimsy, plastic chair. The door could be locked from the outside, however, which told her it wasn't the first time they'd used the room for this purpose.

"I need some water," she told the soldier escorting her as the other one pushed the door open.

"I'll see about getting you some," the woman promised.

"They'll probably say no," Valon predicted. "They want me desperate to talk to them. But don't you have any rules you swore to follow? You're soldiers, aren't you?"

"I'm an airman," the woman corrected her, and Valon frowned.

"Wouldn't you be an airwoman?" she asked, and the female soldier grinned.

"You'd think, by now. But no. Step inside, please."

Valon scanned the room while the absurdly named *airman* unfastened the handcuffs.

"Is there no toilet?"

"Whaddya need a toilet for," the man asked, speaking for the first time, "if you're thirsty?"

"I like to plan ahead." Valon rubbed at the faint red marks on her wrists. "After you bring me the water that it's your human duty to supply, I expect I'll need to urinate. Will someone be monitoring the door to take me to a toilet?"

"Relax," the woman told her, gesturing to the couch. "Take a nap. I'll ask about the water."

Valon said nothing, just watched them lock the door. This room had to be under observation, which ruled out immediately trying to disassemble the furniture to create a weapon, or testing the walls for weaknesses. She considered several options, including finding and disabling the camera and then ambushing the ones who came to repair it, but chose instead to lay down on the couch and wait. She didn't trust any of these people... but she did trust Wash Williams.

He'd be trying to get her out, and she needed to give him the chance.

19

Brian Reeves checked the load on his Glock 43X for the hundredth time since he'd been stuffed into the "guest quarters," and found, just like last time, that it still had seven rounds, six in the mag, one in the chamber. The gun was tiny, which was why he'd chosen it for a holdout years ago, and he was gratified that the Thacians had been slack enough with their prisoner handling that they hadn't bothered to frisk him and find it, but... it held seven rounds. No reloads, because he didn't have anywhere to carry them. It wouldn't do a damned bit of good against demons, but it also wouldn't get him out of *this* mess if it came down to that. It was a gun to use to get a bigger gun, and he wasn't yet ready to do the first part of that, which involved shooting the guy with the bigger gun.

The Thacians were their only hope of solving the problem the American government—well, to be fair, one very secret and compartmentalized portion of it—had created for itself. Even if the Senate decided they needed to keep him prisoner in what was admittedly a very well-appointed cell, Reeves wasn't sure if he should make a violent attempt at a breakout. For starters, he had no clue how to get back to Earth from here.

Reeves sighed and tucked the Glock back into the deep-cover holster at the small of his back, pacing around the living room of the studio-sized guest quarters like a caged lion. At least they hadn't taken his watch. He knew exactly how long he'd been here, which was almost as bad as *not* knowing. If he'd been stuck in the windowless apartment with no sense of time, he could have taken refuge in lying to himself, pretending he'd been there a week and that a decision *must* be forthcoming soon from the Senate.

As it stood, he'd been in the guest quarters for exactly forty-six hours, ten minutes, and thirty-five seconds. Not nearly long enough for politicians to make up their minds about anything, much less something momentous. Reeves played with his phone, scrolling through the media he had stored there, wondering if he could stand to watch any of the movies he'd downloaded yet again. The only one that appealed to him at first blush was *Jaws*, but he didn't feel like trying to watch it on the phone screen.

He wished he could call someone... hell, *anyone*.

And tell them what?

Dos Santos knew where he was and what he was doing, assuming Shaw and the others had made it back in time. The colonel was probably right pissed at him too, for going off on this fool's errand without prior clearance, but Reeves wasn't a squad leader in an infantry platoon, he was a Delta team leader. That entailed a level of autonomy even in conventional times, which these were definitely not.

He looked around at the walls. This place didn't have a TV, at least not one he'd been able to find, but he knew they had video monitors. Maybe the next time his attendants—a euphemistic way of saying "guards," he was sure—brought in a meal, he could ask them if they could figure out how to attach one of the monitors to his phone.

I could be the first American to watch a movie on an alien planet.

How long *would* it be until lunch? Or whatever the meal was called here? Reeves checked his watch again and tried to remember when they'd brought it yesterday. He was still working on that when the wailing, shrieking warble filled the entire room and Reeves threw himself behind the bed, pulling the Glock out again. His heart was thudding in his chest, the drumbeat nearly drowning out the siren.

Fire? Tornado?

The door bounced open under the impact of a shoulder and Prefect Marcos stumbled into the room, his face pale. He scanned the room, finally settling on Reeves, who was standing from behind the bed, still holding the Glock but keeping it at low ready. If Marcos saw the gun, he made no comment.

"What the hell's going on?" Reeves asked him, a sinking feeling in his gut that he already knew. Marcos didn't seem like a man easily intimidated, but the prefect was scared shitless.

"It's the Hive Mind," Marcos confirmed Reeves' worst fears. "Another gate opened just outside the city a few hours ago. A demon horde is on its way, and I doubt we can hold them off for more than a few days at most, even pouring everything into them."

"Shit," Reeves muttered, grip tightening on the 9mm, as useless as it was against demons. "You want me up on the line?" It was a logical conclusion. He probably had as much experience fighting the monsters as most of the Thacian Venators, if not more.

"No, I think I'm going to be forced to do something that would get me censured by the Senate." Marcos snorted a humorless laugh. "Assuming any of us survive. Come with me. I'm sending you home."

Acting like you belong is half of not getting caught.

Wash's dad had told him that when he was thirteen and had got caught sneaking into a party for the high school senior class. His mom had been pissed off that her husband was advising her son how to break the rules, but the advice had served him well through the years in a variety of situations.

Like this one. MacDill Air Force Base was the home of the USSOCOM, the United States Special Operations Command, which meant that everyone there was used to SEALs, Army Special Forces, Marine Raiders, and other groups that didn't even officially exist walking through the corridors and down the sidewalks, and no one gave any of them a second look.

So when he walked through the entrance hallway to Building B at zero dark thirty, the guard at the front just eyed his ID tag, which identified him as being attached to US Army Special Forces, with authorization that went all the way up to the highest clearance that existed in the military, and waved him through. Wash didn't even nod, just kept his head down, slipping off his beret as he headed for the elevators. Not even *his* beret... he'd stolen it from an unoccupied office and gone by the clothing store to pick up the correct rank tab, along with a fresh set of utilities and new boots, because what he'd been wearing looked like he'd jumped through a volcano with it.

And what had Dos Santos said? He'd encouraged buying a new uniform, given Wash the keys to a room at the MacDill Inn and told him to get a shower. Wash, of course, hadn't mentioned the rest of his plans. He would have bought a new beret as well, but a new beret required shaving and shaping, which took days he didn't have, and an unshaved, unshaped one *would* have attracted unwanted attention.

The guard at the door had been the first test, but the elevator was the second. Which way to go, down or up? He had to choose and had to look like he wasn't hesitating, like he'd intended to push that button the whole time. He chose down. He knew Dos Santos a little after these last few months and he felt like the man would put Valon somewhere with no windows, someplace the sun didn't shine, where she'd become disoriented without any clue to whether it was night or day. The basement.

Most buildings in Florida didn't even *have* basements because of the groundwater, but Building B had been built for it, with an elevated foundation. Why, Wash wasn't sure… maybe as a nuclear shelter back in the day.

Restricted Access, the sticker beside the basement button warned him, but he pressed it anyway.

The door closed, taking with it his last chance to back out of this. What would he do if he got to the basement level and the guard there stopped him, called Dos Santos or someone *above* him to check his credentials? Lie, of course. Tell them he just wanted to check on his friend. He might be able to get away with that without winding up in a cell beside her, but for sure Dos Santos would have sent him not just off MacDill but out of Florida altogether, maybe to France where the rest of the team was. If he was lucky and the colonel didn't just ship him back to Wyoming.

It was worth the risk. The elevator ride was smooth, lulling him into a false sense of security, and when the door opened it was a surprise. There *was* a guard at the desk across from the elevator, though she looked as if she was about to fall asleep. No shock there… it was coming near the end of her shift, but not close enough that eagerness to go home would have kept her alert. She blinked and shook her head, offering him a thin, businesslike smile.

"Good… sort of morning, Sergeant," she said. "Can I see your ID?"

"Sure thing," he said with a friendly grin, offering her the tag from his pocket. She was his rank, E5, no deference or saluting required, even if the Air Force kept their covers on indoors.

She looked at his ID a lot closer than the guy up top had, and sweat began beading at the small of his back. Her expression was still pleasant when she looked back up at him, though there was a question behind her dark eyes.

"You've got clearance for this level, Sgt. Williams, but I don't see you on the schedule." She laughed softly. "Hell, I don't see *anyone* on the schedule right now."

He mirrored her laugh, remembering an article that suggested mirroring as a good way to win over a stranger.

"Yeah, I get that. This is all kind of last-minute." He looked around as if he was making sure they were really alone, then leaned in closer, like he was about to share something top-secret with her. "It's about the gates."

Her eyes went wide, her mouth falling open.

"You're *that* Wash Williams!" she said. "Oh my God! You looked so different in that documentary! I didn't recognize you!"

"I try not to advertise it," he said, laying the humility on as thick as he could without overacting. "I mean, I'm still on active duty…"

"I thought it was so damned romantic that you went after your girlfriend on that hell planet," she confided, putting a hand on his arm. "Are you guys still together?"

"Yeah, we've been talking about getting married soon," he said, and at least this part he didn't have to pretend to be enthusiastic about.

"Oh, that is so awesome!" The woman giggled. "You too are so cute together! And excuse me for saying, but she's one tough bitch!"

Wash opened his mouth, couldn't think of a response, closed it again.

"I don't think I'd put it to her in those exact words," he said carefully, "but yeah, she's one of the toughest people I know."

"Is this about that woman they brought in?" the sergeant asked, gossiping now as if they'd been friends for years, though Wash didn't even know her name. That was a part of the instant fame from the documentary he'd never been able to handle, but it was coming in handy now. "I wasn't here, but Johnny, the guy who was on duty before me, told me they brought in a tall, good-looking girl in some kind of weird, foreign uniform."

"I can't say," he confided, feigning regret at not being able to tell her. "It's been compartmentalized. But I need to talk to her… it's important."

He felt it, felt the swing of the situation, what his father had called the *flux*. When the flux changed, he'd said, it was like a shift in the barometric pressure just before a storm, and if a man paid attention, he could feel it.

"Okay, sure." The sergeant pointed down the hallway. "She's in the third room on the left. I'll have to let you in." She rose from her desk and pulled a ring jangling with keys off her belt.

Wash's breath caught in his throat, both at the thought that this was actually going to work and from guilt for what he'd have to do, and how much trouble it would bring for this anonymous, friendly NCO. But he owed Valon his life, and this sergeant getting a non-judicial punishment for breaking protocol was preferable to Valon being confined indefinitely for the crime of being from another planet.

He followed the sergeant to the door, which looked very much like any other door in the hallway, identified only by the number on the door, 014B, though he had no clue what it signified. The sergeant paused with the key in the lock, doubt creeping into her eyes, her right hand going to the SIG M18 holstered at her waist.

"I just thought, is this woman dangerous?"

"Oh, no," Wash assured her, raising his hands palms-out.

"She's being confined here because of the sensitive nature of the intelligence she's been giving us. I'll be fine."

That seemed to mollify her, and she took her hand off her weapon and put it on the doorknob, turning the key and the knob with both hands. The door was wrenched open and the sergeant was pulled inside with it, squawking as she went off-balance. Valon moved so quickly, Wash couldn't follow her, just watched the Air Force staff sergeant flip through the air and land on her back, the air going out of her with a croaking wheeze.

The lights were off inside the room and the glow from the hallway through long shadows, but the darkness solidified into Valon standing over the sergeant, fastening her hands behind her back with her own cuffs. Valon held the SIG 9mm from the sergeant's holster at high ready, not quite pointed at him.

"I thought I recognized your voice, Williams," she said, smirking. "Is this one a friend, or should I leave her handcuffed?"

The sergeant wheezed, still unable to talk, and Wash shot her an apologetic look.

"She's just doing her job," Wash told Valon. "Take her clothes."

"Her clothes?" Valon repeated.

"It's the only way you're getting out of here," he told her, looking back and forth between her and the hallway. "No one's going to be watching the cameras this time of night inside the room, but if you try to leave the building dressed like that, someone's going to notice."

"And what happens if I *do* get out?" she demanded, pulling the jacket from the sergeant, pausing to rip a strip of the woman's T-shirt and gag her with it. The sergeant glared daggers at Wash as she came back to her senses. "I'll still be stuck here, away from my people, among those who distrust me."

Wash wanted to tell her he'd rented a car, wanted to tell her about the device he'd requisitioned, but he didn't want to spill the beans in front of the sergeant, who had every incentive to remember everything he said and use it against him. Valon had taken off her own uniform, down to her underwear, which resembled a sports bra and a pair of long speedos, and Wash fought not to stare. She was a very athletic woman.

"*I* trust you," he assured her. "You have to believe I wouldn't let that happen to you. Right?"

She puzzled for a moment at the Velcro fastenings of the top, but then figured it out, smoothing the front down and putting the woman's cap on before looking up to meet his eyes.

"You're risking your career, Wash. What will your Brenda say about this?"

"What she always says. Do the right thing, no matter what."

Valon followed him out of the room, chuckling softly.

"Does she *really* say that?"

"I'm sure she must have at some point. She's one tough bitch."

20

"Brenda, it's me."

This was a nightmare. She knew it. She remembered going to sleep, remembered setting her alarm and putting the gun on the nightstand and turning off the light. Sometimes in dreams she didn't realize it, like the one she'd had about Wash two nights ago, but this time she did.

She was walking through a cavern, but it wasn't pitch-black like any cave on Earth. A preternatural glow came from the walls, from a bacterial slime mold that coated everything. She'd seen it before. This was Hades. Fear seized her in its talons, clawing at her chest, panic starting to take hold until she reminded herself it was just a dream. She *couldn't* be on Hades, *couldn't* be back in the Hive Mind's lair, because it no longer existed. It had been collapsed by the nuclear warhead.

Brenda tried to wake herself up. She'd done it before in nightmares. Tom, one of her stepfathers, had taught her the trick of doing it, of grabbing at consciousness. It was a matter of concentrating on the details, starting with herself. She looked down at her clothes. She was wearing what she'd worn in Hades, the same blue jeans and flannel shirt, right down to her old boots.

She'd tossed them out after they'd made it back, unwilling to try to clean off the layer of black ichor she'd stepped in, but they were back, unmarked. And still she didn't wake up. It wasn't working.

She stopped walking. Maybe if she refused to cooperate, it would all come to an end. But she couldn't stay in one place. An irresistible panic seized her, the conviction that *something* was chasing her down, that it would rip her to shreds if she stayed in one place, and without even meaning to, she was running. Running in those boots wasn't comfortable, but she didn't feel it, didn't feel the weariness in her legs that she would have clomping through those stone tunnels or the impact from every echoing footstep.

"Brenda, don't run! It's me!"

Jimmy. It was Jimmy behind her. She ran faster, somehow more scared of him than she had been of the demons.

Why? He's dead. I killed him months ago.

And that was why. He *was* dead, which meant this was a ghost... either a real one or the ghost of guilt in her mind, the one she'd shoved down and refused to acknowledge. She'd had no choice, and yet that was little comfort. She'd killed the man she'd once loved, the man she'd been prepared to marry, and Brenda wasn't sure if she felt guiltier for killing him or that she'd been willing to overlook the fact he'd been an asshole and marry him anyway.

"Brenda, please don't run. I can't do this much longer... I need to talk to you!"

She turned a corner, pushing off the wall, the slimy texture making her palms slip. The slime coated her hands and she wiped them against her jeans, feeling every inch of the texture, far too real, and just the granularity of the experience scared her. She needed to get out, to draw away.

This shit is not stronger than me.

Gates of Hope

Deep breaths. In and out and repeat, and she forced herself to stop running.

"Brenda, I'm not going to hurt you! I'm sorry!"

He was there, a ghost of the man he was, a spectral outline she could barely make out in the green-tinted light of the tunnel. He took a step toward her, hollow and wasted away, not quite a rotting corpse, nor yet still a starving man, but more as if coherence was deserting him. Like the world was trying to force him out.

Brenda sucked in a breath and set herself, then screamed aloud.

"Get away from me!"

Her eyes opened. It was dark and she was in bed, soaked with sweat. She didn't jump up, staying calm through a force of will, fumbling for the light switch. The room was just as it had been before she'd gone to sleep, no ghosts in sight. The little SIG 9mm was still on the nightstand, but she didn't touch it. The threats to her weren't corporeal enough to be killed with a bullet.

Instead, she grabbed her cell phone, checking the time. Two in the morning, give or take. She sighed. Too early to get up. She'd have to go back to sleep. Brenda frowned, noticing the flashing red light that indicated a text. She'd had the ringer off and hadn't noticed it before, but a flick of her finger showed it was Wash.

Brenda, it read, *there's a problem. Have to do something that will get me in trouble. Definitely will be going offworld. I'll get in touch with you as soon as I can. Love you.*

She fought back a wave of nausea. Weren't things bad enough? She'd already thought she lost him once, had actually begun to make plans of what she would do if he was actually dead. She'd allowed herself to feel relief, like it was all over with, and now it was starting over again.

"Stop it." She said the words aloud, since that had seemed to work to banish the nightmare. "You're a grown woman, Sands.

Stop whining like a baby. This is the fate of the world, not just your little corner of it."

But what the hell was going on with these lucid dreams of Jimmy? Maybe she should go see a psychologist. Brenda sat up in bed and tried to stop her hands from shaking. Or maybe she should just face her *real* fear and go talk to the Bonners. She had a suspicion that was the source of the nightmares, the hallucinations. The guilt. Not that she'd killed Jimmy, but that she hadn't told his parents what had happened to their son. And if it meant they hated her, well... it wasn't as if she was that close to them since she'd come back.

"You know what you have to do, Sands. Stop running from it."

She looked back at her phone and finally tapped a reply, hoping he'd see it.

Do the right thing, she told him. *No matter what.*

Brian Reeves had been in so many war zones, in so many disaster areas in his career that one seemed to bleed into another, and only the architecture was different. Not this time. This wasn't an invasion as much as it was an infestation. The demons weren't an army moving through the streets in formation, weren't wild animals rampaging through the city... they were a swarm of insects, organized, but not in a way the human mind could grasp, entering through any possible avenue of entry.

Watching them from the roof landing pad, Reeves was reminded of army ants marauding through an African village. People would watch them helplessly, knowing there was no way to stop them. Not so here. The Venators Reeves had seen in the field were far away from their operational base, the heaviest equipment they had the armored personnel carriers, but here in the city, they had heavy armor. The things weren't so much reminiscent of M1 Abrams as they were the M163 Vulcan Air Defense System, an APC with a big-ass gun rotary cannon mounted on it. Except this thing had armor even thicker than an Abrams and the rotary cannon fired rocket-assisted rounds.

They were impressive in action, particularly from above, the continuous streaks of rocket motors looking something like the blasters from a science fiction movie, and where they touched, the demons melted away. Their bodies piled up, hundreds of them at each intersection, smoke billowing up from the carnage, forming a haze over the buildings at the edge of town, lit up in the glare of the streetlights. And beyond the edge of town, the gunships worked the horde with missiles and chain guns, reaping the demons like wheat.

Yet still they wouldn't stop coming, and worse, the spikers were coming behind them. He'd seen them inside the caverns of Hades, but never gathered like this, Hannibal's elephants heading over the Alps… if those elephants had doubled as anti-aircraft artillery. Six-foot long gray spikes traveling as fast as cannon rounds, launched by some arcane combination of internal chemistry and muscle power, slammed into gunships, knocking them right out of the air, the ducted-fan hovercraft spiraling out of control and crashing in dust plumes on the gravel road.

"Can you hold them off?" he asked Marcos, interrupting the man's orders to the gunship crew.

"For a while," the prefect answered once he'd finished instructing the pilot. The canopy of the bird was open, waiting for Reeves to join them as the rotors gained speed, the engine warming up with a petulant whine. "But not forever. The gate's too close and we can't block it. We need your help, and we can't wait for the Senate to okay it. The pilots are going to take you to the nearest gate to your world. It's kept shielded and in a location known only to the senior staff, but once you're there, I need you to do as you promised. We'll leave the gate open, and you have to send through one of those weapons."

"I'll do what I can," he told Marcos. "I'm not in charge, I'm just a team leader, but I think they'll listen to me. Either way, I'll be coming back through to guide the missile, if they let me." He offered a hand. "It was an honor to meet you, Prefect."

Marcos eyed the gesture with a raised eyebrow and Reeves carefully reached out and took the man's hand, shaking it.

"That's a thing on our world," he explained. "A greeting between friends."

"Let us hope," Marcos agreed, staring at his hand as if he thought Reeves might have contaminated it. He motioned at the open canopy. "Go now, while we still have time."

The prefect, Reeves decided as he clambered into the cockpit, had a stick up his ass, like most generals he'd met. Not necessarily a bad guy, but definitely the politician sort of officer, though at least he was one who wasn't afraid to do something that might get him called in front of their equivalent of a Senate subcommittee.

"Get strapped in!" the pilot called back to him once he was settled in the third seat, behind the crew.

The canopy was closing and Reeves sank down in his chair as it came closer to his head, simultaneously trying to figure out the restraint system. The gunship was cramped compared to the transport he'd flown to Thacia in, more like the interior of an AC130. Which, he supposed, was better than an Apache, but not by much.

Wait... did that guy just speak English?

"How do you know my language?" Reeves asked him, shouting over the hum of the engines as the aircraft lurched away from the landing pad, leaving his stomach behind.

"The imprinter," the young officer told him as if that explained everything. He wore a goatee, and Reeves was beginning to wonder if facial hair was a uniform requirement in the

Venators, which would have sucked for people who couldn't grow a good mustache.

"What's an imprinter?"

"If the prefect didn't tell you," the pilot said, eyeing him with suspicion, "then I probably shouldn't either."

Great.

"How far away is this place?" he asked instead.

"Twenty miles northeast." The pilot pointed helpfully out of the cockpit, off toward the mountains, barely visible by the moonlight. "Shouldn't take more than half an hour, assuming nothing goes wrong."

Either military traditions were different on this world, or the man must not have had much combat experience, because *that* was something a combat veteran would never say. And like the trickster god he was, Private Murphy chose that exact moment to demonstrate his existence on multiple human worlds.

The first clue was a panicked exclamation from the copilot, something he was sure was a curse in Thacian, followed closely by the next sign that something was wrong—a sharp, banking turn that threw Reeves up against his restraints and made him immensely grateful he'd figured out how to buckle himself in. And the biggest one was the pale blur that passed by just a few feet from the nose of the plane.

"Spikers!" the pilot informed him.

"No shit."

Brian Reeves wasn't a man prone to airsickness, or motion sickness of any ilk, but the spinning, banking, twisting evasive maneuvers the pilot put the bird through was almost enough to reverse decades of experience and bring up that weird gyro-looking thing he'd had for dinner.

"Yeah, getting it," the pilot murmured, half to himself but also in English, as if he'd spoke last in the language and hadn't mentally shifted back to his own. "Just a couple seconds and we'll be clear of their firing arc."

Reeves scowled at him.

"I *wish* you would stop saying shit like that."

Too late.

Way back in his early days in the Rangers, Reeves had been part of a mounted patrol through Ramadi and an IED had touched off one Humvee ahead of his. The concussion had hit him like slamming his face into a brick wall and his own vehicle had gone up on two wheels, nearly turning over. The impact on the portside of the gunship was nearly as violent as that, and so much more likely to kill him.

The pilot reverted back to his native Thacian, but Reeves didn't need a translated explanation. They'd taken a hit, and by the way the aircraft was listing to port, it had either taken out the main engine on that side or, if they were lucky, one of the steering fans. Reeves had tried not to focus on the blurred kaleidoscope of the night landscape outside the canopy while they'd been in their uncontrolled spin, but now it held acute interest for him.

They'd leveled out and stopped spinning, which was good news, but they weren't more than two or three hundred feet above the trees in the intermittent forests outside the city, which was not.

"Are we gonna crash?" he asked, fingers digging into the armrest.

"Crash, no," the pilot told him, his voice slightly distracted as he concentrated on the steering yoke, which didn't seem to want to cooperate. "Forced landing? There's a good chance. We've lost the forward port steering fan and the main rotor on that side has taken damage. We're down to about thirty percent power on the port, and I'm having to feather the starboard to stay level."

Okay, so not *quite* the worst-case scenario, but not even close to the best.

"Can we make it through the pass?" Reeves pointed past the

man's shoulder to the gap between the mountains. It wasn't the Himalayas or even the Rockies, but it sure as hell looked high to him, given that they were puttering along at barely fifty miles an hour.

"Maybe. But so can they."

The pilot pointed at a display at the corner of the control panel, showing the view from the belly camera. The gunship was following a road through the mountains—not a well-maintained one, but wide enough that they could get cargo trucks up it if they needed to. Also following that road, running at a pace only slightly slower than the wounded aircraft, were dozens of Hive Mine warrior drones.

"Why the fuck are they bothering with us?" Reeves muttered, not so much asking a question as he was bemoaning their luck. The pilot answered it anyway.

"Because there are enough of them that they can afford to. And because the Hive Mind must figure if the Venators are sending a gunship off into the mountains in the middle of a battle for the city, there must be an important reason for it." He looked back at Reeves, his face stricken. "Please tell me there's an important reason for it."

Reeves was tempted to repeat the man's earlier answer back to him, how if the prefect hadn't told him then maybe he shouldn't talk about it. But he knew what it was like to be a soldier who wanted to fight in a battle being sent away from it.

"If you can get me back home," he told the pilot, "then there's a good chance we can shut down that gate to the Beast World."

The man nodded and turned his attention back to the front. He pushed the throttle open just a little more, fighting the buck and sway of the steering yoke to keep the aircraft level, the muscles in his forearms bunching with the effort. The copilot's eyes went wide and he said something plaintive in Thacian, but the pilot responded with a sharp retort.

"I'll get you there," the man promised through clenched jaws. The ship lurched, tilting wildly before he got it back under control. Sweat beaded on the young pilot's forehead and he smiled weakly. "Or somewhere in the vicinity."

Reeves sighed and tightened his seat belt.

21

"What is that thing?" Valon asked, nodding to the pouch on the center console of the rental SUV. It was dark, made from some sort of heavy fabric, and she'd seen him stick his communications device inside of it before they'd started driving.

"Faraday bag," Wash said absently, his eyes flickering back and forth from the dimly lit backroad out of the car windshield to the odd device he'd brought with him from the military base. "My cell phones—the work one and my personal one—both send out a signal that can be traced. The bag blocks the signal so they won't be able to find me."

"Why didn't you just destroy your phone?" she asked, adjusting the stolen Air Force jacket again. It wasn't sized for her and she missed her own uniform.

"Because it's the only way I can get ahold of Brenda if I need to," he explained. "And I don't plan on staying on Thacia once I get you back."

"They'll put you in jail if you return," she reminded him.

"Maybe." Wash didn't elaborate, but Valon sniffed in skepticism. She thought perhaps he was in denial about it, but she couldn't very well criticize his logic when he'd put his life and career at risk to free her.

She *should* have just shut up. She wasn't normally this talkative, but she sensed Wash *needed* to talk, and guilt at putting him in this position made her go against her habits.

"How does the tracker work?" Valon asked, pointing at the device, which was about the size of one of the Venator issue tablets, propped up against the air conditioning and entertainment console of the vehicle. It displayed a grid overlaid with both topographical and road maps, tiny stars showing the location of gates in the area.

"The gates emit a particular electromagnetic signature, or at least that's what the physicists tell us." Wash glanced aside, frowning at her. "You guys have been around these things for centuries. You didn't know about the EM signal they put out?"

"We had no reason to research finding the gates," she said, shrugging—perhaps, she had to admit to herself, a little defensively. "We *knew* where all the gates were and had the ones to the Beast Worlds shielded."

"They couldn't break through any of those shields?"

"It's not impossible." Valon shrugged. "The Hive Mind tries, now and then. That's why we have the outposts to watch over them. But it takes days, sometimes *weeks*, and it's easy to spot. We just put another shield on top of the old one and it's not worth their effort. The Hive Mind mostly concentrates on finding paths on far-off worlds where we can't maintain constant security." She sighed. "Until now, of course."

Wash squirmed in his seat.

"Are you going to tell your people about the ship? The experiment?"

"It's my duty," she said, then winced as she realized how that sounded. "They need to know what's causing the new gates to open," she went on. "If they know the cause, perhaps they can come up with a solution."

Wash snorted.

"You just said they haven't even been studying the gates. Tell me something. All that technology you guys have, the airplanes, the rocket guns, the gizmo you used to learn English... did the Archaion give all that stuff to you?"

Valon's jaw worked as if she was chewing up something distasteful.

"Yes. They gave us the tools we needed to keep the threat of the Hive Mind at bay, to protect Earth."

"And since then," he pressed on, as if he didn't notice how uncomfortable the subject made her, "have you guys come up with anything major on your own? Any new technologies? Medicines?"

"We haven't had the need." Valon realized her voice was stiff and sharp and she was leaning forward as if she might need to jump out of the moving vehicle, and she tried to calm down. "We have all the power we need, all the food we need. No one starves, no one wants for a roof over their head or medicine. People still die from sickness, but not through lack of care."

"And that's all nice and everything," he allowed, "but the point is, telling them about the experiment won't do anything except make them angry at us and totally fuck up any chance we have of us working together."

Valon bit back her initial response, then her second one as well. She was silent for nearly ten seconds before finding a reply that wouldn't sound ungrateful and insulting.

"You have been a... what did you call it? A guardsman?" At his nod, she went on. "You have been a guardsman for several years, and your father was a career soldier. How do you find it so easy to disobey orders?"

Wash laughed softly at first, but then long and hard.

"Things must really be different on your world," he said, finally. "If being a combat vet and a career soldier taught my father anything, it's how totally fucked up and short-sighted generals and especially politicians could be. Most of them have no real clue of the situation on the ground and are more worried about keeping their jobs than whether they're doing the right thing."

Valon nodded slowly.

"Our Senate can be like that. But the Venators are under the command of Prefect Marcos, and he's been like a father to me for my whole career. He's not blinded by ambition because he has none. I've told him many times that the Venators would benefit if he was part of the Senate, but he always says he would rather gnaw off his own leg like an animal caught in a trap than be thrown into that snake den."

Wash's eyes narrowed and he said nothing for a moment. When he did speak, his words seemed carefully considered.

"How many Venators *are* there?"

"Active duty?" She shrugged. "Usually the number is kept at fifty thousand, more or less." Valon frowned. "Why? How many are in your military?"

"In the United States alone," he said, as if he'd been expecting the question, "there are over a million on active duty, another 700,000 in the Guard and Reserves."

Valon's breath caught in her throat.

"Just... just in your one nation?"

Wash nodded.

"I think I read there're like twenty-five million people in the military worldwide." He shrugged. "That doesn't mean as much though, because a lot of countries have shit armies with no real training and poor equipment. But yeah, worst-case scenario, that's how many we could put on the front lines against the demons. Most of them would be speed bumps, though."

Valon's brow knitted.

"Speed bumps?"

"What?" Wash laughed. "Your imprinter didn't explain that one to you? It means worthless troops you just put in front of the enemy to slow them down because they're not good for anything else. Over in Russia and China, they've already used nuclear weapons on their own ground to stop the demons... and you probably don't understand what that means, but it's *bad*. It means there was no way they could stop the enemy coming through and they didn't care that they were making their own land unlivable for the next few decades." He eyed her sidelong. "You guys ever figure out how many demons there are? Like an estimate?"

She laughed, though without humor.

"We have spent decades trying to do just that. It's nearly impossible since the Hive Mind stretches over dozens, maybe even hundreds of Beast Worlds. You know why we call them that, right?"

"Because that's where the demons live?" he guessed.

"Because that's where they're *made*. The Hive Mind grows them, somehow." Valon shook her head. "We've seen the vats... well, *one* of our scouting missions got footage of them. They're like something out of a nightmare, a nightmare *factory*. The only limiting factor is the supply of biological materials... and transportation. In raw numbers, we're talking *billions*, at the outside. We can't get to them, we can't destroy them, all we can do is block the gates they come through to get to us... or to you. Or we *used* to be able to." There was too much bitterness in the words. This wasn't Wash's fault.

"How does that gate tracker device know which one goes back to Thacia?" she asked, changing the subject.

"That's where you come in," he told her. "Your tablet, the one you were carrying, is in that backpack." He jerked a thumb at the backseat. "And trust me when I tell you, it was harder to get hold of that than it was to break you out."

Valon lunged back and grabbed the backpack.

"Is my gun in here?" she asked, rummaging through it.

"No, that was locked in the armory." He winced. "Unfortunately, I couldn't get any guns. If we were in Wyoming, I would have just stopped at a store and picked up a couple, but I don't have a Florida ID."

"I'm sure that should mean something to me, but it doesn't."

"The bottom line is, we don't have any guns, so I hope you can detect one of those signals you're talking about through your gates, because I don't want to be hopping around Beast Worlds unarmed."

"Is there any chance your people will find us before we find a gate?" The thought worried her almost as much as being unarmed. She'd been worried before that they might keep her confined indefinitely, but now it was almost a sure thing.

Wash didn't answer immediately, chewing on his lip.

"There's a chance. I pulled the tracker from this car… my dad taught me where and how they were installed. But we're talking about the CIA, Delta Force, the FBI… I'm sure they have a BOLO out on this vehicle. That means 'be on the lookout.' That's why I'm sticking to the backroads. If we can find a parking lot somewhere, I'll swap plates with another car, which should buy us some time."

"How much time do we need? I thought your team was going around closing all the gates on your continent?"

"All the Beast World gates," he corrected her. "We don't have enough teams or enough portable nuclear warheads to shut down every gate… and we wouldn't even if we did. Those are habitable worlds on the other side of those things, and even if our government was stupid and selfish enough to poison the other side of the gate for decades, they're also too greedy to give up the opportunity to exploit a whole other planet for resources. Gates popped up all over the country and we only closed a handful of them, the ones that led to active sites, and we only find out about those when people report seeing demons."

"Where's the closest one then?"

Wash tapped the screen.

"It's another fifty miles northeast. In a place called the Ocala National Forest. I've never been there, but it sounds like a place where there'll be less people, and that's gotta be a good thing, since we're kind of America's most wanted right now. Should take us about an hour."

Valon didn't know what America's most wanted was and didn't feel like asking. She looked around in the dim light from the dashboard, then felt around at the bottom of her seat until she happened upon a switch that inclined the upper part of her chair backward. She laid back and closed her eyes.

"In that case," she told Wash, "wake me up in an hour."

22

"Do you prefer to hear the good news or the bad news first, Sgt. Reeves?" the pilot asked, having to yell to be heard over the grinding and clunking from the engines and the vibration through the superstructure of the aircraft.

"That imprinter even taught you about good news-bad news jokes?" Reeves asked, fingers wrapped in the "oh-shit" handle mounted on the canopy brace. The pilot said nothing, just stared back at him uncomprehending, and Reeves sighed. "The good news."

He was hoping there *was* some good news, because the rocks and trees of the mountain pass seemed to be getting closer to the belly of the gunship every minute, and the sun was coming up fast enough that he could see the jagged rocks way too clearly... along with the smoke trailing out of the port engine nacelle.

"The good news is," the pilot told him, "we're almost there. Less than two miles."

"Thank God," Reeves sighed. It seemed like they'd been in the air forever, and the column of demons on their trail was still visible, just a mile or two back down the mountain road they were following. "What's the bad news?"

"The bad news is, we're going down." The words were accompanied by a clamor of warning buzzers and rows of flashing yellow lights, none of which seemed like positive developments.

The gunship's engines sputtered, and Reeves wished he knew anything about flying ducted-fan helicopters or could read Greek well enough to figure out what any of the dials and readouts were saying.

"Fuel leak," the pilot supplied as if reading his mind, or at least his eyes. "I nursed it as long as I could, but we're running on fumes. Make sure you're strapped in tight."

"Oh yeah," Reeves said, staring in disbelief at the back of the pilot's head, "I was just relaxing back here till now, seat belt all loose and shit because I wasn't worried at all."

The pilot actually glanced away from his controls to frown at Reeves.

"Really?"

"No, not fucking *really*!" Reeves snapped back at him. "Don't they have sarcasm here?"

"Sure we do." The man smiled thinly as he looked back at the controls. "This isn't going to hurt at all."

It wasn't Reeves' first crash, of course. He'd been in forced landings in Blackhawks, V22 Ospreys, and even a UH-1 Huey once, but this was nothing like any of those. Helicopters autorotated and even Ospreys could kind of glide, but this thing just sort of *dropped*. Not far, thankfully, since the pilot had been taking them lower and slower with each second, but when they hit, metal crunched and screamed and Reeves' seat tried its best to rip free of the battered fuselage and take him right along with it.

His shoulder joints screamed just as loud as the crashing aircraft, though the stars filling his vision from the whiplash dulled the pain... and everything else. Reeves floated in a haze of glowing yellow and red, a dull ache pounding at his head, shoulders, chest, and back from the inside, trying its damnedest to work its way out.

"*That* wasn't sarcasm," he moaned, hands going to his head. "That was just a fucking lie."

Reeves eyes blinked open slowly and painfully, the acrid smell of burning wiring catching in his throat and sending him into a paroxysm of coughing.

"At least we don't have to worry about the fuel tanks going up," the pilot said, sounding just about as worse for wear as Reeves, though he was already moving, slipping out of his restraint harness and reaching over to shake the arm of the copilot. "Kallias! Kallias!" That must have been the copilot's name, but Reeves couldn't understand the rest of his shouted exhortation.

Whatever he said must have penetrated Kallias' fog, because the copilot moaned and raised a hand, feeling around at the release for his harness. Reeves decided that was a damned good idea and tried to figure out where the latch was for the thing. Despite the pilot's assurance that they didn't have to worry about a fire, Reeves wasn't so sanguine.

There. Right at the center of his chest, the big, yellow button. Did yellow mean the same thing here that red did back home? The warning lights had been yellow, the quick-release was yellow. He hadn't seen any individual automobiles, so he wasn't sure if their stop signs would be yellow.

"What's your name, man?" Reeves asked the pilot, grunting in the middle of the question as he yanked hard on the latch, the harness falling away in four parts, the center latch dropping away with one of them.

"Peleus," the pilot told him, then clambered onto his seat, feet braced there, shoulder against the canopy, and pushed.

The unpowered latch resisted, but Peleus' teeth clenched, the muscles of his neck bunching up, and gradually the canopy inched open, finally giving way with a loud crack. Peleus nearly tumbled out the side of the plane with the sudden lack of resistance, but Kallias caught his arm and kept him steady.

"Reeves," Peleus said, pointing behind him. "There's a compartment back there with weapons and supplies. Grab them and pass them up to me."

It took him a minute, more to figure out how the latch worked on the compartment than to find it, but once the panel fell open, Reeves grinned at the row of carbines. Three of them, which was just enough. He passed two up to Kallias and Pelleus, then grabbed the third for himself before bothering with the chest pouches full of spare magazines and two backpacks.

Peleus was already out of the plane, and Kallias gingerly climbed out of his seat and lowered himself to the ground, which finally made room for Reeves. Free of the cramped, spider-webbed, smoke-filled cockpit, he finally got a look at their surroundings. The place wasn't so much the Smokies or the Appalachians, which had been his first point of comparison when he'd flown over them a day ago. Or was it three days ago?

Either way, they were more reminiscent of the Apennines. He'd first seen them on an operation in Italy ten years ago and had been struck by their gentle beauty, something between the weathered and the sharp. The ship had gone down near the top of the pass, almost wedged between two gray slabs of granite, trees and brush crowding in on either side of the road, some of it already lit afire by the splashes of fuel from the tank.

Empty my ass.

Right on the heels of the dawn beauty of the scene was the cold. It had been an early fall feel down in Thacia, but here it was somewhere close to freezing, and Reeves was acutely aware of the holes in his pant leg and shirt. He paused in the dim light from the cockpit and checked the controls of the carbine, not wanting to get stuck with a gun that he didn't know how to take off the

Gates of Hope

safety of. Of course, the safety had tiny printing beside it instead of a handy, multi-lingual image of a bullet with a line through it, and he had no idea whether the gun had been stored on fire or safe.

Cursing under his breath, he slung the carbine over his shoulder and ran after the others, limping on his burned leg. A mile, Peleus had said, and the road was fairly smooth, but all uphill, and they were moving way too slow.

"Those damned things are moving faster than a pissed-off grizzly, as Wash would say," he told Peleus, his breath coming heavy. *Need to do more running. Been operational for too long.* "They're gonna catch us."

"You're probably right," Peleus gasped, and Reeves felt better that the Venator was out of breath too. "But I think I'll keep running, if it's all the same to you."

Which was a good point. Reeves' quads were on fire, and it wasn't just from the burn on his thigh—the altitude and temperature was freezing his lungs and his whole body felt like someone had worked him over with a baseball bat from the crash, but he shoved all that into a tiny compartment and kept moving.

Running maybe a ten-minute mile. The demons are a mile back of the crash site running at thirty-five miles an hour. Yeah, that didn't add up. The things would be within sight in another two or three minutes.

Reeves tried to run faster, but kept thinking of the old sniper motto. *No use running... you'll only die tired.*

The road was strewn with fist-sized rocks and he tripped over one, stumbled forward but caught himself. He instinctively glanced backward, barely able to see and wishing he'd thought to bring his night-vision goggles with him. Or his helmet. But night-vision or no, he saw the movement behind them, not nearly far enough back.

There. Just ahead, the crest of the hill. Steeper, gravity trying to drag him backward, and he fought his old enemy tooth and nail, digging in with each step, spraying dirt and rocks behind him. Over the top, and the path was just as steep going down as it was coming up... but not as dark.

Light around the next curve. Not quite the brightness of a gate, but a glow greater than the moon halo beyond the overhanging clouds. Peleus and Kallias might have begun the run with a head start, but Reeves caught up with them on the downhill, coming up between the two pilots and forcing himself to slow down so he didn't pass them. Not just because he didn't want the Thacians to think he was abandoning them, but because Marcos had told him the gate was shielded and Peleus would have to open it for him.

"They're over the top," Peleus said, risking a look back over his shoulder. He snapped something to Kallias in Thacian and the copilot skidded to a halt, unslinging his weapon and setting himself in the center of the trail.

Reeves slowed down, but Peleus grabbed his arm and urged him forward.

"Keep running... he's going to slow them down."

Peleus' voice was emotionless, cold, but Reeves knew soldiers and knew the man was tamping down the pain. He'd done it before. Reeves wanted to argue, wanted to stop, to turn back and fight beside Kallias, but that wasn't the mission. Kallias knew the mission and knew he was expendable.

Whoosh-crack.

The discharge of the carbine seemed farther away than it had to be, yet somehow also obscenely loud against the silence on the mountain. The shots were a chain-fire, so close together that Reeves couldn't count how many rounds the copilot got off, but he knew when they stopped. The end was marked with a scream that cut off abruptly, the choked-off gurgle tightening claws inside Reeves' chest. He'd never talked to the man, didn't know his language, but he knew enough. The man had given his life to get Reeves back home, hadn't thought of his own family, his friends, his future, hadn't questioned his commander's orders.

He'd bought them enough time to reach the curve in the road, one side up against a rock face, the other dropping off a couple hundred feet into a gulch until it twisted around to the right. The road grew wider, the shoulder flatter, and off to the right side, hugging a niche in the bare rock face was the gate. It was easy to forget how huge the thing was when it was a vague discontinuity in space, its edges poorly-defined, but this one was different. Fifty feet in diameter but not simply hanging in mid-air, this gate was covered by an iris of what looked like solid tungsten resting on a base six feet thick and half-buried in rock. Yet still the light from the effect shone through the edges, through every crack, as if something inside was trying to get out.

Peleus stumbled to a halt, ripping open a thigh pocket and pulling out a tablet, shaking it to wake up the screen. Reeves unslung his carbine and took up a position at the side of the road, waiting for the inevitable, for the demons to round the curve and rip them to shreds. Before they could, Peleus touched something on the screen of his tablet and a solid *thunk* echoed off the rock.

Reeves looked over his shoulder and his mouth dropped open. The iris was sliding open. It seemed impossible, seemed as if the thing was too damned heavy to move without a motor the size of a semi-tractor, but whatever was inside that base was powerful enough to slide the twenty-five-foot sections sideways into the perimeter of the circle. Through the gate was the glare of mid-day and the red, burning sands of a desert.

"Shit," he murmured. That could be anywhere... could be in the middle of the Gobi or the Sahara, and here he was without so much as a hat or a canteen. He'd brought his sat-phone, of course... as long as someone had a chopper ready to go, and he wasn't in the middle of a hostile country.

"Get through!" Peleus yelled over the *whoosh-crack* of his rocket carbine. Fireflies swarmed from the barrel, miniature rocket engines intersecting the incoming horde of demons, still a hundred yards away.

"Come with me!" Reeves told him, waving at the gate. He shouldered his carbine and added his own suppressive fire to the Thacian's, sweeping across the line of Hive Mind warrior drones, dropping three of them and creating a bottleneck on the path.

"I have to close the gate!" Peleus insisted, motioning with the tablet.

"Close it from *my* side, dammit! I can get you back here through another gate!"

That seemed to convince the pilot, and he sprinted across the road, firing from the hip as he ran. Reeves' weapon locked open on an empty magazine and he clawed for a spare in the chest pouch, but the fastenings were some sort of toggle and eyelet and he fumbled with them for just a half-second too long. The demons broke through the bottleneck, moving so fast they were on Peleus in an instant.

Reeves finally smacked the new magazine home and chambered a round, but by the time he had his carbine up and ready, two of the things had the pilot cornered against the rock wall. Peleus fired his weapon, putting a wild round through a demon's thorax, but the gun was swept aside by a slash of wickedly curved talons that continued right on through the man's chest.

Reeves bellowed wordlessly, incoherent with rage as he pumped half a magazine into the monsters, explosive rounds carving tunnels through their torsos, sending them collapsing nearly atop Peleus. The pilot was alive, but barely, blood gushing from the deep slash, more of it bubbling out of his mouth. Reeves skidded to a halt beside him, originally intent on pulling the man free until he saw the injuries the pilot had suffered. There was nothing to be done.

"Take this," Peleus said, his voice a wet gurgle from the blood in his lungs. He pressed the tablet against Reeves' chest. "Yellow... control... closes the door. White... opens." The man's eyes lost focus and his body went limp, fingers sliding away from the tablet, leaving a trail of red on the back of the device and down Reeves' shirt.

Reeves felt an irrational compunction to try to bring Peleus' body with him, but that went into that box of pain where he'd stored his weariness and strained muscles, things to be dealt with later, either in a psych counselor's office or the bottom of a bottle. Clutching the tablet to his chest, he fired off the rest of his magazine at the hulking figures squeezing between the bodies of their own dead, bringing down one of them only ten feet away.

A jagged, spiked scorpion tail whipped inches from his head, close enough for the cold wind to brush against his bare cheek, the bitter smell of whatever acid the thing contained filling his nostrils. And then he was through, rolling on his shoulder in the sand, the high-altitude chill of the mountain pass replaced by a rush of breathtaking heat, jumping from a refrigerator into an oven.

His instincts told him to reload the rifle, to pour a burst back through the gate behind him, but his intellect had other ideas. Reeves dropped the rifle into the sand, turning around the tablet, finding that yellow, flashing button on the screen, and tapping it over and over, just in case once wasn't enough. A demon lunged through the portal behind him, its black carapace glistening in the sun, but only its torso was past the edge of the gate when the shield closed.

The metallic *thunk* was dull and distant, but the effects were drastic and immediate. The gate seemed to fade to nothing, the edges still there for someone who knew where to look, but the center faded to a ghostly pale. The only hint of the thing's existence was half of a Hive Mind demon, bisected at the waist, gushing black ichor across the red sand. Talons clawed at the ground, the demon trying to drag itself toward Reeves in one last desperate attempt to kill him. But even a demon could die, and this one slumped to the ground, the last of its vitality drained into the desert wastes.

Reeves sat back on his haunches, motionless, catching his breath. One second ago he'd been inches from a cold, bloody death, and now he was sweating in some desolate badland, possibly thousands of miles from the nearest help.

No use sitting here feeling sorry for myself.

Reeves grabbed the rifle and used the butt to lever himself to his feet, giving the dead demon one last, cautious look before he turned to survey his surroundings. It was high noon, so he had no clear idea of east or west, but in one direction were red mountains, beaten down and weathered, the sort he expected in the high desert. He turned and his eyes went wide.

Houses in the near distance, suburban neighborhoods. Power lines stretching off forever. The crosshatch of dull gray highways heading past the suburbs to a city, far away yet still visible. He might not have recognized it except for the tower. It was 1,149 feet tall, the tallest tower in the United States, second tallest in the western hemisphere. It belonged to the Strat Hotel, Casino and Skypod, and he'd stayed there with his ex-wife on their last vacation before the divorce.

He pulled out his sat-phone and dialed Colonel Dos Santos' number. It rang once before the man answered.

"Reeves?" Dos Santos' tone was annoyed. "Jesus Christ, Sergeant, where the hell are you?"

"Las Vegas, sir. And I'm gonna need a ride."

23

"The gate's down this way another couple miles," Wash said, rubbing at his eyes, then slapping himself lightly in the face.

"You all right?" Valon asked him. "You want me to drive?"

He eyed her sidelong.

"You've never driven a car before," he reminded her.

He honestly wouldn't have minded. The road was dead-black, not a single streetlight, no houses, just ditches on either side of the narrow road, and even on high-beam the headlights didn't seem to be penetrating more than a few car lengths ahead. He'd tried turning up the air conditioning, tried turning the radio up, even tried eating some beef jerky, though he wasn't at all hungry and all that had accomplished was to make him thirsty. And all drinking water had done was make him need to pee.

"It doesn't look that hard," Valon objected. "You push the right pedal to accelerate, the left pedal to brake, and you turn with the wheel, though I must say, I find the whole wheel thing a lot less efficient than a double control yoke."

"It's just another mile or so." *I hope.* Well, he knew the gate was *there*, but the question was, would it be reachable? Or would it be in the middle of a lake? Or deep in the swamp?

"I'm not getting any signal yet," she warned him. "That's not to say it's impossible, since the trees are so thick here, but there's no guarantee it won't just be to a dead end with no connecting gate."

Wash's eyes went to the mirror. Headlights met them, turning off a side road he hadn't seen. And gaining quickly. He looked down at the speedometer. Sixty-three miles an hour... and he had no idea what the speed limit was on this road.

"Shit."

Red and blue strobes lit up the night, accompanied by the beep of a siren.

"What is it?" Valon asked, twisting around in her seat.

"Police. I was going too fast."

"That's a *crime*?"

"Not a serious one. But they probably have warnings out to all police agencies about this vehicle... or if not the car, then at least about me." Wash sighed and pulled off to the edge of the road, putting the vehicle in park.

"Then why are we stopping?" Valon demanded, looking back and forth between him and the sheriff's car behind them. "Shouldn't we be running?"

"He'd catch us before we could get to the gate." Wash fished in his pocket for his wallet, then grabbed the rental agreement from where he'd stuffed it into the side pocket of the door.

"Do you want me to disable him and tie him up?" Valon asked, reaching for the door handle.

"No. Just let me handle this."

The sheriff's car pulled up behind them, his spotlight playing over the rear window of Wash's rental SUV, the red and blue flashes lighting up the thick trees and brush around them. Wash turned the detector's screen downward, not wanting to have to explain what it was.

"When he walks up to the car," Wash instructed, "keep your hands in your lap and don't say *anything* unless he asks you a direct question. If he asks who you are, you're my cousin Matilda."

"*Matilda?*" She stared at him. "Is this considered a noble name in your world?"

"Matilda Johnson," he expanded, remembering the last name on the uniform jacket's name tape. "From…" He racked his brain for the name of a city in Florida. "From Tallahassee. You're in the Air Force, but you forgot your ID because I was driving. Keep it simple."

"I'm from another planet, Wash," she said, way too calm for his taste. "I have no idea what your people consider *simple.*"

It was a good point, but there wasn't time for anything else. The deputy was out of his car, approaching the driver's side window. He was a big man, maybe twenty or thirty pounds overweight, and it looked worse because of the body armor. He had his hand resting on the butt of his holstered Glock, the other holding a flashlight at shoulder level. Wash rolled down his window and tried not to look into the glare of the light, preserving his night vision.

"Good evening, sir," the man said, polite and professional. "I pulled you over because you were doing sixty-five in a forty-five zone. Can I see your license and registration?"

Wash smiled apologetically and handed over the ID, along with the papers.

"It's a rental," he explained. "Sorry I was speeding, I'm not from around here, and it's so dark and deserted out here, I lost track of what the speed limit was."

"Wyoming, huh?" The deputy looked from the driver's license to Wash's combat utilities. "Are you in the military?"

"Yeah, Army." Wash had his military ID already in hand and passed it to the deputy.

"Kyle Washaki Williams," the man read, then frowned. "Don't I know that name from somewhere?"

"Well, there was the documentary…" Normally, Wash wouldn't have mentioned it. Being recognized in public still bugged the hell out of him. But if it could put this guy off his defenses and get him to let the two of them go, he'd sign an autograph for the man.

"That's it!" The deputy snapped his fingers, grinning ear to ear. "You're the kid who won the Medal of Honor for fighting them damned alien things! Holy shit!" He looked over at Valon. "You guys here on business?" The deputy scanned the woods around them. "Are there more of those monsters here?"

"No, no," Wash assured him. "I was at MacDill for training and my cousin Matilda is stationed there." He nodded at Valon, who hadn't said a word. "I had a rental car, so we decided to visit a friend who lives out this way."

"You know someone who lives out *this* way?" he asked, eyebrows raising, and Wash knew he'd screwed up, had activated the deputy's curiosity.

"Well, we *thought* it was out this way," Valon piped up, and Wash tried to keep from wincing. "We might have gotten turned around."

Wash pictured the map he'd examined, just going with the one name he remembered.

"He, um… works at a kind of hotel out here. Mill Dam Lake Resort?"

"Oh!" The deputy smiled. "Yeah, you *did* miss that. It's back about five miles that way." He pointed the way they'd come. "Okay, give me one second and I'll try to get you out of here as quickly as possible."

He took Wash's ID and rental agreement back with him to the cruiser and slipped back inside his vehicle. Wash watched him in the side view mirror, trying to control his breathing, trying to think.

"What are we doing now?" Valon asked, arms folded.

"If he comes out of the car holding my ID," Wash explained, "then we're good. He's going to let us go. If he comes out holding his ticket book, we're *still* good. It means he's going to give me a fine for driving too fast, but he's not going to arrest us. If he comes out with his gun in his hand or with his hand on it, then there's a BOLO for me or the car and he's about to arrest us."

"I find it troubling that you know so much about how your police deal with criminals, Wash."

"I told you about my father, didn't I?"

The door to the cruiser opened, and Wash knew from the look on the man's face before he even saw that his right hand was on his gun. He knew.

It took all the patience Wash could muster, but he waited until the deputy took a few more steps toward his door before he shifted into drive and jammed down the accelerator. The SUV peeled away from the side of the road, spraying mud and gravel.

"Grab the gate tracker!" he snapped to Valon, fighting to keep from fishtailing as they hit pavement. "Tell me when we're there. We're going to have to jump out quick and get to it before he gets to *us*."

In the rearview mirror the deputy ran back to his cruiser, threw open the door, and jumped inside. The lights had already been on, but now the sirens screeched to life as the car pulled away and raced after them.

"Half a mile," Valon told him. "I believe it's going to be on the left side of the road…" She squinted at the screen of the device. "It's a short distance off the road, maybe one fourth of a mile?"

Wash wasn't listening, trying to figure out how fast he could go and how quickly he could stop. On the left the ditch had ended and the trees were thinning out, which was promising.

"Now! Turn now!"

Wash slammed on the brakes and cut the wheel, the SUV fishtailing, its rear end sliding to the right, the nose pointed off into the trees. There was a gap right in front of them, not particularly wide, but maybe big enough for the SUV to fit. Wood scraped across the driver's door, screaming in protest, and Wash cringed, then jammed on the brakes as another stand of trees loomed ahead of them in the headlights.

"Glad I got the extra insurance," he murmured, throwing open the door. "Let's go!"

The sheriff's car was close, almost to where they'd gone off the road, the lights still strobing through the night. There was no time, but Wash reached back into the back of the SUV, grabbing the backpack there, counting on Valon to get the other one.

"This way!" Valon urged, still holding the tracker.

Wash followed her, boots pounding into the sandy dirt, off to the left of the glow from the rental's lights, sprinting past the broad leaves of palmetto bushes. Mosquitos buzzed past his ears and the ground turned muddy, clinging to his boots, each running step a wet squish. The headlights provided enough light to not run straight into a tree, but it was fading with each step farther from the car, and he was following a woman who was looking down at a video screen that probably killed her night vision. There was a flashlight in the backpack, but using it would draw the deputy right to their position.

No... wait. Up ahead there was another source of light, more diffuse than the headlights but unmistakable, bright enough that Valon was silhouetted against it through the trees. She was heading straight for it, not even looking at the gate tracker anymore. There was no need for it. They'd found the gate, now they just had to get to it ahead of the deputy.

"Williams!" The shout came from far too close behind him, accompanying a cone of white from the deputy's flashlight. Or maybe the weapons light attached to his Glock. "Come out of there with your hands behind your head! You know there's nowhere to go! I've called for backup and the K-9s are going to find you if I don't! Trust me, you don't want that!"

No, I don't, Wash agreed silently. He wondered if the K-9s would follow them through the gate.

"Here!" Valon cried hoarsely.

The gate wasn't as bright as others he'd seen, and as they cleared the last stand of trees, Wash could see why. It was parallel to the ground, only three feet above the mud, swallowing up most of a knurled oak in its extradimensional maw. Valon ducked through it and Wash followed, going down on one knee, the watery mud soaking into his pant leg. He imagined he'd be climbing through the gate and up into the connected world, but he was quickly disabused of that notion when gravity flipped around and he tumbled to the ground almost six feet below.

The air went out of him and stars filled his vision, but he shook them away, trying to assess the area for threats. The ground under his fingers was dry, almost desiccated, a stark contrast from the swampland they'd just left. The portal to that land still loomed above him, though it was nothing but a black circle against the sky, the wet muck below the Florida side barely visible.

Wash scrambled out from under the gate, not wanting the deputy to decide it was worth popping a few shots through the portal for spite.

"Williams?" The man's voice carried through from the Florida side, more plaintive and doubtful than commanding this time. "Did you go through this thing? Come on, man… if this is a military operation, why didn't you just tell me? Dude, I'm not going through there… you're on your own."

"Yeah," Wash murmured a reply, "thank you for your fucking service."

The other side of the gate was night, but not the cloud-wrapped, inky night of central Florida. This night was lit nearly to twilight not by one moon but two, each at least as large as the one he was used to. He stared at them for a moment in awe, each chasing the other across the sky, huge and crystal clear. Finally he tore his gaze away from the sky and looked around him. They were in a valley surrounded by jagged mountains, devoid of any work of man, populated only by short trees and rough scrub. No game trails, or at least none large enough for him to make out even in the bright glare of double moonlight, but something with bat wings and a long, trailing tail flew across one of the moons, impossibly large or uncomfortably close.

"Where the hell are we?" he wondered.

"Well, we're not on Thacia," Valon announced, the gate tracker in one hand, her tablet in the other. "Whether this is a Beast World or simply a barren waste, I can't say."

"Can't be a Beast World," Wash said, shrugging into his backpack. "We'd have had reports of demons coming through by now... we would have shut it down."

She arched an eyebrow at him.

"I'm gratified you're so sure, but I am not. The gate was close to the ground, with no light coming through it, facing the dirt on both sides. It's quite possible the Hive Mind hasn't even discovered this gate."

"Tell me there's another one in walking distance," he pled with her. "Please." Their only other choice was to sit around and wait for the cops to abandon the gate and double back. Which wouldn't work, because the Army would be all over the site once the deputy called it in.

Valon smiled, pointing out to the front of them, toward the moons.

"There is. Ten miles in that direction." She squinted at her tablet, frowning. "And I *think* there's a signal that way. It's very faint... I can't swear it's from this gate, but it might be the one beyond it, if it's close enough."

"Ten miles," Wash sighed. "Well, at least it'll get us out of the area before Dos Santos arrives looking to slap me in the stockade."

"Look on the bright side, Wash," Valon urged him, passing over the gate tracker. "The Venators are always looking for good soldiers. And maybe Brenda would learn to appreciate Thacia..."

Wash snorted in disdain, pulling the flashlight off the side of his pack and using it to light up the trail.

"Shit. You expect me to learn Thacian?" He shook his head and set off through the thin scrub, hoping there were no snakes here. "Hell, I can't even manage Spanish."

24

"You want us to do *what*?" Dos Santos demanded, eyes wide, face so red that Brian Reeves thought the officer's head might explode.

"It's simple," Reeves told him in-between sips from the water bottle the medics had provided him while they checked his leg. "I have this." He motioned with the Thacian tablet. "It'll open up the gate to Thacia. Me and the boys plant a radio signal at the other side of the gate outside Vegas, then we ride Light Strike Vehicles through and find the gate back to the active site the demons are using to invade Thacia… and we guide the Tomahawk right into it."

"You want us to launch a *nuclear* warhead over Nevada?" Dos Santos looked as if he either thought Reeves had gone nuts or maybe he was himself. "And you think there's a chance in hell that the president would approve that?"

Reeves winced as the medic probed the burn. They hadn't even gone to a proper hospital, instead settling for the same tent city the Army had set up just outside the Vegas limits when the initial incursion had happened months ago. Like most things in the military, the place had stuck around because of bureaucratic inertia and it had seemed like a nice, handy, private setting for the briefing he'd had to give the colonel.

"I'll tell you what I think, sir," Reeves said, eyeing the medics doubtfully, wondering whether they were cleared to hear any of this. "I think Thacia is about to be overrun. I think they were about to be overrun *hours* ago. And I think if the president wants us to have *any* allies who know what the fuck is really going on, we need to save their asses before it's too late." He shrugged. "Plus, they'll be really fucking grateful and share all their advanced technology with us, so that'll be cool."

Dos Santos sighed, but then nodded almost reluctantly.

"Maybe I can sell that." He pulled a sat-phone from his pocket and punched in a number, walking away from the examination table and out the door of the tent.

Through the door was the burnt orange of twilight, reminding Reeves how much time had passed since he'd arrived at the gate, and how little time the Thacians had. He waited patiently as the medic applied a burn cream, then waved the man away.

"Hand me those clothes," Reeves told the medic, motioning at the fresh combat utilities Dos Santos had brought with him.

The colonel was thorough and had even brought along clean underwear and socks and fresh boots, and since the jacket had Reeves' name on the tab, he assumed Dos Santos had sent someone to raid the go bag he'd left in his locker back in North Carolina. There were male and female medics and doctors in the medical tent, but he'd figured they'd seen everything before, so he stripped out of his torn and soiled clothes right at the examination table and pulled on the fresh ones. Reeves winced at the feel of clean clothes on top of dried sweat and funk. He'd managed to grab a shower in Thacia, but felt grubby all over again after the uphill climb to the mountain pass and then languishing in the hot sun for two hours in the Nevada desert, waiting for pickup.

His Glock 43 holster snapped into place on his belt and he

shoved the little holdout gun away before fastening his jacket. He glanced around the medical tent, suddenly annoyed.

"Anyone know where they put the rifle I came in with?"

The medics met his demand with confused glances and shaking heads, and Reeves sighed. That rocket carbine was a cool gun and he intended to hold onto it for as long as possible, but now it was probably locked away in an armory somewhere.

Dammit. Dos Santos had better at least have brought me a sidearm.

He was about to go find the colonel when the officer pulled open the door, his phone still pressed to his ear, and motioned for Reeves to join him outside.

Don't make me talk to the president, Reeves pled in the privacy of his thoughts. *Don't make me talk to the president. Please don't make me talk to the fucking president...*

Dos Santos lowered the phone and covered the receiver with his palm.

"It's the president. He wants to talk to you."

Fuck! Reeves closed his eyes for a moment and took the phone.

"Yes, Mr. President?"

"Sgt. Reeves, it's good to speak to you again." The man seemed awfully enthusiastic, but then he always did. "We've been using quite a lot of nuclear weapons lately, you know? That's gotta be problematic for the environment, doesn't it?"

"Not on this planet, sir," Reeves said patiently. It was wise to be patient when talking to the president, particularly if you technically worked for him. "I think the Chinese and Russians and maybe the Indians have used them on-planet, but we've strictly used them on other worlds."

"Wow!" the president said. "That just really blows my mind, you know, Brian? Do you mind if I call you Brian?"

"Not at all, Mr. President." *Particularly since I've already told you three times before I didn't mind.*

"Well, Brian, like I told my wife, it just blows my mind that we're using terms like 'on-planet' and 'other worlds' like it's nothing, like we've been doing this forever. I mean, it's other *planets*, man!"

"Yes, sir, Mr. President." It took a lot of self-control for Reeves not to sigh, but he settled for rolling his eyes since this wasn't a video call.

"And now you think we should launch a nuclear cruise missile at a planet full of humans?"

"Thacians, yes, sir. Not *at* their planet, just through their airspace, if you will. They're under attack right now and I don't think they can hold out much longer."

"And there's no way to just take a warhead through and plant it manually, Brian?"

"No, sir. The gate to the active site is overrun with tens of thousands of the enemy warrior drones. There's no way we could get through."

"Warrior drones." The president laughed hoarsely. "That's another of those freaky things I'll never get used to. I guess it's better than calling them *demons* though. Some of those people in the press really pushed *that* idea, you know? The whole satanic thing. Makes me remember the early eighties. Well, hell, Brian, you probably weren't even born then!"

And you probably don't remember what you had for breakfast.

"Late eighties, sir."

"And you're sure these Thacians won't take offense at us sending a cruise missile? I mean, what if there's some kind of technical error and we wind up setting off a nuclear warhead right on top of them?"

"At this point, Mr. President, it would be the choice between being burned ashes quick by a nuke or having bug-eyed alien monsters rip them to shreds with talons. I know which one *I'd* pick. Either way, they'll all be dead." That might, he realized, have been too curt for a conversation with the president. "But if we do our job right, the missile will hit through the gate to the Hive Mind world and the Thacians will owe us, big time."

He wanted to point out that none of this would be happening if the government black project hadn't been fucking around with alien technology they didn't understand, but he wasn't sure the president would appreciate him spilling something that sensitive out loud.

The president was silent for a long few seconds, and Reeves was mentally laying odds that either the man had fallen asleep or forgotten that he was on the phone, but he finally responded.

"All right, Brian. We'll do this your way. Put your boss back on the line."

Reeves let out the breath he'd been holding and handed the sat-phone back to Dos Santos. The colonel listened silently for a moment, nodding as if the president could see him.

"Yes, sir. The sooner, the better. Yes, sir. We'll get it done. Thank you, sir." Dos Santos' shoulders sagged as he hung up the phone and tucked it back into his pocket, like the whole conversation had been a physical effort. He closed his eyes for a moment before turning back to Reeves. "The launch is in six hours." Reeves was about to blurt an objection, but Dos Santos raised a hand to forestall it. "It's the best we can do. Anyway, it'll give the rest of the team the opportunity to get here and get geared up."

Reeves nodded, still not happy but realizing it was the best he was going to get.

"You haven't heard anything from Wash yet, have you?" he asked, thinking that he needed to give Brenda a call.

Dos Santos' face turned just as red as it had been when he'd explained they needed a cruise missile.

"Funny you should mention that…"

"Hey, you hear something?" Wash asked, looking up from the tracker screen and shining the flashlight around them.

The valley had narrowed as they'd followed the course of an ancient, dried-up river, canyon walls closing in on them as the miles passed. Three hours had gone by and the moons had traveled across the sky, out of view now behind the rocky cliffs rising up on either side. The whole time Wash hadn't seen anything bigger than what might have been a rabbit, but something...

"I think you just want an excuse to stop walking," Valon accused, hand on her hip as she eyed him with obvious skepticism.

"And you don't?" They must have gone at least eight miles now, and under normal circumstances it wouldn't have been anything he couldn't handle. But normal circumstances didn't involve jailbreaks, car chases, and no sleep for the last two days. His feet were sore, his quads were aching, and he felt like he might fall asleep on his feet at any second. But he *had* heard something.

"There!" he said, stopping in his tracks, turning and pointing the flashlight behind them. "What's that scratching?"

No, not just behind... up. Wash played the beam ten feet up the partially collapsed canyon wall, and his blood ran cold as he saw the insectoid creatures making their way down the slope. He tensed up, ready to run, thinking at first glance that the things were demons, but then he noticed the baskets they carried, their shorter size.

"Shit," he hissed. "Workers."

He'd seen the worker drones back on Hades, marching purposefully through the tunnels, bringing the biological material they'd collected back to the Hive Mind to feed it. If they were here, that meant...

"We're on a Beast World," Valon declared, lips peeling back from her teeth in a snarl. And they didn't have a gun between them. "We have to get out of here... those things are harmless, but the Hive Mind can see through their eyes."

The workers kept coming, not showing urgency, but still heading straight toward them, and there were over a dozen of the insectoid drones.

"Harmless unless they think *we're* food," Wash amended, backing away from the things.

The drones filed down the earthen ramp in the side of the canyon, spreading across the trail in a line, as if they were getting ready to march on the two humans abreast. Valon frowned, staring at the workers in obvious confusion.

"What the hell are they *doing*?" she asked.

The things had mouths, but they were mandibles, never meant to speak any language, much less a human one. And yet they all opened as one and spoke.

"*Williams*," they said in chorus, "*it's me, Jimmy. Jimmy Bonner.*"

"What the fuck?" Wash blurted. "Jimmy? You're dead!"

"*My body died, but... something survived inside the Hive Mind. Don't ask me how.*" And somehow, the drones shook their head as one, just the sort of gesture Wash would have expected if a human had been standing there speaking to them. "*Maybe it's just my memories, or maybe it's my soul, if I have one, but I'm trapped inside the Hive Mind. It's hell in here, Williams.*" The familiar voice broke. "*I want to die... I want you to kill me.*"

"I thought we already had!" Wash said, throwing up his hands, feeling ridiculous talking to the drones. "How the hell do we kill you when you're living inside the thing's head?"

"*When it dies, I will. You have to kill the Hive Mind.*"

"Well, that's the idea. But we're doing everything we can do just to survive."

"You have to understand, Williams. It knows. The Hive Mind knows everything I know. It knows all about us, our capabilities, it has access to all of my memories. But because I'm part of it, I know what it know, too, and it knows what's causing all these new gates."

Wash's mouth went dry, and not from the macabre chorus Jimmy was speaking through.

"How? How the hell would it know?"

Valon wasn't saying anything. Wash had been too dumbfounded by the situation to notice, but she'd stayed silent. His first thought was that she was silent from disbelief, but the look on her face was cautious, discerning.

"It recognizes the technology of the Archaion."

Now Valon's eyes went wide, mouth forming an "o," and if his expression didn't match hers, it was only because he had too many questions.

"It's impossibly old," the collective voice of Jimmy Bonner went on. *"The Hive Mind was around before the gates, and it remembers when the Archaion created them. It fought the Archaion to a standstill across the galaxy, and destroyed their civilization on dozens of worlds. All that's left of them are pockets of survivors, living like primitive savages. The Archaion are gone, so it believes either us or the Thacians did something with Archaion technology to make these new gates, and it knows there's nothing we can do to stop it."* As one, the drones looked back over their shoulders. *"It's found me. I don't have much time, and neither do you. Demons are coming... you need to go. Tell Brenda... tell her I'm sorry."*

The drones shuddered as if they'd been possessed by an evil spirit and were finally free of it, then they wandered off, totally ignoring the two humans. Wash stared at them, frozen in place, feeling as if he were stuck in a nightmare.

"Wash," Valon said, and his head snapped around, sure that she'd called his name more than once. She motioned down the canyon. "You heard him. They'll be coming."

"Yeah," he agreed, unable to keep from staring at the workers foraging for food. "I heard him all right."

The tracker said it was less than two miles to the gate, but Wash would have sworn under oath that the run through the canyon lasted hours. He expected demons to rampage down from the canyons, expected the canyon to wind up stretching out forever like the nightmare his life had become, but there was... nothing. Not even the furtive rabbit things he'd seen before. When the gate appeared, it was almost a letdown, if a fifty-foot-wide hole in space could ever be considered a letdown.

"You getting a signal still?" he asked Valon, trying to see through the gate. The other side was shrouded in darkness, as if it was pressed against the dirt or facing a cloud-covered night sky. She nodded, checking her tablet. Wash was impressed with the battery life on the thing and wondered if that was another piece of Archaion technology. If so, there were a bunch of EV manufacturers who would kill to have it.

"Still a bit faint, but I'm getting it." She shot him a look. "You want me to go first?"

Wash shook his head and stepped through, tensing up in case they were high up or upside down or something else unpleasant. There was no guarantee the thing wasn't on the edge of a cliff, and he wished he'd brought a drone along to check.

If wishes were fishes, we'd all swim. Or something like that.

When the ground on the other side was absolutely level with the ground he stepped through, it was a surprise and he nearly stumbled. He also discovered that it was so dark because the gate was pressed up less than a foot from a rock wall... inside a cave. Valon was beside him, and he fought back a surge of annoyance.

"You *should* have waited until I yelled back that it was clear," he chided. "I could have gone straight off a cliff or something."

"I didn't hear a scream," she said with a dismissive shrug. She moved to the end of the gate, squeezing between the faint glow of the portal and the unyielding rock wall, and looked around the cavern. "This explains why the demons haven't found this gate. There's barely room for us to get through here, much less one of them."

Wash wasn't so sure there was even room for *him*, and he had to slip off his backpack before he felt comfortable following her. The cave wasn't deep, but past the chamber with the gate it narrowed sharply and headed upward to an entrance a good twenty feet above them. And it was *cold*.

"Shit," Wash said, shrugging back into the pack. "This is a hell of a change from Florida."

Valon wasn't listening, frowning at the screen of her tablet.

"We need to get up to the surface," she said, tucking it away in her pocket and scrambling up the slope.

Wash followed her, having to dig his fingers into the dirt and rocks to pull himself up, his legs too spent to push him. It was lighter outside than Wash thought it would be, early morning he thought from the hint of gold on the horizon above the mountains. Valon wasn't looking at the sky though, she was looking at the tablet again.

"The signal was being blocked by the cavern," she told him, visibly excited, holding up the screen for him to see. "This *is* Thacia! We're home!"

Wash didn't look at it, instead following the line of mountains down to the valley below... to the city. It was different from anything he'd seen in the US, bringing more to mind the few Mediterranean towns he'd visited since he'd begun operating with the team. That wasn't what attracted his attention though. It was the fire. Smoke poured up from one end of the valley, consuming the buildings at that edge of the city, and even from miles away the distant crump of explosions echoed off the mountains. Aircraft that looked very similar to the gunship Valon had crashed on Hades swooped downward to where the fires raged, flashes of light coming off their chin cannons.

"We're not the only ones."

25

"I can't tell you how relieved I am to have you back," Marcos said, pulling Valon into an embrace. "I thought when I decided against children, it would mean not giving my heart a hostage to the fates, but such still seems to be my destiny nonetheless."

Valon gently disengaged herself from the prefect, somehow embarrassed at the show of emotion in front of Wash. For the Earther's part, he seemed to be pretending not to notice, studying the interior of Marcos' office instead.

"I wish I came home to better news," she said, motioning at the walls and what was beyond them. "How long can we hold them off?"

Marcos sighed, leaning back against his desk.

"The terrain has been our only ally." He made an encompassing gesture. "It funnels their forces into a bottleneck just outside the southeast walls. But if they break through our lines there, they can flank us and spread throughout the entire valley, and then there'll be nothing we can do." The man's mouth worked as if he wanted to spit. "We've slaughtered them by the thousands, yet they still come. There's no end to the demons. I pray to the gods and the Archaion that your Sgt. Reeves keeps his word."

"Reeves was *here*?" Wash asked, jumping out of the chair beside the door. "In Thacia?"

"Not but a day and a half ago," Marcos confirmed. "He came in with a Venator patrol his team had encountered on a Beast World and I sent him alone at the beginning of the incursion to ensure his word got back to your government."

"What word?" Wash asked. "What was he wanting to do?"

Marcos smiled thinly, looking between Wash and Valon.

"I assume your Earther friend has told you about nuclear weapons."

"I've seen one close up," Valon said, feeling an odd twist in her stomach. "Is Sgt. Reeves proposing his team somehow can get one of those warheads through the ranks of the enemy to the Beast World gate? That's insane."

"No. There is, apparently, something in their arsenal called a cruise missile."

"They're gonna launch a fucking nuclear missile through the gate?" Wash squawked, sounding horrified. "How? Those things have to be guided somehow, usually by GPS satellites. You don't have any satellites, do you?"

Marcos frowned, looking as confused as Valon was.

"I'm not sure what the word means in this context," Marcos confessed. "The best the imprinter's translation can do is... something moving around something else?"

"They're machines we shoot into space to orbit the Earth," Wash explained.

"For *what*?" Valon wondered, brows knitted in confusion.

"A lot of things," Wash said, waving it off. "How do they plan to guide the missile?"

"I imagine they'll tell us when they return," Marcos said. "He made it clear he intended to come back in person."

"Are you certain this is a good idea, sir?" Valon asked, pacing across the office. "The weapon they used... it was enough to bring down an entire hive. The gods alone know what it could do to our city if it were to detonate before it hit the Beast World gate."

"If you have an alternative idea," Marcos told her, cocking an eyebrow, "I'd be delighted to hear it, Primus."

"Nukes are the only way to close the gates," Wash agreed, shrugging. "At least the only one we've been able to figure out."

Anger flared behind Valon's eyes, and she let it out without thinking, despite the fact that Wash was hardly to blame for it.

"I'm not certain you Earthers are the ones we should ask for solutions," she snapped, "given this is all your doing."

Valon realized what she'd said a half a second after the words came out, and she tried too late to bite down on the statement. Wash's mouth dropped open, but the reaction that concerned her was the narrowed eyes of Prefect Marcos.

"What is that supposed to mean, Primus?"

Valon hesitated, torn between her duty to Marcos and the debt she owed to Wash. In the end, Wash saved her from having to make the decision.

"She's talking about the new gates," he confessed, sinking back into the chair, unable to meet Marcos' eyes. "It's our fault they're opening up. I don't know all the details, but I guess from what Valon told me that my government found at least some part of an Archaion spaceship. They were experimenting with it somehow and a gate opened up. We buried it, but then more and more of the gates started opening up... on our world. I guess on a bunch of others too."

Marcos looked as if the Earther had committed blasphemy, coming to his feet and backing away from Wash like he expected the lightning bolt of Zeus to strike him at any second.

"You damned *fools*!" Valon knew Maruos well and recognized a storm coming, a minutes-long rant that would culminate with him running to the Senate and telling them that the Earthers weren't to be trusted.

"Fools without doubt," Valon agreed, interrupting the train of thought that would lead to that end, "but whose fault is that? We've known the truth for hundreds of years and we've told them nothing. Are you surprised they would tinker with the tools of the gods when they weren't even aware the Archaion existed, or the Hive Mind, or the demons? As far as they could tell, this was their gift from the ancient gods, a chance to become as wise and powerful as the Archaion, and where were any of us, any Thacian, to warn them otherwise?"

"You would have me trust these people after they unleashed this hell on us?" Marcos demanded, throwing his hands up as if in appeal to the gods for patience.

"I grant you that their leaders may be idiots, but are ours any better?" She raised an eyebrow, pointing in the general direction of the Senate. "Do I have to remind you how close we came to being overrun just a few months ago while our government did nothing?"

Marcos' jaw was set stubbornly, but there was some give in his eyes, a grudging acknowledgement of the wisdom of her argument.

"And as you say," she went on, "what other choice do we have?"

The tablet on Marcos' desk pinged and the prefect glared at it in obvious annoyance. He swept the device up and then blew out a breath, turning it to show the message to Valon.

"I suppose we're going to find out if we can trust them. They've arrived."

"This place would be pretty nice," Victor Shaw declared, "if it weren't for the alien demons and like half of it being on fire."

"It's not half," Reeves said, arguing with the man automatically, whether it was worth it or not, just out of habit. He squinted down the mountainside at the city below, trying to judge the extent of the damage from the fighting. "Can't be more than a quarter, max."

He glanced over the crest of the mountains on the opposite side of the valley, catching the glint of the sun off high-flying aircraft. The glint wobbled and black dots dropped from the planes, tumbling downward into the faint, dark mass of the enemy still swarming up the river valley from the gate there. The explosions were flashes of red, the sound of their detonation lost in the distance.

"I still wouldn't want to live there," Flanders insisted, looking at the distant towers through the optic on his M250, adjusting the magnification. "What you told me, boss, this is like the twentieth time or something they've had a demon invasion."

The rest of the team was spread out in a semi-circle across the trail, only a half a mile from the gate. Reeves had thought about waiting at the gate site itself, but Peleus and Kallias had still been there when they'd arrived. Ideally he would have taken the time to bury them, but the schedule was tight, and that missile would be arriving in two hours whether they were ready for it or not.

"There's the transport," Nyland said, pointing nearly straight up.

Reeves squinted against the midday sun, finally spotting the black dot against the cloudless, blue sky. The pilot had learned a lesson from the crash of the gunship that had brought Reeves to the gate the night before—they were coming in high, well beyond the range of the spikers, an arc up from the city and then down on the other side. That didn't keep the Hive Mind army from trying though. The spikes rose and fell, impotent, spiteful, coming down somewhere inside the city.

Reeves hoped the civilians were under cover. He thought of what Flanders had said and what it would be like to live under the constant threat of the demons... and whether American cities would get the chance to find out.

The transport landed nearly on top of them, taking up the whole road, from the edge of the cliff to the tree line. Rotors whined, then hummed as power was leached away from them, dust and debris billowing around the aircraft, forcing Reeves to slip on his sunglasses. The side door opened downward into a set of stairs and Wash Williams descended them, the smile on his face awkward and sheepish.

"Hi, guys," he said. "Glad to see you again."

"Kid!" Shaw yelled, jumping up from where he'd been kneeling and running over to Wash, grabbing him up in an enthusiastic hug. "I swear to God, you must be the luckiest son of a bitch I've ever met! I thought sure you'd bought it after that shit that went down in Romania!"

Reeves jaw clenched against the reflexive curse that wanted to force its way out as he stalked up to the younger man.

"You know," he said tightly but in a normal volume, "that was a damn stupid stunt you pulled at MacDill."

"I know," Wash admitted. "But she would have done it for me."

"Yes, I would have," Valon agreed, coming down the steps behind him. "Sgt. Reeves, it's good to see you again."

"Primus Valon," Reeves returned, nodding to the woman. Her eyebrow rose and he suppressed a smug smile. She hadn't expected him to remember her rank. "Glad to see you're okay." He nodded to Wash. "Thanks for taking care of our boy."

"And thank *you* for coming back to aid us in our time of need." She motioned up the trail. "You left the shield open, I assume?" Reeves nodded. "How do you intend to direct your weapon to the other gate? Wash tells me they're usually guided by satellites or terrain mapping. You have neither for our planet."

"Sgt. Williams is correct," Reeves told her. "But this missile has been modified." Reeves patted the backpack Nyland was carrying. "This is an AN/PED-1 laser designator."

"And it's fuckin' heavy," Nyland added.

"We just have to set this thing up within sight of the gate and we can bring the Tomahawk right through it." Reeves checked his watch, which had a countdown running on it. "And we have just over an hour and fifty minutes to get there." He shrugged. "We'd appreciate a ride and any interference you could run for us."

Valon nodded and waved at the transport.

"Come aboard. We'll get you as close as we can, but the only way to approach is from behind the gate… and that's going to take a long flight. We need to go now."

The transport was set up for passengers, thankfully, which meant there were actual seats instead of just netting or cargo boxes, which was what Reeves was used to out of long-range birds. He was still strapping himself in when the door swung shut and the ducted-fan aircraft lurched upward.

Wash was seated across from Reeves, chewing on his lip, nervous as a kid waiting outside the principal's office. Wash had one of the Thacian carbines tucked into his side, slung across his chest, fingers tapping on the receiver rhythmically. Reeves sighed. He'd pulled off his backpack before he'd strapped in, and he reached into the top flap and pulled out Wash's Canik 9mm, along with a chest holster and spare mag pouch.

"I think you left this behind in Tampa," Reeves said, handing the pistol off to Wash.

The kids eyes went wide, and he smiled as he took the weapon.

"Thanks, Master Sergeant," he said, strapping on the weapon quickly.

Reeves closed his eyes for a second, debating what he was about to say.

"Dos Santos left it up to me, you know," he told Wash. "What to do about you, I mean. And God knows, I *thought* I'd made the decision about twenty times on the way here. I'd settled on sending you home once we got through with this mission, kicking you back to the Wyoming National Guard." He shrugged. "No charges, but just out. Because there's one thing you gotta understand about what we do. We have a mission, and we accomplish it, whether we like it or not. We work with some bad people sometimes, because we're trying to take down *worse* people. I've had to do a lot of things I didn't like, things I lay awake at night and wish I could go back and undo." He snorted a humorless laugh and shook his head. "Which is why I admire the hell out of what you did, even though it was so fucking stupid. But if you *ever* do anything like that again, you won't be going back to Wyoming, you'll be heading straight to fucking Leavenworth, we clear?"

"Clear, Master Sergeant!" Wash barked like he was locked up at attention in basic training.

"And that's another thing." Reeves wagged a finger at the kid. "Stop fucking calling me *master sergeant* all the time. This isn't the Army. It makes you sound like you don't belong here, like you're the fucking water boy or something. Call me Reeves, or *boss*. You're fighting next to us, you're one of us. Got me?"

A smile spread across Wash's face, and he nodded.

"I got it, boss. Thank you."

"Don't thank me, Williams." He shook his head. "Why you want to keep risking your life on other planets when you have that girl Brenda waiting at home for you, God only knows. You'll be lucky if you don't come home after one of these ops and find out she's cleaned out all the furniture like I did." Reeves chuckled. "Of course, *my* wife didn't shoot her ex-boyfriend in the head to save my life, so maybe your situation is a little different."

The smile faded and a haunted look replaced it on Wash's face.

"Oh, yeah… about that…"

26

Wash Williams never thought he'd miss the SIG M5. It was a heavy gun with a heavy, complicated optic and he would rather have hauled around a short-barreled AR10, but he'd grown used to it. The Thacian carbine was probably a good weapon, but there was something off about the balance, probably a cultural thing. He wasn't about to give the thing back though, not after seeing the pulsating mass of demons coming out of the gate. Even several thousand feet up, the unending swarm was terrifying.

Even more terrifying were the spikers, because he'd seen what they could do. Even this high, the things still took shots at the transport, not caring that the six-foot darts fell back into their own ranks.

"Holy shit," Carver said, not concealing his awe. "We're dropping in the middle of *that*?"

Wash didn't know Carver that well. He was one of the replacements, like Greenway, though usually much quieter, and seemed to be trying self-consciously to cultivate the whole *quiet professional* image. But he couldn't blame the man for breaking character in the face of what lay below them. Wash had faced worse and his stomach was still churning, and he couldn't blame all of it on the bumpy, turbulent flight.

Valon heard the man and raised a finger as she hung off a safety strap just outside the cockpit, conversing in Thacian with the pilot of the transport. She swayed back and forth, feet shifting like a surfer, as if the intermittent, violent shaking didn't bother her. The pilot nodded, then touched the headphones he wore and made a radio call. Valon turned back to them, moving back to her seat.

"The gunships are on their way for a fire suppression run," she explained. "They'll clear us a landing zone and then the high-altitude bombers will launch another strike to try to keep the area open for you as long as possible."

Reeves looked at his watch. The man had been doing that a lot as the flight had dragged on.

"We're cutting it close," he said. "The missile transits the gate in fifteen minutes, and it won't take more than a couple minutes to get here from there."

"If you want to go down *without* air support," Valon told him, arching an eyebrow, "I'm more than willing to let you."

Reeves scowled at the woman but didn't respond, turning instead to Wash.

"Tony's going to be setting up the designator." Reeves gestured at Nyland, who waved casually, as if it was nothing. "I want you and Flanders to go with him, find some high ground off to the side and keep the bastards off him. The rest of us will be laying down Claymores and setting up a perimeter."

Wash nodded. He wasn't sure if Reeves was sending him off someplace safer or hanging him out to dry. With how many thousands of demons were pouring through the portal, it didn't seem to matter.

"Here come the gunships," Shaw announced, twisting around to stare out the aircraft's side window.

Wash had to loosen his restraints and lean forward to see out that side, but it only took a second for him to spot the Thacian ducted-fan helicopters. Their formations reminded him of the Hueys in the old Vietnam War movies his father had used to watch with him, tight and fast and low to the ground, coming straight along the valley. Missiles shot out from hardpoints on the stubby wings of the aircraft, one squadron banking out of the way of the next to allow them space to fire, the explosions distant thumps as they carved chunks out of the enemy column.

Fire consumed hundreds of the Hive Mind warrior drones and, more importantly, missiles traversed through the gate, smoke pouring out of the opening as the stream of enemy troops paused. Not without a heavy toll though. Spikes peppered the air as the gunships attempted to pull out of their firing run, spearing through a dozen of the aircraft in the space of a heartbeat. The wounded birds tumbled downward, trailing smoke, and Valon leaned forward in her seat, teeth clenching.

Even with the losses the gunship squadrons didn't falter, swinging around again for another pass, this time laying down a barrage of fire from their chin cannons, the rocket-assisted rounds red and white pulses stitching rows through the enemy lines.

"There," Valon said, pointing to a spot a half a mile down from the gate, where the narrow confines of the ancient river valley broadened out by a few dozen yards on each side. The gap in the enemy column had nearly reached it, the demons moving past the wide spot and continuing on, while the other side of the gate was jammed up by the bodies of the ones killed by the missiles. "There's our landing spot."

Whether she'd been instructing the pilot or had already told him and was just informing the rest of them, the plane descended sharply, shoving Wash back in his seat and hauling his stomach up into his throat.

"We won't have much time when we hit the ground," Valon

said, her voice obscenely calm and casual despite the abrupt descent. "Get out quick, or this transport will catch a spike or three before it can take off again."

Which was fine and all, but Wash was curious how she expected them to get back *out* of the valley without the plane staying to pick them up. There was no time to think about it now though. The landing gear slammed into the ground with enough force to throw Wash forward against his restraints, his teeth clacking together, colored flashes filling his eyes.

"Out!" Reeves yelled, the sharp command piercing the haze of the impact and bringing Wash's hands to the quick-release of his safety harness without thought.

Sunlight flooded the interior of the aircraft as the side door flew open, and Flanders somehow managed to be the first out, despite carrying the machine gun, leaping through the gap before the stairs were even down. Wash managed to be third through the door right after Carver, though he didn't try to skip the stairs, clambering down them instead as fast as he could. Wash lunged away from the aircraft, falling into a perimeter position to the left of Carver, automatically leaving ten meters between them because that was what he'd been taught at infantry AIT, despite the fact that the enemy wasn't likely to throw a frag grenade at them.

The others hit the ground off to his left in a synchronized ballet possible only through intense and ceaseless training, and before Wash could get to a count of ten, the engines of the transport roared to life, the massive craft, as large as a Chinook, leaping back into the air, keeping low, nap of the earth as it evacuated the area. Leaving them alone.

Wash had seen the area from the air, but now that he was down in the midst of the terrain, he finally got a better sense of it. The path from the gate to the city was a dry riverbed, though it was old enough that anyone might have been forgiven for their ignorance of its origin. It was over a hundred yards wide, the banks sloping gently but inexorably upward on either side, one hemmed in by thick forest, the other by the face of a cliff leading up to a plateau, evidence of some ancient earthquake.

And at the center of the ancient waterway was a gate. Guilt gnawed at Wash's insides from the knowledge that Valon had been right, that this was the responsibility of the American government, of Earth in general. The Thacians had spent hundreds of years protecting Earth from the Hive Mind, and they'd been repaid by their charges acting recklessly, causing the deaths of thousands of their people.

Out to the side, at the edge of his peripheral vision, four of the Delta operators rushed out into the center of the riverbed, emplacing Claymore mines with practiced speed, then unspooling black wire back to their position. One of them trailed behind, scooping loose sand and dirt on top of the wires just in case one of the demons was smart enough to see the wire and follow it to the pesky humans.

As if reading his mind, a row of demons four across jumped through the gate, leaping from a few feet up as if they'd had to climb over the bodies of their own dead. They were only a quarter of a mile away, and Wash's finger tightened on the trigger of his carbine, the intersecting arrows of the electronic sight hovering over the chest of the center one, but Reeves' soft but insistent voice overruled him and anyone else with similar thoughts.

"Hold your fire," he insisted. "Wait until we're sure they see us. We're here to shut that gate, not to shoot the enemy. Tony, you got that shit set up yet?"

"Getting there," Nyland replied, voice distracted. Wash was tempted to risk a glance back at the man but kept his eyes on the demons.

They showed no sign of noticing the humans set up at the edge of the old riverbank, loping forward with single-minded intensity, proving Reeves correct. More ranks passed through the portal behind them, and in their wake a wobbling, lumbering spiker, squeezing past whatever was blocking the bottom half of the gate on the other end. Wash grimaced. Even worse than the demons, the spikers set his teeth on edge, as if the things were an affront to nature... or maybe just because he knew there was nothing his rifle could do against the things. He didn't even know if a Claymore could kill one of the things, and worry nagged at him that the spiker would rip the wires up as it passed.

"Got it," Nyland announced. "Painting target now."

And where the hell is that missile?

He'd been listening for it even if he couldn't watch, and all he heard was the wind howling through the trees behind them. No, that couldn't be the wind. Nothing was moving, no trees swaying, no debris blowing. Wash turned, looking over his left shoulder, and saw the thing coming in low along the riverbed, subsonic. It was an older one then. The new ones were supersonic. Of course, the official story was that there were no nuclear-armed cruise missiles in the US inventory, but the official story and five bucks might get you a cup of coffee.

He wasn't the only one to notice it though. The spiker did too. The thing's hide flexed and half a dozen of the six-foot darts whipped out toward the missile.

"Mines!" Reeves shouted, and the clackers were loud enough that they nearly drowned out the jets of the cruise missile.

The chain-fire explosions certainly did, battering his ears even through the tactical earbuds he wore, shrouding the spiker in smoke and dust. Wash didn't know if the detonating Claymores injured the spiker, but they certainly distracted it, and a moment's distraction was all they needed. The cruise missile was going hundreds of miles an hour, but Wash was sure he saw a flash of it as it passed, the glow of its jets just before it darted right through the gate.

"Yes!" Nyland exulted.

"Down!" Reeves yelled, drowning him out. "Duck and cover!"

Oh yeah. The nuke.

Wash buried his helmet in the sand, putting his hands over his ears and opening his mouth, just the way he'd been trained before they'd sent him on his first mission with a nuke. The flash was the same as before, and something rebelled in Wash's mind about the idea that he was becoming accustomed to witnessing nuclear explosions. But the results were also the same… no shockwave, no concussion, just the initial burst of heat.

And then nothing. No sound except the hot wind and the crackle of fires. Wash cautiously raised his head, searching for the gate. It wasn't there, which he'd suspected, since he was still alive, but there was a scorched cone of blackened earth just ahead of where it had been and a row of smoking corpses laying in front of it, the remains of the demons that had been just a bit too close to the initial burst of heat and radiation.

Wash wanted to cheer, knowing they'd saved Thacia, but that left one little problem. Or, more accurately, several thousand *big* problems. The demon horde that had been monomaniacally focused on invading Thacia was cut off now from the Hive Mind that had aimed them at their target, which meant they looked instead for the closest available human to take out their wrath on. Which was the Delta team.

It made no logical sense, since the smart thing to do would have been to press their attack on the city and do what damage they could, but it was at least consistent with what the demons had done in LA when they lacked any real guidance. The closest of them was four or five hundred yards away, yet somehow they still detected the small group of humans and turned back to them, falling into a loping run that sped up with every step.

"Shit," Victor Shaw said in a mild tone. "Really wish we had some more of those Claymores."

"Pick 'em off as far away as you can," Reeves ordered, following his own suggestion on the heels of the words, the suppressor at the end of his M5 barking hoarsely.

Wash couldn't tell whether any of the demons went down, but if the shot accomplished nothing else, it at least got everyone else firing. The suppressed SIG rifles coughed individual shots or the occasional three-round burst, but they were all drowned out by the full-auto fury of Flanders' M250 machine gun. The thing *sounded* impressive, and there was no mistaking the enemy who fell to the swathe of its fire. Wash had to remind himself to add his own weapon to the fight, though he had no idea how accurate it would be from this range.

It was, as it turned out, pretty damned accurate. The scope seemed to adjust to the range of whatever he was targeting without needing to be adjusted, the electronic reticle moving on its own, settling on the head of one of the demons just before Wash pressed the trigger. The recoil was negligible, though the optical signature of the thing was jarring and garish, a factor of the weapon not being designed to fight other humans, he supposed. The burst of fireflies swarmed down the targeting screen and a demon's head burst in a spray of black clearly visible in the scope.

He adjusted automatically to the next target, but it was much closer... they all were. Three hundred yards, and if the dozen men firing had attrited their numbers, it hadn't been by enough.

But they weren't alone. High-caliber cannon rounds raked across the front lines of the demons, chopping them down by the dozens, the stutter of the guns coming just a second ahead of the whine of the rotors. The gunships had come back. Missiles followed the guns, taking down the ranks farther back, and Wash let out a relieved sigh.

High-altitude bombs sent plumes of fire into the air a half a mile away, the ground shaking under him with their detonations like the petulant foot-stomps of an angry godling, something the Thacians might worship. Not that he was about to complain. He rolled over on his side and raised the muzzle of his weapon, watching the show like the rest of them, their rifles seeming hopelessly inadequate beside the overwhelming airpower on display.

The cacophony of the bombing was so distracting, Wash didn't even notice the transport returning until its shadow passed over them, blotting out the sun. They didn't need to clear a path this time, since there was nothing threatening the landing except the torn bodies of dead warrior drones, and when the massive aircraft touched down the tone of the engines descended with it, powering off rather than staying active for a quick takeoff.

Valon was smiling when she exited the aircraft, and Wash thought maybe it was a sign that she was taking her elevated rank more seriously that she hadn't insisted on undertaking the mission alongside them.

Reeves went to meet her and, lacking anyone to tell him otherwise, Wash tagged along.

"How's your Senate gonna like *that*?" Reeves asked her, gesturing to where the gate had been.

"I believe," Valon said, nodding to the man in recognition, "that the Senate will have the same question for you that I have right now." There was naked hunger in her eyes. "When can we do this again?"

27

"I can't believe we're making a phone call between planets," Wash mused, shaking his head in wonderment.

"Theoretically," Reeves amended, waving at the collection of mismatched electronic gear scattered across the worktable.

Dornan, the communications specialist, was working on getting the American equipment connected to the Thacian antenna systems, which was being supervised by a skinny, elfin Venator technician who didn't seem impressed by the Earther gear at all. She kept arguing with the man in Thacian, which had to be translated through Valon since there hadn't been time to get the technician imprinted with English. Dornan would argue back, and Valon was stuck in between the two and didn't seem happy about it.

Finally though, Dornan gave Reeves a thumbs-up and the little Thacian woman nodded to Valon and Reeves sighed and switched on the radio. He adjusted the frequency and winced in anticipation as he keyed the mic.

"Pirate Base, this is Pirate One, come in, over." He looked to Wash and shrugged. "Cross your fingers."

"Why should he cross his fingers?" Valon asked, squinting at Reeves.

"For luck," Wash supplied. "Like when you guys make the sign of the horns." He'd seen them do it and assumed it was done for the same reason other cultures on Earth did it, to avert bad luck. Valon snorted a humorless laugh.

"We make the sign of the horns to keep away the demons. Obviously, it hasn't been working."

"Pirate One, this is Pirate Base." The radio's speaker crackled to life and everyone lurched toward the worktable as if they were vying to be the one to reply. "Over."

"Base, we have positive ignition on the device," Reeves reported, sitting on the edge of the table. "Objective accomplished, no casualties. Over."

"Copy that, good job, One." A pause. "Did you locate our prodigal? Over."

Warmth filled Wash's face as he realized Dos Santos was talking about him. Reeves shot him a grin.

"That's affirmative, Base. He's back on the team. Over."

"Well, I did leave that up to you, One," Dos Santos acknowledged, as if he would have made a different call. "Tell him we returned his rental car, but he'd better not set foot in Marion County again unless he wants to see the inside of a jail cell. Over."

Shaw's laugh was the bray of a jackass, and the warrant officer made no attempt to conceal it. Wash and Reeves both glared at him.

"Copy that. We have contact with the locals and they want a repeat performance with a different target. *Several* different targets...Including the enemy strongholds they've been using to hit us. Over."

A longer pause this time, stretching into almost a minute, and Wash looked between Reeves and Valon, wondering if the connection had been lost or if Dos Santos had hung up on them for suggesting something so idiotic.

"I copy that, One," the colonel finally replied, hesitance in his voice. "That's going to take some arranging, but I just received an indication from higher that it's not impossible. How would you scout the targets? Over."

"The locals have volunteered to help us in that. Pirate team will be staying on this side and using one of their transports, laying comm relays along the way. The... devices need to be calibrated to follow the relays, and then we'll guide them to the final targets with the laser designator. The upshot is, if we can locate the active sites, we can shut down, or at least slow down the incursions back home. Over."

"I copy. I'll run it up the flagpole and see if I can get a salute, but indications are positive. Higher is very pleased both with the results and the lack of casualties. I'll get back with you in less than twenty-four hours. Over."

"Roger," Reeves said, something of a relieved sigh making its way into his reply. "Pirate One, out."

Wash pumped a fist, unable to keep his enthusiasm in check.

"Yes!" Reeves cocked an eyebrow at him and Shaw chuckled, but Wash refused to be cowed, throwing his hands up. "You guys know what this means, right? We can finally start killing off the Hive Mind!"

"How do you figure?" Shaw asked, frowning in confusion.

"Yeah," Reeves agreed, shaking his head. "Even a nuke isn't going to be enough to take out one of the hives, not unless we get dead lucky and the gate is right in the middle of it, like on Hades."

"I think I see what you're saying, Wash," Valon put in, but she fell silent, allowing him to complete his thought.

"It's those worker drones," Wash explained, pacing around the communications room, a radio shack filled with electronics equipment and what looked to him like computer servers. "The Hive Mind needs them to gather food... it's immortal, sure, like one of those giant slime molds you read about that live under the ground, but it still has to *eat*, and the drones gather biological material to process and feed to it. We can slaughter demons all fucking day long and the Hive Mind'll never notice, but we get rid of enough of the workers, the hive *will* starve. We might never be able to kill all of the hives, but if we shut down enough of them, the thing is going to start thinking about its own survival."

"Maybe for the first time since it went to war with the others of its kind," Valon agreed, clasping her hands in front of her chest. "This could be the chance we've been looking for. We've constantly been on the defensive, but with your weapons and our knowledge of the gates, we could go on the offensive, finally." The woman seemed as enthused as Wash, and the others were nodding now, slowly becoming convinced.

"We could take the heat off our European allies," Reeves suggested. "That would definitely make the White House happy. And maybe offer to do the same for the Russians and Chinese… *if* they agree to start behaving."

"Shit," Shaw drawled, making a sour face. "I say let 'em nuke themselves to cinders, then launch a few of our own to shift the rubble."

"Which is why you'll never be anything but a door-kicker, Vic," Reeves told him to a chorus of chuckles, Wash included. But another thought struck him, one that stole his enthusiasm and wiped the smile from his face.

"What about Jimmy?" he asked. "You heard his warning. The Hive Mind knows what he knows, knows about our weapons. Are we worried about that at all?"

Reeves brows crunched together, and he was silent for a beat as he considered it.

"I'm worried," he finally said, "but not worried enough to sit around and do nothing. Valon, if the word comes down that we're doing this, we're going to need a transport with gunship escorts. Can you swing that?"

"You're going to need more than that," she told him. "Many of the paths to the Beast Worlds will be through shielded gates. You'll need someone authorized to open them, which is a responsibility not given to many."

"Who can do that for us?" Reeves asked her, but Wash wouldn't have had to, as well as he knew the woman. Valon smiled.

"Me, of course. You think I'd let you go do this without me?"

———

"That was a lot faster than I expected," Wash confessed, checking the bolt of the SIG M5. "I mean, considering we're talking about Washington."

Reeves snorted a laugh, loading 6.8mm rounds into a magazine.

"Yeah, DC can be glacially slow most of the time, but this is a no-lose situation. What's the worst that can happen if this all goes to shit?" Reeves gestured expansively with the partially full mag. "They lose twelve guys and a handful of modified Tomahawks and no one outside the Pentagon and the White House ever knows it happened. But if it all works, they eliminate an existential threat and can hold that over everyone's head for years."

"I'm just glad they dropped a resupply through the gate," Flanders said, dropping another ammo box for his machine gun into his backpack. "I know the Thacians offered to arm us with their shit, but I'd rather stick with something I know."

"You'd have sex with that thing, Flanders," Nyland accused, barking a laugh, "if only the hole in the barrel was a little smaller."

"She's been more reliable than my ex-wife," Flanders shot back.

The team had been quartered in an unoccupied Venator barracks, bare and white and unadorned, reminding Wash of the base where his National Guard unit held their annual training every summer. Except it smelled better. The laughter of the team echoed hollowly off the wooden interior, the only furniture to interrupt it the metal-frame cots they'd slept on last night.

Wash knew what Flanders meant though. The Thacian carbine had been effective and accurate, but he felt better with the M5 in his hands. It had the benefit of familiarity. The cargo drop had also included a set of ENVG-Bs for him, and he'd had a nightmare last night that the Defense Department had decided to deduct the cost of the rifle he'd had destroyed on the active site from his salary and ordered him back to the worlds he'd traveled through to find his night vision goggles.

He sighed, tapping a loaded mag against his Kevlar before he tucked it into a chest pouch. This wasn't the Wyoming guard anymore. Delta went through high-dollar equipment faster than a CSU college student went through Daddy's money.

The door to the barracks banged open and Valon walked through with Marcos at her heels.

"Hey, manners!" Shaw objected, miming covering himself. "What if we'd been naked or something?"

"It's nothing I haven't seen before," Valon assured him. "Except probably larger."

A chorus of hoots, and Shaw responded by shooting them all a bird. Wash joined the laughter, although a flush of instinctive embarrassment sent heat through his ears.

"Gentlemen," Marcos interrupted, "and I use the term loosely, the transport is ready for you to board."

"The gunships are already in the air," Valon added. She was as geared up as any of the Delta soldiers, decked out in body armor from head to toe, a carbine hanging off her shoulder. Marcos was a stark contrast, still unarmed and dressed in the Thacian equivalent of Class-Bs. "We'll be heading through one of the shielded gates in the primary field outside the city, one that was sealed because it leads to a world with a connection to a Beast World. This one was sealed off decades ago, but the records say that the Beast World gate is a good distance from the connecting portal… at least twenty miles." She shrugged. "The demons may or may not be occupying that world now, but if they are, we'll have to fight our way through them. And if they have spikers, we may have to go to ground and emplace the relays on foot."

"You trying to scare us?" Shaw wondered. "We've spent the last few months carrying fucking nuclear warheads on foot with nothing to guide us but our Goddamned noses."

"Then you should be perfect for this mission," Valon said, jerking a thumb over her shoulder. "Let's move it out."

"Come on, guys," Shaw said, waving everyone toward the door. "Time to take this fight to the bad guys."

Wash grabbed his helmet and pack and moved to the exit just behind Reeves, so when Marcos paused the master sergeant with a hand on his shoulder, Wash heard his low, nearly whispered words.

"I'll tell you the truth, Reeves, I'm troubled by this plan. Not enough to advise against it, but enough that it kept me awake last night. The Hive Mind's greatest weakness has always been its overconfidence. I fear we are beginning to make the same mistake."

"Prefect Marcos," Reeves replied, smiling wryly, "if I've given you the impression that I have an overabundance of confidence about *anything* after spending the last few months hopping from one planet to the other, fighting actual bug-eyed monsters, then I apologize. It's more like I'm desperately clinging to the one thing we've done that's actually worked."

"You pushed this plan through the Senate, Prefect," Valon pointed out, still standing in the door, her expression troubled. "Why would you do that if you didn't think it was the right thing?"

Marcos sighed, the stiffness Wash had noticed in his spine when they'd first met seeming to melt away.

"I suppose because I'm just as guilty of grasping at straws as any other drowning man." He offered Reeves a hand. "From what I've seen, this is how your people offer a wish of good luck."

"It is," Reeves agreed, shaking Marcos' hand. "And I'll take all the luck I can get."

"And *you*," Marcos said, spearing Wash with a glare. The corner of his mouth turned up and he shook the younger man's hand. "You've been stranded with Valon twice now with no other help, and both of you have managed to keep the other alive. Can I count on you to do the same this time?"

"I don't need anyone to protect me, Prefect," Valon insisted, but Wash noticed that when she glanced at him, it wasn't with annoyance but with fondness… and for some reason, that scared him.

"We all need someone to protect us, child," Marcos said, waving his hand dismissively. "Whether it is a comrade or simply the gods. A wise warrior turns down help from neither."

28

"What the hell are these things made out of?" Wash asked, watching in wonder as the shield over the gate winked open like a camera iris.

He'd somehow scored a seat close to the cockpit in the transport this time, and since he was right next to Valon, he had to assume it was her doing.

"Tungsten," she told him, then arched an eyebrow. "It's incredibly expensive and hard to obtain, but nothing the Hive Mind can muster will break through it."

One of the gunships went through first, the image of the thing wavering as it passed through the gate. Valon's eyes narrowed, her jaw clenching as she watched the Venator attack aircraft enter the portal. Wash had spent a grand total of five or six days with the woman, but he thought he knew her well enough to say she was worried about the crew, about her people. She was the kind of officer his father had spoken of with respect, the kind who cared more about their troops than they did about their reputation or their career.

"Funny," Shaw said, "that this Hive Mind thing never figured out shit like heavy industry or nukes or anything."

"It manufactures biological robots," Reeves pointed out, "and big jelly monsters that can launch anti-aircraft and anti-armor missiles they grow on their damned skin. That's different, but not inferior."

"*I* say it's inferior." Shaw waved at the aircraft around him. "It's fucking inefficient. We can launch a nuke and it'll blow up thousands of those demon things. They have to kill each of us individually. That takes longer, and the only way they've been able to get away with it is because there's a shitload more of them than there are of the Thacians."

A crackling, staticky voice in Thacian came through the cockpit speakers and Valon blew out a relieved breath.

"The other side is clear," she told Wash and the others. "We're going through."

The order to the transport pilot was curt, and the man accepted it with a nod. Wash's teeth went on edge as the whine of the rotors rose an octave and the aircraft urged forward. He was sure the heavy troop transport was going to be just a hair too wide to fit through the gate, or that the pilot would drift just a few feet too far to one side or the other and the edge of the gate would rip one side of the aircraft clear off. It would be a damned silly way to die after all he'd gone through.

But the pilot was a professional, and they slid through with just the slightest hint of turbulence, the difference between air pressure and ambient temperature from one side of the gate to the other. Though the differences weren't as great as Wash had expected. After what Valon had told them, he thought the world through the shielded gate would be a wasteland, something like Hades, devastated by decades of Hive Mind occupation, devoid of any life.

The morning sun painted golden highlights on a lush, green forest that could have been anywhere from northern China to the Pacific Northwest all the way up to Vancouver, but wasn't. Valon seemed just as surprised as he was, staring at the living world beneath them with no sign of the touch of the Hive Mind, no demons, no ransacking worker drones.

"Are we sure this is the right planet?" Wash asked her.

"The gates don't move. This shield was put in place nearly a century ago and the records are clear. The demons were coming through here." Valon shook her head. "I've never known them to abandon a world once they owned it. They strip it bare, take every possible resource, and build a new hive. Once they own a planet, they never leave."

"Until now," Wash said.

"The nearest gate is forty-eight miles south by southwest," Reeves announced, holding up the tracker so Valon could see it. "Is that the one we're looking for?"

"It's the gate the demons came through," Valon said cautiously, as though she was afraid to commit to anything more certain. "But I think we'll have to investigate it when we arrive." She relayed the coordinates to the pilot and the transport lurched off to their left.

Wash frowned at the terrain below them. There was something familiar about it, though it was hard to say seeing it from a few hundred feet up.

"Hey, boss," he said to Reeves, "have we been here before? I swear I've seen this area before."

"Looks like every other temperate rain forest I've ever seen," Reeves said with a shrug.

"Glad we caught it on a sunny day," Shaw commented. "Nothing I like better than flying low-altitude in a fucking thunderstorm."

"I know what it reminds *me* of," Valon said, nudging Wash. "The place where we found the Archaion."

Something clicked into place behind Wash's eyes, and the view shifted into a familiar pattern.

"It *is*," he insisted, pointing at the cockpit windscreen. "That's where we are."

"How the hell can you be sure of that?" Reeves asked. "It's a whole planet… you saw one small part of it for a couple days."

"I don't know how," Wash admitted. "I just have the feeling that this is the same place. Not just the same planet, but right around the gate we went through."

"That gate went to Florida," Reeves said, "not an active site."

"The gate back to Earth was one of the new ones," Valon said. "The ones you…"

Her mouth snapped shut and the hackles went up on the back of Wash's neck. He glanced sideways at Reeves, wondering if the man had noticed.

"The ones you discovered on your world," Valon corrected herself. Reeves' eyes narrowed, but he said nothing. "And it was in a remote area, not something they would have stumbled upon accidentally. But if the gate to the Beast World was the one we came through, then it would already be closed."

"Oh, great," Flanders muttered. "Then this whole thing is a waste of time. Brass is gonna love this shit. Wonder how much those fancy, specially made Tomahawks cost?"

"Hold on," Valon said, pulling out her tablet, scrolling through map layouts. Wash leaned against her armrest, looking over her shoulder. The map might have been made by an unfamiliar culture, but it looked very much like the conventional topographic model used by the US military. Valon tapped on a red arrow displayed at the right edge of the screen. "This is the estimated position of the Beast World gate, according to the records. Look here." She held the screen up so Reeves could see it as well. "This map shows it being in the middle of a river delta. The gate we came out through from the Beast World was in a pond at the edge of a forest."

Gates of Hope

"Two active site gates on the same planet, that close together?" Reeves asked. "And the demons haven't overrun the place?"

Wash shared a look with Valon, and he was sure they were both thinking the same thing.

"The Archaion?"

"I think," she said, "that we should try to talk to them again."

Valon had expected the Archaion to scatter at the approach of the aircraft, to run screaming into the woods like the primitive tribe they appeared to be. That didn't happen. Instead, the Archaion tribe stood and watched as she descended the boarding ramp of the transport, as if this sort of thing happened every day and was barely a passing curiosity.

"Holy God," Victor Shaw murmured, coming down behind her and Wash, just ahead of Reeves. "It's fucking *cat* people. Cat people, man. And I thought bug-eyed monsters were the strangest things I'd ever see. Brian, I gotta get some PTSD meds for this shit. I've shot and been shot at by assholes on every continent except Antarctica, but this is just too much."

"Shut up, Vic," Reeves said quietly, as if the words were a long-ingrained habit by now, although from the expression on his face, Reeves was just as astounded as Shaw.

Valon scanned the crowd of Archaion, noting there were more of them this time than she'd seen gathered in one place when they'd been here before. More males, more children out, watching silently, even the infants barely making a sound.

There. The matriarch stood behind the others, watching the outsiders, watching Valon. It was hard to read the face of a non-human, but Valon would have been willing to swear to the gods that the old female was disappointed with her somehow.

"I know you can understand me, Mother," Valon told the

297

matriarch in Thacian. She waited for the female to reply, but the matriarch said nothing, simply stared at her with those slitted eyes, disapproving. Valon sighed and motioned at the Americans, who had disembarked from the transport and fallen into a loose defensive perimeter. "We've come to this place because the demons came through here long ago. We're looking for the place they came through back then, on a river delta."

She paused again, and again, there was no reply. Valon bit down on the impatience roiling in her stomach.

"Are you sure they speak your language?" Reeves asked her, and though he kept his voice low, Valon wanted to snap at him, like somehow him speaking had been a sign of disrespect for the matriarch.

"The older one did last time," Wash answered for her, perhaps sensing that Valon wasn't in the mood to be interrupted. "She took us to the gate through to Tampa, and it sounded like she even spoke a couple words in Thacian."

Valon reined her temper in and tried to make the mental shift from English back to Thacian.

"Mother, you had two gates here that lead to Hive Mind worlds. How have they not overwhelmed you and stripped this place of every resource? How have you lived here all this time?"

Nothing. No response from any of them except blank stares, unless the soft cooing of one of the infants counted. It was eerie. They didn't even speak to each other, though they had when she and Wash had stayed with them. Frustration tried to force her to give up, but embarrassment insisted she keep trying.

"We need to know if there's something we can do to close these gates," Valon insisted. "If not, these men are going to have to use a weapon against them, and when they do, there's the possibility it could harm you, could harm *all* of you, everyone in this area." She sighed, tugging at her hair like she was ten years old and back in algebra class. "If there's anything else we can do, you have to tell us!"

The matriarch still didn't speak, but she strode past Valon and straight up to Victor Shaw, the closest of the Americans to her. Valon didn't completely understand the American rank structure, but the tall, rangy man was some sort of in-between rank as close as she could tell, something below most of the officers but above everyone else... except Reeves. Shaw was subordinate to Reeves, but she had the sense that was more because of the sergeant's position rather than his rank. Which meant that Reeves was the only one who could tell Shaw to shut up and get away with it.

"Why's this cat lady eyeing me?" the older man asked, looking as if he wanted to take a step back but didn't want to seem cowardly. "This is freaking me out, boss. She looks like a girl I met at this convention in Atlanta once. She was one of those furries, you know what I mean? Thought she was a cat, and you won't believe how she pinned that damned tail on..."

The matriarch was less than a long step away from Shaw now, yet still the man didn't try to avoid her, clearly not regarding the frail, wizened female as a threat. Until she snatched the rifle out of his hands with blinding speed and pushed the barrel into his chest. Shaw's eyes went wide, and there was the space of less than a second before a dozen voices began shouting at the matriarch to drop the gun, their big, heavy rifles pointed at her... some of them. These men were well-trained and only the ones who could shoot at the matriarch without hitting one of their own actually had their rifles raised, the others merely holding them at the ready.

"Don't shoot!" Valon shouted, pitching her voice to carry above their bellowing demands. She rushed up and interposed herself between Reeves and the matriarch. "Wait, don't shoot!"

The matriarch stared into Shaw's eyes for what seemed like an eternity but was probably less than ten seconds before she tossed his rifle on the ground. It clattered to the dirt and the old female turned and walked away from the Americans, ignoring all the weapons still pointed her way. She tried to pass by Valon without pausing, but the Venator had enough and grabbed the old female by the upper arm, spinning the Archaion to face her.

"Can't you understand that I'm trying to protect you and your people?" Valon demanded, nearly screaming at the matriarch.

"So quick to trust in weapons." Finally, the female spoke, the words barely intelligible. "Weapons can be used by anyone, by any side." She made a sound that might have been a cat coughing up a hairball and pulled her arm out of Valon's grasp with deceptive strength. "Do not be concerned for *us*."

The matriarch kept walking, and as she did, the entire village turned and walked with her, withdrawing from the landing zone, back through the village. They didn't stop there, every last one of them disappearing beneath the banks of the river, filing down the trail that ran beside it. Valon watched them go, and so did the Americans, none of them saying a word until all the Archaion were gone from view.

Wash shook his head, mouth working but no words coming out for a moment until he finally found his voice.

"What the hell did she say?"

"We're on our own," Valon said, still staring after the Archaion. "And so are they."

29

Jimmy Bonner screamed.

He shouldn't have been able to scream. He had no body, no physical existence. All that was left of James Bonner was a collection of memories living in the scattered brain cells of the Hive Mind, yet somehow the thing was able to inflict pain on those paltry remains.

Maybe, he thought, it was simply the *memory* of pain, replayed over and over, the worst pain he'd experienced. Not all of it was physical. There was the time he'd realized that the boy he'd considered his best friend in middle school had only hung out with him because Jimmy's parents had money and would take him out on their boat or buy him gifts. There was his first real girlfriend, Trish, who'd broken up with him after his father had sued hers over a property line.

But some of it *was* physical pain. The time he'd broken his ankle in a fall while hiking with his father and then the man had forced him to walk the three miles back to their truck. The time he'd burned his hand setting a bag of dog shit on fire on Wash Williams' doorstep. The whiplash of the impact when he'd driven his truck into a tree after the first time he'd gone drinking with his friends in high school.

The bullet passing through his brain when Brenda had shot him.

"You thought I wouldn't see," the Hive Mind taunted him. "You thought you could use me to warn them and I wouldn't notice. I am everywhere. I see everything. You're a part of me, the smallest, most worthless part, a toy I keep for my own entertainment. It's almost as amusing to allow you to believe that you still possess free will and self-determination as it is to torture you with your own pitiful past."

"If I don't have free will," Jimmy ground out, clenching muscles he didn't have to keep coherent against the wave of pain and despair, "then how did I take over your drone slaves?"

Why am I arguing with the thing? What does it matter?

The question seemed to upset the Hive Mind, and the pain intensified.

"I *let* you have enough freedom to make you believe you're still a sentient being, you worthless cretin. Do you think it matters if you tell the humans that I have your knowledge? Do you think they'll act differently? More cautiously?" The Hive Mind wasn't human, but it had apparently learned something of them since its interactions. It laughed. "If anything, they'll rush in headlong, desperate to act before I have the chance to use the knowledge I've gained. You've acted just as I wished, and as a reward, I will allow you to continue to exist."

"You call this a *reward*?" Jimmy snapped back, and the anger overwrote the pain for a moment.

"You can tell me honestly, human, that you would prefer nonexistence? I know you can't... I can read your thoughts. They're part of me, as are you."

"Why are you punishing yourself then? You're like some

stupid-ass teenager cutting himself because he doesn't like his parents."

"You're right." The Hive Mind sounded as if it had actually considered the issue. "Internal pain will accomplish nothing other than inuring you to it. What's needed to teach you your place is an *external* lesson. Hurting someone you care about."

"Good luck with that." Jimmy hadn't meant to sound so bitter, though in retrospect, what difference did it make? "There's no one left."

"You say that, yet I know more than you do that it's a lie. The female called Brenda is still heavy in your thoughts."

Jimmy snorted.

"Sure. The woman who hooked up with my worst enemy and shot me in the fucking head."

"And yet you don't blame her. Perhaps you've grown from the experience of dying. I've come to understand the human concept of love, as ridiculous as it is, and though you lack the body chemistry that is so very much a part of that emotion, you're still nostalgic for it. And you've come to attach this nostalgia to Brenda Sands."

Jimmy was about to reflexively deny it but decided there was no point. The Hive Mind wasn't lying about knowing his thoughts, though he had his doubts that the thing could actually interpret his emotions.

"What are you going to do?" he demanded. "You think you can threaten her? I know you don't have access to any gates in the United States anymore. They've shut them all down."

"For now, James Bonner. For now."

"There it is," Wash said. It was redundant, inane, but he needed to hear *someone* talk, even if it was just himself.

The whole bird had been quiet as a grave ever since they'd left the Archaion village, all of them lost in their own thoughts. His were bewildered and muddled, uncomprehending. Why would the Archaion act that way? They'd been friendly, if inscrutable, when Valon and he had been there, had fed them and sheltered them and even led them to the gate back to Earth eventually. The matriarch had acted as if she was angry with them, disappointed somehow.

Maybe she hadn't wanted them to come back? The thing that wouldn't let his thoughts rest was the idea that maybe she was right. Maybe they were making a mistake and should leave this place alone.

The appearance of the gate had put those thoughts to rest. It stood waiting for them, dark and menacing and out of place sitting in the center of the river delta. The delta wasn't large, reflective of the narrow size of the river itself, just a half a mile or so across, narrowing to a point where the freshwater emptied into the salt, the bay enclosed on the other two sides by rocky promontories. White birds that could have been seagulls circled high, one of them diving now and again to pick up a meal, but none came anywhere near the gate, as if they could sense its menace.

Yet for all the ominous foreboding the gate possessed, nothing came through it, and there was no swathe of devastation surrounding it as evidence of past battles.

"That's weird as shit," Reeves said, the tone and the words out of character for him, though Wash couldn't blame him for it. "Where are they? Why haven't they come through?"

"Maybe," Wash guessed, grasping at any theory he could come up with, "we already nuked it? Maybe the connection went through a hive we buried under rock when we hit some other part of it?"

"That's not a bad idea," Reeves admitted, though Valon made

no comment at all. Reeves motioned at her to get her attention. "Take us down. We need to send a drone through."

Valon snapped an order at the pilot and the transport descended quickly, leaving Wash's stomach several hundred feet up, and not just from the precipitous drop. He'd faced enough of the alien demons in the last few months to not let the idea of fighting them again panic him, but there was something different about this gate. The Hive Mind hadn't come through again, even though there was an outbound gate to Earth, and the question of why was more frightening than the actual threat of the demons.

Wash couldn't shake a paranoid certainty that something strange and awful was going to storm through the gate the second they touched down, though he couldn't imagine anything stranger or more awful than the demons. Nothing disturbed the shimmering darkness though, as the ramp lowered and Nyland walked down carrying the heavy, plastic drone case.

Wash grabbed his rifle and followed the man, not because he particularly wanted to be out there but because he'd expect the others to do the same for him. It was still light outside, but he pulled down his ENVG-Bs to activate the link between it and the rifle's optics, and if he was being honest with himself, to create a barrier of unreality between himself and the gate. Its lines were cartoonish, the darkness less stygian through the goggles, though he still couldn't see anything through it. The goggles couldn't keep out the stench though. Dead fish and brackish, swampy water, and the ocean. Shallow, Wash judged just by the smell and the sound.

The drone looked off-the-shelf and probably was, since Delta could pretty much requisition whatever they wanted, a quadcopter with a mounted camera. Nyland held the control pad in one hand, tossed the drone into the air with the other, the rotors screaming as the thing jumped upward, well above the top of the gate. Nyland cursed and his thumbs stroked the touch-screen of the control pad, bringing the drone lower, ducking it through the gate just a few feet from the upper edge.

Wash flinched as the thing passed through, as if the passage would cause some devastating backlash, but there was nothing.

"Getting a signal," Nyland announced. His own control tablet had the picture, but so did the one Reeves was holding, and Wash pushed up his goggles and looked over the master sergeant's shoulder at the feed from the drone.

He frowned. On the other side was an arctic wasteland, snow blowing wildly from one drift to another, the sun low in the sky over distant mountains painted in solid white. Not a dead world though. Thick pine forests rose majestic in the middle distance, the green of their boughs peeking through the frosting. The sky was clear, the snow from storms days distant. Something moved on the ground at the edge of the drone's view, and Nyland grunted, bringing the quad-copter lower.

It was a rabbit. Not some alien creature, not a Hive Mind creation, just a rabbit.

"What the fuck?" Wash asked. He didn't elaborate, but he didn't have to. Reeves was shaking his head.

"That's not an active site."

"This makes no sense," Valon objected, her tone plaintive, sounding unsure of herself for perhaps the first time since Wash had met her. "Unless the records are faulty... but I've never known them to make a mistake when it came to the gates."

"Hey, boss," Nyland said, "check that out." He adjusted the course of the drone, taking it higher, drifting it to the left. The view skewed through the rolling, snow-covered hills into a draw. Something glinted, not reflecting the last rays of the dying day, but instead shining from within. Valon pushed Wash aside to get a better view at the tablet's screen.

"That's a gate."

"That might explain it," Wash said softly. A half a dozen sets of eyes turned his way and Wash gulped but pressed on. "Look at this place." He nodded at the icy terrain. "Those demons, I haven't seen them anywhere cold. Every active site we've been to has been pretty hot, hasn't it?"

"The Hive Mind needs warmth to thrive," Valon confirmed. "That's why the hives are always underground. The demons can survive in the cold, but they don't spend much time there, and the workers never bother to scavenge there."

"Your ancestors said the demons came through the gate that led to the Archaion village," Wash went on, nodding. "They didn't follow them through, just put up a shield, right?" At Valon's nod, he continued, though he could see understanding crystalizing in Reeves' eyes. "The demons came through, like scouting or something, but once they got driven out and the gate to Thacia was closed, they didn't bother trying to come back through to the Archaion planet because this place is covered in ice."

"Yeah, I can see that," Reeves said.

"Whaddya wanna do, boss?" Shaw asked, sounding more bored and impatient than fascinated. "Do we turn back, try another gate?"

"No," Reeves decided. "Nyland, bring back the drone. Perez, set up the relay. We're going through."

30

"Yeah, there it is," Reeves said, nodding in satisfaction. It was cold as hell outside the transport, his face going numb with every gust of the wind through the hills, but he didn't let it show.

The view on the screen wasn't of some icy mountain pass this time, wasn't anything as unexpected as the Archaion world. It was an active site... a *very* active one. There was very little native life left in the scene on the tablet's screen, just the devastated, scorched dirt they were used to seeing on Hive Mind worlds. The gate was outdoors, not squirreled away inside the hive, but the nest was within sight of the drone, perhaps a mile away, dug into the side of a rocky outcropping like a termite mound.

Demons swarmed out of the entrance to the mound, their movements jerky and unnatural in the night-vision filters of the drone camera, forming into rows like toy soldiers, preparing to go... somewhere. Spikers stomped among them, tails sweeping back and forth like some artist's rendition of a stegosaurus... assuming the artist was high on crack. Lots of spikers and something else, something he hadn't seen before. They were just as huge as the spikers, but while the spikers were bulbous, jiggling with each movement, these things were cadaverous, spider-legged, skinny and cylindrical. To describe them as spiders would have been inexact though. Their upper torsos were hinged, upright, their upper sets of limbs articulated... and dangling from them were billowing sheets of what looked like webbing. Reeves shuddered, and he wasn't sure it was the chill wind.

"You know what the hell those things are?" he asked Valon, holding the screen where she could see it.

"I've never even heard of anything like that," she said, eyes wide, shoulders shaking. She wasn't dressed for this weather, but then, none of them were. Of everyone, Wash seemed to show the least effect from the cold. Wyoming boy, of course. "There's nothing in the records, I'm sure of it. These are something new."

"Why would something like the Hive Mind," Wash said, "that's been around like tens of thousands of years and never changed the way it did business ,all of a sudden create some new monster?" He met Reeves' eyes. "There's only one new thing that's happened to it."

"Us," Reeves agreed. "It has to be getting ready to go after us somewhere." He made an instant decision, because what other sort was there? "Perez, we need the final relay on the other side of that gate." He squeezed his eyes shut, debating this next part. It was something he wanted badly to do himself, but also something he knew he shouldn't, as the team's leader. "I need two people to go through and paint the target with the laser designator. We need that Tomahawk right through the hive entrance."

Valon glanced at him sharply.

"There are tens of thousands of them and they're on full alert. If you're seen, they'll be all over you before you can return back through the gate."

"They will," he acknowledged. "Volunteers only."

"I operate the designator," Nyland said, jaw set stubbornly, though his attention was still on the drone controls.

"We need you to operate the drone, Tony." Reeves shook his head. "Any one of us can use the designator."

"I got it," Shaw said, yelling the words over the wind, then jogging back up the ramp.

"I'll go with him." It was Wash. Of course it was.

The kid's eyes were hidden behind his night-vision goggles, but Reeves knew what he'd see behind them. Wash wanted to pay Reeves back for breaking Valon out. Reeves wanted to tell him he didn't need to do it, but that would have been unfair to the others, as well as to Wash. Reeves just nodded.

"I got it," Shaw said, holding up the case on the way down the ramp. "Let's get this over with."

Reeves got the thumbs-up from Perez that the relay was operational and tuned his radio to the frequency. It would be bounced back through the last three gates all the way to Las Vegas, to Dos Santos. And probably from him directly to the POTUS, or at least the SecDef.

"Pirate Base, this is Pirate One, you copy?"

It took a moment. Reeves didn't know what time it was back in Vegas, but the colonel might have been sleeping, or eating, or taking a dump. Whoever was monitoring the comms would go get him rather than answering themselves, because if there was anything in the history of the world more top-secret than this, Reeves hadn't heard of it.

Shaw and Wash were already walking toward the gate, the rest of the team setting up a perimeter, the two gunships still on overwatch, buzzing a few hundred feet overhead in gentle arcs.

"Pirate One, this is Base, I copy, over." Dos Santos sounded exhausted, probably running around like a madman, trying to organize all the moving parts for this operation.

"We're in position. Have discovered enemy active site with troop buildup. Sending images now, over."

The tablet was hooked into the communications network,

though Reeves wasn't enough of a tech nerd to understand how they were able to send the picture files back through it. He dragged the files into the folder to be sent and waited for the progress bar to creep toward one hundred percent.

The pause between completion and Dos Santos' reply was undoubtedly filled with cursing. The colonel was too professional to let it go out over an open signal.

"Message received, One. Do you have any idea of the purpose of these... previously unknown entities? Over."

It was a dumb question. If Reeves had known, he would already have told the man.

"Negative, Base. They're obviously prepping for something. I doubt we have much time. Recommend immediate launch. Over."

And there it was. Reeves didn't have the final call, but he'd made the field recommendation to launch a nuclear missile.

"I copy, One." Weariness dragged down Dos Santos's voice, perhaps from the same realization. "Passing it up to higher. Will get back to you shortly. Over."

"Pirate One, out."

Reeves let his hand fall away from the mic switch, watching Shaw and Wash plodding through the snow to the gate. Wash led the way, rifle at his shoulder, and both men disappeared in an instant, leaving a weight on Reeves' shoulders that made asking for a nuclear launch seem light by comparison.

"Goddammit, Brenda, listen to me!"

Brenda Sands' eyes popped open... yet they didn't. She knew she was in a dream, waking up in a bed that wasn't hers. It was the one she'd shared with Jimmy at the house his parents had built for him on a corner of their property. It looked the same as it had months ago, the last time she'd been there before she'd moved her things out, but her quilt still hung from the headboard, her paintings still on the wall. The haze of unreality left no doubt where she was, and she resisted the urge to sit up, to look around, yet she seemed to lack control over her own actions.

It wasn't like before, when Brenda had known she was in charge. Something... *someone* was in control of this place, this experience. She could feel the strength like a hand pressing down on her. The strength coalesced into a figure at the head of the bed... a figure she knew very well.

"Jimmy," she breathed, eyes going wide at the sight of him.

He didn't look like he had the last time she'd seen him, lacked the maniacal tinge to his expression, the hollowed-out cheeks and circles around his eyes. This Jimmy looked like the man she'd been engaged to, right down to the clothes he'd been wearing the day he'd proposed.

"You're dead," she insisted. "I killed you..."

"I deserved it," he admitted, taking a step forward.

Brenda shrank away from the specter, hugging her knees to her chest, her back against the headboard.

"I won't hurt you," Jimmy assured her, raising his hands, palms out. "I'm not really here... I'm only able to talk to you in your subconscious."

"How are you able to talk at *all*?" Brenda demanded.

"What's left of me is part of the Hive Mind," he explained. "And I can talk to you because..." He blinked and shook his head. "I'm not sure. I think it has something to do with the time you spent with me in the hive, on Hades. We're connected somehow, and I need to talk to you. I tried to warn Wash and the Hive Mind found out... it wants to punish me, and since I don't really exist except as memories inside its head, the only way it can do that is to try to hurt you."

"But Wash told me his team closed off all the gates to the

Hive Mind in the states," she said, and hated herself a little for the desperate hope in the words.

"That's what I thought too. But the Hive Mind is planning something." Jimmy paced, which seemed like a strange thing for a ghost to do, and Brenda wondered why he would need to walk at all in a dream. "I tried to find out what, but it doesn't think like a human... I think that's why it can't keep track of what I'm doing as close as it would like, because trying to interpret my thoughts is like reading a different language. That's the same problem I'm having."

This version of Jimmy was intense, thoughtful, everything she'd loved about the man, and Brenda suddenly remembered why she'd fallen for him years ago, before the jealousy and the constant clashes with his parents. He'd been a different man in college, far away from them. Brenda shook her head, dragging her mind back to the problem.

Was this real? That was the number one question. This could be nothing more than a nightmare. She'd had enough of those since Hades... although, if this *was* Jimmy, and he *was* telling the truth, then maybe that was the reason for them.

The second question was, if this was real, what did it mean?

"You think it's actually coming after me?" Brenda asked, loathe as she was to converse with the phantom, since talking to it meant that it was real. She swung her imaginary legs off the imaginary bed and stood up, facing Jimmy. She was dressed in sleep clothes, a tank top and shorts, her feet bare and cold on the wood floor. "Maybe it's just saying it to torment you. Maybe it can't get here at all and it just wants you to panic."

"Maybe," Jimmy assented. He took a step toward her but stopped abruptly, eyes darting to the floor, as if remembering how they'd parted. "But like I said, I don't know that it has a firm enough grasp on human thought to know that would work. Either way, you should get out of here. Get as far away as possible, and do it now." He shook his head. "I've got a really bad feeling about this, Brenda. I already fucked everything up. I don't want to drag you down with me."

"Okay," she said, trying to sort through her options. "I can go to…"

"*No!*" he snapped, raising a hand. "Don't tell me. Whatever I know, it knows. Just go."

Brenda nodded, then remembered that their connection was mental, however that worked, and he might be able to read her thoughts. She banished the train of reasoning she'd been heading down from her mind, made her thoughts a blank, white page, and concentrated on nothingness.

"I don't know if I'll be able to talk to you again," Jimmy said. He was getting paler, fading from existence like a ghost. "This has taken all the concentration I've got. Take care of yourself, Brenda. I always loved you, and I guess I always will."

Brenda froze on her reply. She didn't love him anymore, but she *wanted* to lie, wanted to tell him she did because she felt bad for him. Which was how she'd gotten herself mired in a toxic relationship originally.

"Thank you, James," she said instead. She reached for his hand, expecting hers to pass through it, but found flesh instead. Not exactly warm, but not corpse-cold either. She squeezed it. "Thanks for trying to help."

Brenda sat up in bed with a gasp, looking around in the darkness. She was back in her room, the only light coming from the clock beside the bed. She didn't even waste a second considering whether it had all been a dream. Instead, she switched on the bedside lamp, then raced to the closet and grabbed a suitcase. While she packed, she debated where to go and decided there was only one person she could ask.

Punching in the number, she tucked the phone into her shoulder while she yanked open the dresser and pulled clothes out, jamming them into the case without bothering to fold them. The phone rang but no answer until she hit voicemail. Brenda nearly hung up—no one used voicemail. But she was dealing with the military, and they did all kinds of old-fashioned, useless things because it had become habit.

"This is Master Sergeant Brian Reeves. Leave a detailed message and I'll get back to you."

"Brian, this is Brenda," she said, her voice hoarse with interrupted sleep. "I have a big problem and I have to get out of here. I don't know where else to go, but the last time I talked to you, I think you told me you were in Las Vegas, that there was a temporary base there. I'm coming there. I have to talk to someone who knows what's going on and Wash isn't here… I can't get hold of him. If you're not in Vegas, have someone meet me. You have my number."

She hung up and tossed the phone down. Pausing, she looked away from her clothes and pulled aside the window shade, sneaking a look outside. The night was deep and dark, dead quiet. Nothing moved. She grabbed the little SIG P365 from the night table and shoved it into her purse, but it seemed inadequate against the outer darkness. Brenda licked her lips and yanked open the nightstand drawer, finding the key concealed beneath some insurance paperwork and went to the closet, and the gun safe inside it.

The 12-gauge pump was heavy, awkward in her hands, but it was also loaded with three-inch magnum one-ounce lead slugs. She tossed it on the bed. Maybe she was being paranoid, but Vegas was a long way.

31

"At least it's not cold here," Wash said softly.

It was stupid to talk at all, but the ranks of demons were a good half a mile away, and none of them had shown much in the way of keen hearing since he'd been dealing with them. The demons had left this gate unguarded, as if it had been forgotten, tucked away as useless in a draw away from the hive. He couldn't see the demons from inside the narrow draw, but he could see those giant, spider-like things.

And it *was* warmer here, like on every active site they'd found so far, and dry as the high desert.

"I thought you were from Wyoming, kid," Shaw said, creeping slowly toward the end of the draw, peering off toward the hive mound. "Don't it get really cold there in the winter?"

"Sometimes. And I have a nice down jacket I wear when it does." Wash brushed snow off the top of his boots before it could melt and soak his feet. "The colonel could have sent us some cold-weather gear along with the guns and ammo."

"Goddammit," Shaw murmured, hugging the edge of the rock wall. The dirt and stone might have been black, or brown or even dark red, but Wash couldn't tell in the utter darkness. The ENVGs provided clarity and delineation, even depth perception, but there wasn't much they could do to give accurate color. "Can't get a clear look at the entrance. Really didn't want to go out in the open."

Wash trailed behind him, rifle at his shoulder, breath coming shorter than he would have liked. Maybe he just wasn't getting enough cardio, or maybe it was the sudden and drastic temperature change. *Or maybe I'm just scared shitless.*

"Yeah, I was hoping to avoid that too."

Shaw paused, pulling the laser designator and its tripod out of the case and assembling the thing with deft, practiced motions.

"Why'd you volunteer to come with me?" Shaw didn't look up from his task, not that it would have made any difference with the goggles on. "No one would have thought any less of you if you hadn't, you know."

Wash stared out at the motionless night and didn't immediately reply.

"I felt like I had some stuff to make up for," he finally told the older man. "I didn't do anything I thought was wrong, but it still felt like I'd let you guys down."

"Shit, kid," Shaw murmured, hefting the laser designator. "Ain't no one here who thinks you let anyone down. You ain't got no training and honest, once upon a time, I was thinking you didn't belong here. But you've done everything everyone asked and haven't fucked up yet, and that's more than I can say for every newbie that pops up in this unit. Come on, let's try to live through this."

Wash's first instinct would have been to low-crawl once they left the cover of the draw, but even a high-crawl would have been impossible for Shaw carrying the laser designator, so they settled on a crouching jog. Wash wanted to look at the hive mound, wanted to see when the entrance came into view so they could go to ground and not get spotted, but his job was to watch Shaw's back. Which meant watching the demons instead.

Did they think about anything? Was there any sentience at all to the things, or were they just biological robots? They didn't communicate verbally, didn't seem to have any aspirations of their own, simply shifted back and forth, their scorpion tails twisting and writhing as if searching for something to kill. There were so many he couldn't count them, more than he'd seen before, more demons than he'd seen people in one place since basic training. He wasn't good at estimation, but he figured there had to be over a hundred thousand of the demons, plus a few hundred, maybe a thousand spikers.

Only a couple dozen of the spider things though. Not that a couple dozen weren't enough to freeze his blood in his veins. And all of them seemed to be staring straight at him. That was his imagination of course. They weren't staring, because they weren't looking for enemies here... they couldn't be. They couldn't know anyone was here. That was what he kept telling himself.

"Here," Shaw said when they were about a hundred yards out of the draw, smack in the middle of the open plain in front of the mound.

"You're kidding, right?" Wash ground out, going down to one knee. "We couldn't do this from cover?"

"Nope." Shaw unfolded the tripod and set the legs into the dark and unyielding dirt and rock. "This is where we can see the entrance."

And that much was true. The entrance to the mound was blocked off by the mass of demons from this point on, leaving a narrow corridor between the draw and the entrance, over a mile away. The valley sloped downward so that just the top ten or fifteen feet of the broad entrance was actually visible from where they were, and if they moved back at all, they'd lose sight of it.

Wash licked his lips, tasting sweat, sure with each second that passed they'd be spotted.

"Come on, boss," he muttered under his breath. "Send that fucking missile."

"Pirate One, this is Pirate Base, over."

Reeves didn't jump, not *quite*, but it was only through supreme self-control. It had only been five minutes since Wash and Shaw had passed through the gate, and his eyes hadn't left the display scene from the drone camera. He'd wanted to scream at the two of them when they'd walked right into the middle of the plain, right out in front of God and everyone, but he knew Shaw wouldn't have done it unless it was the only spot with a clear view of the hive entrance.

"Base, this is One, we have personnel on the other side and we need deployment ASAP." He didn't *quite* snap at Dos Santos, but it was close. "Over," he added belatedly.

Valon turned at the words, looking expectant. She'd seemed as worried as he was about the two men. One of them at least.

"The weapon has been deployed," Dos Santos told him, calmer than Reeves was, calmer than any of them had a right to be. "We estimate delivery in fifteen minutes. Over."

Reeves stifled a curse. The missile had to have been launched from a ship off the California coast, which would mean a minimum flight time of a little over twenty minutes just to get to the Las Vegas gate. That meant they'd launched the damned missile five minutes ago and either hadn't bothered to tell Dos Santos until just now, or the colonel hadn't bothered to tell *him*. Either way, Reeves was pissed.

"Copy that. Will keep you advised as to delivery. Over."

He didn't even listen to Dos Santos signing off, already switching frequencies to Shaw.

"The missile's launched," he told the man, not bothering with radio protocols since there was absolutely no one else on either planet using radios. "ETA fifteen minutes. Can you hold out that long?"

"Well shit, Brian," Shaw replied, his voice staticky and distant, "I'm sure you'll be the first to know. I mean, we're just hanging our asses out to dry here, but you tell the colonel that I'm pleased as punch that the brass finally got around to launching the fucking thing."

Reeves snorted a laugh despite the situation. Shaw knew as well as he did that their conversation was private, and the warrant officer wasn't holding back his innate snark.

"You keep your heads down. If things turn bad, we can send the gunships through for support."

"Yeah, tell 'em to get ready. All it's gonna take is one of those damned things looking the wrong way and the Hive Mind paying attention, and we'll be bugs on a plate out here."

"Hey boss," Flanders said, "why don't a couple of us go through and stay by the gate, cover them in case they get spotted?"

Reeves glanced sidelong at the man. Flanders could have only heard his half of the conversation. The offer was tempting, but still he shook his head.

"Not yet. The more people we send through, the better chance we'll get discovered."

Valon paced back and forth, checking the drone screen over Nyland's shoulder every few steps one way, looking in the direction of the gate to the Archaion world when she walked back the other.

"I don't like this," she told Reeves.

"Yeah, I got that impression," he admitted. Reeves looked around at the others, seeing that they were far enough away not to overhear him if he kept his voice down. "You like the kid, don't you?"

She stopped in mid-step and scowled at him.

"Of course I like him. He saved my life multiple times."

Reeves chuckled. It was easy to forget that, high-tech mind-imprinting gadgets aside, the woman hadn't been raised in his culture.

"I mean, you're attracted to him," he clarified. Valon's face reddened, her teeth baring, and Reeves thought he'd broken some Thacian social more and was about to get punched in the face.

"He is betrothed to another," the woman said, her tone stiff and formal. "This is not something a respectable person would speak of."

"Sorry," Reeves said, raising a palm in surrender. "I didn't mean to pry… well, yeah, I guess I did. But I was just gonna tell you, it's okay to feel that way. He's a good kid, he's got plenty of guts and a good head on his shoulders." He shrugged. "And yeah, he's with someone else, and maybe he doesn't think of you the same way right now, but don't beat yourself up."

Her brow knitted.

"Do people in your culture beat themselves up?"

"More than you'd think."

"Hey, boss," Nyland said, a strained edge to his voice. "We got a problem."

Reeves had looked away from his tablet, but now he raised it again. The drone was wavering a little, blown side to side by the warm wind on the active site, and it took Reeves a second to compensate for the shifting image and spot what Nyland was talking about. There was a squad of demons—well, it was a group of around a dozen, and that was how *he* thought of it—running

Gates of Hope

from the rear of the huge formation up the gap where Wash and Shaw were positioned, the only clear view of the hive entrance.

"Vic, you're about to have company," Reeves said, yelling over a gust of cold wind. "A squad of enemy heading your way."

"Yeah, I see them," Shaw told him. "Any suggestions that don't involve both of us dying horribly?"

Reeves's brain churned along with his stomach, trying to figure out how much time they had before the missile arrived and how much of it he could buy.

"Remain in position," he said, finally. "Open fire if the enemy gets within three hundred meters and we'll send air support through to cover you."

It wasn't a satisfying answer. Two gunships weren't going to be able to hold the enemy back for long, and once they were gone, there'd be nothing standing between the demons and the laser crew.

"Pull them back," Valon suggested. "The weapon will still close the gate and kill the army assembled over there. If it doesn't destroy the hive, it's still worth it."

She wasn't wrong, but he was loathe to withdraw before trying to carry out the objective. Reeves searched her eyes, wondering if Valon was suggesting it because she was worried about Wash.

"If the demons follow them through, the whole mission is fucked," he reminded her. "They'll overrun us here and destroy the relay, maybe follow us right back to those cat people and slaughter them too. We have to hold them back. Tell your gunship pilots to get ready to go through and support the team."

Valon looked like she wanted to argue with him, but she nodded curtly instead and ran back up the ramp of the transport, presumably to use their radio. Reeves attention went back to the screen, to the demons. They weren't running full-speed, which was probably an indication that they didn't know that Wash and Shaw were specifically human soldiers. They just knew they didn't belong, and the Hive Mind had finally noticed the smudge of camo dark against what should have been open ground.

There was still a chance.

32

"Not a chance," Shaw said, shaking his head. "There's no way they don't know we're here."

It wasn't the answer Wash wanted to hear, but what was it that his father had said?

Don't ask questions you don't really want the answers to.

Speaking of answers he didn't care to know, the rifle's optics module had a very handy rangefinder built into it, and it kept warning him that his chosen target was getting closer. Through the night-vision filters the demon looked like a bad guy from one of the vintage video games his father liked to play, something from the 90s or early 2000s, but Wash didn't have a BFG-9000 handy to take them down. And the closest, the one he'd set his targeting reticle on, was only five hundred meters away.

"He said three hundred meters, right?" Wash asked, careful not to let the rifle waver.

"He did." Shaw chuckled. "Wish we had those movie silencers for our rifles. Maybe then they wouldn't even know we were shooting at them."

"How the hell," Wash wondered, "do you stay so fucking chill?"

"I don't see you turning and running, Junior."

"Yeah, but I sure as hell *want* to. I'm about to piss my pants and you're making jokes."

"I got two ex-wives, kid. Death would be a financial relief. Naw, seriously, it ain't the first time I've been about to die. Not even the tenth time. At some point, you either start laughing at it or you get all cold about it like the boss, or you just fucking quit. Which one you figure you're gonna do?"

"Quitting's not an option," Wash told him. He was surprised how much he meant it. "I'm not much of a funny guy. Guess I'll have to try being a machine."

Four hundred meters. The things were moving faster now, dust kicking up behind them, tails curled over their shoulders. They moved *so* damned fast.

"I'm gonna fire in a couple seconds here," he warned.

"Yeah, I figured. Shoot a couple of them for me, will ya? I'm a little busy." Shaw murmured something too soft for Wash to hear, and he guessed the warrant officer was radioing Reeves to update him on their situation.

Wash's eyes wanted to flicker to the draw where the gate was located, wishing the gunships would come through and save their ass. He didn't because he needed to stay focused... and because part of him realized the aircraft would only buy them a little time.

Three hundred meters.

Wash squeezed the trigger. The report of the rifle wasn't painfully loud, but he couldn't imagine any of the things not being able to tell where it came from. The warrior drone leading the pack staggered, a spray of black erupting from its skull, and when it went down the next one in line tripping over its body and tumbling back to its feet with the agility of an Olympic gymnast. Its reward for the maneuver was Wash's second round, then his third through fifth, which was probably a slug or two more than it would have taken.

The rest of the cluster broke into a sprint, either the demons themselves or the Hive Mind controlling them finally understanding that the two of them were a threat.

Not big enough of a threat.

The things would be on top of them in seconds, and there was no way he could shoot them all. Wash was so focused on the demons that he didn't notice the gunship until it opened fire. The rocket-assisted cannon rounds chopped up the ground on either side of the loose formation of demons and took them down along the way. The hum of the rotors came hot on the heels of the echoing bang of the cannon rounds, and the wedge-shaped aircraft banked around above their position, throwing down a breathtaking wash of warm, dry air.

"Thanks for the assist," Shaw yelled up at the aircraft, "but you're kind of putting a huge spotlight down on us for all those fucking monsters!"

As if the flight crew had heard him, the gunship lurched forward, moving fast and low, barely thirty feet off the ground. The chin cannon opened up and a rank of demons fell to it, which made Wash want to cheer, except that the dead numbered in the dozens while the living were in the multiple tens of thousands. The things shifted like a wave breaking on the shore, reacting to the incoming fire in a completely un-human way, not trying to protect themselves, not running for cover, but simply watching, waiting.

The gunship pilot had kept the aircraft low to avoid the spikers, making the incorrect assumption that they wouldn't fire this close to their own army. Or maybe just hoping against hope. Either way, the creatures disappointed. It wasn't just one of the spikers, because there was, apparently, nothing the Hive Mind liked more than overkill. Four of the things were on this side of the assembled army of demons and all four bracketed the area with biomechanical missiles, not caring that most of the projectiles arced downward and ripped into their own ranks.

Two of them did their job. Metal screamed and rotors shattered, sending shrapnel spattering into the dark rock and soil across the valley floor. Wash ducked instinctively, though he knew that it was too late, that if any of it had been on a trajectory to hit him, he would already be dead. As dead as the crew of the gunship. The aircraft broke apart at the spine, hitting the ground in three parts and shattering into jagged pieces pinwheeling across the plain.

Right toward Wash. The stray rotor sliced through the air like a guillotine, heading straight at his head, and Wash threw himself to the side, arms and legs pulled into a protective ball. Cool wind kissed the bare skin of his neck, and he could almost taste the razor-sharp edge of the rotor as it passed. Wash stayed curled up for a full second, certain he was about to be crushed by a falling slab of metal. When it didn't happen, he rolled onto his side, using the buttstock of his rifle to push himself back to his feet. Smoke and dust billowed around him from the crash and the outline on thermal showed Victor Shaw still hugging the dirt, the laser designator knocked over on its side.

"You alright, Shaw?" he asked, coughing at the thick dust, spitting dirt. Wash stumbled over to the man and grabbed his shoulder, shaking him. "Come on, man, we gotta get this laser thing back up."

Shaw didn't move, but the smoke did, drifting away, revealing a jagged shard of dark metal a foot long protruding from the man's chest. The body armor hadn't stood a chance and neither had Shaw. Wash yanked the man's goggles off, along with his helmet. Shaw's eyes were wide open, his face pale from the blood disappearing into the thirsty, dry soil.

Wash's breath was chuffing, heading out of control, and he

struggled to get it back to something approaching normal while he activated his throat mic.

"Shaw's dead," he gasped, scrambling over to the laser designator, yanking it back up onto its tripod feet. "This is Wash. Shaw's dead and the gunship is down."

No response, and Wash grabbed at the radio on his belt, trying to make sure it was turned on, but then Reeves' voice came over his headset, so quiet he could barely hear it.

"I copy. Do you remember how to use the laser designator?"

Wash didn't even consider the question, struck first by how cold it seemed. Shaw had been Reeves' friend, and the man was blowing off his death, all business. Cold, that was how Shaw had put it.

"Yeah, I remember," he said, looking over the controls for the thing. It had been a short class to refamiliarize the rest of the team, but he'd paid particular attention since he'd never even seen one of the things before. He pushed his goggles out of the way and put his face to the screen. "It's still working. I don't know how much longer I have here before the enemy gets organized and decides to come finish the job."

Wash didn't look at them. There was nothing he could do if the Hive Mind noticed and sent a hundred demons after him.

"We just received a signal from the relay. The missile is through the Thacia gate. Get that laser in place and get ready to run just as soon as the thing comes through the gate. You copy?"

"I got it."

Getting out would be a chancy thing. The nuke *should* go off underground, in the tunnel, but should was a slippery word when they were talking about a nuclear warhead.

Do your job. Be cold. The voice was in his head, but it seemed to come from Shaw's lifeless body, his eyes frozen on Wash.

Everything was deathly quiet, just the whisper of the hot wind and the scratch of a hundred thousand feet on dirt and stone, and then jets screamed their defiance. It could only be one thing. The cruise missile was louder than it would usually have been because it had to slow down and take a hard turn in the draw, going from over five hundred miles an hour down to almost stall speed as it adjusted course.

Wash wanted to look at it, wanted to watch it curl around, but he knew he should keep that laser on the target. He looked.

The thing almost seemed to be going in slow motion, either that, or the giant spider-legged creature could move a lot faster than he'd thought. It rumbled across two hundred yards of open ground, the gigantic, cone-shaped pads at the end of its legs sweeping demons aside as if they were inconsequential, pebbles and twigs to be kicked out of the path.

"What the hell is it *doing*?" he blurted aloud.

Then a spindly, skeletal upper arm raised high, fifty feet in the air, and the strange webbing attached to its underside swung upward... like a net. And he knew.

"Abort!" he yelled. "Abort the strike!"

Too late. Wash would have thought the webbing couldn't be strong enough to stop the missile, even going this slow, but he would have been wrong. The wings crumpled, the engine stalled, and the missile was trapped inside the webbing. Wash stared at it, frozen in disbelief.

"Get out!" Reeves yelled in his ear. "Get out now!"

Wash didn't think, he just grabbed the metal shard in Shaw's chest and pulled it out. Not much blood came from the wound, most of it already soaked into the ground, and the body was limp and lifeless over his shoulder. Leaving the man behind hadn't even entered his mind, but he abandoned the laser designator without a second thought, running for the draw with a short, stomping gate.

They were following. He knew it, knew they were coming after him, but he didn't look back. His rifle was a useless weight banging against his shoulder, his night-vision goggles still up and out of the way, leaving him in the blindness of deep shadow, the only light a very dim glow from the gate itself. Loose rock collected in the base of the draw tried its best to trip him up, forcing Wash to drag the soles of his boots through the dirt, the impact of the sharp rocks painful reminders of the disaster unfolding around him.

Movement ahead, dark shapes against the light of the gate, and his first thought was that somehow demons had circled around to the other side of the draw and cut him off, until perspective snapped into place and he realized the shapes were humans.

"Give me him," Jansen said, grabbing Shaw off his shoulder. Wash wanted to tell him that the man was beyond the help of a medic, but he didn't have the breath for it.

Others pushed him along, the hand grabbing his arm familiar somehow… Valon. It was Valon. Flanders' M250 stuttered hoarsely and grenade launchers barked sharp warnings, their warheads delivering on the threat with the distant bang of detonations. He wanted to turn, grab his rifle and join them, but Valon was insistent, and before Wash could get his brain working, the brutal cold wind slapped him in the face.

He couldn't see a damned thing, though it wasn't because of the darkness so much as the wind and the snow. Wash yanked his ENVG-Bs back into place, shielding his eyes from the snow and throwing everything back into false day. The remaining gunship hovered above them, waiting, while the transport sat a hundred yards away, tempting, taunting with its distance, bathed in the glow of its running lights.

"What are we doing?" he yelled over the wind. Valon was beside him, but the others had retreated with them through the gate… Jansen was beside them, keeping up despite carrying Shaw's body over his shoulder.

"Retreating," she told him. "Back to Thacia. There's no other choice."

Explosions behind them, and he twisted around, watched the gunship unleashing a barrage of missiles and cannon fire into the gate, demons blowing apart as they tried to press through. By the time he turned back, the transport was only a few yards away, two of the Thacian flight crew waiting at the bottom of the ramp, manning their version of a heavy machine gun. Valon pushed him up the ramp and he moved off to the side, making room for the others.

Helmets came off along with night-vision goggles, and the entire team seemed to wear the same expression, a mixture of disbelief and anger. Reeves was the last one up, the ramp powering shut behind him as the flight crew ducked inside, carrying the machine gun with them.

Valon snapped something up to the cockpit and the rotors roared obedience, the transport leaping skyward before any of them had a chance to strap in. Wash caught himself against a safety strap, hanging just above Shaw's body, resting on two of the seats beside him.

Trying to force his breathing back to normal, Wash pushed away from the body and fell into a seat in the center row. Reeves was sitting across from him, staring at Shaw's face until Jansen slid a body bag over the man, zipping it closed, shutting out the unseeing eyes.

"What about the mission?" Wash asked, not sure if he was asking Reeves or perhaps Shaw's phantom presence. Reeves gave the only answer he was going to get, not looking at him.

"It's over. We failed."

33

Brenda rubbed at her eyes, squinting against the rising sun reflected in the rear windshield of the car in front of her. She'd driven straight through, stopping only twice for gas, running on bad gas-station coffee, and now the city skyline of Las Vegas rose above the desert plain ahead of her, silhouetted against the distant mountains.

She hadn't thought about how to find the Army camp until she was already on the road, but during a bathroom break at a Shell station outside Provo, she'd thought to google it and found the answer on a local UFO enthusiast's message board. She'd *used* to call them crackpots, but given recent history, maybe she'd been too hard on them.

Nellis Air Force Base had been the obvious choice, but the temporary special operations center had been set up outside the actual base itself, though within the grounds on US government property. Brenda knew she'd reached it when she saw the fence. It looked new, one of those tall, chain-link things the government could seemingly throw up in a day. The guardhouse at the gate was similarly temporary and quickly erected, though the concrete barricades were solid.

Brenda took a deep breath as she pulled up to the guard, hands on the wheel, driver's license ready in the center console.

"Can I help you, ma'am?" The guard looked younger than her, no older than nineteen, the divots of old acne scars painting a map over his florid cheeks. The carbine held across his chest looked serious enough though. "This is a restricted area."

"My name is Brenda Sands," she told him, offering her driver's license. "I need you to contact Colonel Dos Santos and tell him I'm here. He's going to want to see me."

"Ma'am," the kid reiterated, "this base is highly restricted. No civilians allowed without prior authorization."

She scowled at him, using the expression she'd seen from her late grandmother when the weathered old woman had browbeat her mom into doing as she was told.

"How the hell are you going to know if I'm authorized if you're too fucking lazy to contact Colonel Dos Santos, Corporal? I repeat, he's going to want to see me. And if he doesn't, *he* can tell you to send me away."

Her stomach churned at the thought that the kid would just get pissed and have her detained, and that they'd find the guns in the trunk and she'd wind up arrested, but she didn't let the doubt show on her face. The corporal scowled but turned back to the guard shack and grabbed a radio microphone there. The conversation was beyond her earshot, but it went on for long minutes, and at one point the younger man read off her license to whoever was on the other end.

When he returned, he shoved her license back at her, not seeming pleased about what he was about to say.

"A car is coming from Colonel Dos Santos. Stay behind it and don't try going anywhere other than where it leads you, understand?"

"I copy five-by-five, corporal."

She'd expected a Humvee, but the vehicle that came for her

Gates of Hope

was a black Suburban, like something the FBI or Secret Service might use. She couldn't see the driver through the tinted windows, but the corporal waved her through, gesturing at the big SUV, and she obediently followed it through the gate.

Canvas tents lined the unpaved road, interspersed with prefab sheet-metal storage sheds and a handful of CONEXes, the sort of military shipping containers converted to housing and offices that she'd seen pictures of from Wash's father from his time in Iraq. Humvees and other, newer vehicles she didn't recognize, as well as more of the Suburbans were parked beside nearly every building, and walking purposefully between the tent buildings were soldiers in camouflage utilities, civilians—maybe contractors, maybe intelligence—in polo shirts, vests and khaki pants, and others who were clearly something *else*.

These were the kind of people Wash had been working with the past few months, walking around in faded blue jeans, flannel shirts and vests and sunglasses, their hair longer than regulation, most of them bearded and scraggly. Some had pistols in drop-leg holsters, others carried rifles slung over their backs, but all of them looked like they had a plan to kill everyone they met.

A lot of them were clustered around the tent the Suburban led her to, and they gave her the stink-eye when she pulled up behind the huge SUV. Brenda closed her door quickly when she got out, wincing at the beep of the alarm when she locked the car up. As if that would stop any of them who decided her car needed to be searched.

Dos Santos stalked out of the open door of the tent, dressed in combat utilities, a pistol at his hip and aggravation on his face.

"Ms. Sands," he said with the air of a man who was barely containing his rage, "this is not a good time. I know you haven't heard from Sgt. Williams in a while, but I assure you, he's fine, and…"

"I'm not here about Wash," she told the colonel. "I've been... contacted. Somehow. By Jimmy."

Brenda expected Dos Santos to mock her, to say something condescending about how she'd gone through a traumatic experience and if she needed counseling, he had a number she could call. Instead, he froze in his tracks like she'd slapped him in the face.

"Come inside," he said, waving at the tent.

It was warm here, and she stripped off her jacket. It hadn't been warm in Wyoming and she hadn't left her car long enough to notice the weather warming up on the drive. The inside of the tent was cooler, out of the sun, but also much darker, and she paused, blinking to let her eyes adjust. Brenda had an image in her head from old war movies how the operations center of a military unit should look, much of it involving maps on the wall and men hunched over radios. This wasn't anything like that picture. No maps, unless the one on the flatscreen monitor on a stand at the center counted. No radios, at least none like she imagined with big, black, metal cases that took up a whole desktop and awkward, padded headsets connected by tangled wires.

There were a few uniformed soldiers in the tent, but they had Bluetooth headsets and cell phones, like stockbrokers in some Hollywood version of a Wall Street brokerage. All of them seemed to be talking at the same time, and she couldn't understand any of them, each of them huddled over laptop computers on folding tables.

Dos Santos led her over to a corner of the tent where there a metal desk was set up, the only personal adornment on it a single picture of a young girl who shared a family resemblance to Dos Santos. The colonel waved her into a chair beside the desk, and she sank into it with a sense of relief. She'd made it farther than she'd thought she would.

"What I'm about to tell you goes no further," he warned,

raising a finger in warning. "If I hear it anywhere, on the news, on the internet, I'll know the source." He searched her eyes as if looking for deception or ulterior motives, then finally sighed and went on. "Sgt. Williams was with the Thacian Venator, the woman called Valon, heading through a series of gates between here and Thacia. They happened upon an active site and were confronted by a group of worker drones." His eyebrow went up. "You know what those are, right?"

"I was on Hades," Brenda reminded him, arms crossed. Dos Santos nodded.

"They later linked up with Sgt. Reeves and the rest of the team and told them that James Bonner spoke to them through the worker drones, told them he was somehow part of the Hive Mind now."

"That's what he told me," she said, enthused not by the idea of Jimmy still existing as a subroutine running in an alien hive mind, but by the fact someone else had confirmed she wasn't crazy. "He said that the Hive Mind knew what he'd done, that it was trying to punish him... by coming after *me*."

"There're no gates to active sites in the contiguous United States." The statement was a flat declaration, without doubt, almost a religious conviction, as if that assurance was central to his view of reality.

"Jimmy said that the Hive Mind believed there would be. And soon. He told me to get out of Riverton now, and this was the only place I could think to go." Brenda looked around the tent. "You said Wash and the others were on Thacia. Are they still there?"

Dos Santos' expression was guarded.

"That's a long and highly classified story, I'm afraid."

"Sir!" One of the stockbroker-looking technicians jumped up from the table full of laptops, holding his cell phone out like he wanted Dos Santos to watch a cat video. "There's a call for you from Pirate One!"

Dos Santos held a hand up at the man and jogged over to the doorway off the tent, waving at Brenda to follow.

"Mr. Donner," he called to the driver of the Suburban who had escorted her to the tent. The man was one of the clean-cut polo shirt types, mid-thirties, a service pistol holstered at his waist, *almost* concealed by a Patagonia vest. "Take Ms. Sands to the mess tent." Dos Santos shrugged an apology to her. "Sorry, it's the only place we have set up for visitors. Get some breakfast if you like. I'll get back with you as soon as I can."

"That's them on the radio, isn't it?" she asked him. "Pirate One? That's his team."

"I can't say," he told her, though the look on his face told her she was right. "I promise, I'll tell you everything I can when I can." He put a hand on her arm. "You'll be safe here."

He was wrong. She didn't know how she knew, but she was certain of one thing as the man called Donner led her to the mess tent.

Nowhere was safe.

"I don't understand," Prefect Marcos said, shaking his head. "How in the name of all the gods is that possible?"

"I've told you, Prefect," Valon said dully, cradling her head in her hands, leaning forward in the folding chair in the aircraft hangar. "The Hive Mind grew a new beast, something huge, with webbing along its upper arms to catch the missile."

"Yes, and that's the part I don't understand, Primus," he insisted, voice rising along with his hands. "That would take *time*. We don't know exactly how long it takes the Hive Mind to grow a demon or a spiker, but it's at least weeks, and it has to take even longer to design an entirely new creature out of nothing! We didn't even launch one of your missiles at it before a few days ago!" He scanned back and forth across the room, though none of the Americans would meet his eyes, not even Reeves. They were slumped in their seats, some simply sitting on the concrete floor, backs against the sheet metal of the walls, the ones not staring at the floor instead fixated on the black, plastic bag holding the body of their friend. "How did it *know*?"

Wash was the one who answered. Not that the young man seemed any less devastated by their losses than the others, but perhaps he saw Marcos as an authority figure more than the experienced, battle-hardened special operations team did.

"Jimmy told us. We didn't know what he meant, but now we do. The thing knows everything he knew."

"This James Bonner wasn't a soldier," Marcos protested, still furious, though he couldn't honestly say at who.

"No, but he was what we call on Earth a 'wannabe.' He learned all he could about the military, said he wanted to join, but when it came down to it, he was afraid of the discipline, of not having his mother around to spoil him, of being away from his room and his bed, and all the friends that his parents' money bought him." The young man's voice had started neutral, but with each word it grew heavier with bitter cynicism, so much for someone his age. "This is my fault. If I'd just humored him like everyone else did, let him get his way, not tried to antagonize him, maybe he would have just ignored me and we never would have been fighting at his parents' place, neither of us would have fallen into that gate, and a whole bunch of people would still be alive." Wash didn't actually turn to look at the body bag, but his eyes flickered toward it.

"We all signed on for a dangerous job," Reeves interrupted, gently chiding. "That includes Vic. Even if Bonner hadn't been taken over by the Hive Mind, it would have found someone at some point."

"I don't mean to dismiss your friend's sacrifice," Marcos

interrupted, fighting against the impatience burning inside his gut, "but if Bonner has given the Hive Mind all this information, does that mean your nuclear weapons are useless against it?"

"No," Reeves insisted. "We can still use the portable nukes to close gates." He pushed up from the edge of the transport ramp, hands shoved in his jacket pockets, walking to the open door. It was near to midnight and the lights of the city were gentle, paltry competition for the moon. "It's gonna be slow and costly, but the tactic is sound. The demons can't be everywhere at once."

"It would have been so damned handy to be able to drop a cruise missile right in their lap though," Nyland lamented. He blinked and looked over at Reeves, then at Wash. "Hey, not to be too paranoid, but there's like... a nuclear *warhead* on that Tomahawk. There's no way the Hive Mind could use that against us, is there?"

Reeves looked at Wash, and the younger man shook his head.

"No. Jimmy was a lot of things, but a nuclear physicist wasn't one of them."

Of the many things that sucked about being a residual memory stuck inside the diffuse brain of an alien Hive Mind, Jimmy Bonner wasn't sure which he hated more, the lack of sleep or the lack of any sense of time. Either was likely to drive him mad eventually, but he thought the timeless nature of his existence was the worst.

No, wait... it was more likely that the loneliness would do it. No sense of time, compounded by no sense of movement all shrank to nothing next to the sheer isolation of it. He'd managed to get a reprieve from all that while communicating with Wash and Brenda, but now it was building up again. Jimmy was floating free in nothingness, eternally alone, and with each time-

Gates of Hope

less moment that passed, it became harder and harder for him to summon the mental energy to concentrate, to summon the link to Brenda or take over one of the drones.

"Hello? Is there someone here?"

It was impossible for Jimmy to jump, or he would have. The voice came from nowhere, or it seemed to until he focused on one area of the nothingness and it solidified into a human shape. A woman, older, maybe sixty, her hair short and silver, eyes wide behind thick glasses. She wore a thick, woolen sweater, though the rest of her was harder to make out, vague and shadowy.

"Who the hell are you?" Jimmy demanded, surprised at his own outrage, as if he'd been looking forward to the solitude, to fading away to nothing. "How did you get here?"

"I... I don't know where *here* is," she stammered, looking around furtively. Did she see anything he didn't? "I was driving home from work and these... *things*, the demons they call them on the news, came out of nowhere and slammed into my car, drove me off the road. They took me back through one of the gates and into this cave." The older woman shook her head. "After that, everything got hazy and my head hurt really bad. And I was here. I don't know for how long. It could have been days, it could have been *months*." Fear set her face in a rictus mask. "Am I dead? Is this Hell?"

"I'm afraid the answer to both is yes." Jimmy cursed. He didn't need the woman going catatonic. She was the only other human he'd had the chance to talk to in here, a welcome change from the torments of the Hive Mind. "Wait a second." He frowned. "You're the only other person who the Hive Mind has absorbed into itself besides me."

"Is *that* what happened to me?" She was near panic now, pulling at her hair as if she *had* hair or hands to tug it with. "Oh, Jesus! I'm dead..."

"Calm down," he told her, trying to take a step closer to put a hand on her arm but unable to move. Their proximity was just as illusory as their physical bodies. "What's your name?"

"Helena," she told him, sounding as if it was almost a reflex, the word breaking through her panicked sobs. "Dr. Helena Winters."

"You're a doctor?" Jimmy asked, now even more confused. What would the Hive Mind want with a *doctor*?

"Not a medical doctor." Again, the words were reflexive, as if she'd gone through this explanation a million times. "A physicist."

Frost danced on a spine Jimmy no longer had, just an idea that seized his thoughts and wouldn't let go.

"Dr. Winters," he said, "you said the demons grabbed you on the way to work. Where, exactly, would that be?"

"Lawrence Livermore," Winters said as if the answer was obvious. "I work for the Department of Energy. I'm a nuclear physicist."

34

Wash Williams stood on the roof of the Venator Headquarters in Thacia City and watched the dawn crawl over the horizon.

"What are you doing up here?"

He half turned, knowing it was Valon before he saw her. She'd gotten cleaned up sometime in the last few hours, changed into a fresh uniform. He had too, of course. Shaw's blood had stained the back of his shirt, gone down his shoulders. Wash had used the excuse of taking a shower and changing to get away from the others. It was probably irresponsible, but he couldn't stand the looks he knew they'd be giving him.

"Just needed some time alone," he told her. A cold wind slapped him in the face, stronger up here above the city. "Didn't feel like talking to anyone."

Take the hint. It wasn't that he didn't appreciate Valon coming to find him, but he didn't want sympathy at the moment. Unfortunately, cultural differences couldn't be translated even by Archaion technology.

"Was the man Shaw your friend?" she asked, moving up beside him at the edge. The Thacians didn't, it seemed, believe in railings.

"Not really," he admitted. "Most of the time, I thought he didn't want me along on the team. But at the end, I think he'd accepted me."

She frowned at him, perhaps in consternation.

"You've seen others die before, I know this. You told me. Why does this man's death affect you so?"

Dammit.

"It's not his death." He closed his eyes, shrugged. "I mean, it's not *just* that he died. It's that he died and we didn't accomplish a damned thing. Since the beginning of this, we've been fighting a holding action, playing whack-a-mole, we call it. Demons pop up and we close the gate, and lose lots of people doing it. But the gates keep coming. This *finally* seemed like something we could do that would win the war, not just a battle."

Valon's smile was sad, wistful.

"Welcome to the life of a Venator, Wash." She swept a hand across the horizon, gradually growing lighter behind the low clouds and fog. "We lose people and we put up shields and there's always another battle to fight. It's our purpose."

"It's not *mine*," he snapped, then took a deep breath and forced himself to calm down. "I want this to be over with, Valon. I can't keep doing this forever. I can't do that to Brenda." He shook his head. "She understands. She knows I have to do this, knows better than anyone what's at stake. But she's not going to sit there at home the rest of her life and wait to get the call that my luck ran out."

Valon's hand was warm on his shoulder, and he looked at her in surprise but didn't pull away. Her eyes were gentle, understanding.

"You're following a false assumption to an errant conclusion," she said, and he blinked, not expecting that. "You still think you can leave this and go back to a normal life, but you make the false assumption that things will go back to normal." Valon shook her head. "The gates aren't going to stop popping into existence. The Hive Mind isn't going to stop sending the demons. The world you knew is over."

Wash pulled away from her, breathing hard, realizing abruptly that he was squared off as if he wanted to fight her. He forced himself to calm down.

"I don't believe that. I *won't* believe that."

"You can go back to your Brenda," Valon said, pressing the argument like she was going into battle. "You can get as far away from the cities as possible, you can hide... but the world will fall apart around you. Is that how you want to go down, Wash? Hiding, running? Waiting for the last of humanity to fall while you do nothing?"

"We'll close those damned gates as fast as they open." The words rang hollow in his ears.

"Even if you have thousands of those nuclear charges, you won't be able to get to them all in time. And you've already told me that other countries aren't cooperating with you, that they're destroying themselves trying to kill the demons. How long before a gate opens there and they aren't able to close it?" Valon jabbed a finger at his chest. "You're a brave man, Wash Williams, and the brave face up to the truth, no matter how ugly it is. Reality is what it is, whether we like it or not."

The sun broke through the clouds, shining across the distant plains, almost painfully bright even through the clouds.

No. Sunrise was the other direction. Wash held a hand over his eyes and grabbed Valon, shielding hers as well until the glow faded. The noise came next, trailing the light, miles distant, too far to damage the city, yet still as loud as the thunder from a lightning strike just beside them, shaking the building to its foundations. Wash nearly stumbled over the edge, saved by Valon's arm around his waist.

Out over the hills, in the plains where the Thacians guarded their collection of gates to the Beast Worlds, a mushroom cloud rose high into the morning sky.

"Oh, my God," Wash breathed, more a prayer than a curse.

"What is it?" Valon asked, face slack with confusion. "What did that?"

"It's a nuke," he told her. "It's the nuclear warhead from the missile. The Hive Mind intercepted it, rigged it up to blow somehow." His eyes went wide, the realization hitting him like the warm wind of the shockwave. "Used it to blow a hole through your shield."

She stared at the cloud for a moment, looking as lost and overwhelmed as he felt before she turned to him.

"What have we done?"

"There's nothing we can do to stop them," Primus Calista said, background noise and static nearly drowning out her words. The air was full of static electricity, the smell of ozone plain even from this far away, and the only way the outpost was able to communicate at all was by buried fiber optic cable. No radio signals were getting through. "There's too many, Prefect! Hundreds of thousands pouring through the minute the shield came down! And the watch stations were burned to ashes by the blast, along with the static defenses. There's nothing but open ground between them and the city!"

A scream and a burst of static, and the line went dead.

"Calista!" Marcos yelled into the microphone. "Primus Calista!"

His breath caught in his throat and he put a hand against the wall of the hangar to steady himself, pressing his eyes closed for a moment before he trusted himself to turn back to Valon and the Americans.

Gunships streamed from every hangar here at the Venator headquarters compound, and they'd be taking off from the strongholds outside the city as well, while armored vehicles rumbled through the streets, heading for the gates. Infantry went to fortified positions at the walls, missile turrets and artillery moved into positions to rain hell down on the primary approaches... and still, it wouldn't be enough.

"This was the army we saw on the other side of the snow gate," Wash Williams said. The young man's face was pale, his fingers gripping the stock of his rifle as if the thing was a totem of the gods, ready to deliver him from evil. "This was the plan all along."

"How the hell did it figure out how to trigger the warhead?" Nyland demanded, nearly spitting with anger, as if he thought the Hive Mind had cheated him somehow. These Americans were fierce warriors, but far too naïve.

"It doesn't matter," Reeves snapped, cutting through the noise of the deploying aircraft and through the panic of his people. "It's happened, and we need to get word back to Colonel Dos Santos. The Thacians need help."

"We ain't getting shit back from here," Nyland told him, slapping a hand against the radio on his belt. "The EMP from the nuke is still scrambling all the signals. We have to get closer to the relay... or just go right through the gate and tell the colonel face to face."

"You should go," Marcos told them. "Get back through to your side and get your people mobilized. We're going to need any help they can give us."

"And it won't be nukes this time," Reeves said. "There's no way the government will okay their use at all, now that we know the Hive Mind has figured them out."

"Get on board the transport," Valon said, motioning up the

ramp. "We won't have the luxury of a gunship escort, but I'll get you as close to the gate as we can."

"You'll do more than that, Primus," Marcos told her. "You're going through with them."

She goggled at him, shocked. He'd expected it and had allotted her thirty seconds for outraged protest.

"Are you serious, sir?" she exploded. "You need me here! Besides which, the last time I went over there, they put me in a holding cell and Wash had to break me out!"

"I think I can keep that from happening again," Reeves assured both of them.

"I need you over there," Marcos said, forestalling another eruption, "because we don't have enough Venators to hold down a full-scale invasion. We *have* to count on the Americans for support, and while I'm sure Master Sergeant Reeves is a good man, he's loyal to *his* people… I need someone over there who's thinking about *us*." The struggle was clear on her face, though the fact she hadn't started yelling was encouraging. Marcos pressed on, sensing victory was near. "I trust you to fight for us here, Valon, but the real fight will be over there. Will you go?"

"Damn you, Marcos," she spat, shaking her head. "You know I can't say no."

"I know, daughter." Marcos smiled fondly. "You've always done your duty without complaint. May the gods go with you."

She threw herself into his arms unexpectedly and hugged him tight.

"And with you, father."

Marcos closed his eyes, allowing himself to imagine a life where he'd married and had a family, yet even in this fantasy life, he couldn't picture a daughter who would have made him prouder than Valon. She pulled away and headed up the ramp, followed by the American troops, the tromp of their boots a marching drum signaling the start of the battle.

His tablet was buzzing for attention and an aide was waiting patiently, hand clutching physical paper reports, but Marcos waited and watched until the transport's boarding ramp ascended and thumped closed. The engines roared to life, the rotors spinning up, yet still he stood there, eyes slitted against the dust and particulate debris the fans threw up. Marcos only turned to his aide once the ducted-fan helicopter had lifted out of the hangar, soaring quickly upward, heading for the mountains.

"The Senate has contacted us three times, Prefect," the man told him, clearly anxious and just as clearly trying not to show it. "They want to know if they should evacuate to the bunkers."

Marcos smirked.

"Of course they do. Send runners to each of the evacuation centers and make sure the civil defense volunteers have begun checking every housing block for stragglers." He sighed. "And send a protective team to the Senate offices, get their regal asses to the shelters."

"Yes, sir." The younger man hesitated as he turned to go. "Sir... this is the fourth time just this year that we've had to send the populace to the shelters. I don't remember it ever happening before, not even when I was a child. Is... is the end coming?"

He thought about lying, but Dolon was a good man, a steady soldier.

"I fear it may be here." He motioned to the man's chest holster. "Give me your sidearm. And have my personal transport brought around to the front of the hangar."

"Where are you going, Prefect?" Dolon asked, handing over the weapon.

Marcos sighed, knowing what he was about to do, what the penalty might be, but beyond caring. He tucked the gun into his belt.

"The temple."

35

"Do you think they'll send troops through?" Wash asked, keeping his voice low, hoping Valon wouldn't hear. She was seated across the troop compartment from Wash and Reeves, but the woman's hearing was as sharp as her mind.

"Hard to say," Reeves admitted, just as quiet, his eyes also on Valon. "I'll recommend they do, and I think the colonel will, too, but..." he shrugged. "Drones with Hellfires, sure, and special ops teams to guide them. Maybe even Apaches. But armor? Conventional infantry?" The shake of his head was brief, curt. "You know this administration. You think they're going to send in the 82nd Airborne? The First Marine Division? You think they're going to tell Congress or worse, the press, that they've had two or three *thousand* troops killed in one battle, fighting not just for another country but another *world*?"

Wash bit down on a curse, then on the argument that threatened to follow it. There was nothing Reeves could do about it. He leaned forward and tried to get a look out one of the side windows. The rising sun glared off the glass, but he could make out the green of the mountain beneath them.

"We have any radio contact yet?" He addressed the question

to Valon this time. She looked up sharply, as if he'd startled her out of a fugue, then blinked and shook her head.

"Still too much static. And every established position with wired connections has already been overrun. We have scouts out, but there's no way for them to report back except in person." Valon looked down at her tablet and frowned. "I can't even reach the control unit for the shield."

"Fucking bastards couldn't have done this better if they planned it this way," Flanders commented.

"They did," Wash said. "*It* did, somehow. And it had to have done it months ago, back when it had gates available somewhere in the US. The thing isn't stupid." He opened his mouth, then shut it, the train of thought leading him into a conclusion he didn't like. "Valon, you left the shield open so we could keep up the relay, right?"

Valon was one of the smartest people Wash knew, and it didn't take her a second before her eyes flew open wide, realizing the implications of what he'd said. She leaned toward the cockpit, yelling a warning to the pilot.

It was too late. The transport was coming over the top of the pass, just a quarter mile from the gate, and by the time Wash saw the writhing stream of demons winding up the pass from the other side, saw the cluster of spikers coming up the sides of the trail, the streaks of white were already incoming.

"Look out!" Wash yelled, but the final syllable wasn't out of his mouth when something hit them like a freight train smashing through a car stuck on the tracks.

The impact threw Wash against his safety restraints, pain lancing through his shoulders and back, taking his breath away. The world spun around crazily and everything went black.

Brenda wasn't a picky eater. Her mother was, and maybe the fact Brenda could hoover up any food put in front of her was a reaction to that. But Army scrambled eggs and sausage tested her resolve, and it was only through a determined application of mind over matter that she was able to force down the last few bites. The fact that she was starving helped only slightly, and she had to wash the mouthful down with coffee to finish it.

"You should have picked the shit on a shingle," Donner told her.

Brenda looked up sharply, having forgotten he was still there, seated across the table from her. The man had a generic look to him, the short-cut hair, strong jaw and clear eyes of someone who'd either come up through the military and transitioned to DoD contractor or else a fed. She was betting on the former, not because she knew the community that well but because she didn't think Dos Santos was the kind of guy who trusted the feds.

"The what?" she asked, sure she'd heard him wrong. Donner laughed, though not in a mocking tone.

"Shit on a shingle. It's military slang for creamed chip beef on toast. Some people hate it, but I think it's better than the scrambled eggs and sausage."

Brenda smiled.

"Thanks, but I think this sufficiently killed my appetite. You must be former military then?"

"What makes you think I'm not still?" he asked.

"Too clean cut."

"You got me. I used to work for the colonel till I got medicaled out." Donner patted his left shoulder. "Caught an AK round through here. Almost lost my arm, did lose about a third of the mobility in my shoulder. But Colonel Dos Santos brings in a lot of contractors from the unit." His clear gray eyes looked her up and down. "I know who you are, of course. I watched the documentary."

"Oh, Jesus," she moaned, covering her eyes. "That thing made everything seem so dramatic." Donner laughed again, louder this time.

"Yeah, you just got abducted by aliens sent by your ex-boyfriend, then shot him to keep him from taking over the Earth. Nothing at all dramatic about *that*."

Brenda's face was warm, and she hoped to hell she wasn't blushing. She hated blushing—it made her look like a little girl. She was about to give the stock answer she'd practiced for her clients, that it had all happened fast and she hadn't had the luxury of thinking about it, but their conversation was interrupted by a wailing, warbling siren.

There were only twenty people inside the mess tent, but every one of them snapped to their feet, looking around at the walls as if the answer to what was behind the siren was projected on the canvas.

"What the hell is that?" Brenda asked.

"We need to get back to the Ops Center," Donner snapped, pulling his sidearm from the drop-leg holster at his right side, grabbing her arm with the other hand.

"Why?" she demanded, resisting his pull. "What's that siren mean?"

"It means the gate's been breached," he told her.

"The demons," she hissed. Donner pulled her toward the exit, and this time she didn't fight him.

Outside the tent, all was chaos, men and women streaming out of tents and CONEXes, weapons in hand, running toward the center of the camp where she'd seen a motor pool of Humvees and armored vehicles. A few of the vehicles were already on the move, rumbling down the center of the street and not waiting for anyone to get out of their way, heavy machine guns and automatic grenade cannons scanning back and forth, looking for targets.

Donner hugged the side of the packed dirt street and Brenda

stayed behind him, letting him block for her like he was an NFL fullback. The siren wailed, unceasing, wearing at her nerves, the howl of a wolfpack at her heels, and she willed Donner to run faster. She didn't remember the mess tent being so far...

There. There was her SUV, the Honda sitting tiny and desultory among the military vehicles, parked behind the Suburban in the lee of the Ops Center. Brenda wanted to just jump into the vehicle and take off, drive north and not stop till she hit Canada, but she followed Donner into the tent.

If the technicians had seemed like stockbrokers before, now they were in martial mode, each of them marking maps and transferring them to the one on the central monitor, red dots peppering the area around the base, around Nellis. The red dots moved though, as if they weren't content to simply sit where they were placed, bunching up, forming into a spearhead.

"Is that them?" she asked, half out of breath.

Dos Santos turned, glaring at her as if she were a student who'd interrupted during his lecture.

"General, I *need* those fighters at position Alpha and I needed them *ten minutes ago!*" His lips peeled back from his teeth in a grimace. "Yes, I know you need presidential authorization, but if you wait to get it, we're all going to be fucking dead!" A pause, and his features relaxed. "Thank you. Contact me as soon as they're wheels-up." Dos Santos jammed a button his phone and then looked over to Brenda and Donner. "Donner, get her into that Suburban and get the hell out of here! Show your credentials at Nellis—I've already called ahead and they'll let you both into the underground shelter there."

"Sir," Donner objected, "I want to stay and fight."

"Incoming!" The call was distant, out past the fence line, barely audible above the clamor outside.

The gunfire was *not*. The thump was deep inside Brenda's chest, the explosions rattling her sinuses along with the furniture inside the tent, drowning out the sirens. Brenda wanted to steady herself against something, but the tables seemed too flimsy and she wound up grabbing Donner's shoulder.

"Too fucking late," the contractor murmured, just close enough for her to hear it over the shots. "Come on!" he said to Brenda, running out to his vehicle.

Brenda followed but split off from him at the exit, going to the rear of her Honda, yanking up the tailgate. The Remington shotgun was concealed under a blanket in the back, the sling dangling from swivels at front and back weighted down with spare shells in the loops there. All slugs. Wash had loaded it that way months ago and she'd never questioned why. The little 9mm was in her purse in the front, but she didn't bother with it, figuring all it would be good for was putting herself out of her misery.

She didn't bother to close the hatch, just ran to join Donner, who had pulled a rifle out of the back of his own vehicle. Not the M4 she would have expected, but something larger, heavier, probably a thirty-caliber, though she wasn't enough of a gun person to know what kind. It had a scope and looked like it was geared for long-range work. Donner grinned at the shotgun.

"I hope we're far enough away you won't need that," he said, then gestured at the passenger's side. "Get in."

The interior of the vehicle reeked of cigarette smoke, which would normally have made Brenda gag but barely registered. The diesel engine roared to life before she even had her door shut and the Donner cranked the steering wheel around, throwing dust in a quick U-turn, cutting off a Humvee that didn't seem inclined to stop. The violent turn threw her against the door and she cursed loudly, pulling on her seatbelt.

Donner didn't apologize, his face a mask of concentration as he steered around running soldiers and airmen. Brenda rolled down the window, letting in fresh air and letting out the stale smell of cigarettes. And giving her a clearer view of the fence.

The view between the tents was a kinetoscope, every frame showing a wall of demons washing across the desert, closer with every interval. Scores of them went down with every gap as well, falling to the crew-served weapons lining the perimeter, but more replaced them.

Brenda remembered videos she'd seen in history class of human-wave attacks by the Japanese in the Pacific during World War Two, by the Chinese Army in Korea. None of them had been as inexorable, as inevitable as the dark rush of alien monsters trying to breach the wire.

"Son of a bitch!" Donner exploded, and Brenda was thrown against her seatbelt as he hit the brakes without warning.

Two Humvees had collided at an intersection of two of the graded dirt roads, blocking all but a narrow gap off, but Donner didn't stop, jerking the wheel to the left and scraping the driver's side of the Suburban against the sheet metal of a storage shed. Aluminum smacked against the side mirror, folding it inward, and Donner made no attempt to push it back out. The drivers and crews of the Humvees yelled at him, as if this was the Vegas strip and they were waiting for a traffic cop to arrive.

The front gate beckoned, finally, yawning wide open for the stream of vehicles heading outward, the guard shack abandoned, the soldiers who'd manned it firing from behind one of the concrete barricades. They were dead men, Brenda realized with a sinking feeling in her gut. They had no shelter, no way out unless they jumped in one of the escaping vehicles, and the enemy was so close...

An ungainly armored vehicle was in front of them in the slowly moving queue out the gate, multiple turret-mounted weapons firing as it went, and it followed the rest to the right, off the road into the teeth of the enemy. Donner kept straight, though Brenda thought he would rather have joined his brothers and sisters in the battle.

Clear of the fence, Brenda finally got a good view of the entire mass of enemy, and she couldn't suppress a gasp. There were tens of thousands of them, maybe a hundred thousand, maybe more, more than she could even begin to estimate. More than even the jets she knew were coming could begin to defeat.

"Our Father, who art in heaven," she prayed softly, the words coming automatically, though she hadn't said them since she was a child and her father had taken her to church, "hallowed be Thy name."

"Yeah," Donner agreed, fingers white on the steering wheel. "While you're at it, put in a good word for me."

36

TO BE CONTINUED…

Pearl-white columns towered above Prefect Marcos as he slipped out of the driver's seat of his rover. It was built for traversing the wilderness, not for the city, but the oversized wheels could handle the cobblestone streets as well as they could the dirt roads beyond the pass. He never drove it himself, of course. Not since he was a pilum.

Marcos checked the load of the sidearm he'd taken from his aide. Something else he hadn't done for years—carried a gun. Guns were for soldiers. He was more of a politician, and often he lamented the choices that had led him down that path. Not today. Today, Thacia needed this version of him, not the one who might have died a war hero.

Taking a deep breath, he ascended the steep and narrow steps to the temple of Zeus. They seemed eternal, just like the gods that had followed them to this world. Just like the struggle with the forces of darkness, with the Hive Mind. Never-ending.

Except today, it has *to end.*

The entrance hall to the temple was broad, expansive, showing all were welcome to worship here, though there were no priests or acolytes present this day, no worshippers come to leave donations or make sacrifices. They'd heeded the warnings, the sirens, the City Watch fliers sent to make sure all civilians made it to the shelters. The place was deserted.

Almost.

"Prefect Marcos." The man was short, slight, almost frail, his head shaven as clean as his face. Androgynous in his off-the-shoulder robe, Marcos wouldn't have known if he was male or female except for his voice and the fact that they'd met before. "It has been many weeks since I last saw you here. Has adversity and danger driven you back to the arms of the gods, finally?"

"Hiereus," Marcos said, nodding respectfully. "No, High Priest, I have never left the arms of the gods. It is not disbelief that keeps me from this place."

Hiereus had emerged from the primary chamber of the temple, and through the arched entrance the massive statue of Zeus watched over them, his disapproving scowl directed straight at Marcos.

"What is it, then?" Hiereus wondered, hands folded, dark eyes full of curiosity, as if the soul of this one man was more important than the fate of the city, of the planet. "What has kept you from the house of the all-father?"

"Temptation," Marcos confessed, nodding at the statue.

He paced through the entrance to stand near the base of the thing. He'd always found it so intimidating as a child, and if he was honest with himself, no less so as an adult. Twenty feet tall, the marble-skinned god wielded the thunderbolt, ready to strike down the unfaithful.

"It was different when I was younger," he continued, still looking up at the god. "Then, I thought only of placating the all-father, of gaining his favor and someday being brought before his presence as a great warrior." Marcos offered the priest a wry smile. "But that wasn't to be my fate. Instead, I am burdened with the life of a politician, a diplomat, a go-between." He nodded at the statue. "I feel like he disapproves. But that didn't keep me away either. What began to keep me away was when I found out about the Archaios."

Marcos expected the priest to stiffen with shock. Speaking of the Archaios was a taboo thing, something that could only be done in private, under the tightest security. But Hiereus simply nodded, unfazed.

"It is a great burden," the priest acknowledged. "A responsibility passed down through the line of the priests back to the beginning. It is why I remain here while the others flee."

"You think you can keep it safe from the Hive Mind?" Marcos asked him. "From the demons?"

"My job is not to keep it safe from such as them, Prefect," Hiereus corrected him. "It's to keep it safe from such as *you*."

Marcos laughed softly, circling around, putting himself between Hiereus and the statue.

"You believe that the gods would have us sacrifice our people, our *existence*, rather than use the gift they gave us? Look outside your temple, priest!" Marcos motioned at the walls with the barrel of the handgun. "Is not *this* what it was meant for? Why would they entrust it to us if they didn't want us to use our judgement for when it should be used?"

"*Our* judgement, Prefect... or yours?" The priest made no move, yet somehow Marcos felt as if the man had stepped closer to him, as if those dark eyes were threatening storm clouds. "You arrogate yourself, thinking the circumstances make it right. But the gods care not for our individual lives, only for our duty."

"The gods will be my judge, then, priest," Marcos told him, half warning, half pleading. "I am here to activate the Archaios, and I will let no man stop me. Not even you."

Hiereus smiled almost gently, as one would to an errant child.

"Prefect Marcos," he said, "no *man* will stop you."

Marcos frowned, wondering if the priest was speaking in

vague, religious wording, assuring him that heavenly forces would work against him... until he heard the scratching against the marble floor behind him.

The demons filed out from behind the statue of Zeus as if the god had given birth to the three of them, silent and unfeeling, their bulbous red eyes seeing all, their scorpion tails waving like cobras charmed by a mystic. Talons clicked together, mandibles clattering, all three moving slowly in a patient dance across the floor, as if they were part of some ceremony to Zeus.

Marcos flicked the safety off of the handgun and moved. There was one chance... take down the one in front, block the way for the others. He could make it back down the steps to the car. Something tripped him up before he took a step and he fell at Hiereus' feet, hitting hard on his right elbow, the gun spinning away. Marcos tried to get up, tried to lunge for the weapon, but a wickedly clawed foot stomped down on his arm, pinning it to the floor, the crack of the bone echoing in the silence of the temple. Marcos drew in a shocked breath, but the scream caught in his chest, refusing to come out.

Hiereus' face hovered over him, that gentle smile turned into something harder, more pitiless.

"Hail to the Master," he said, crossing his arms over his chest in an X. "Hail to the Lord of Demons. Hail to the Hive."

Marcos wanted to ask him why, but a jagged spike dripping acid sliced downward, obscuring all light, ending all questions.

The story continues in Gates of Victory.

ALSO BY RICK PARTLOW

If you are enjoying Gates of Eternity , you will love Drop Trooper and Holy War!

Start a new adventure today!

Start a new adventure today!

ALSO IN THE SERIES

GATES OF HELL
GATES OF HOPE
GATES OF VICTORY

FROM THE PUBLISHER

Thank you for reading *Gates of Hope*, book two in the Gates of Eternity series.

We hope you enjoyed it as much as we enjoyed bringing it to you. We just wanted to take a moment to encourage you to review the book on Amazon and Goodreads. Every review helps further the author's reach and, ultimately, helps them continue writing fantastic books for us all to enjoy.

If you liked this book, check out the rest of our catalogue at www.aethonbooks.com. To sign up to receive a FREE collection from some of our best authors as well as updates regarding all new releases, visit www.aethonbooks.com/sign-up.

JOIN THE STREET TEAM! Get advanced copies of all our books, plus other free stuff and help us put out hit after hit.

SEARCH ON FACEBOOK:
AETHON STREET TEAM

ABOUT RICK PARTLOW

RICK PARTLOW is that rarest of species, a native Floridian. Born in Tampa, he attended Florida Southern College and graduated with a degree in History and a commission in the US Army as an Infantry officer.

His lifelong love of science fiction began with Have Space Suit---Will Travel and the other Heinlein juveniles and traveled through Clifford Simak, Asimov, Clarke and on to William Gibson, Walter Jon Williams and Peter F Hamilton. And somewhere, submerged in the worlds of others, Rick began to create his own worlds.

He has written a ton of books in many different series, and his short stories have been included in seven different anthologies.

He currently lives in Wyoming with his wife, two children and a willful mutt of a dog. Besides writing and reading science fiction and fantasy, he enjoys outdoor photography, hiking and camping.

www.rickpartlow.com

Made in the USA
Columbia, SC
06 December 2023